DEAD RECKONING

PX DUKE

Print books

Jim Nash, Investigator

Jim Nash The Beginning
Gun Crazy
Gun Crazy 2
Gun Crazy 3
Fallen Angels
Last Stop to Nowhere / The Last Goodbye
Revenge is Justice
Escape / Forget Me Not
Wedding Bell Blues / Breakdown
Mexico Time
Lobo
No Free Ride / Gone
Stealing America
No Escape

Harry Delaney Adventures

Dead Reckoning
Uncharted
Go-Around
Sand Storm

Frank Ross Biker Tales

No Way Out
Bank Robber Dames
Bad Girls

Other

The Last President

DEAD RECKONING

Copyright ©2025 P X Duke
All Rights Reserved

ISBN 978-1-928161-51-6

Dead Reckoning is a work of fiction. Any resemblance to persons living or dead is purely coincidental. Places mentioned by name are entirely fictitious and purely products of the author's imagination, and are not meant to bear resemblance to actual places or locations.

Publisher: P X Duke
Web site: https://pxduke.com
E-mail: peterxduke@gmail.com

9 8 7 6 5 4 3

Printed in the United States of America

For Delissa, Jean-Marc, Bob, and Stan.
They reckoned wrong.

For Irit, wherever you are.

Make my bed and light the light,
For I'll be home late tonight,
Blackbird, bye, bye.

When you don't have a plan, you often end up doing something called flying by the seat of your pants. In the world of aviation, that's known as Dead Reckoning, and for good reason.

If you reckon wrong, you can end up dead.

DEAD RECKONING

Some of this could be true.

PROLOGUE

We were living on the cheap, going native and spending our days and our money in a broken-down country in a broken-down town in a broken-down cantina. We were on the run from too much drink, too many women, a shortage of cash and East African desert—not necessarily in that order.

There was nothing too desperate in any of that. It was hardly enough to force us into being desperados.

My friend Mike Williams and I took up space in the small cantina in an attempt to while away the endless days and nights. By force of habit adopted from experience, we always sat with our backs against a wall. We liked to keep an eye on the doors and windows and what they might present beyond our control.

I learned to speak the language from the local señoritas who took a liking to me. Maybe it was my friendly manner. Maybe it was my ability to laugh at myself or to let them laugh at me. Or maybe it was the dancing I did with the girls on the cantina's dirt floor.

Perhaps even all of that. But mostly I figured it was the bit of cash I sent in their direction from time-to-time. That was all right with me, and it seemed like the thing to do.

The day was no different from the countless others that went before it. It was getting on to noon. We had been in the place for an hour, maybe a little longer. When you drink your lunch, you tend to lose track, and if you started early enough and waited long enough, the dark inside would eventually match the night outside.

We were flirting with the local color, but we weren't making any headway. Perhaps the girls started figuring us to be regulars. They might have known by now we were the only game in town.

The cantina picked up the lunch crowd, such as it was in the small town. It was looking like the pickings would be slim today. Such as it was, the crowd had already thinned. All the regulars were long departed.

Whatever was going on wasn't up for discussion. With nary a word to the gringos, the girls drifted away as well. Even the bartender disappeared.

Never one to miss an opportunity, I grabbed two teary, wet-stained Sol from behind the bar. They were cool and damp in my grip. I set them on our table and sat down to enjoy the fruits of my labor in the day's heat and humidity.

Mike nodded his thanks and tipped his head toward the door. The cantina darkened even more when an enormous man hesitated in the doorway. He blocked the entrance and the sun streaming past the door. It was replaced by a dark shadow cast on the dirt floor.

The stranger looked around for what I thought was a little longer than if he were only on the lookout for drinking buddies. He must have been satisfied by what he saw, because he entered.

Both hands clutched a dirty canvas bag tight against his body. He looked over at us, nodded, and took a seat at the deserted bar. He didn't stay long, probably because there was no one behind it to serve a drink. He looked around again, sweaty and shifty-eyed. Seemingly satisfied there was no one he knew, he stood up and shuffled toward the cantina's open back door.

A car door slammed. Tires slipped on gravel. A car pulled away. It left behind a cloud of dust that drifted into the cantina's dead air thanks to the breeze blowing outside.

I returned to the bar to refresh the Sol. My foot caught on something. I stumbled. Looked down in the dim light.

Squinted to recognize the bag on the dirt floor by the deserted barstool. The cantina stayed empty, but I didn't care about that. I was too immersed in trying to know if I should leave the bag where it was, or investigate further.

I figured I should investigate.

Bad idea—but I didn't think about that.

I made a grab for the bag and mumbled to Mike. "It's time to go." We stumbled our way out the door. Blinked our eyes and squinted into daylight. Climbed into our broken-down Jeep and took off for parts unknown. At a respectable distance down the road, we pulled over to investigate our purloined treasure.

One look inside the bag told us without a doubt the parts wouldn't remain unknown for long.

PART 1

Baja sur y norte

1

It's all about the money

"Do you have the money?"

"Yes. You know we do. We always do. Have we ever not had the money?"

"How much do you want?"

"We have the cash for ten."

"Hand it over. If the count is good, the boat will hook you up at the usual place."

"The count is good. We'll be waiting."

2

Harry Delaney and Mike Williams spent a week or ten days roaming parts of mainland Mexico. They mostly kept out of the major centers and wandered into the more out of the way places. They tried paying out good money for information.

That didn't work, so Harry rolled with the punches and used his gringo Spanish to attempt to verify local rumors. He got a little gun-shy about the trail he was leaving, but it was probably too late. He stopped worrying about it.

Mike had about enough of the wandering around as though they were lost in a desert. He had a belly-full of that in East Africa. So did Harry. Mike was the one who needed a break, so he took up residence in a cantina he thought he'd like. It turned out the girls were friendly and the dance floor was smooth. He decided to call it home for a few days before rejoining Harry to continue their research.

It wasn't so long after that when it all came together. They were about a hundred miles east of the Mar de Cortes. Or the Golfo de California. The locals used both names.

Harry fell into what had to be a former military airport. Two old hangars looked long-lost and deserted. Broken windows and cracked floors and walls said they had seen better days, but not recently. There were a few concrete pads that probably had Quonset huts on them at one time.

He needed to know how isolated the strip would be before they could put it to use. He camped out about a quarter-mile away in a deep depression obscured by desert scrub. It would help to keep him invisible while he kept eyes on the place.

In the daytime, with the sun beating down on that depression, it was hotter than a bitch. At night, it was as cold as the East African desert nights he was more familiar with. Sometimes he would wake up from a sweaty dream, thinking he was back in the thick of it.

Toward dark on one of his scouting expeditions, he discovered a small creek a hundred yards from his campsite. When the urge struck, he relieved the boredom by washing off the dust that accumulated thanks to the wind and the sand that drifted into the hollow.

It reminded him of a ghibli, the hot, dust-laden wind that comes up out of the Libyan desert. Minus the abundance of water he found in the creek, that is. That dry, dusty wind had shut down their North African operation more than a few times.

During daylight hours, he'd siesta in the afternoon with the best of them. By night he chanced cooking over an open fire. He would wait until the dead of morning when there wasn't much chance of anyone spotting the smoke.

By mid-week, there was no sign of anyone. The place was so isolated, it could only be meant for something illegal. That something illegal would put it right up their alley.

It was toward the end of his stakeout in the early morning, on his only recon of the buildings. Harry stumbled across a rickety-looking old Cub tucked away beside a hangar. It was hidden on three sides behind a scrub-covered berm. The berm kept the plane out of sight from everyone but the most determined—or the people who stashed it there.

Harry took time giving it a quick once-over. He dropped the cowlings. Visually, the engine appeared good and clean. There were no oil leaks. Fabric covering the wings and body was in good shape. Hell, what could go wrong with a Cub? It was an airplane meant for stick-and-rudder flying if there ever was one.

It came together fast. He had the airstrip. He had the airplane. It was everything he was looking for. He and Mike would be able to make their escape without leaving a trace.

All he needed was Mike Williams, his business partner in this fantasy they found themselves in.

Harry stood back, surveying the expanse of airport. He swiped at a sweaty forehead with the back of his hand. Clouds of dirt-road dust grew on the horizon. He scurried for cover behind a hangar wall. He needed to know for sure. He waited, concealed by a corner of the vast wooden building. The beater wheezed and backfired its way across the tarmac, finally screeching to a halt in the shade of the open hanger.

He stepped out to reveal himself and greet the driver. "I thought I recognized the sound of that wreck. How did the trip go?"

"Harry Delaney. As I live and breathe. I was starting to think you were a figment of my imagination," Mike Williams said.

Mike didn't look so good. He looked like he had spent too much time in a cantina. He was hung over. Shaking hands and the bloodshot eyes gave it away. He had to be coming off a drinking spree like nothing ever witnessed. Mike's eyes resembled two piss-holes in a snowbank. There was a problem with that, though. They were on mainland Mexico. Snow was at a premium.

"It must have been one hell of a party." Harry moved upwind just to be safe and grinned mightily, glad he wasn't in that condition. Whatever Mike's condition was. He still couldn't figure it out.

"Let me tell you. It lasted day and night," Mike began. "I think I wore holes in my shoes dancing with the señoritas." He looked down at his boots and swayed. "Then the locals took it upon themselves to get jealous. When the fist-swinging began, I was forced to do a quick-step dance to the baño to find a window out of that cantina."

He laughed at Mike's description of the hombres trying to get the girls onto the dance floor and away from the gringo with the money. Hell, he'd have been right there with him if he wasn't stuck in this shithole.

"Would you like to see your reward?" It had to be a reward

after everything they went through to find it. He led Mike to the Cub squatting in the dirt between the berms.

Mike said, "So this is it. She looks ugly as hell just sitting there, Harry. Does it have the range with those wheels?"

Someone had outfitted the Cub with tundra tires. They were huge, oversize tires normally found on the much larger DC-3. Low air pressure in those wheels would give the Cub the ability to land almost anywhere in the dirt. Considering the huge amount of dirt in this country, those wheels would be a definite asset.

"You'll need to watch the winds, but this is the one to do the job," Harry said.

Together they pushed the Cub into the shade of the hangar where it was marginally cooler. Mike groaned and cursed at the effort. He found and old push broom and lightly swept the ground to remove traces of tire tracks in case anyone came looking. When he finished, he wandered off to catch some much-needed shuteye in the truck's cab.

Mike looked like he needed just a little more of the hair of the dog that bit him than he needed shuteye, but he didn't let on.

Harry didn't let Mike close his eyes for long. He'd thank him for that when mid-afternoon arrived and the heat radiated off the tarmac in waves.

"Hey, partner, give me a hand—if you think you're up to it, that is."

He figured he wouldn't point him toward the creek until he didn't need him. If Mike fell in, he might not be capable of crawling out in his present condition.

"Cut me some slack. I'm up to it. I need a minute, is all." Mike held up a hand. He staggered across the cement slab burning up under the noon-day sun. He made it to the edge before stumbling and falling to his knees. He gagged twice. Clutched at his stomach. Convulsed and threw up.

"Are you going to need help to get back on your feet?" Harry asked.

Mike reached to pull a rag out of a back pocket. He managed a swipe at the sweat running down his face. "Damn, that's better. All right, I'm ready." He got half-way up, swayed from side to side, and went back on his knees.

The man didn't even get any puke on them. He must have had plenty of practice in that cantina he liked so much. He pushed himself up the rest of the way and grinned a shit-eater before dancing a jig. Fresh sweat poured down his face.

Harry shook his head, but they both knew he'd be in the same condition were he the one enjoying the sins of the cantinas and the girls. It had been a long month for both of them. Now that everything looked to be coming together, they had the end in sight.

"That's one ungainly looking airplane," Mike said, taking in the view.

"She's no beauty, but she'll do the job. And the price is right. Did you bring everything?" he asked.

"Yes. It's all here."

"I have to look over this tin can. We'll do a run-up when I'm done."

Despite throwing up, Mike still didn't look so good.

"Five days in that Mexican cantina pretty much tore me down and spit me out. I need to wash the stink off."

He was right about that. He took pity on him. "Follow the trail to the creek." I waved a hand in the general direction.

He'd have to cross the heat emanating from the tarmac before he'd find relief in the cool of the tall grass.

"The water isn't so bad. Don't drown before the job is over."

Harry retrieved his tool kit and went to work. He popped the engine cowlings. Inspected the engine with a fine-tooth comb. Pulled the fuel bowl and took a look at the filter. He drained the fuel line.

There was no rust. No water. No nothing.

He slipped off the leads and pulled the plugs. The color was good. The plug wires looked to be new. This airplane was somebody's baby. Whoever owned it would be some pissed when he showed up and found it desaparecido. Disappeared.

Even the control cables were new. He knew, because he

checked. No way would he take a chance on anything going wrong that would endanger Mike.

Mike showed up from the creek looking clean and refreshed. He was just in time to help push the Cub toward the open hangar doors.

With wheels chocked, he climbed in. He called out, "Magnetos off. Fuel on. Carb heat off. Prime two pumps."

Harry walked around front and pulled four blades.

"Magnetos on!" Mike yelled.

Harry pulled on the prop one more time and stepped back. She fired right up. He was right. This was one well-maintained airplane. In the cockpit, Mike did his run-up in a cloud of dust.

He pulled the wheel chocks, and Mike got to work taxiing figure eights inside the hangar. When he was satisfied, he shut down.

"What's with that fancy dancing?" Harry asked. It couldn't be.

"Bonus. Someone rigged the brakes," he said.

It was a definite bonus. Someone had set up the brakes to be used individually on those huge tundra tires. It turned a plane that could turn on a dime into one that would turn on the head of a pin. He hadn't told Mike.

"Yeah, I left them the way they were. I wondered how long it would take you. So what do you think?"

"Damn but she started like a dream," Mike said. "I can hand-bomb it by myself, no problem. She runs smooth, too. It's a bear looking over that nose on those wheels. Angle taxiing should take care of that."

"I wouldn't sweat the taxiing. She'll be good to go from wherever you park her with those tires. Hell, you could land on a shore swell wearing shoes like that. You could probably take off from one, too."

Harry didn't need to tell him. Mike was too experienced not to know.

To celebrate, they cracked a couple of Sol and sat down in the shade. He noticed right off Mike smelled a lot sweeter after his trip to the creek.

"We're good to go," he told him.

"Harry, the sooner I fly her out of this place, the happier I'll be." Mike was almost too eager to get on with it. Already he had a chart out and was contemplating the blue-colored expanse of water it presented.

"I'm with you on that. I've been leaving a trail a mile wide. I don't think your generosity in the cantinas has gone unnoticed either."

They settled back and relaxed, knowing they'd be heading out soon.

"El Dorado is an eighty-mile hop to the west. I plan on keeping a low profile and staying away from the cantinas. For a change, I'll count the churches while I'm waiting for your call," Mike promised.

As far as counting churches went, they both knew it would be an impossible task in this country.

"I didn't get any puke sacks for you," I joked. The wide grin told me he was coming around.

"I won't need any if that engine performs. The pucker factor will be high until I nurse her across to dry land."

"I don't envy you on that first leg to Los Muertos, but that engine is as good as gold, I promise you that." It didn't need to be said, but he did anyway.

"I'll hold you to that, Harry."

They clinked bottles and chugged, celebrating as only they knew how.

"I'll see you across the water," Mike added.

"You know it, partner."

3

On a road trip down the Baja more than a few years ago, Harry had heard rumors of an old fly-in fishing camp at Los Muertos on the Golfo side. The place was once popular with the moneyed crowd in the 50s. Times changed. The camp fell out of favor and ended up being unceremoniously dumped and deserted.

Unseen, Los Muertos became their plan A, and thus critical to the operation. It was to be the first stop on their trek north up the Baja. It was the closest point of land, separated as it was by the Gulfo de California, from the mainland and El Dorado. If the old Los Muertos strip was usable, Mike would have a place to land the Cub after his 200-mile flight over the Gulfo's open water.

They had no plan B.

Mike had already agreed to do the flying.

Harry was tasked with confirming the existence and usability of the Los Muertos strip. It took two days of hard driving through wind and heat and dust and dirt. It didn't help that the Jeep impostor was an old, uncovered, broken-down excuse for transportation. Miraculously, it got him from the mainland and down the Baja. He could have taken a more direct route overnight on a ferry. He'd have a good night's sleep, too. The downside was the required permits would create a paper trail for the vehicle and for him.

Mike's problem wouldn't be one of time, unless he

considered three hours over open water on a wheeled Cub a problem. He didn't envy him. Mike would need all the nerve he could muster to nurse an ancient, single-engine plane on oversize wheels across two hundred miles of open water.

Harry made the turnoff from Mexico 1 into La Paz. After the non-stop overland drive, he was looking forward to a shave and a shower. He wanted to flush the Baja grime, thanks to the open Jeep, down the drain. First things first, though. He picked up a phone card and checked the number before dialing Mike on the mainland. Mike had taken up residency in a small cantina while he waited. By now the girls were probably calling him el loco gabacho behind his back.

Mike's comeback, after someone tracked him down, took him by surprise. "I'm not spending any money on the cantina girls. They stopped talking to me. I can't find any more churches to count. Tell me you're somewhere close to Los Muertos."

He did just that. "I'll be stocking up on refreshments when I hang up. Another hour of driving and I'll be there."

The line went dead. The man wasn't kidding when he said he was tired of counting churches.

Harry spent the last of his pesos and loaded up with fuel, food, and ice for the Sol they both found an appetite for before threading his way south out of the city. Only an hour later, the Jeep was rattling down the rough overland trail to a beat-up shack off the west end of the old Los Muertos landing strip.

He picked a spot in the shade and leaned back against the ramshackle building. If he leaned too hard he thought it might collapse. He tested a few times before settling in to wait. What could be more boring than that?

Harry drank cold Sol to wash away the dust that accumulated in the back of his throat. It was a long, sun-burned, two-thousand-mile trek in the open, broken-down Jeep. With luck, there might a bottle or two for Mike when he showed up.

His mind started to wander. Was Mike airborne yet? He closed his eyes and allowed himself to imagine easy street being a lot closer than it had been back on the mainland.

His eyes closed for a well-deserved siesta. His head banged against the shack hard enough to wake him up. The building didn't fall down. He grabbed a beer and began walking the strip. It was rough and uneven. There were sharp rocks scattered around, capable of puncturing normal tires on a heavy twin or even a single-engine aircraft. He didn't bother with them. The strip was usable for our purposes. The low-pressure tundra tires on the Cub would make short work of the rock-covered, unstable ground of the deserted landing strip.

He congratulated himself on the ease with which this make-work project of theirs had finally come together. The rest of it would be a piece of cake.

When he and Mike landed in Mexico, they were on the last legs of an adventure that began in East Africa. What once started out to be just another flying job turned into something else when it went south and made the news. He and Mike got nervous. When two guys on the same wavelength got to talking, they had to agree their days were numbered.

Harry extricated himself in time, but not before having to contribute a little baksheesh in the form of bribes to the local economy. To say it didn't benefit his health and well-being would be an understatement.

Thanks to Mike and a welcome escape from a North African jail, he was loaded into the back of a truck. What followed was a long, cross-country driving adventure across North Africa to Tangier. From there, they boarded a flight into Spain. Along the way, they collected a few battle scars.

They carried those scars from Spain into Mexico City. From there they headed north into what was, for them, uncharted territory in northern Mexico. They figured on the anonymity and isolation to keep them out of the frying pan they'd somehow stepped into across the ocean.

So far, they were lucky that way. They were completely unaware they had stepped into an entirely new frying pan on this side of the ocean. That it didn't appear to be non-stick didn't figure until much later.

Harry finished walking the Los Muertos strip in time to hear faint engine sounds. It took him out of his thirst-induced reverie and he allowed his eyes to sweep the sky over open water. He cupped an ear. It had to be Mike and the Cub. Who else would risk a chance approach to this hellish bit of real estate? He waited, impatient for the sound to grow louder.

He shaded his eyes against the sky and squinted. Sure enough, Mike and the yellow Cub were on a distant final, low and slow over the water.

He checked his watch. Mike was about on the edge of his usable fuel.

The Cub's wings waggled. He recognized me. Excited, Harry waved and danced a jig, picturing the gleeful grin Mike had to be wearing. He had just crossed 200 miles of open water in a wheeled aircraft. He would be on the ground in minutes.

The engine coughed. It caught and then coughed again. Sputtered. Came back to life. He'd make shore. Barely. The smile would be gone, and he'd be sweating it to touch down on land. The engine sputtered and died and Harry knew his thinking Mike would make it jinxed him.

The sound of silence followed the Cub on its downward glide toward the shoreline.

Mike's only option was a dead-stick landing. The Cub disappeared from Harry's vantage point at the base of the rise. Did Mike have the altitude to make it over the strip's threshold? He ran to the crest in time to spot a single puff of dust turn into two as oversize tires grabbed for dirt, one after the other.

The Cub's high wings fluttered as it rolled and bumped on oversize tires on the uneven terrain of the unkempt landing strip. As though in a dream, the Cub coasted to a silent stop. Harry grabbed a fuel can and the handful of tools he'd need to troubleshoot and made for the Cub to greet Mike.

Already Mike was out and making his way toward the shack.

"Running out of fuel in the air will get you fired from any reputable company," he told him.

They stopped and regarded each other. Mike was pale as a ghost and shaking. It wasn't from booze. It was the reaction taking over when he realized the job could have had a different outcome had he not been within gliding distance of shore when the engine quit.

"That's true, partner, but we both know this outfit is being run by the seat of the owner's pants."

"So then you're calling our operation fly-by-night," Harry said, to emphasize the point.

"Pretty much." Mike's comeback was better. "Even in daylight."

Mike swiped a forearm at the sweat running down face. His sweat-soaked shirt told the tale, too. It had been a close call, and they both knew it—Mike most of all. It got a lot hotter in the cockpit when the engine sputtered and quit.

"You made it just in time, Mike."

"She never skipped a beat coming across. I'm pretty sure the engine quit due to fuel starvation. If it isn't, I won't be happy about the next leg. There's a lot of open water I have to fly to make our next stop."

He was right.

"How does she handle?" He wanted to keep him talking so he didn't think about it.

"She flies like a dream, even with those oversize tires grabbing for all that air," he admitted. "Once I had her aimed for the strip, she floated right in, dead engine and all."

"There's food and water in the shack." He knew it wasn't what he was looking for after his experience with two hundred miles of open water and a dead engine on final.

"Did you pick up any Sol?" Mike was having a love affair with the Mexican beer since he arrived in-country. He was no stranger to it, either.

"You need to ask? I think I might have left you a couple or four in there somewhere. It'll be warm by now," he added. It was true.

"Never stopped me before. You either." That was true too.

Mike wasn't the only one wondering why the engine failed. Right off, Harry turned the carb drain. Nothing came out. He yelled back to Mike with the results. With both of them satisfied, he got busy with tape, paintbrush and a small can of paint and drew out a made-up N-number on the port side of the Cub's tail. He left the Mexican registration on the starboard.

It was simple reasoning. If Mike was forced to land the Cub in civilization, they figured it would keep the local authorities confused long enough for him to make a flying getaway.

He pulled the plugs. They were clean and clear. He pulled the oil dipstick to check the level and found it good. He opened and closed the carb drain again. Still nothing. That was a good sign. He added fuel from the can and walked around to the cockpit to check magnetos on and the throttle setting on ground idle. He pulled the prop through and the Cub fired right up. He got in and taxied to the shack before shutting down.

"You were right. It was fuel. I noticed something else, too."

"What's that?" Mike asked.

"You've got fabric peeling off the top surface on the starboard wing. Past the wing brace."

They weren't expecting anything like that. The fabric was perfect last he had checked on the mainland.

"How the hell did that happen?" Mike wanted to know.

How indeed?

"The entrance point on the fabric wing's bottom is a perfect circle. Did you notice anything when you left El Dorado?"

"The underside has a hole too? That can only mean one thing. I saw a cloud of dust on the road to the strip. I was airborne by then. How bad is it?"

"The shooter missed all the good parts but for the fabric," Harry said. "I have what I need to make the repair. Good thing it wasn't buckshot."

Buckshot would have ripped an enormous hole in the fabric and torn up the wing ribs. It would have hit the spar, too, causing the wing to fail. The Cub and Mike would have been a smoking pyre off the end of his departure strip.

"It's fifteen hundred miles of dust and dirt to get this fly-by-night operation up to the cabin in Colorado. I still have a sea of open water to cross. The last thing I need is a problem with the fabric, Harry."

"Don't worry. The repair will be good." He took a roll of duct tape out of his bag and held it up. "Whoever took the shot missed the good parts." He tried to make it a positive. "Besides, you're here to talk about it."

"I know you're more than capable. I'm not sweating it. The gas we'll have to use won't do a thing for the valves." Mike wasn't happy about that.

One of his concerns was using automobile gas in the Cub's aircraft engine. Modern car gas was already low lead. It might not be as low as aircraft gas, but it was good enough for our purposes. We'd already talked it over, but with the dead-stick landing he was forced to do, he was running it through his head again.

He couldn't say he blamed him.

"We have to keep away from airports. We can get auto gas anywhere, even by the side of the highway when we need it," he reminded him.

The locals were happy to provide gas from 55-gallon drums to gringos who drove the trans-peninsula highway. It wasn't the best fuel for a piston aircraft engine, but it would keep us away from airports and the questions that would come with them.

"Did you paint the registration?" Mike asked.

"Yes."

Mike was definitely on edge. He'd crossed two hundred miles of open water known as the Sea of Cortez. The Golfo de California, the Mexicans called it. He did it in an airplane outfitted with wheels. His engine had quit on approach. Furthermore, he'd just found out his airplane was shot up back on the mainland.

As far as Harry was concerned, Mike could be as edgy as he wanted. "I know crossing that water was no picnic. If you want, I'll fly the next leg." He wondered if he was being tested, but at this point, he didn't think so. He and Mike had been friends too long and been through too much for that.

"No, I'm good," Mike said. "You have your hands full with everything else."

They walked around to check out the cargo in the back of the Cub. The butt of Mike's double-barreled sawed-off stuck out from a bag. It was something he picked up during their last African adventure, a souvenir thanks to a woman who saved their grateful asses.

"Rough night last night, or the jitters?" he asked.

Mike continued to nurse his Sol. He'd shown remarkable restraint so far. "The jitters. I'm still on edge from being over that water for two hundred and change. I'm not accustomed to being beyond gliding distance without a set of floats beneath me. The kicker was hearing about that hole in the fabric."

Harry wondered how long Mike's restraint would last. "I'd be shaking like a leaf if it was me that jumped over all that water sporting wheels. Don't be concerned about the wing patch. I'll tape it up good. It will hold one hundred percent—top and bottom."

"I need to unwind, is all," he replied.

"So you know, everything looks good, just like back on the mainland. Oil burn in negligible. The fuel line and filter is clear. That airplane is as good as gold. It's the wind that isn't. I wish it would be as reliable."

For good measure, he told him once more it was fuel starvation that caused the engine failure.

"I trust your judgment, Harry. You know that. As long as there's food, I'll be okay." He grinned at me. "And a Sol or two."

Were it him in Mike's position, he'd trust his judgment, too.

"I picked up a gas stove. There's a week's worth of canned goods and water in the shed. I didn't drink all your beer," he assured him. "If it takes longer than that, I'll be back with supplies. In case I miss you, I'll spot fuel at Coronado on the beach."

"I'll go over the charts again before I leave," Mike said.

"How was your dead reckoning crossing the water?" Dead reckoning was a familiar turn of phrase, known to every bush pilot in the world. If you reckoned wrong during a flight over unknown territory, you could end up dead.

"I was off by a couple of miles. Maybe three," he assured me.

That wasn't so bad for two hundred miles across open water

in a lowly Cub. He doubled down on the ask. "Are you sure you don't want me to take this leg?"

"I'm good for it," Mike insisted.

The next stop for fuel was a hundred and eighty miles to the north.

"Since you're not offering me one of your treasured Sol, I'll be heading back to the highway," Harry said. "I'll see you again in Coronado on that stretch of beach south of town."

Mike nodded. "Count on it."

On the way north, he stopped to fuel the beat-up Jeep on the outskirts of La Paz. Across the road, a taquería called his name. He went looking for fish tacos and Sol, found both, and settled in. Damn but the tacos were just what he needed. The breath of humidity on the bottle of Sol wasn't so bad either. He didn't have time to waste, though. He grabbed a couple to go.

He had somewhere he needed to be in a hurry.

4

All right, so he changed his mind. How could an oasis surrounded by a shady grove of coco palms be all that bad? It couldn't.

Except.

Mike warned me about los Cocos. It was a good place for a relaxing meal and a cold beer, he said. Next door was a place he called the crazy snail with cheap beer and girls. He never said if the girls were cheap. He never mentioned it might be trouble, either.

It was called *El Caracol Loco*, according to the sign. So it was the crazy snail. Mike was right. He was probably right about the rest of it, too.

Harry opened the burn phone and checked the time. He had enough to spare for one, at least. He'd take a quick look around and be back on the road in a flash. When next he met up with Mike, he'd file a report and they'd have a laugh.

He pulled open the door and walked in to the darkest bar he had ever been in. It took at least a minute for his eyes to adjust to the cantina's dark interior. He tried not to trip as he groped his way to the long bar running the length of the room. On the way, he mentally rehearsed his gringo Spanish for what would probably turn out to be a lazy bartender. What he wanted a nice cold cerveza with a dash of humidity running down the side, but he'd settle for anything.

He made it to the bar without tripping over anything. Just

as he thought, the bartender ignored him. He apparently found it easy to spot the gabacho. That, or he didn't want to be disturbed. Perhaps it was both. Obviously, he didn't think the dust-covered, sweaty gringo had money to spend.

"Sol, por favor," he ordered, in case the bartender was looking for something to do.

He didn't notice the girls right away. The dirty, faded mirror behind the bar he was attempting to use to watch his back wasn't reflecting much of anything in the dim light.

He turned and headed for the baño and a quick wash. That's when he noticed them. In all their brightly-colored glory. They were sitting at a table with their backs against the wall where they could survey the bar for incoming fresh meat.

The prettiest one looked to be about eighteen, but it was hard to know for sure in the bar's dingy light. She had a low-cut top, just low enough to show off what she had. Given his experience, he figured that until they were around thirty, they all looked to be eighteen.

That low-cut top wasn't so low that it made her look like she was bragging. Or begging.

On his way past, he gave her the eye and smiled. She smiled right back. In the baño, he scrubbed down with a whore's bath and slicked back his hair with water. He swiped at the mirror to wipe away the fog. A quick glance convinced him he looked about good enough.

He made his way back to the bar and the full beer he had called for and there she was, sitting beside it like she was its protector.

He chugged the beer, in a hurry to wash away two days of road dust and dirt and hot wind. Slammed the empty bottle down on the bar. Waved for another. He wanted to be sure it was gone before he tempted fate. It didn't help. He knew right off he was in trouble. The sooner he got the temptation done with, the faster he'd be able to get back on the road.

At least, that was the plan. It seemed more than reasonable. In fact, the more he thought about it, the more reasonable it became. He sat down and succumbed to temptation. How could he refuse? It was sitting right beside him, just like a devil.

"Hola, señorita." He was feeling a tad tongue-tied. It was the best he could do. He checked his phone one more time in the drab bar and snapped it shut. It was still early. He had plenty of time.

"Buenos d'as," she replied.

The woman's voice was soft and sweet. He could barely hear her. He leaned in. Shoulders touched. His head came up against soft hair and a wisp of perfume. "Habla inglés?"

She tilted her head. "Poquito. A little."

"Bueno. Permit me to buy you a drink." It was the least he could do for a woman who smelled so good.

"Si. Limonada, por favor."

No beginner, that bartender. He couldn't ignore him any longer. He had the lemonade in front of her in an instant.

He made a grab for the Sol he slid down the bar in his direction. Now that he was flirting with the local color, the bartender must have thought he deserved better service. Either that, or he was working on a percentage basis now.

He went with the percentage.

"Gracias." He tipped the bottle in the barkeep's direction and took a nice, cool slug.

Her name was Medianoche. Midnight. He hoped it wouldn't be the harbinger of things to come. He had to get back on the road. They parlayed back and forth, neither making much sense to the other. He began to think Medianoche was a lost cause until her older sister showed up. Or maybe it was one of her compatriots in the bar.

Lupita's command of English wasn't as bad as that of Medianoche. His Spanish only improved as he pounded back the Sol. On the uneven dance floor, he stumbled his way through a couple of sweaty juke-box numbers while clutching at each of the girls in turn.

He checked the time again. Past midnight. Mexico time worked better for him so he turned the phone off. The girls would keep me nice and safe as the hours passed. Or until my money ran out.

The only thing remaining for my newfound amigas was to get their hands on my wallet. Not to be outdone, he only wanted to get his hands on both of them.

In his drunken stupor, he thought it about evened them up.

It was hours later. He found himself wide awake on top of sweat-dampened sheets. He felt around the empty bed. There were no warm spots. He worked at an eye and got it open. The room was empty. The girls were history.

He felt for his wallet. It was missing, too. He reached down to the floor and felt for his clothes. He looked over the edge for his socks. Double bonus—he had both, and they were on my feet. The money stash he kept in them was there, too, wrapped in tinfoil.

He had no idea what the bartender fed him, but it had knocked him down and out for the count. His head throbbed. He got out of bed and stood up, and the throbbing turned into pounding. He wasn't completely blameless for his misfortune, no matter how much he told myself it was no fault of his own.

It was time to get back on the road. He picked up his pants and checked the pockets for the keys to the Jeep before pulling them on. He did a walk of shame past El Caracol Loco's open door as la musica blared, calling his name. He wouldn't be searching out last night's compadres, though. There would be no fond adiós. Las hermanosas and their lazy bartender would have to enjoy his money without him. Surely it wouldn't be a great difficulty.

His head pounded so hard his eyes hurt. The suspension on the Jeep was no help. HIs head wobbled like a hula-skirted dashboard dolly. Such were the hazards of drink—not to mention the hazards of sweet Medianoche. He knew how Mike felt when he had to get down on all fours to steady himself so he could throw up.

Not that he was unfamiliar with the maneuver.

By the time he passed the beach fifteen miles south of Coronado he was so hung over he missed the palapa across the dune. No way was he turning back to sleep beneath palm fronds. All he wanted was to climb into a bed and snore.

He backtracked to the Hotel Las Palmas on the malecón. It worked for him.

Yesterday's hangover became all but forgotten in the fresh light of morning and a sunbeam leaking through the open patio door. He felt like a dog snoozing in the sun. Around noon—or maybe it was afternoon—he roused himself without giving an old dog's shake to make for the bathroom. He needed a refresher and a quick shower to wash away last night's sins.

The trusty old Jeep fired right up. He steered for the beach south of town. It was where he and Mike had agreed to meet for his next fuel stop. It's where he was to set up camp and wait out Mike's arrival.

And then he remembered.

He didn't have fuel for the Cub.

Okay, so maybe he wasn't over yesterday's drunken orgy. He herded the Jeep back to town one more time to fill the jerry cans. In the mercado he stocked up on fresh food and beer and ice for the coolers before making for the beach.

He groaned the Jeep over the dune to the beach and the sole palapa and halted beside it. He dug out the tent and the poles and got it assembled with a minimum of cursing. He gathered a stash of driftwood to burn hot and bright in the firepit. Glowing embers would soon rise into the night sky.

So far, in my estimation the day went pretty well. Everything he and Mike would need was at the campsite. He waited for the sun to finish dropping below the hills to the west. The cold Sol went down with it. In the dying twilight, he enjoyed what was left of the fire's lazy warmth before it died to glowing coals. The rest of the world didn't exist in the darkness beyond.

Isolated and content in a world of his making, his only concern was for Mike and the Cub. Exhausted, he dozed off into a much-needed and relaxed sleep while thinking about the drawbacks to their plan.

There were a few.

The Cub wasn't known for its long-distance abilities. That was the flaw in their attempt to fly it north. They were stretching it to stay on the edge of civilization, and it was chancy. That became obvious when Mike ran out of fuel on final to the Los Muertos strip.

The biggest problem Mike would encounter on this leg would be the wind that flowed out of California's Imperial Valley far to the north. It funneled south, trapped between the Baja peninsula and the mainland for a thousand miles along the length of the Golfo. That wind could last for days at a time. When it did, it was in the wrong direction to benefit Mike and the Cub's limited range.

Mike would need a tailwind to help get him up the coast. In this neighborhood, that wind was known as a Coromuel. A Coromuel occurred whenever a Pacific wind blew in and dumped down the mountains west of La Paz. If Mike got lucky and hit the back side of La Paz at the right time of day, he'd end up riding the leading edge north over the islands and across to Coronado.

He settled in at the campsite, prepared for a long wait.

5

A vehicle groaning in low gear was attempting to work its way over the top of the dune hiding the palapa Harry was camping under. The dune helped conceal the palapa from the main road. That invisibility drew him to the site from the beginning. Either they were locals out for a party, or touristas who had been there before.

The engine whined as it drew closer and then died to an idle when headlights crested the dune and the vehicle began its descent. The lights tracked him where he stood by the fire, blinding him.

High-pitched voices cut through the night. Female. Laughing and giggling. Drunk, by the sound of it.

Just in case, he sand-crabbed beyond the fire and out of range of the headlights. The engine groaned and started. He recognized it as a microbus. Headlights aimed for the tent beneath the palapa. Whoever it was, they weren't strangers to the beach. The lights went out and the engine died. Doors slammed.

Two gringas. How the hell would he get rid of two of them, drunk or sober? He stepped back into the blazing orange light of the fire.

"Hola!" one of them called out. "We thought we saw a campfire from the highway and thought we'd come down for a look. We were right. You took over our palapa."

Christ. They thought they owned the place. He grabbed a

stick and poked at the fire. His .45 was in the tent. If this encounter went south, he'd never get to it in time. He kicked himself in the ass for being complacent.

"Well, it's all mine now," he said, not to be outdone. "How long are you planning on hanging around?" He figured he might as well get to it, obvious or not.

"A couple of days. We need to get home by the weekend."

Two days. That sounded about right if Mike got lucky with the wind. He'd have some female company while he waited out Mike's arrival on the back of the Coromuel.

"What the hell. Unload and we'll share."

The one with the long, dark hair walked back to the van. Nervous, he followed her with his eyes as she almost disappeared into a dark shadow in the night. He chased after her. He needed a look inside.

The van's interior turned out to be empty but for suitcases and clothes scattered on a foamy. No stray men that he could see.

"What's your name?" he asked the dark-haired beauty.

"Sasha. That's Barbara by the fire." A blond. That was all right with him, too.

"I'm Harry. When you get set up, come on over to the fire and I'll spot you a cold one for that warm trash in your cooler." He was guessing their ice had run out.

Sasha made another trip to the van and returned with a chair. The other one disappeared.

"Where did your friend get to?" He was more than a little curious. He was worried, too.

"Barbara's in the van. She'll sleep there tonight."

Gringas. They no sooner arrived, and it was all figured out. Either he was the luckiest bastard in the world or come morning he'd be fresh meat hung out to dry in the back of that van.

He never learned, but he kept right on trying.

"How long have you been down in this part of the world?" he didn't really care, but if she was looking for conversation, he was her man.

"About a month," Sasha said. "We ran out of money so

we're headed home."

"Money. I know all about running out of it, all right. What are you heading home to?"

"Not so much. We don't have jobs. No one is waiting for us," she admitted.

So then, he had two good-looking chicas with no boyfriends. Hard to believe. "I need another beer. You want one?" All she could say was no.

"Sure."

On the way, he grabbed the full water bucket warming by the fire. He climbed onto the hood of the Jeep to reach the palapa's roof.

"What the hell are you doing?" Sasha asked. "Is that where you keep your beer? I'm not going to steal it."

"I've got a home-made shower spotted up there. I'll be under it in a few minutes."

"No shit." Sasha jumped up and began tearing off her clothes. "Turn it on, dammit." She was bossy, but he forgave her the instant he saw her naked in the full light of the fire.

"There's only enough water for one." Now why the hell had he added that?

"Then we'll share. I don't mind."

He didn't, either. Sasha wasn't a shy one. The water cascaded down her long, dark hair and flowed over her breasts. To get a better look, he shifted her hair out of the way behind her neck.

"Are you done looking yet?" she asked.

He figured he wasn't the first man to hear that question. He didn't look up. His eyes were busy admiring her breasts. His hands joined them, cupping and lifting. Nipples grew hard, and he admired those, too.

She sighed.

He finally answered. "No." He hoped his answer didn't come too late.

"Good."

The water ran out and he handed her a towel. "We're out of beer, too."

"Good." She permitted me to feast on her performance before handing over the wet towel.

"You're not much of a talker, are you?" He wasn't expecting an answer.

The early morning sun warmed the tent enough to make it comfortable. Harry pulled the covers back to take a fresh look at last night's body in the light of a new day. It was the right thing to do.

He wasn't disappointed.

He unzipped the tent and stepped out to discover Barbara had the fire going full tilt. He smiled and she and he forgot all about her when he got busy frying bacon and cracking eggs.

"I found your shower. Have you got a spare towel?" Barbara asked.

She was in front of him, naked and dripping. She hadn't bothered to cover a thing with arms and hands. Erect nipples stared at him. He stared back. She wasn't a shy one by any stretch, either. Damn. One he could handle. Two and he had some doubts. She had great legs, though. Among other things.

And she was a bottle blond. That was all right, too.

"Right. The towel." He handed her one. She didn't bother turning around. Hell, he'd have checked out her ass, too, if she did.

"Did you forget your glasses?"

That was a question out of nowhere. She was the one performing, after all. What the hell? He didn't wear glasses. Then he got it, finally.

"I need to check on the eggs. I don't want to ruin anything."

Barbara snickered as the long buzz of the tent's zipper broke the ice, and Sasha stepped out. She had her long dark hair tied back. Her bangs framed the dark brown eyes of a true beauty. This was getting too good to be true.

"Something smells good," she said. "I had to investigate."

He dug into a box in the back of the Jeep and broke out plates and cutlery while the women carried on.

"How did you sleep?"

Barbara's question wasn't directed my way. He piled eggs and bacon on three plates and sat down to busy myself with a fork.

"Not so good. The mattress was a little lumpy in places," Sasha complained.

He ignored his eggs and glanced up to catch the women trading looks before bursting out laughing. "That must be an old joke."

"Kind of, but we don't mean anything by it. It's not a dig at you. If anything, it's a compliment."

He almost pinched himself. Maybe he should have. Instead, he announced breakfast.

"Sit down. Shut up. Eat. Or I'll toss it out. Anyone who wants toast will have to walk to town."

When the women finished, there was nothing left to throw out.

Harry convinced the women to climb into the Jeep and the headed to town to play at being touristas. He had a ton of questions that needed asking. He hoped they'd break the ice by asking their own. When that didn't happen, he decided not to ask any of his.

They walked the sleepy streets until they tired of it. They piled into the Jeep to head for the market. They finished picking out fresh fruit and returned to the Jeep.

Barbara lifted the tarp to load the grocery bags. "Why do you have so much gas? There's plenty on the way north. Does this old crate burn that much?"

"I thought I might pick up a generator for the campsite." That stopped the questions, but when Mike arrived, he knew Mike would have his own about the company he was keeping. The man would be very nervous. Hell, he would too if he found himself in his place.

"Does anyone want to rent a panga and take a cruise?" No way did he want to spend the day at the campsite making idle conversation. It occurred to him he might be too friendly for his own good.

They tracked down a pangero on the malecón and loaded up his panga with a cooler of Sol. He pointed the panga south toward Isla del Carmen. On the way, he caught sight of a huge cabin cruiser moored a long way offshore in the low tide.

"Now there's something I'd like to own one day," he said à propos of nothing.

"You'd need a crew," Sasha said.

"You're right about that. Are you available?" he asked.

"When you get the boat, try giving us a call," said Barbara, the smartass.

He took it as a definite no.

Out in the channel, the panga bounced in the chop. The wind strengthened. It appeared to be changing direction. He couldn't wait any longer to question the captain. "Is this the start of a Coromuel?"

"It could well be, señor." He took off his cap and wiped his brow with a handkerchief. "For the past week, there has been a strong northerly. There is no doubt a change is due. The wind appears to be coming around, but it is slow."

He didn't want to take any chances. "Capitán, it's time we headed back."

It was late afternoon when the pangero tied off on the malecón. The cooler was empty. The women had lapped up most of the Sol. He didn't care. The prospect of a favorable wind had him on edge. He needed to get back to the beach.

If Mike was on his way, he'd be cutting it fine. If he was in a hurry, he'd fuel up, steal the Sol, and leave a note. He'd be well on his way north to the next stop. They had agreed there would be no waiting around. He'd be doing catch-up. Hell, he'd do the same to him.

There was one slight problem. The fuel was sitting in the back of the Jeep. In its place, he'd have to be satisfied with drinking the Sol.

By the time Harry turned off the highway backtracking to the beach, the girls were singing at the top of their drunken lungs. The Jeep crested the rise and the top of the palapa came into view. He could finally unload his drunk passengers.

Suddenly, the singing halted.

6

Mike Williams leaned casually against the Cub, a lone sentry waiting to see what was up. He would have recognized the Jeep and the tent beneath the palapa.

Harry figured the shotgun was high on his mind right about then, given he had just showed up with two women in tow. The double-barreled sawed-off would be hanging off his right shoulder beneath his jacket.

No doubt it was cocked.

He gave him the sign saying everything was all right, and he answered with his own before walking up to greet him.

"When did you get here?" Harry asked.

"About a half-hour ago," he replied. "The tail-wind from La Paz turned into a roller-coaster of a ride."

"You're here now. That's all that matters," he assured him.

"And glad of it. What's with the company you're keeping? Is it accidental or on purpose?"

Harry knew it was killing Mike to find out. "They pulled into the campsite late last night. I think it was accidental. There are no tells so far."

"Good. In case you didn't notice, I'm a little nervous."

The shotgun.

"Yeah, I noticed all right. That's a good thing. Barbara is the blond. Sasha is the dark-haired beauty."

"Let me guess." He didn't have to. He knew my proclivities when it came to women.

"Why would you guess? You already know the answer. Old habits die hard."

They grinned back and forth.

"Chicas, I'd like to introduce you to Mike." He wanted to keep it light.

They grinned. Mike's return smile wasn't so friendly. At least it was a smile.

He felt he had to explain. "These two crashed into my campsite last night in a drunken stupor. I made the mistake of taking pity by inviting them to stay. As you can see, they're still here."

Mike had a wary eye on the van. The suspense finally got to be too much. "That's a nice-looking van for being so old."

"We bought it together for this trip," Barbara replied. "It saves us a lot of money and time when we don't have to set up a tent."

"Mind if I look?" Mike didn't wait for permission. He made his way to the van. Sasha followed him. He opened the doors, front, side and back, all while feigning interest.

"It looks to be in good shape for a 67," he said.

"Barbara picked it out. It was already set up for camping. Everything works, including the old tape deck." Sasha halted and then added, "We like it because we don't have to pay for hotels."

Mike made his way back to the tent.

Harry heard the clicks. He was emptying his shotty and stowing it in the tent. He talked at him through the walls. "Are you happy now?"

"Yes. I need to get something to eat. I haven't had anything since I stopped to fuel up out in the boonies."

"What? Say that again," he insisted.

"I landed on a playa across from the old salt flats. I didn't want to chance another dead-stick landing, so I borrowed some fuel."

Harry couldn't resist the crack. "Don't worry. You won't be fired any time soon. How are those tires working out?"

"Those things are the cat's ass. The oversize tires float that crate over the sand."

"We got lucky, didn't we?" They both knew it.

"That we did. Now let's stop talking shop and start paying attention to your company, beach bum." Mike grinned.

"They're our company now." That made it plain.

The beach bums devoured supper like it was the last meal they would see. The dregs of the Sol came in handy to wash it down. When no one could eat nothing more, Sasha cranked up the tunes, and they danced up a sandstorm around the fire like there would never be a tomorrow.

"How did the two of you end up down here with an airplane and a Jeep?" Sasha wanted to know.

Here we go.

Still, it surprised me that the questions hadn't started sooner. Truth or lie? Half-and-half worked for him, but he always had a hard time remembering which half he lied about.

"Mike and I were in East Africa working for an exploration company."

That was the truth.

"When the job ended, we got out on an R&R. We were sitting around in Spain with nothing to do but get into trouble. First thing we jumped aboard an airplane for Mexico City and here we are. Now that we're almost broke, we're headed home. It's time to go back to work."

That was putting it mildly. The sooner he and Mike could get out of this place, the better. Added bonus, no one asked how the plane fit into the equation.

Harry turned to Sasha and asked what he knew Mike wanted to know. "What's the deal with you and Barbara?"

"It sounds like we're in the same boat as the two of you—minus the trip overseas. We got fed up with our dead-end jobs in the city. We quit and here we are, broke-ass and homeward-bound."

Mike was looking back and forth at the Cub. He'd been doing it for most of the evening.

He managed a kick at a foot, but it didn't dissuade him. Now in the pitch-black surrounding our campsite, his unease was getting on Harry's nerves.

"I'm not comfortable with that airplane sticking out on the beach like that," he said.

Mike was making sense.

He couldn't disagree, but the night was as black as the inside of a box.

"If someone floats by and sees it, we'll be caught out in the open," he said. "That's not where I want to be."

What were the chances? Slim to none, Harry figured.

"I'll be back in a couple of minutes." Mike stood up and retrieved his sawed-off.

Harry lost sight of him in the dark. He went for his .45 in the tent and met him at the plane. "You've been worried about this all night."

"I don't like leaving this thing in plain sight loaded up the way it is," he said.

Harry agreed. "Then we should get the hell out at first light."

"I'm good to go. The sooner, the better. What about the women? Are we going to slink out of here like the dogs we are after sending them off to town in the van?

He and Mike thought the same way. "I've been wondering about that. I've got a good feeling about Sasha. She seems cool with whatever the hell it is she thinks we're doing. I'm not so sure about Barbara. She hasn't even blinked an eye looking in the direction of the plane."

Mike went on. "We could take them along for the ride. That van might come in handy. The two of them would be good cover for two gabacho tourists like us."

He had to agree. "Let's play it by ear and see what they want to do."

Mike said, "I'll fuel up first thing in the morning. One thing for sure, eventually one of them is going to notice the Cub is stuffed with sea bags."

Harry sniffed at the damp air. With the onshore breeze, the distinct odor was noticeable.

"I know. Sasha asked me earlier about the two registrations.

I told her we didn't have time to paint over both. She gave me an I'm not that stupid look. For about a second, I felt bad for lying, but what the hell was I going to tell her?"

"We'll work it out in the morning." Mike was pretty confident.

He wasn't so sure.

Sasha and Barbara, head-to-head and deep in conversation by the fire, clammed up as they approached.

"Mike is going to pull out of here tomorrow morning and head to El Coyote for a day or two. Are you interested in coming with us?" It never hurt to ask.

"We were just talking about that. We're out of money and we have to get back home, the sooner the better."

"In that case, Mike and I can help with gas for the van."

"You only want us for the CD player."

Perhaps. But why would the two of them want Mike and I tagging along? Our Jeep didn't even have a radio.

Harry scrambled out of the tent with Mike's shotty in hand. He reached in and made a quick grab for Sasha. He connected and dragged her out. He shoved her toward the van before calling to Mike. "I've got Sasha. Is Barbara with you?"

"No. Who's doing the yelling?"

"I don't know."

He handed off the shotty to Mike.

"Have you got yours?" he asked.

"You bet," I said.

"Sasha, stay here. If Barbara shows, keep her here. Understood?" He didn't wait for an answer. "Get in the van and stay down."

In the shadowy darkness, he spotted a white-hulled panga beached beside the Cub. It showed up distinct against the rolling surf that had picked up with the wind. Two shadows crouched under a wing. A third lay on the ground at their feet. It was too dark to tell what was going on.

"It sounds like they're arguing. Can you hear what they're saying?" he asked Mike.

"Shit. That's Barbara. And no, I can't make out anything. They're speaking Spanish."

"It's go time," Harry said. "We can sort the bullshit out after the dance. Are you good?"

"You bet," Mike said. "I'm good."

"Head to the right. I'll go left. When you think the time is right, see if you can blast a hole in that panga. If they come my way, I'll try to hold them to the shore."

The shotgun blast scattered the men. The body on the ground rolled beneath the plane. Mike let another one go at the feet of one and he headed for the hills.

He recognized the sound as the shotgun snapped open, ejecting empty shells. It clicked shut with a determined snap. The sound made him happy. Mike had reloaded.

The fat one made for the panga. No doubt he'd have a tough go pushing the beached panga out by himself. Harry sent one toward el gordo trying to climb aboard and the fat man slouched forward over the bow.

Mike caught up to the second man behind a dune. He dragged him back to the panga and pushed him over the side into the panga. He landed with a hard thud. His head had connected with the gunnel.

7

Hiding Places

"Were you able to get the goods into the van without those two losers noticing anything?"

"Yes. The confusion on the beach in the dark made it easy. I got into the compartment when they were wrestling with the panga."

"Do you think the couriers got hurt in the process?"

"Bad luck for us if they did."

"We'll hear about it, that's for sure. Sooner rather than later."

8

Harry and Mike struggled to push the heavy flat-bottomed panga off the beach. The weight of the added bodies wasn't helping. Feet sunk into sand as they rocked and heaved the heavy, awkward boat. Inch by inch it scraped off the shallow, sandy beach. It hung up again and again as they manhandled it through tide pools until they hit one large enough to allow it to float free.

Mike huffed as he climbed aboard and fired up the engine. He nodded, satisfied, as the engine settled into an easy lope. He swiped at a sweaty forehead before handing off the shotty. Harry took it and made for shore and the Cub. It was slow slogging through the tide pools of water-logged sand.

Ashore, he found Barbara crouched beneath the plane. She was shaking like a leaf. Sobbing. Barely keeping it together. She was on her side, knees up, with her arms surrounding them. She looked up at him, pale, questioning, apparently unsure if she should say anything.

"Are you all right?"

Harry pulled her up and steadied her. He gripped her arm and squeezed, hard, remembering this was her fault. "What the hell was that about?"

Her response came too quick for his liking. "I went for a walk behind a dune. I wanted to go to the bathroom. Those two jumped me."

"What did they want?" His mind raced. Was he followed down the Baja? Was Mike tracked across the Cortez?

"I don't know. It sounded like they were asking about two people and drugs or two people who got away with some drugs."

Shit. Now they were stepping in it. Or were they? It had to be too soon to think it was about Mike and the plane. He had only just arrived. It occurred to him that these two could be doing the same thing he and Mike were doing.

He helped Barbara to the palapa.

Sasha was waiting, pacing back and forth beside the dead fire. She looked about ready to kick sand or spit nails any second. He couldn't tell which.

"I broke down the campsite and stowed everything. Are we going to ditch camp right away?" Sasha wanted to know.

She had the foresight to prep for a get-away, he had to give her that. She even had the tent down. The woman had a clue, at least.

"We can't. The plane needs fuel."

"Where the hell did you get that thing? What are you doing with it?" Sasha was adamant. "And what's with the two registrations? Don't tell me you can't decide which way you're going."

Harry had enough. "Not now, okay? Maybe you should keep Barbara company. She had a scare from those bandidos."

The woman ignored me and instead began looking around. That couldn't be good since my partner was missing. He wouldn't be capable of distracting both of them at the same time.

"Where's Mike? Is he all right?"

That was easy enough.

"He took the panga out into the bay. Once he kisses our company goodbye, he'll be back. We'll all sit down for a few minutes before we pack up."

He wondered if that would hold her.

Sasha scowled like she wanted to bury a foot between his legs, and not in a good way. He was in deep shit, but it couldn't be helped. He sat down with Barbara beside the dead fire. She continued to tremble. How much of it was fear and how much cool night air?

"You did good out there. When the lead started flying, diving under the plane kept you from getting hurt."

They sure as hell weren't about to shoot up their reason for being there.

That wasn't enough for Barbara. "Who the hell are you guys? What the hell are you doing? And where's Mike? Is he hurt?"

The blame was already being cast. He and Mike were prime suspects according to these two. "No. He's fine. He's in the panga."

"With those two? By himself? Will he be all right?"

Barbara's care and concern appeared genuine. He didn't think it was the time to mention the men were dead. "He'll be fine. In fact, he should be back any time. We'll break camp and get out of here."

The woman wasn't satisfied. "We can't leave Mike all by himself."

Harry looked at Sasha for a bit of help, but he knew right off she wasn't having it. She was giving him the look again. For good measure, she was shaking her head in disgust.

"We won't be leaving Mike anywhere. By the time he gets back, I'll have our camp packed up. Sasha has you ready to go. If you want to leave now, go."

And good riddance.

Barbara and Sasha made for the beach, heads bent, whispering.

He attempted to listen in, but the surf on the incoming tide made that impossible. He figured they'd come up for air announcing they were getting out as fast as they came in. He pictured being left behind in a spray of beach sand from the van's spinning tires as it raced for the highway.

Something was settled following their confab. The pair headed straight for him. He grinned, and for a second, he thought about running the other way. He tried hiding the grin.

"What are you smiling at?" Sasha asked.

Apparently I hadn't concealed it very well.

"We'll wait for Mike," Sasha said. "Then we'll all leave at the same time. Is Mike going to fly that thing out of here?"

"Yes, he is," he said. "I'll be meeting Mike and the plane down the road. Are you sure you want to tag along after what happened?"

"Judging by how you and Mike handle yourselves, there's

safety in numbers. We decided we want to stay with you." Sasha's decision sounded final. "Is that going to be a problem?"

"It's fine with me, but Mike might have other ideas when he gets back."

"Other ideas about what?" she wanted to know.

Other ideas about you two tagging along with us.

"Mike and I have to talk it over before deciding." He changed the subject. "We need to fuel up."

Sasha helped carry the jerry cans to the plane. He showed her how to set and hold the funnel. He hoisted the cans one at a time and filled the Cub's tank. When he finished, she carted the empty containers back to the Jeep.

Mike sloshed his way through the surf on foot and made his way to the beach. Barbara ran to meet him. She screamed and threw her arms around him like he was long-lost family. Hell, they only met a few short hours ago. It looked like she was already making plans to settle down and move in. He was a likable guy, but the performance was a tad over the top.

Harry listened in to the sideshow just the same.

"You're soaking wet. Did you fall out of the panga?" Barbara asked.

Mike peeled Barbara's arms from around his neck. He took her hand and looked my way. Call me cynical, but he had a hard time believing the performance. Call me Mr. Negative, too, but love at first sight wasn't a strong point at this stage of his life. Mike's either, if he knew him.

"Sort of. It's all good now. The panga is headed for open water and dos cabrones are on top of things. We need to get out of here right now," he said.

He and Mike were in deep shit, and not only with Sasha and Barbara. The policías would take a dim view of two men floating in the Sea of Cortez aboard an abandoned panga. If the bodies could be linked to them, he and Mike be growing old in a Mexican prison—if they lived that long.

He waited until he had him alone before asking. "How did it go?"

"Not so good. I think they finally caught up to us," Mike replied.

"Well, we knew it was a possibility when we discovered the Cub's wing fabric took a hit after leaving El Dorado."

Mike's frown deepened. "There's a boat sitting out in the bay."

"A boat?"

"A cabin cruiser. A big one. And it's way out." Mike was obviously concerned.

He had noticed it yesterday and gave it a pass. Maybe he had guessed wrong. "It could belong to anyone. No one could have figured on heading out over two hundred miles of open water with an airplane on wheels."

"Maybe so, but we don't need to be wasting more time on the beach. What about those women, Harry?"

The women. It always seemed to come back to that for them, no matter where they were in the world. "They want to come with us. What do you think?"

"I wouldn't blame them if they want out," Mike said, "especially after last night. You've spent more time with them. What do you think?"

He might have spent more time, but it was time measured in hours, not days or weeks. "I say trust but verify. That fake display of affection on the beach got my alarm bells ringing a little too loud."

Mike nodded. "Yeah. I wondered if you caught that vibe. I feel the same way. What do you want to do?"

"They're asking a lot of questions. Yesterday, Barbara was wondering about the gas in the back of the Jeep. Sasha threw a skeptical eye at the dual registrations painted on the Cub." He hesitated. "Who knows what the reaction will be when they find out our two friends are dead in a panga aimed at the mainland? The questions will come hard and fast if they find out."

"You need to clue them in after we pull out of here, Harry."

I looked at Mike. "Me? Why me?"

Mike's grin almost went to his ears. He looked over at Sasha. "I'll say one thing. I'm glad it's you that has to deal with that one. Judging by the pacing she's doing she looks to be one pissed-off woman right about now."

It was obvious Mike was happy to be getting out alive in the airplane. He'd be in the back seat with him if there was room.

"Thanks for letting me have both of them all to myself, Williams. Sasha has been kicking sand in my direction since the sun came up. I've been trying to avoid her, but it's tough when we're all under the same palapa. I'll fill them in when we get down the road. After that, it'll be do or die."

"They need to decide if they want to stay on or not, Harry. If it was us and the situation was reversed, we'd want to know where we stood."

Mike was right, but there was something still bothering him.

"Shouldn't we be asking some questions of our own? It sounded like Barbara was arguing with those men last night. I wish to hell my Spanish was better. What if they're not after us? What if they're chasing after the two of them? And if they are chasing them, why?"

"They've been down here for about as long as we've been on the mainland," he said. "Maybe they have their own problems, just like us."

Harry considered. "Maybe, but I hope not. Let's get the hell out of here. Sasha helped fuel the Cub. It's ready to go. Do you want a hand firing up?"

"No. This beauty starts like a dream. Get everyone going and I'll see you down the road."

Mike reached into the cockpit to set the switches. He walked around to the propeller and hand-bombed it. The engine started first-pull.

He climbed through the open door, belted up, and advanced the throttle to taxi the Cub to the water line and the smooth sand on the edge. They all watched as he jockeyed into position to aim the nose down the beach. He waved and closed the door.

Mike held the brakes and firewalled the throttle on the Lycoming 65 engine. The back end came off the sand and he had the Cub airborne in a hundred feet. He waggled the wings before heading low and slow over the water.

"Why did he do that?" Sasha wanted to know.

"The wing waggle? It's our way of saying hello-goodbye. Everything is okay. Don't worry, be happy." He grinned.

She returned my grin with a raised eyebrow and a skeptical look. "Oh really?"

That was the end of that discussion. He had a suspicion the questions coming up on the road trip north might get a lot more demanding.

9

There wasn't a lot of conversation as they finished breaking what was left of camp. They loaded vehicles. Doors slammed. With Mike long gone, he was on the receiving end of sullen looks and side-eye glances coming from the women. He took my cue from them and kept his mouth shut until they had everything loaded. He couldn't figure what the big deal was. Everyone was safe, no thanks to Barbara and her dos cabrones.

It was time to circle the wagons.

"Okay, chicas, we need to get out of here right now. We can't afford more company since no one seems to know why it showed in the first place."

Disgusted, Sasha stuffed her hands in her pockets. She stopped kicking sand long enough to look hard at me.

"The plan for the day—" Harry began, until Sasha interrupted.

"I'd say there hasn't been much of a plan up to now. Why the sudden hurry?"

"Cut me some slack, woman." He was hoping to buy some time.

Sasha wouldn't let him. "It's true, and you know it. Get your ass over here, gringo. We're going to go over a few things if you want us along for the good times."

How could he refuse? "All right, but shake a leg or it'll be bread and water and hard times in a Mexican jail for some of us. For the good-looking ones, not so much." His humor fell flat.

Sasha addressed Barbara. "Mr. Plan-for-the-day here is going to ride with you in the van and fill you in on what's going on. I already have a good idea. When he's done with you, he's going to sit his ass down in the Jeep and explain why we should keep him company past this morning. Are you okay with that?"

Barbara cradled Mike's sawed-off. "I don't know about you, sister, but I'm ready just in case some of us don't have an airplane to hide under."

He gasped, shocked that Mike had left behind the sawed-off behind. It had done duty with them in East Africa.

"Dammit, woman, don't be flashing that shotty. Down here you'll end up in jail. You'll lose more weight than you want to on a bread and water diet."

"Somebody has to cover the good guys, Harry. Come on, get your ass in gear."

He looked over at Sasha. She was doing a good job of ignoring him. He wondered if that was what it felt like to be married. It seemed that was all she could do now that both of them had agreed to team up with them.

Sasha climbed into the Jeep. "Get on the bus, gringo. It's time."

Not quite. "There's been a change of plan, chica. We're heading into town to pick up fuel. We'll catch up with Barbara and your bus later."

All things considered, Sasha took it well. If the woman was pretending, she was doing a good job.

Sasha wasted no time getting behind the Jeep's wheel. She gripped it so hard her knuckles turned white.

He was thinking she was about ready to head off without him. He said as much. "If you do, you won't be able to grill me in the hot seat."

"Yeah. No. You're good. What's the deal with the airplane?" she asked.

"At least give me a chance to get in and sit down."

He reached back under his shirt and adjusted the .45

tucked into the small of his back. Seeing Barbara with Mike's shotty made him nervous. He didn't want to be caught unaware with these women.

Sasha turned off the sand trail road onto the highway and put the Jeep's pedal to the rickety floor. If she pushed any harder, her foot would punch through to the asphalt.

"All right. You're in. You're sitting down. Talk or walk, stranger."

Where had he heard that before? The woman didn't waste time.

"We picked it up on the mainland across the Golfo from the Los Muertos cape. It didn't look like anyone was using it, so here we are."

That wasn't enough. "What about the two registrations?"

"We figured it would confuse people long enough that we could get away if the policía or the federales caught on to us. I still think that's true."

He already knew what the next question would be.

"What's in the back?"

Shit. She knew. She must have smelled it. "Well—"

"No bullshitting. What's in the back?" If nothing else, Sasha was persistent.

"Dope."

"That's what I thought, the way you two were fussing over that thing. The smell wasn't easy to miss, though. Overwhelming, I'd call it."

So she knew what a lot of grass smelled like. Chalk one up for something else going on here.

He clammed up.

Sasha didn't say another word.

He wondered if she thought she'd said too much. There was no way he and Mike could back out of taking them along for the ride now. They knew too much.

The Jeep's engine was sounding like it was on its last legs. Sasha's foot didn't let up. It was still glued to the floor.

We covered the short distance to Coronado in record time. Sasha slowed and turned right off Mexico 1 onto a gravel road. It became obvious she had made that turn at least a time or two. She drifted to a dusty stop at the side of a taquería. She got out and returned with a bag of shrimp tacos and a couple of long-neck Dos Equis.

He didn't have the heart to tell her he preferred Sol.

The plan was to gas and go, but Sasha ended up crossing a dry river bed. She turned right onto the malecón. She followed it for a way until the harbor came into view. She screeched to a halt. This morning's yacht was anchored outside the harbor. It was a huge, white beauty perfectly set off by the deep blue of the sea. It said money. Lots of it.

"Look at that." He pointed. "Where the hell did that huge-ass boat come from? It has to be the cabin-cruiser Mike saw offshore last night."

"Isn't it the same one we saw yesterday out in the bay?" Sasha asked.

He studied it for a bit. It was. "Now what?"

An inflatable loaded with people came around from the seaward side of the yacht. It wasted no time making for the shoreline. A huge wake trailed after it. Harry wanted a better look at what he suspected was coming our way.

"That dinghy makes me more than a little nervous. Take a right and park us at that hotel on the malecón. We won't stand out like sore thumbs there. If they man up with vehicles, there's only one place they'll be going."

"Where's that?" she asked.

"The airport south of town. It should buy us time."

They made the hotel in time to hear the engine die on the inflatable. It bumped into the rocky shoreline. Two men climbed out. Two more lifted a heavy sea bag onto shore and began handing out weapons.

"Are you seeing what I'm seeing?" Like he needed to ask. The men weren't being shy about it.

"They look like rifles," she said.

"Automatics. They're AK-47s. They're well-armed. Experienced, too. I can tell by the way they handle them."

The men separated into a pair of waiting SUVs and set out toward the airport. There was no doubt. They were after someone. Or something. That something had to be the Cub.

"All right," he said. "I can safely say we're all in deep shit."

Sasha regarded him across the Jeep. "So you think they're looking for us?"

That was a loaded question. Last night's action on the beach left me wondering if perhaps the gringas had something to hide, too. He wished he could understand what Barbara and her two compadres had been yelling about.

"They're looking for someone. I'm thinking it's the two gringos with the plane—unless you have something you want to tell me."

Sasha ignored him. That one proved good at doing that. "Let's catch up to Barbara. She needs to know what's going on."

He needed to know what was going on too, but he figured he was last on her list.

Sasha might not have had any secrets she wanted to confess, but it left him wondering if this was part of a huge screw-up. No one knew where Mike and I headed off to from the mainland. Setting out over two hundred miles of open water in a Cub on wheels was foolhardy.

No one sane would chance that. Except, he and Mike did.

The encounter with the women on the beach had to be coincidence. No one outside of Mike knew about their rendezvous points as they headed up the Baja. Even if the women went through their bags after they encountered them on the beach, there was nothing to give up the route. All he and Mike had was two well-used triple-A road maps. We took great care not to leave a mark on them.

Harry's suspicion was the cabin cruiser's arrival coincided with Sasha and Barbara. That was when the shit passed through the fan on the beach. Unfortunately, it was covering all of them with the same odor. Did the people manning the cruiser think they were involved in what Sasha and Barbara were trying to do?

It was impossible for the fan to have been aimed at he and Mike at the outset. It had to be directed at the women. What was it the two of them were up to?

They stopped to fuel the Jeep and the jerry-cans. They made a quick stop at a mercado to stock up on food and beer and water and then made a beeline for Mexico 1 north.

By the time they caught up to Barbara, she had the van holed up in a dry riverbed. Sasha pulled in behind her and he left the Jeep behind. By the time he slammed the door on the van, Sasha was already disappearing in a cloud of riverbed dust and sand, headed north. The haste with which she departed was one more thing to convince him we weren't the only ones on the run.

The women had to be, too, but instead of speeding off behind Sasha in the Jeep, Barbara switched off the van's ignition. It sputtered and died. It was time for another explanation. "I let your friend in on most of it. Now it's your turn."

"It's about time." Barbara twisted in the seat to face me.

"With the flying experience Mike and I have, we figured we could do a job by borrowing an airplane on the mainland and ferry it across the Sea of Cortez. Once we got onto the Baja, it would be a straight shot north. We hoped what we were doing would pay us some petty cash to invest in a business back home."

"Do you know who the men were in the panga?" she asked.

Good question, but Harry figured he was the one who should do the asking about that. For the time being, he ignored it.

"We picked up the airplane on the mainland. I suppose last night could have something to do with the former owners. The Cub is the perfect size for the low-level flying and canyon-hopping we need to do to get across the border," he explained. "Maybe someone had the same idea. We tried to keep a low profile, but you never know."

"What have you got filling up the back seat?" Barbara was going to force him to spell it out, too.

Christ, but these two were almost twins. "It's a load of pot we're moving north. You must have smelled it last night."

She ignored that.

"So then, what you're telling me is that Sasha and I are

traveling with a couple of amateur drug smugglers, learning as you go."

She had him there. "Pretty much. But we've got the airplane thing down pat. It's our area of expertise."

"Do you two need help or what?" It wasn't a question.

Barbara didn't give him time to respond. She cranked the engine and steered the van back onto the highway.

Barbara said, "We'll take a break when I catch up to Sasha. It'll be her turn to ream your sad ass."

"Already done," he admitted.

A cantina appeared ahead.

"Pull in," he said, welcoming the change of scenery.

10

Sasha turned off Mexico 1's well-worn faded blacktop into the cantina's rough gravel parking lot. A dusty cloud kicked up by our two-vehicle convoy followed us until the light breeze chased it away. It wasn't enough to cool the growing heat of day.

Sasha jumped out of the Jeep and hurried to greet Barbara, who was already out.

Harry joined them and they exchanged a glance before ignoring him. He might as well be back in Coronado, but he knew the silent treatment wouldn't last long before the questions began all over again.

"Did he tell you anything we didn't already have figured out?" Sasha asked.

His ears perked up.

"Not really. But damn, these two gringos have cojones." Barbara seemed impressed with their prowess, at least.

"Should we show him?" asked Sasha.

He was within listening distance, but they didn't seem to care. "Show me what? I've already seen you both naked."

The humor fell flat. It earned him a scorching look from Sasha.

"Oh, really?" It was Barbara's turn to be on the receiving end of Sasha's scornful look.

Harry's foot went a little deeper into his mouth. "Yeah. No. Not like that. She was taking a swim, and I managed a peek at her assets, is all."

He caught myself blushing like a guilty teenager. Why was he still able to talk with his damned foot hanging out of his mouth?

"If you say so," Sasha said. "Open the back of the van, Barbara."

Barbara looked skeptical. "Are you sure we should do that?"

"I'm sure. Open it."

It was my turn to ask a question. "What's going on?"

Barbara made a beeline for the cantina and he wondered why she was in such a hurry.

"You. Gringo. Get over here."

Harry sensed yesterday's palapa picnic was over. HIs instinct was to make light of it along the lines of You're not the boss of me. Instead, he followed Sasha on her way to the back of the van. She raised the door and shifted the foam mattress, revealing an opening to a hidden compartment.

"Take a look."

He lifted a panel and peered in. "Holy shit. You're packing a load of dope. What is it?" He knew, but he asked anyway. Idle conversation was worth a try, at least.

"It's coke. Our only problem is we're out of cash, but now you've solved that for us."

Sasha pointed the suddenly too-huge muzzle of Mike's sawed-off at my knees. When did Barbara hand that off? This wasn't looking so good.

His hand moved out of sight until it fingered the grip on the .45 he had tucked into the small of his back. Sasha's eyes didn't move. She didn't appear to notice.

"You're robbing me? The dope is on the airplane, remember?"

Sasha stared into my eyes for what seemed like an eternity before opening the shotty with a satisfying click. She cradled it in the crook of her arm. I tucked the .45 back into my belt. She still hadn't noticed.

"We think you've got a brilliant method. It's the plan that's not so smart."

"To be honest, Mike and I know that," he said. "But this is our shakedown cruise. With all the exploring we're doing, next year will be a cakewalk."

"It will, if dos cabrones in the panga don't come back to haunt you for the rest of this trip," she said. "Judging by what we saw at the malecón in Coronado, they're already back with fresh faces armed to the teeth."

Harry left out the part about the cabrones they had dispatched on the beach never coming back. Instead, he wondered how she could recognize fresh faces.

"I never told Barbara about the men coming ashore. It's time."

"Tell me what?" Barbara was back with ice.

"There are men on our tail," he said. "What I don't know is whether they're after me and Mike or both of you."

The women exchanged looks before turning eyes on me. "Did you show him?" Barbara asked.

"Yes."

"And?" she wanted to know.

"He's on board. Let's get this dog and pony show back on the road. Harry, get in the Jeep. We need to catch up to Mike."

"Do I get a say in any of this?" he asked.

Apparently, he didn't.

Sasha slammed the Jeep into gear, popped the clutch, and screeched onto the highway in a cloud of dust and dirt. She pretended to ignore him, but she couldn't pretend to be so interested in the road to keep it up for long. He looked across at her.

"What?" Her look was too innocent.

"You know what."

"I had no intention of pulling the trigger," she said. "I wanted you to see how vulnerable you are."

"Vulnerable?" He pulled the .45 from the small of his back and set it between the seats.

"I wondered about the hand I couldn't see. You've always got yourself covered. That's one thing I like. Better yet, you've got your partner covered when he's on the ground. I like the way you two operate, even if you are amateurs."

Yeah, maybe, but he didn't believe her for a minute. At least, not yet. Would he ever?

"How many trips have you made down here to buy up product and run it north?" He expected to find out this was her first, too.

"This is our fifth."

"Your fifth?" What the hell? No way did he believe her, but he let Sasha go on.

"The first was eighteen months ago. We were like you, feeling our way around. Trying to learn the players. Getting a feel for things," she explained. "Small buys helped us get established. We got screwed over a time or two. We were too eager to make big money."

Learn the players? Get a feel for things? Damn, but he and Mike were flying—literally—by the seat of their pants. With no plan. They only wanted to get the hell out of Mexico before anyone caught up to them now that the chase was on. No way was he about to tell her how he and Mike crossed paths with their dope.

"How much searching did you have to do to find a reliable supplier?"

"We were small-timers until Barbara hooked up with somebody connected. She played him and then let him screw his brains out. She made him feel good. He expressed his gratitude with product, and now he's a regular."

"So you both screwed your way to where you are."

"No. I told you. Barbara did that. I played the heavy as best I could. Women get little respect down here—especially gringa women. I dug in my heels and made sure Barbara didn't get screwed over for real. When she fell for the guy, I kept her head above water."

"So then, given Barbara's grand sacrifice to the cause, you would be the martyr under the palapa." He knew it.

"I was being obvious that first night, but I figured you wouldn't notice. You were by yourself, so I thought in typical male fashion you'd just grin and lie back."

So it was a setup from the start—although one they hadn't planned on. That was good to hear, but he still needed convincing.

"You were right. I did both, didn't I?"

"When my problem became the same one Barbara had, she didn't step up to extricate me from the situation. Here we are."

He ignored that. Whether she was telling the truth would work its way out eventually. He changed the subject. "From what I can tell, there's plenty of product down here looking for a way north."

"The only problem is getting it past the border. Find a way around that and you'll be home-free."

"I wish. Now tell me again the meet-up on the beach was an accident and I'll mostly go along with you about the rest of it."

"It's our cover," Sasha explained. "Barbara and I try to overnight in those kinds of places on our way north. That's why we bought the camper van. It keeps us away from towns and hotels and people when we're headed north with a load of product. That stretch of beach is a regular for us. We saw the fire glowing and figured it wouldn't cost anything to check. We were short on cash, too."

"Yeah, and looking for a patsy to pick his pockets." He had no doubt. That he was alone had to figure into it, too.

"We thought we could spend two or three nights and maybe borrow a little cash when you weren't paying attention. In case you didn't notice, we're broke."

"I'm always trying to pay attention," he told her.

"Yes, you are. Then we took a liking to you. If you weren't the man you are, we'd have been long gone with your cash in our pockets."

"Someone tried something similar. Not so long ago, in fact." He thought back to Medianoche and her crew. "Does all this mean you and Barbara are going to stick it out?"

"I don't know." She was obviously uncertain.

"Don't take too long to decide. We'll be in El Coyote soon. We won't have a lot of time there. If Mike doesn't have any mechanical problems with the airplane, it's going to be a quick turnaround. It won't be anything like the picnic in Coronado. It'll be gas, go, and gone."

"Do you know where your next stop will be?" she asked.

"No," he told her. Even that was an understatement. Neither he nor Mike had any idea what they were going to do past El Coyote.

They had never planned that far ahead.

11

For most of the morning the wind couldn't decide whether to turn nasty or disappear. They drove through valleys where small dust devils floated listlessly across the road. In the hills it strengthened, buffeting the vehicles. The old open Jeep offered no protection, with only the front window to keep the wind out of their faces. It did nothing for the blowing sand.

In the rearview, low black clouds darkened the landscape already traveled. Eventually, the clouds overtook them. The horizon in front changed from blue to gray. The wind accompanying the storm caught up.

Harry chased after Barbara in the van, waiting for a straight stretch to pass. She battled the wind too, struggling to keep the boxy van on the road as it rocked from side to side.

The wind grew stronger, turning into its own version of a nightmare. On a straight stretch, he floored the accelerator on the old Jeep. It wheezed and caught up to the madly swerving van. Barbara over-steered. The van drifted toward them. He swerved with her and slipped past.

He glanced in the mirror and witnessed the near miss. Shaking hands tightened his grip on the wheel. He tried to stay calm. He slowed and waited for a place they could pull off the road.

South of El Coyote near Bahía Concepción, he found a spot and Barbara followed them into it. The sky overhead went from light to dark gray as the cloud base caught up and passed them.

A relieved Barbara shook the cramps out of her hands and flexed her fingers. She turned to face the wind. Her sweat-soaked shirt billowed and dried. Her enthusiasm to get on the road in the morning hadn't lasted.

She didn't sound happy any longer. "That wind is going to force me into the ditch. Can we change out for a while?"

The wind was working against her. The bulky van was taxing her abilities.

He sympathized. The old Jeep was only marginally more comfortable with its antiquated suspension and loose steering. That it was open was lost on her. To make his point, he took off his shirt and shook it. A cloud of dust disappeared with the wind.

"Barbara, when you were getting ice in the cantina did anyone say anything about a storm?"

She considered for a moment. "I thought I heard someone mention el huracán. I wasn't paying that much attention since we were going north."

"A hurricane? Damn it, Barbara. We have to catch up to Mike." Mike and the Cub would last about a minute in a hurricane. "We have to get the airplane fueled. If he gets get caught out in the middle of the storm he'll end up blown out of the sky."

"I'm sorry," she said. "I didn't think it was important. I forgot about the airplane."

"Don't worry." He didn't allow her to see the look of concern taking over his face. "Just get going."

Barbara took off in the van and was almost instantly lost in a windy cloud of swirling dust.

A new-looking Jeep raced around the bend and halted abruptly in its own dust cloud. He recognized it as one from the breakwater in Coronado. Dark tinted windows concealed the interior. The doors opened and AK-47s sprouted from between the front seats.

They would be okay if los cabrones weren't paying attention. It would be a bonus if they didn't recognize Barbara in the van as she pulled onto the highway.

Sasha's frightened, high-pitched voice resonated. "Harry. Look."

"I see them. Let Barbara get away. Then we'll take them." He sounded more optimistic than he should have.

The goons concentrated on what they thought they knew. They were out of the Jeep as Barbara turned onto the highway. The dust cleared and eyes turned into saucers when they got a look at Sasha sporting Mike's shotty, close-up.

Damn but the woman had cojones of her own. She motioned up and down with the twin muzzles. Two sets of hands reached for high ground.

Harry reached around and pulled out his .45.

"Collect the guns while I figure out what we're going to do. Don't put yourself between me and them. Approach them off to the side so they have to turn to keep you in sight."

Sasha steadied the shotty. She kept it aimed where the twin barrels would do the most good. "Throw out the guns. Slowly."

The AKs came out from between the seats and ended up on the ground.

"Pistolas, por favor." Sasha wasn't taking any chances.

"Nada, gringa puta.

She smiled and nodded. "Si. Gracias."

The shotgun's twin muzzles moved from side to side in a narrow arc. It stayed aimed where it would do the most damage. "Pistolas. Now! Ahora!"

Sasha allowed the muzzle to drop. If they thought that was an opportunity, they were sadly mistaken. The shotgun jerked in Sasha's hands. A single barrel exploded. An explosion of sound, sand and rock erupted at the feet of dos cabrones. They couldn't jump back fast enough. Shocked expressions appeared on sweat-covered faces. Feet stumbled as they backed against the shiny new Jeep halting their rapid retreat. A pair of automatic pistols dropped to the ground.

Sasha smiled. The shotgun only nodded its approval.

Harry wasn't happy.

Well, okay, he was happy they were in a good place, thanks to Sasha. He wasn't happy he had two more to be concerned about. Where were they coming from? And who were they coming for? The women? All of us?

There was more to this chase than he could figure. He had to trust Sasha. He had no other choice. "There's rope in back of our vehicle. I'll keep these assholes busy. Don't walk in front of me."

"You said that already, gringo." Sasha gave me side-eye before moving off to our Jeep. She kept her eyes on our travel companions. The shotty's double barrels barely shifted an inch from its targets. Even with the single remaining, she could do a lot of damage and the men knew it.

"What are we going to do with them once they're tied up?" she asked.

"On the other side of the highway there's a washed-out trail that leads up the side of that hill. It's a good place to keep two men alive who wanted to see us dead."

How many more were on a fast track in our direction?

"I'll hog-tie them and then I want you to follow in our Jeep. It looks to be a rough go, but it'll work. When we get on the back side, we'll get rid of these cabrones, set fire to ours and take the nice shiny one. It's in better shape. Got it?"

Sasha nodded.

"Follow me."

It took a good twenty minutes to walk the Jeeps in low gear up the rough, washed out, dusty trail to the crest of the hill. The wind curled around the hill and whipped at us. At the top on the back side, we dumped the cabrones in the dirt. He bent to check the ropes one last time and collected the AKs and the magazines. They climbed into the Jeeps and backtracked.

Halfway down the hill, he pulled over out of sight of the highway. Sasha pulled in behind him and got out.

"We'll do it here," he said.

The white sand beach and blue water of Bahía Concepción sparkled in the distance. He pointed it out to Sasha, but she chose to ignore the postcard vision. Instead, she looked at him like he was in trouble again. "Now what?" he asked.

"Are you going to tell me, or do I have to beat it out of you?"

Harry feigned ignorance. "Tell you what? You know we need the AKs. At the least, we have them if we need them farther down the road."

"Yes, but it seems you know more about them than you're letting on."

"Oh, that. Where should I start?" He was still trying to ignore it.

"How about at the beginning?"

It became obvious she wasn't going to give up. "We don't have time."

Sasha reached into the Jeep and pulled the key out of the ignition. She made a show of tucking it into the top of her shirt. She didn't take her eyes off me until she finished the job.

He didn't take his eyes off her while he waited for the keys to drop.

They didn't.

"We do now. Talk or walk, cowboy."

Familiar-sounding words. "You won't quit, will you?"

"You know it, partner."

Harry didn't like the sound of that, but what the hell. If he let her in on what kept him awake, she could do what she wanted with it. "I spent some time in parts of Africa. I was bumming around, getting the lay of the land, when I fell into a job flying a Pilatus on the supply route for a mine. Mike was there, too. He maintained the plane."

Still not satisfied, she wanted to know about the Pilatus.

"It's a short-takeoff fixed-wing aircraft. It has plenty of power in hot temperatures and it carries a good load."

Sasha wasn't yet satisfied. "So you two are a team when it comes to planes."

"Yes, we are. We can work with airplanes or helicopters. Whatever suits the customer's fancy." He hesitated.

"Don't stop on my account."

He went on.

"Before long we found the head crook in the supply chain. Soon we were using the Pilatus for just about anything that walked, talked, crawled or couldn't. There was always a payment for the privilege, and it didn't take long to add up.

The need for weapons was a prime motivator for putting cash in our pockets."

"And?"

Damn but the woman could be annoying. "And everyone and their dog had a firearm to hang onto. I figured I should learn what the natives could teach. That, and a few words of the local dialect worked for me. It all helped to gain trust. I figured if we ever got ourselves in a jam, it wouldn't hurt to have allies within the clan we were working with."

"It sounds to me like there's more to this than you're letting on."

"There could well be, but I think we better get our asses in gear. It's time we hooked up with Barbara." Finally. A way out.

We loaded the AKs and the magazines and our water and food from the old Jeep into the new.\

He crawled under and punched a hole in the beater's gas tank and waited for fuel to build up on the ground. He added the padded seats from the interior into the mix.

When he was happy, he tossed a match. In seconds, the job was done. All they had to do was watch.

Sasha handed over the keys. They were warm. Unsurprising, considering where she had stowed them.

Harry worked the brakes, careful to keep the Jeep in gear to help slow down on the steep descent. At the bottom of the hill, he halted in a bend, out of sight of the main road.

"It's time to stash the AKs in the back. We need to keep them hidden. As much as I might appreciate the look of you wearing an AK across your front, it's probably best to keep everything out of sight and stowed."

All Sasha could do was grin, but she did as she was told. He felt like a clown without the makeup.

"Everything?" She unbuttoned her shirt and climbed onto his lap. One hand lifted a breast. Another snaked to the back of his head and forced his mouth to it. He never could resist a woman with a will of her own.

"Damn, woman, don't do this now." Like she was going to listen.

"Why not?"

He didn't answer. She pushed his head away. A swollen nipple popped out of his mouth.

"You don't talk much." She smiled down at me.

"It's difficult with a full mouth."

He grinned like a teenager and went back to work.

They separated and re-arranged clothes, grinning like teenagers parked in the dark at a drive-in movie. Except it was broad daylight.

"No smirking, woman. You're not getting off that easy. It's your turn."

"I just had a turn. I think I'm good for now."

"You know what I mean. Talk, or I'll never allow you to put a hand on one of those AKs for as long as I know you." He figured he had her with that.

"You know the way to a woman's heart, don't you?"

"I know the way to your heart. And smiling at me like that won't save you—at least not this time."

Sasha shook the dust out of her shirt and turned toward me before putting it on. She took her time buttoning up, starting at the bottom and grinning the whole time like a cat playing with a canary.

"I grew up saddled with a father that pulled up stakes when I was a kid and a mother who wouldn't let me get past the front door to the outside without subjecting me to a screaming match. I know now she was only trying to keep me out of the trouble she knew I'd be getting into. But back then it was too much for me, so I up and left.

"How old were you?" he asked.

"Fifteen going on twenty-one." She finished tucking in her shirt.

"Fifteen? Damn. You were a kid."

"I was, and I wasn't. I had the assets, so I figured I'd put them to use before I got old. I thought twenty-one was old."

She paused, and he waited for her to go on.

"I found my way to southern California. Eventually, I hooked up with an older man. He wanted to take care of me. He had money, so I let him. He treated me pretty good. Took me everywhere."

She stopped, as though waiting for him to object. He didn't, and she went on.

"He owned a couple of power yachts. By the time I screwed my way through the yacht clubs, I was on just about every boat you can imagine—except sailboats. I never got used to the way they would heel over on one side."

"After all that water you're stuck in the middle of a desert in a foreign country with two guys looking for a place to call home."

"Well, I wouldn't quite put it that way, but yes. I guess so."

"You need to know we're not even yet," he told her. "We've got to get moving if we're going to pull this off."

He started the Jeep and turned north onto the highway. Eventually they caught up to Barbara, parked on the side of the road.

She got out of the van and approached us. "You made it. I started to worry when I saw the black smoke. What's with this?" She gestured at our new Jeep.

"Upgrade," he said. "Let's get our asses moving. We need to catch up to Mike with the fuel before that hurricane gets close."

12

Barbara worked the van over the soft sand toward the Cub's tail, sticking up like a flag. The bus hung up in the sand, and when she couldn't get closer, she flung open the door and ran. She circled the crashed plane in a frenzy. She screamed Mike's name over and over before running back to the Jeep.

"He's not here! Mike's not here!"

The Cub's nose was tipped down, stuck in the sand. Only splinters remained of the wooden propeller. That meant the engine was running when it hit the sand. It looked to be low-speed damage. Most likely, Mike was on the ground when the plane came to a sudden halt and nosed over, damaging the prop. Holes in the tail fabric told the tale. Someone had shot it up. They knew what they were shooting for.

"He's not on the beach," Barbara said.

Harry looked into the cockpit. When the engine dug into the sand, the sudden stop ripped the seat from its mounts, thanks to the seat belt bolted to it and Mike's weight. The seat was resting against the bloodied dash panel, where it probably tilted when Mike extricated himself. Blood spattered the cockpit. Part of the door lay on the ground.

He tried to reassure Barbara.

"It happened at low speed. That's why there's no damage beyond the shattered wooden propeller and the shot-up tail. His head must have smacked the panel, thus all the blood. Head wounds leave plenty of it. Someone might have pulled him out."

Perhaps that was why he wasn't with the wreck. The explanation was for Barbara's benefit. Going by the blood, Mike was in no shape to get out on his own. Our four sea bags filled with product were missing. Mike wouldn't have been able to carry them far. Whoever it was would have taken them first.

Harry walked an ever-widening circle and picked up a trail of footprints and blood leading to the water. The trail disappeared where a boat, probably a panga, had been pushed out to sea. There was hope. Mike had to be alive if they took him.

It was that, or someone wanted them to think he was still among the living.

He went back to the Jeep to retrieve a can of gas. Barbara paced back and forth, her eyes on him. He knew she was hoping Mike was somewhere nearby.

"He's gone."

On hearing the words, she dropped to her knees and screamed.

"Not that way! Sasha, help me get her up."

Together, they got Barbara on her feet.

"He's not dead. He's missing. Someone took him. Look after her, would you?"

He carried the jerry can to the plane and doused the airframe with gasoline. A match took care of the rest.

Barbara's eyes shifted from the burning wreck to him and back to the Cub. "What did you do that for?"

"If we can't use it, nobody can."

"What are we going to do about Mike?" Sasha asked. She was worried, but she wasn't off the rails like Barbara.

"Whoever did this is long gone. The panga has to be from the cabin cruiser. I wouldn't know where to look. I don't know if Mike is even on board."

Sasha fumed and glared. It seemed as though her hands never left her hips every time she looked my way. He was used to it. There was no satisfying that one. The woman was an exercise in man's frustration with women. "Is there something you're holding back?"

Her expression didn't change a whit. "Dammit, we need to

do something.”

If he looked surprised, it was because Sasha seemed to care.

“If you think I’ll be leaving him behind, you better think again. I’ll start with the lighthouse in El Coyote. If we’re lucky, someone saw the cruiser. It’s too big to ignore.”

“What about the vehicles?”

“If we keep together—” there, I said it. “If we stay together, we’ll keep the van and unload the Jeep. I’ll set fire to it north of El Coyote. You two should head out right now. I don’t know how long I’ll be tracking down Mike.”

“We’ll wait for you off the highway, like last time,” Sasha said.

He took it to mean the women were five minutes from hightailing it north once they left him in the dust and he was out of sight. No blame there. He would, too, but for Mike. Beyond sharing a shower and a sweaty mattress, he had no ties that bind with either of them. They wouldn’t have the cojones to do what needed to be done when he located Mike. If he located Mike. There was no guarantee he’d find him alive.

Even if he knew where to look.

“You don’t have to wait. We’re all in this pretty deep. Consider hitting the road without me. I’ll be busy tracking down Mike. I don’t know how long it will take or what I’ll do when I find him.”

That last was an outright lie. He knew what he’d do to get to Mike, and it wouldn’t be pretty. He took out the borrowed AKs from the front of the Jeep. Dropped the magazines. Found some duct tape and spare mags in a canvas bag in the back of the new Jeep. There was plenty of ammunition. Our friends had come prepared.

He got busy taping. It was a simple thing, but it took his mind off of the missing Mike and the women that would be in the way.

“Do you want help with any of that?” Sasha asked.

“You could make yourself useful and load the cuernos des chivos.”

“The what?” she asked. “I thought you didn’t speak Spanish.”

"Two magazines taped together resemble a goat horn when they hang out the bottom of an AK. Load the magazines. If you don't know what you're doing and need help, ask. If you stick around, your life might depend on getting it right."

Harry covered the AKs with a blanket borrowed from the van and drove Mexico 1 to cross a lethargic river into El Coyote. He turned right and followed the gravel road to the end. The lighthouse turned out to be some modern piece of work. He was forced to park some distance away. He walked a trail up a hill to the base. He wasn't able to climb the lighthouse, but that was all right. The hilltop gave me a good view of the Sea of Cortez.

It was a good view of nothing. Not even a boat's faint wake on the water remained, a calm before the storm. It made the walk back to the Jeep long and slow. That was okay.

He needed the time to think.

He didn't hold out hope the women would be waiting down the road. If they were smart, they'd lose him right there and high-tail it to the border. While they did that, they could chalk the experience up to adventure.

As much as he hated to admit it, that's exactly what he and Mike would do. They already did something similar in East Africa. That shit-show went a long way to getting them to where they were now.

Wherever the hell that was.

The vehicle in the rearview was coming up fast. Harry recognized it immediately. In his enthusiasm, he almost forgot to brake when he pulled off the road onto a dry riverbed. The women pulled in behind him and got out.

"Well, well. This is a surprise." It surely was.

"Was there any doubt?" Sasha asked.

"The truth? Yes. Plenty," he replied.

"Good to know. Not every woman likes a man who thinks she's predictable."

That took him by surprise. "I've never been happier to see

two women together that I've seen naked. Usually, I'm busy slinking out the back door of one and on my way for a quick visit to another." He chose not to allow a stupid grin to cross my face.

"We kind of figured that about you and Mike," Sasha added.

"You wouldn't be figuring wrong."

"Fair warning, I suppose. Did you get anything on the cabin cruiser?" she wanted to know.

"Nothing. If they want to unload drugs, they need to get as far north as they can. It will make for a shorter run across the border. In fact, I'm betting Mike's life on it."

"Do you think Mike will be all right? There was so much blood," Barbara said.

The blood in the cockpit was still spooking Barbara.

"When the plane did its low-speed nose-over," he explained, "the engine dug into the sand. That's the reason for the broken prop. The sudden stop caused Mike's face to hit the panel pretty hard. Head wounds bleed a lot. I know. I had one a long time ago."

"It sounds serious."

"His nose was likely broken, too. More reason for so much blood." There was no sense lying. "A concussion wouldn't be out of the question. I know what that's like, too. Whoever hauled him out of the cockpit took him alive. If not, he'd have been sitting there, stone cold. I'll find him."

Barbara appeared relieved.

"He was alive when they carried him to the panga," he said. "If he wasn't, there'd be no blood trail."

Sasha looked at me with no expression. She didn't ask how he knew. She knew he was kicking up sand for Barbara, too. He couldn't help it. He wanted Barbara to have hope, at least.

"So what now, Harry?"

Sasha and her questions. He couldn't allow himself to believe Mike wasn't alive. He owed him too much.

"Santa Agueda has a fair-sized port with a breakwater. It's the last big town on the Sea of Cortez before Santa Esmeralda. I don't think they'll make for there. It has no port and no breakwater. No docks, either. The offshore tide runs shallow for quite a distance into the bay. They'd have to drop anchor a long way out."

An antsy Sasha continued to pace back and forth. "Then we're making for Santa Agueda. Break out the gas. It's time to get this circus back on the road."

Barbara began dousing the Jeep with gasoline.

"Hang on a minute. I need to get something for your partner." He grabbed the AKs and the magazines. "We're going to pull off down the road. Your partner needs some practice, Barbara. I have a feeling she's going to need a lot."

Barbara looked puzzled. "Practice? At what?"

"Sasha is going to learn how to use an AK-47 to its best advantage."

"Enough jaw-jacking, Harry. Let's get to sighting that thing in." Sasha had a one-track mind, but that was all right with him. Sometimes enthusiasm could make up for inexperience.

"Sighting is going to be the least of your worries, woman."

Barbara emptied the jerry can into the Jeep.

He flicked a lighted match. The gasoline fumes ignited with a whomp. The Jeep turned into history. If the women changed their minds, he'd be walking from here on out.

Barbara drove.

He rode shotgun in the passenger seat.

Sasha sat in back with an empty AK. The butt rested against the floor. The muzzle pointed at the roof. It was good to see the woman enthusiastic about something.

Harry studied Sasha's reflection in the mirror. She had plenty of cojones. Both women did. Still, he wasn't certain they'd be capable of doing the dirty work needed to free Mike.

Mike would do the same for me. In fact, he already had. He owed him, and owed him big. Come hell or high water, Mike would be a free man or he'd be dead trying. No way would he leave the man behind.

Still, he didn't know if he was alive. Sure, they'd taken him from the plane. Was that to make them think he was alive? Did they want us to think so in order to keep them going?

What could they possibly want now? They had the drugs.

As far as he knew, they had all of them.

Except.

Except they didn't. The van was loaded with coke.

How long would it be before the people that took Mike would come calling for Sasha and Barbara?

13

We need them more than they need us

"We need these guys."

"I'm thinking that, too. I kind of like Harry. Despite his who-gives-a-shit attitude, he's got the cojones for the deal. There are times when I'd like to give him a good kick in the ass, though."

"Even I know you had your eye on Harry from the beginning. What the hell is it about you and men that you always get a soft spot for the one with the most problems?"

"Call me irresponsible. Like you're any different, girl."

"You're right, but I'll never admit it. Mike is a sweetheart, too. So, what are we going to do with those two?"

"I'm thinking."

"Well, don't think too long. Show time is coming up fast, and we're going to have to do something. Our supplier won't like what we might be bringing down the pipe with the missing Mike."

"You're right. It's looking more and more like Harry could be a one-man army."

14

The dirt road coming up swung off the highway at a sharp angle. It disappeared around and behind a rise. The isolation appeared ideal for what he wanted.

"Take that turnoff and follow it for a mile or so."

Sasha slowed and turned off Mexico 1. She passed the hill and Harry let her go on for about a mile before telling her to stop. He got out and looked around. What he needed was a place where he could put Sasha through the paces. He had to know if she could handle pressure. He needed to teach her how to handle the AK-47 he had rescued from the burned-out Jeep.

"Wait here while I have a look."

He spent five or ten minutes walking around, satisfying himself that the hill would block the sound. He stuck his head in the driver's window and surprised Sasha. She leaned away and threw him a dirty look.

He wasn't in the mood to waste words or time. "You have work to do, woman. I need to know if you've got what it takes." He was pinning his hopes on the woman. That she'd be capable of backing him up when he went in to retrieve Mike. He still didn't believe he was dead.

"If I knew I was going to be taking a test, I would've tried harder," she said.

He had enough of Sasha's sarcasm.

"Have you ever field-stripped an AK-47?" He already knew the answer, but he wanted to shut her up.

She only rolled her eyes.

He waited, hoping she'd understand she knew nothing. About anything.

"Christ, Harry. Where was I supposed to learn how to do that? I've never even seen one until today. Better yet, in what hellscape did you learn? Was that a part of one of your desert adventures?"

She had to know he was serious.

"You need to learn the capabilities of the extremely versatile AK-47. In some parts, it's known as the African credit card. Don't ask. It's going to be an adult-ed course. Pay attention and you'll learn something."

"I'm not afraid of learning," she insisted. "It's what I'm about to learn that worries me."

"Sure you are. Get out of the van, pay attention and show me you're not afraid."

He picked up one of the AKs. Racked. Cleared. Safetied and then released the empty magazine and re-inserted it. He handed the rifle over to Sasha.

She gripped it with both hands like a piece of wood and hefted it. "It's heavy." She fumbled and it almost slipped but for her white knuckles and tight grip. The muzzle ended up aimed at the ground.

At least it didn't point in my direction. "It's a little over nine pounds with an empty magazine. Turn it on its left side and find the safety lever on the right. It rotates."

He dropped the Jeep's tailgate.

"Sit down. It'll make it easier to familiarize yourself."

She sat and allowed the AK to rest on her lap.

"Wrong side. Turn it over."

Her fingers found the safety and touched it tentatively. "Got it."

"Be sure the safety is full up and in position so the action can't move. And stop being a girl. Move it like you own it."

"It's that way already," she insisted. "Did you do that?"

He ignored the question.

"There's a small lever on the front of the trigger guard. Find it."

Sasha fumbled and almost dropped the heavy weapon

again before turning it back on its side. He waited patiently for her unfamiliar hands to locate the lever. "Pull it with a finger and let it go." She did, and the back side of the magazine slipped out.

She picked at it. The front broke free. She held it up. "What am I supposed to do with this?"

"You figure out the front end and slip it into place. Then you rotate back and it will click into position. Do it now."

She cursed and fumbled while he waited for the click. Finally, it came.

"Good. Now release it and do it all over again."

She did. And then did it again. That was good. He needed her to learn fast. He needed her to be capable. He needed her to be more than capable.

"Now find the safety. Rotate it. Try to pull the action. Find the lever for the mag release. Do it all again.

She fumbled and cursed. Failed. Succeeded. Failed again and succeeded again.

"Is that it?" She looked at me hopefully.

"No. Do it all again," he insisted.

She hesitated before complying. Closed her eyes to shut everything out, and succeeded.

"Fantastic. Now rotate the safety full down and rack the bolt. When you do, look to check that the chamber is empty. If it's empty, pull the trigger on the empty chamber.

Sasha racked and looked. Nothing ejected. She pulled the trigger.

"Did you look?"

She squinted against the sun and looked at me. "Yes, I looked. Empty. It was empty. Did you know?"

"Yes. I wasn't about to put a loaded firearm in your hands while standing beside you."

He caught her smiling.

"Well thanks for that vote of confidence," she said.

"Dos cabrones weren't expecting to find us. If they were, the chamber would've had a round in it from the start. Now engage the safety. See how it prevents the charge handle from being pulled back?"

She did as she was told, observing her handiwork while pulling back on the handle. "Yes."

"Try it again," he insisted. "Then we need to make it unusable."

"But I thought—"

He interrupted. "Don't think. Do. I'll explain later, okay?"

The woman gave him stink eye, but he was accustomed to it.

"Turn it up and I'll tell you how to take out the bolt and the recoil spring."

"Why don't you do it? I'm a girl, remember?"

"I remember it well. You have a fantastic body. You're much too smart for your britches, though. See the black cover on the top that starts in front of the wooden grip? That's the receiver cover."

"If you say so."

Smartass.

"I say so. Now pay attention. There's a button. Press it in with your thumb and pull up on the cover."

She struggled to get it right, cursing at her ineptitude.

"It's stiff. Ouch!" She brought her thumb to her mouth and sucked at it.

"Yeah, you have to watch out for that. Push the thing that pinched your thumb forward until it slides out of the slots. Throw the spring out the window. Pull out the bolt carrier and throw that out, too."

"Am I done?"

"You're done. How hard was that?"

"Not so bad with you helping. I'm getting to like the new things I'm learning since I started hanging with you and Mike."

Oh shit. Here we go.

"Walk with me while I get rid of what's left. We wouldn't want it to fall into the wrong hands."

Sasha followed him as he disposed of the parts and kicked dirt over them. The questions never stopped. He ignored her. He'd rather she thought about the consequences of what she was learning. Who in their right mind would teach an American girl to use an AK?

They made our way back to the van. Sasha only had eyes for

the single functioning AK on the floor. "What are we going to do with that one?"

If she only knew. "For starters, while you've got nothing to do, you're going to hook us up with what the uninformed call jungle clips."

"Jungle clips? What the hell are jungle clips?" The woman seemed genuinely curious, at least.

"Jungle clips. Some might call them banana clips. When you saw all the news feeds of mercs in the desert or the jungle, do you remember anything about the firearms they carried?"

"Mostly I went to eat when the news came on."

Why was he not surprised?

"Those curly things hanging off the bottom were magazines taped together. Cuerno de chivo in Spanish. The magazine resembles a goat's horn."

"If you say so."

There it was again. Would this one ever learn to listen? He was beginning to think Barbara might have been a better choice. The trouble with Barbara was she had become too involved with Mike to think straight.

"I say so. Basic firearms, baby. He who has the most arms, wins. If he doesn't have the most arms, he'd better know how to use the arms he has."

"Really."

The refrain was too familiar. "Yes, bitch. Really."

Sasha stepped back and took a long look in my direction. Finally. He'd hit a nerve.

"Your new job is to tape those magazines together. In pairs. When you have two taped, you should be able to release, rotate, and insert when one is empty."

He stopped explaining to let her figure it out. Sasha didn't know it yet, but when the time came, she'd be the one handling the AK. Do or die, she better know how.

She fumbled with the mags, adjusting, re-arranging, switching them out, doing it all again. Satisfied, she tore off a short run of tape and used it as a guide for positioning.

"Good idea. Keep trying until you get it right and then do them all the same way."

She continued fumbling with the magazines, attempting to get the setup right. She wrapped and unwrapped the tape until she had one to her satisfaction.

"You've got it. Is the safety on?"

"Yes," she assured me.

"Show me." He needed to see it for myself.

"How will I know when you're happy with my work?" she asked.

"I'll let you know. Show me the safety. Insert the mag. Does it bind with the one you piggy-backed? If they don't match up, you'll have to do them over."

"Not so fast. Shit. I've never done this. I don't think it binds.

He raised his voice and fired commands at the woman.

"You don't think? Then you'd better start. Insert the magazine. Does it lock? Rock it back and forth. Did it stay locked? When you inserted, did it fit nice and smooth? If it didn't, do it again. Now release it. Tip it forward. Did it come out? If it didn't, why?"

Sasha's hands shook. Her face turned beet red with frustration. She fumbled and dropped the mags she'd taped. She looked like she wanted to cry.

He stopped talking and waited. She had to be the one to figure it out.

"Insert. Release. Rotate. Insert. If it doesn't work for you, release it, unwrap it, and tape it until you get it right. Then do it all over again."

She went through the exercise, again and again. He was fed up watching her. He needed a break. He left her to work it out on her own. He went over to Barbara and pulled her aside. He needed her to be our backup. He had to get a feel for whether she'd be capable of functioning when she was needed.

He had the answer when she reached into a jacket pocket and pulled out a handful of 12-gauge shells and held them up.

"Did you get those from Mike?" I asked.

She nodded.

He looked her hard in the eye. "Do you know how to use it?"

"Yup."

That was good enough for me. "Do you think that one will get it?"

He tilted his head in Sasha's direction. "She has to. It's going to be important." He couldn't emphasize that enough. He didn't even try.

"Yup. Wait her out. You'll see," Barbara assured me.

He leaned against the van.

Sasha's quiet cursing floated away in the wind.

He was nervous and unconvinced that putting a killing machine in the hands of a woman who'd never seen one was a smart move on his part. "I hope you're right."

He returned to Sasha in the back of the Jeep. "All right, woman. I'm back, and it's time."

"You know I heard you, right? I'm in here. You're out there."

He ignored her.

"Release it like I showed you, then rotate the mag and insert it as fast as you can without screwing it up. When you've got a pair matched up that work for you, do the same thing with the others. And then do it again."

She had the mags taped in record time. She walked to the van and put the rifle on the floor. She held up her hands as though in celebration. "Six magazines. Three jungle clips. Will that be enough for you, sir?"

"Yes, it will be enough," he reassured her. "It's all we have. Now you have to check all three of them. Go ahead. Do it. And they're magazines. Clips were part of a different war."

He waited for her to finish. He studied every move. She was rough around the edges, but she was just good enough. It would have to do.

"I want to try it out."

He knew that was coming. What took her so long? "You know how to work the safety. How to tape the magazines. How to check your work. You know how to unwrap the tape and do it again until you're satisfied."

"Yeah. So?" She sounded exasperated.

"So when push comes to shove, you'd better know or you'll

die trying. Trying isn't good enough. You being dead is not the prize I'm after. Mike is the prize."

It finally dawned on her. He knew, because she straightened and looked at Barbara.

"If we're lucky, you won't have to use that weapon. An AK can do a lot of damage in the right hands. Even without pulling the trigger, just the sight of one with taped mags hanging off of it can make an impression."

"That didn't stop you and Mike back in Coronado," Sasha insisted.

"Coronado is behind us. You know that. And they had your friend."

That shut down the questions he figured would be coming. In case it didn't, he had a few of his own.

Sasha's handling of the heavy, unfamiliar weapon impressed him. Still, she was no pro. She never would be. But she was willing to work to learn the basics. She was a quick study. She'd been a party to his talk with Barbara. He made sure to let her know in front of her friend that he valued her help.

Even so, the exercise coming up would make her or break her. "It's time for the actual work to start if you're going to feel confident with the AK-47."

A huge, shit-eating grin pasted itself on Sasha's face. She'd better enjoy it while she could. She'd soon be on the ground and sweating dirty. But not right away.

"Show me what you learned," he insisted. The grin disappeared in a hurry.

One by one, she demonstrated what she needed to know to familiarize herself with the weapon. She called each step out as she did. "Check it's loaded. Full or empty, magazine unlatched and set aside. Charging handle pulled back. Look into the chamber for a round. If none, pull the trigger. Release the handle. Flip the fire selector full up to the safety position."

"You did good, woman. Now we're going to find out what you're made of. Confidence is everything. If you look like a scared little girl, you'll lose. The first thing you'll do is rack it. Why?"

"To be sure the chamber is empty." Sasha pulled the slide all the way back, looked inside, and released. She put the muzzle on the floor and kept the stock up.

"It looks like you've got your basic gun safety figured out."

Except she didn't.

Barbara used the lull in the conversation to lay down the law. "No holes in the roof. I want to keep the resale value up on this thing. That, and my mother taught me a bit when I was a lot younger. We didn't have a man around."

"What did you forget while you were listening to someone tell a story, woman?"

Sasha cursed and fumbled with the rifle. She racked again, checked the chamber by looking into it, and released. She pulled the trigger on the empty chamber and then safetied. She replaced the muzzle on the floor.

"That's better. Do it again."

He never even got a dirty look for his trouble when she did. "Find the lever on the right side. Check the position."

He was about to get that look.

"The safety. It's down," she said.

"All the way?"

"Yes," she replied.

"Why isn't it up and engaged?" he wanted to know.

Sasha turned beet red.

He felt sorry for her, but he didn't let on. "Are you planning on shooting one of us?" He figured he knew which one it would be.

"Sorry. I'm sorry."

Harry bit his tongue while she went through the exercise again with the empty AK before flipping the safety up.

"Down is semi-automatic. For accuracy, you want the lever all the way down. What does down mean?"

"It means semi-automatic. One round for every trigger pull," she insisted.

"Funny you should know that. What's full up?"

"Safety." She rotated the safety down, then up. Each time it clicked into place.

This woman was no slouch with an empty rifle. All he was left to worry about was how she'd react when the lead started flying. The answer to that would come when they located Mike.

"You're going to insert one of the magazines you taped." He had been loading it while he watched her. "It'll be a lot heavier with cartridges in it. Pay attention to what you're doing."

She grasped it firmly and tipped it forward and caught the lug in the recess before rotating the magazine back until it clicked into place.

"If there's lead flying and adrenaline pumping you won't hear that sound. You'll have to push on it to verify.

"What happens if I don't?" she wanted to know.

"You'll be bent over picking it up off the ground to do it all over again until you get it right." He hurried to continue. "If you aren't running the other way, that is. Now release it."

She did. Racked. Checked. Pulled the trigger.

"Good. Safety?"

"Up."

"Show me."

She did, and he was happy. He smiled encouragement. "After you insert the full magazine, how do you chamber a round?"

"Rack. Then safety."

That was good enough.

Barbara was even more impressed. "Damn, girl, you're getting scary. Don't tell any of the men we know about this or you'll scare every single one of them away permanently."

Harry shook his head. "That's not my experience. Hell, a woman who knows how to use an AK to its full advantage would be an asset anywhere in Africa." He knew Sasha wouldn't let that go.

"Is that how you pick your women?"

"If it was, you wouldn't be here now." He didn't wait for a response. "Let's go. We have a job to do."

He wasn't satisfied with the spot he had picked out to test the firepower. He had the women pile into the van and had Barbara take us back to the highway.

"We need to find a place to experiment. We want to put high hills between us and the highway to muffle the gunfire. While you're standing around, maybe you could use the time to come up with a story to get us across the border.”

He wanted Barbara to have something to do that would take her mind off of Mike and the possibility he might not be alive.

“I completely forgot about that. No thanks for reminding me,” she added.

“Remember, we didn’t find Mike sitting cold and dead in the plane. Someone went to the trouble of hauling him out. That has to mean he’s alive. They want us to come looking for him. The most likely spot for us to find him is Santa Agueda.”

“Do you think they have him on the boat?” Barbara asked.

“Yes.”

It was that, or they pulled a dead man out of the cockpit and hoped we’d come looking because we would think he was still alive. He didn’t want to bury Mike yet, even if he was floating in the Golfo. Something was nagging at him, though. The bandidos had the drugs from the plane. Why would they take Mike, alive or dead?

Why would they want us to come looking?

15

Sasha's basic firearms training had gone as well as it could, given her inexperience and the limited time they had. She had the dry run part of the exercise down as best as he could show her. It was time to make her sweat.

The excuse for a road they were on forked. "Take the trail that goes left."

Barbara eased into the turn and followed the trail. The van bumped and shook and rattled for a mile as she fought with the steering over the rough ground.

"Okay. This is good. We'll stop here."

The van halted. Harry got out and surveyed the location. It was prime, given the hills that came between their location and the highway. They would shield the noise.

"Chica, it's time to show me what you've got."

Sasha sported a grin like a Cheshire cat.

Barbara couldn't resist. "What did you do? You look like you've eaten something, and I don't mean a canary."

He chuckled. He couldn't help it.

"You've already seen what I've got, gringo." Sasha could barely talk past the wide grin glued to her face. "It wasn't so long ago you attached yourself to me while we were on the side of that hill." She looked around in an attempt to find it on the horizon.

"Well, you didn't give me a choice, did you?"

A look of sudden realization took over Barbara's face. "So

that explains it. No wonder you took so long to get back on the highway."

Sasha hoisted the AK, aimed it skyward, racked, and cleared it. She pulled the trigger on the empty chamber. She inserted a mag, racked it again and rotated the safety up.

Barbara repositioned herself by moving to shield herself behind the van. Not that it would do any good, given the AK-47's firepower. "I'm getting my rear out of the line of fire. If you two need me, I'll be on the ground eating dirt and dodging ricochets. Say, isn't there an old song about a ricochet romance?"

"That's probably a good idea until gun-girl gets it together." He recalled this wasn't their first rodeo smuggling drugs. "If you want something to do, you could think about where we'll cross the border to get the least amount of hassle."

"I'll come up with something," Barbara assured him.

He kept my eyes on Sasha and the AK's muzzle. He didn't want to take any chances. "Show me what you know."

Her finger was inside the guard, on the trigger. That didn't make him happy.

"It's on safety," she said.

"Is it?" he asked.

She checked the lever before turning the side of the AK toward me. She took her finger from the trigger and pushed the safety full-down to semi-auto. Her finger returned to the trigger.

He reached for her finger and placed her trigger finger outside the trigger guard. "Put the safety back on, please. Do I need to explain that?"

"Yes."

She complied, and he went on. "With your finger off the trigger and outside the guard, there's less chance of firing while you're moving."

"I'll get it right next time," she assured him.

"There is no next time if you pull the trigger by mistake. I've got one jungle magazine to teach you what you need to know. For Mike's sake, you better be a quick study."

"So you do think he's alive. Why else would you be doing this?"

The woman was right. There was no way he could let himself believe Mike wasn't waiting for him to show up. He had done the same for me. It was payback time.

"Let's get to it, woman."

It became his job to impress upon Sasha she had her hands on a powerful weapon. Words alone wouldn't do the job. He allowed his mind to wander back to East Africa and the two female mercs that had rescued his ass. What he wouldn't give to have just one of them at his side now.

"The thing about a rifle like this is it can lay down a lot of fire in a hurry. We don't want to do that. That's why you're set on semi-auto. One pull, one round. The thinking woman's way to impress."

She attempted to aim and squeezed one off before I could go on. It was obvious she was unprepared for the result. The rifle kicked at her shoulder. She looked at me with wide eyes.

"How did it feel?" he asked.

Sasha sputtered and slipped the fire lever to the safety position. "Holy shit. I felt the kick."

If the woman didn't start to listen, he'd be forced to get down and dirty to make her pay attention.

"Pull the butt back tight against your shoulder. Do it now." He moved behind her and covered her wrists with his hands to steady her. "Before you let another one go, step into it this time. Lean your body into it, too."

She flicked the safety off. He stayed in position behind her. "Now pull the trigger."

The rifle kicked against her shoulder. She held steady. Not a problem with me supporting her.

"That felt better. Not so much kick."

"Use your left arm for support. Get that left elbow under your grip. I know, it's heavy. That's why you want your elbow under it to support the weight."

She did as she was told. "Now give me three in a row."

She leaned in. Kept her weight distributed. Kept her balance even. He followed her movements with his own. "You need to raise your right elbow. Do it now."

"You're right," she told me. "I need to lean into it. I can

handle this, no problem."

"Yes, you can. Keep your right elbow up. Give me three more."

She did, and said, "That's eight."

"Good, you're counting, too."

"Well, I figure if they're 30-shot clips, I have 22. Are they 30?"

"First of all, they're mags. Short for magazines. Clips are from another generation's war," I reminded her again.

"All right. All right. For crying out loud. I get it."

But did she? He'd find out when he needed her to back him up.

"Don't do the math. Just count what's gone if you think you have to. Or do it this way—one, two, and many." He wanted to keep the woman guessing to take her mind off what she was learning to do with an AK.

"You're a tough taskmaster."

"You'd better believe it. Now get down on your knees."

"Hey. We're not done yet."

It was my turn to grin. "There'll be plenty of time for that once the job is done. In the meantime, down, woman. Put your left foot flat on the ground. Right knee on the ground. Do it, and be sure of your balance."

Sasha did as she was told, and fired once. "When you're down, place your left elbow on your knee. It'll give support and better accuracy with your arm supporting the weight of the AK. Now stand up and give me two."

The AK barked twice.

"Down again and give me two. Elbow on the knee. What's the count?"

The bluff worked. He hoped giving her something to do would take her mind off of the firepower. It wasn't necessary, but it kept her thinking.

"Thirteen."

Harry had no idea if she was right. "When you swap ends with that jungle mag, it's best to be in the down position. You'll be a smaller target when it takes you a couple of tries."

Sasha got off another three, then stood for what remained.

She pulled the trigger on the empty magazine, kneeled, released, and flipped it. She fumbled getting it in and he jumped on her.

"I thought you practiced that. You said you were fine with it. Why are you screwing it up now? Someone's firing back at you. Are you going to run and scream like a little girl? How many times did I show you?"

Tears streamed down Sasha's face as she wrestled with the magazine. Finally, she had it seated properly. She racked and let go with three from the down position before swiping at her sweat-covered face with her sleeve.

"All right. That's enough. I like what you just did. It'll show whoever is on the receiving end you mean business. It doesn't matter if you score any hits. The intent is what matters. The noise that thing makes and the flying lead it produces will keep whoever is on the receiving end looking for a way out."

If there was return fire from an AK pointed in our direction, she'd be the one looking for a way out. Hell, he'd be running with her. He didn't mention any of that. It was early to tempt fate.

"I'm liking this a lot."

"You're doing a pretty good job." Too bad the job was one that could get them both killed.

He wasn't finished yet. "You need to learn how to aim."

He smoothed out an area on the sand and drew diagrams of the iron sights.

"Your turn. Look through the sights. Align them. Look away. Align them again. That's how you hit what you aim at. Do it again and again."

I waited while she practiced with the heavy rifle. "Are you bored yet?"

"Pretty much."

"Then do it again. Keep your finger off the trigger and outside the guard," he reminded her. "Remember?"

"Nag nag nag."

"Don't get cocky. Someone will be shooting back. It's been my experience that there's no telling how anyone will react to that. That's why it's training, training, and more training." As if anyone considered two magazines enough training to do anything with an AK-47.

"I can believe that."

"Now I want you to try this. But first, how many did you get off?" It didn't matter, but I didn't want her getting cocky.

"Damn you. Three. I think."

"You think, or you know? What is it?"

"I know. Three."

"Give me two when you're down. Then stand, advance and fire. Down, and fire. Up, advance and fire. By twos. When you're finished with that, I want you to retreat the same way until the mag is empty. That's the end of your first magazine. Then turn and run your ass off. Get down on one knee until you get your last magazine loaded. Turn and repeat as needed. What's the last thing I said?"

"Get my ass in gear and evacuate while firing."

"Exactly. Now move that ass, woman."

Harry advanced beside her, hoping to give her a level of confidence. She was a going concern. She didn't hesitate even once. Sweat poured down her face and soaked her shirt. "That's my girl. What's the count?"

"There is none. It's empty," she assured me.

"You're a fast study. You performed like a trouper." He swatted her on the ass, hard. "I'm only doing that because you're out of ammo."

"You should try it more often." She racked, checked, and pulled the trigger on the empty chamber.

"The thing about counting is, you'll never get it right when there's no pressure. Don't even bother. Under fire, you'll forget all about it anyway."

"Then why did you tell me to do it?" The woman was almost stamping her feet.

"Would you have paid better attention if I hadn't told you to do it?"

"Point taken. So, what do I do?"

"Keep squeezing the trigger until you get nothing," he said.

"In that case, I have a question."

He waited and she went on.

"There seems to be a middle position on the fire lever. What's that for?"

He pretended ignorance. "A middle position? What do you mean?"

"There's a click stop there, or whatever it's called." She held up the AK and flipped the fire lever with her index finger.

"Oh, that. That's spray and pray. Otherwise known as rock-and-roll."

She cast a questioning look and aimed a raised eyebrow at him. "Spray and pray?"

"The chances of someone untrained, such as you, hitting anything in full automatic fire mode is slim to none. Even for battle-hardened veterans, it's a feat to hit the target on full-auto when lead is flying in both directions."

"I'll keep that in mind," she assured me.

The ground crunched under his feet as he walked to the van.

The noise drew Barbara out from behind it. He called to her. "It's time to stop hiding and come up for air. We're done."

"How did she do?"

"Not too shabby. She surprised me. She's got it together, at least as long as no one is shooting back. We'll find out how good all of us are when the time comes."

"I'm kind of worried about that." Barbara appeared more than kind of worried.

"Try not to think about it." He changed the subject. "What did you come up with to get us across the border?"

He wanted Barbara's mind to be off Mike's predicament. What he didn't need was a wailing, whiny woman on his hands.

"That depends on where we cross. We have choices. You probably know already."

"What do you think of Tijuana or Otay?" They were the worst of the lot, in his opinion.

"I'd say those are both out," she confirmed his suspicion. "Too many border guards and they're all looking for trouble. They thrive on it."

"I'm with you on that. What about Tecate? It's in the middle of nowhere."

"It's pretty sleepy. Sometimes people who don't have enough

to do like to make work."

"Yeah, you're probably right about that. Border guards are only human."

"I think it has to be Santa Esmeralda."

"Santa Esmeralda? The border is north of there," he told her.

"Exactly." Barbara looked pleased with herself. "It'll look like we spent the weekend and want to get out before what's left of the hurricane blows through. What do you think?"

"Mexicali is a busy crossing, but it's no Tj by a long shot. It's pretty laid back. Plus, there's the newer crossing to the east," he said.

"We can play it by ear when we get there, Harry," Barbara said.

16

The sun began sinking behind the hills. It left behind a haze of salt air blowing in off the Golfo. He rolled down the window in the boxy van, but it didn't help to dissipate the clammy humidity. They were approaching Santa Agueda. The darkening twilight helped frame the town's lights and the harbor through the van's windshield.

They drew closer to the harbor. His eyes locked onto the yacht moored in plain sight at the end of the wharf. He recognized it immediately. He'd seen it before, a long way offshore. Every light was on, as though fighting the encroaching darkness. If they were trying to hide, it wasn't working. It was like they wanted to be seen by anyone who was looking.

They were looking.

Harry scanned the approach to the wharf. There were no barriers. They could drive onto the huge dock and ram the van into the cabin cruiser if they wanted. Given the feelings Barbara had for Mike, the injuries we knew about, and his kidnapping, he didn't say a word. She was doing the driving and she might take him seriously.

"See the taquería ahead? Pull off past it. I have a plan." A plan? Did he say that out loud? Hell, if he had a plan, he sure as hell didn't know about it.

Barbara halted the van a hundred feet past before putting the van in reverse and backing up to halve the distance. The move put them in an excellent position. All they had to do was turn around and they had the full length of the wharf in sight. There was no avoiding the cabin cruiser. It sat, lit up at the end of the wharf, like a cheap circus.

There was no doubt now. Santa Agueda would be their point of no return. All he had to do was come up with the plan he had been so eager to brag about. He crawled into the back of the van and pulled aside the curtain. He stared out the window, studying the wharf and the yacht hanging off the end of it. What he knew about boats would fit on the end of a finger. He couldn't even remember any movies he'd seen. Maybe Oceans 11. Did it even have a boat?

They would have to do a straight run down the length of the dock. From where he sat, the few light standards running the length weren't big or heavy enough to offer cover if they needed it. On the advance down the wharf, they'd be out in the open all the way to the yacht. There was no cover whatsoever. He didn't want to think about the retreat with a wounded Mike slowing them down.

He ran through it again in his mind.

If they made it down the dock unannounced. If they got aboard. If they found Mike. Would he be below deck? Where, exactly? Once they located Mike, retreat would be slow and more dangerous. Not knowing his condition, he expected to be forced to carry him. It would slow the retreat even more.

Harry gave his head a shake. Already he had Mike rescued, and he hadn't done a damned thing except consider how dangerous his rescue would be. He put it out of his mind and kept looking. Kept taking mental notes.

No sentries that he could see. Perhaps they'd be on guard after dark. How many men would greet them if they heard them coming? It was a given they'd be facing AKs if what he saw coming ashore in Coronado was any sign. They were out-gunned, and they hadn't left the safety of the van.

An approach with no cover. No idea how many opponents they would face. No clue where Mike was being kept on the yacht. A retreat while carrying Mike across the wide-open expanse of dock. A woman with an AK as backup who'd never fired a shot in anger.

"Damn!" he exclaimed. Had he said it out loud?

"What? What's wrong?"

He had. "Just about everything."

Harry couldn't admit he had no plan. He was stubborn that way. Between now and go time, he had to come up with something. Anything. Mike was depending on it. On him. Hell, he had busted me out of a jail in East Africa with only a deuce-and-a-half and an AK to back him up. He owed Mike big time.

"It's time to settle down, get organized and get Mike off the boat. The screwup we've been working up to now hasn't been a success." Easy for him to say. Even easier for the women to believe. But did they?

"Finally. I was about to give up on you," Sasha confirmed.

He heard Sasha's words, but he was past caring. He went on. "Now isn't the time to be talking about past failures—yours or mine."

"Now he gets personal. Where's the shotgun?" asked Barbara.

He smiled at the woman's retort. He couldn't help it at this point. Could they know it was a nervous smile? Maybe not. It was darker in the van than it was outside.

"I don't think we need to waste time checking out the harbor. We can see it from here. It's a simple setup." He thought he was talking to himself until Sasha chimed in.

"Yes. The dock seems to have a good line of sight. But how are we going to keep those guys from chasing after us once we get our hands on Mike?" she asked.

"Good question. And my answer to that is another question. Where's the nearest semi parked? I'm thinking the taquería is a suitable spot to wait for one to show up."

"What are we going to do with a semi? They're huge. Explain please."

Exactly. And once they're parked, tough to get around.

"Barbara will climb in, grin at the driver like a hooker, thus engaging him with her winsome smile. Using her feminine wiles, she'll convince him to park it across the road, behind the van.

Then she'll disable it any way she can to keep it from moving."

It was clear the tension was getting to Sasha. She realized they were in it past their ears. Before going on, she swiped at the perspiration covering her face in the van's hot interior. "She shouldn't have any problem smiling like a hooker. You should have seen how she worked over the guy we got the drugs from."

Maybe it wasn't tension after all. "Yeah, I know. I've seen her naked and smiling, remember?" That wiped the smile off Sasha's face. He was nervous all over again.

"If you know what's good for you, you should probably stop bringing that up. You know what's good for you, right, Harry?"

He couldn't change the subject fast enough. "So then, does the truck thing work for you, Barbara?"

"It does. As long as it gets parked behind the van, I'll be good to go. I'll jam it into first and crank the wheels."

"Sasha?" He looked at her in the dim light.

"What she says," Sasha said. "But what are we going to do about finding Mike aboard the yacht?"

"I've never seen the inside of one," he admitted. "I have no idea what to expect."

"In that case, let me tell you all about it," Sasha said.

He looked at the woman. Obviously, she'd been holding out on us. For good measure, he looked at Barbara, too. She wasn't any help. She only shrugged.

He leaned back against the van's tin wall and stretched his legs. Wiped his sweaty face dry in the crook of his arm. He wasn't sure what to expect from Sasha, but he was all ears.

"Listen up, you two. The test will come when we do the deed." Sasha glanced at them before going on. "It's a Constellation. About fifty or fifty-five feet. Maybe a little more. If the interior lights are on, we should be able to figure out where Mike is located. It's not complicated."

Harry looked across at Barbara. Her mouth was open, and she was staring at Sasha like she didn't know her. The woman definitely had our undivided attention, because he caught himself doing the same thing.

Sasha went on. "You step onto the stern and make your way forward. The elevations are such that it's no big deal to see and to get below for the dirty work. If that's where Mike is. The sight lines are pretty generous. There's nowhere we won't be able to see from the dock to get a line on those bastards."

"Is there anything else you think we need to know about the yacht?" he asked. He was still shell-shocked she knew anything about the boat.

"No, that about covers it. You'll see what I mean when we get close."

Night was on the way. To seal the deal, they needed a semi with a hungry driver. He wanted to ask Sasha how she knew about the yacht. He opened my mouth to speak, and Barbara shook her head. He took that to mean not now.

"While we're waiting, we need to talk out how this will work. If anyone has something to add, please interrupt."

They had to block the road any way they could. The semi was the key. They needed it to carry out the raid. It was their best bet to keep anyone from following once they got Mike off the boat and into the van. "It will depend on the semi. No truck, no assault on the cabin cruiser."

Nobody voiced an objection.

"Barbara, you're the linchpin. We need that truck parked across the road. It's our blockade. You'll have Mike's sawed-off to convince the driver to do your bidding."

"I can do that. I've already got a couple of options figured out."

"That was fast. Do we need to know what you came up with?" he asked.

"No, I don't think so," she said. "But I know one of them will work for sure."

"Thanks to Mike's shotty."

"Yes. And I know how to use it," she affirmed.

"It has a sling. You should be able to wear it on your shoulder beneath your jacket."

"I noticed that. I'll try it when we're done."

"One more thing, Barbara. When you're finished seducing the driver with the shotgun, you can cover our backs from the shoreline. We'll need you while Sasha and I are on the dock doing the dirty work to get Mike to the safety of the van."

It should keep Barbara busy. He hoped it would take her mind off what was happening inside the cabin cruiser. He and Sasha wouldn't have time to worry about Barbara getting in the line of fire over her concern for Mike. If she rushed the cabin cruiser with them, he was pretty sure the element of surprise would go out the window.

It was time to take inventory. "There are four shells for the shotgun. I've got my .45 and seven. Sasha?"

"Two jungle mags, 120 rounds."

Damn. She remembered.

"We'll work the wharf together. Stop when you can see into the boat. You have to be able to see inside to cover me off. Got that?"

"Yes."

"If you can't see inside, position yourself where you can. Concentrate on what's happening inside the boat. Barbara will have your back. You shouldn't have anyone come up on you without warning."

"What if I can't see inside from the dock?" Sasha wanted to know.

"Then you'll have to come aboard with me. If that's the case, under no circumstance do you advance past the stern. You stay there. You wait. Understood?"

She nodded.

He asked again.

"Yes. I understand."

"Good. I'll do the searching for Mike. Two of us don't need to be doing that in the cramped quarters. Once he's free, it's up to you to cover our retreat until I can get him off the boat."

"This isn't going to be easy," Sasha said.

She had that figured right, and she was concerned. That was good.

"We can count on plenty of lead flying. Your job will be to keep peppering whatever moves on the boat with the AK. The way we rehearsed. I'll try to stay out of your line of fire, but there are no guarantees. You better be paying attention before you pull that trigger."

"I'll try my best. I hope there's no trouble while you're still down there with Mike."

He tried to reassure her. "Don't be shy about changing your position to your advantage."

"We'd like both of you alive," Sasha said.

That was an understatement. "It would be nice. Once I get past you with Mike, you'll cover our retreat up the dock to the road. Remember, stop and drop when you have to, but keep up with us. I don't want to go back for you with an empty .45 in my hand."

"Just like before, but without unbuttoning my shirt and flashing you."

"Exactly."

Tension in the van was at an unbearable level. No one laughed. There wasn't even a smile.

"Once we get ashore, Barbara will be ahead of us with the shotty. She'll cover our walk around the semi's trailer to the van. With any luck, there won't be anyone waiting for us."

"What if Mike can't walk by himself?"

Barbara was thinking too much.

"Then I'll carry him. For now, just concentrate on what you have to do. That's what's going to get Mike to safety. If you think about all the things that could go wrong, you'll end up useless to Sasha and to me. More important, you'll end up being useless to Mike. He'll still be sitting on that barge at the end of the dock."

It was the best he could do. When the time came, it would be up to a rag-tag team of two inexperienced women and a man who had seen it before from the other side.

"If you want something to take the edge off, think through how the plan is going to work. Rehearse your part in it and what you'll have to do to free Mike."

17

Harry's gut churned. His mouth felt and tasted like it was coated in East African desert sand. Cold sweat poured down his back, soaking through his shirt. He blinked uncontrollably. His eyes wandered the dim van in a vain attempt at looking somewhere, anywhere, but at the women.

He concentrated on the floor before trying to focus on their target at the end of the dock. Mike had to be there, alive, injured, even tortured. The simple part was over. All the talk in the world wouldn't get him back. He had to act. They had to act. The plan had to work.

Would it? Two out of three of them never saw action, through no fault of their own. He tried to lead, tried to encourage, tried to train. Success or failure was up to a woman he found on a beach, who had never been on the receiving end of live fire.

Bonus points for all if they got out with everyone alive.

If Mike's recovery went off without a hitch, I might consider going to church. After all, he'd been the one counting them before we got ourselves into this mess.

It would be a way of doing penance.

For what, he wasn't sure.

He still couldn't take his eyes off the women. He tried. Across from me, Sasha's back was against the front seat. Her knees were up. Her feet were flat on the floor. The AK rested between them against her shoulder. Measured breathing. In.

Out. In. Out. Closed-eyed, she fumbled with the AK's strap, twisting and untwisting and twisting again.

Barbara rocked back and forth. Contrary to what she said earlier, the twin muzzles of the shotgun pointed at the roof of her beloved van. Eyes shifted from him to Sasha and back, again and again.

He couldn't smile. He managed a nod. He didn't know what else to do.

There were so many ways this op could go sideways. No semi. Sasha running off again. Mike dead. Mike alive. Mike not on the boat. The Federales show up. The yacht departs before they can board. On and on and on and circling back to begin again.

It was always the waiting. And then it became about the van's cramped interior. The heat. The unbearable humidity. The sweat soaking everything. There was nothing to do but wait and think and worry and think again about saying Screw it and running north to the border before everything went to hell.

Hands swiped at sweaty faces until the sweat returned with a vengeance and they had to do it again. It kept them busy doing something. Doing nothing.

The silence in the van was unbearable. The atmosphere electric. The tension beyond comprehension. Any minute, he expected one of these women to slide open the door and order him off the bus. With their part finished, they'd make for the border without him. Without Mike.

Leave me with the AK at least, he prayed.

Harry already knew what Mike was made of. When the chips were down, he saved his wounded ass in East Africa by dragging it to Benghazi. He proved he had the cojones. He owed him big. It was his turn to repay the debt. With or without my recruits, Sasha and Barbara, he'd soon be doing just that.

They'd find out what they were made of. If they were lucky, they'd collect Mike and be back on the road. If not, well, that was a thought for another day. He was too caught up to worry about not being able to repay the debt Mike had so willingly and without question gone into for him.

The semi's diesel exhaust roared as the truck downshifted,

announcing its arrival. The engine groaned into a lower gear. Nervous silence and calm within the van broke. Feet shifted. Water bottles doused dry mouths. Nervous throats cleared. Shoulders tensed. Eyes remained locked on the van's floor.

"Yes!"

Was it Barbara, or Sasha? No matter. This was it. The much-anticipated semi was here. Headlights penetrated the rear window curtains and lit their faces in dim shadow. The plan was falling into place. In a few minutes, it would all be a done deal.

Barbara slipped the handle on the van's sliding door. In the interior's forced silence, it unlatched with a sound loud enough to draw us out of our fear. We were minutes away from the goal.

"Let him get his food and then follow him back to the cab," he told her.

Three heads turned. Three pairs of eyes focused on the truck driver as he passed by the side windows. Eyes followed him as he walked around the front of his cab. He halted to light a cigarette and inhaled a lungful of smoke. They inhaled, too. He exhaled a cloud of smoke and they gratefully matched it with sudden breathing.

Cigarette smoke surrounded his head in the still air. He shuffled away and plodded toward the taquería. In the van, the slow-motion walking took its toll.

Sasha's voice trembled with nervous tension. "Go. Go. Get it done, you fucker."

Maybe she was saying it to them. Maybe she was talking to the trucker. At the rate he was going, he'd get there tomorrow.

"You want him to pick something up for you?"

Sasha made a grab for the door and slammed it open. It bumped the stop and bounced back. She pushed it again and stepped out. Her knees gave out. She went down, hard. She coughed. Gagged. Choked. Spit. Threw up. She coughed again and swiped at her mouth with the back of a hand.

The trucker didn't notice. He was too busy thinking about food, maybe.

Sasha forced herself upright. Got a foot in the van.

He reached. Pulled her in. The AK rattled against the door. He slammed it shut behind her.

She couldn't look at either of them. Instead, she checked the action on the AK before leaning back against the seat. The muzzle mimicked the shotty in Barbara's hands. It pointed at the roof.

"I couldn't help it," Sasha insisted.

He couldn't blame her. He made light of it, not wanting to scare her off. "It's nerves. You don't know what's coming down the pipe. I'd do it too if I could. Better to get it over now than on the dock. When you're in the thick of things."

Sasha's eyes found mine, warning me. "I'm ready."

Harry knew then he didn't want to be on the receiving end of her AK, ever. "Do good out there and I'll keep you."

She looked at me with cold eyes. "We'll soon see about that, won't we?" She wiped her face with a forearm, loosening a strand of long hair she'd tied at the back of her head. She ignored it and went back to tapping her foot and patting the outside of her thigh in a tuneless rhythm.

The trucker whistled as he backtracked his way past the van. He had tacos and beer in hand. Mike's rescue was on them now. If they screwed up, he'd be a dead man for sure. There were no guarantees. The deal was all or nothing.

"It's go time, gringas."

On cue, Barbara adjusted the shotty beneath her jacket before standing, bent over in the van's interior. She silently slipped the door and eased out. She straightened and threw back her shoulders, hot on the trail of the trucker.

Harry nodded at Sasha. She exhaled and headed out the door.

He joined her and checked Barbara's position. She was almost caught up to the truck driver.

He slipped the action on the .45, tucked it into his belt, and strode past Sasha.

18

Harry led the walk to the foot of the wharf. The lights were still out. Turned off or broken. His eyes roamed the dock. On the lookout. Searching. The darkness served its purpose. They hesitated and stood still. Waited.

For what? They were out in the open. Exposed but for the dark.

Water slapped at the footings. The yacht bumped, heavy and rhythmic, against its moorings. It rocked and squeaked against the fenders, wailing into the night in mock complaint.

There were no lookouts that he could see. It was too good to be true. Still no lights on the dock. That was good, too. Faint light glowed through a porthole. They were still too far away to tell if they had a guard posted.

It looked too easy. It was turning out to be more like a Sunday stroll, minus the sightseers, rather than a full-blown assault.

They made their way down the wharf. Still no dock lights on automated switches. Still no lookouts on the cabin cruiser. Were they headed toward a setup? It was too late. They were committed. There'd be no pulling back until they got our hands on Mike.

"The lights are out," he whispered. "That doesn't seem right."

"It's weird," Sasha responded. "Like everyone has been chased off. Chased away."

"If these guys aren't paying attention, it's a bonus. We have to use what we have."

He fast-trotted the length of the dock. Sasha followed. Even on rubber soles, it seemed every footstep slammed onto the ground to announce their arrival.

Sasha held the AK level in front of her. Everywhere she looked, it pointed. Where the hell did she learn to do that? She shrugged when he questioned her, their voices a whisper.

"It feels more comfortable," she said.

They halted off the stern, away from any portholes. Out of sight. The dock was too low, the yacht too high in the water to allow a look inside. He climbed onto the stern, one foot at a time, careful to keep his weight from causing sudden motion.

"The view isn't good." He beckoned to Sasha. "Come aboard. Keep to the stern and stay in the shadows like we talked about. Try to keep out of sight for as long as you can."

They whispered, back and forth, in the dark.

"Don't worry about me. I've got your back," she reassured him. "And no, I'm not overconfident. I'm shaking like a leaf."

"I am too. When the action starts, you'll be too busy to shake. Trust me on that. And don't forget to breathe."

"I trust you. I'll bet you haven't heard that from one of your women in a while."

She was right about that. "There's a first time for everything. Will I get to keep you now?"

"I'm still thinking about it."

He couldn't manage even a grim smile. He was on edge. Instead, he went to work. "I'm going in," he announced, still whispering.

The dock's overhead lights stayed off. Maybe a timer would come on later. He eased forward from the stern and peered into a porthole. A dimly-lit room confronted him. Anyone inside looking out would see their own face staring back in the glass, it was that dark.

Muffled voices floated past a cabin door. Two goons were shooting the shit playing cards. He moved to get a better look and spotted Mike off to the side. He didn't look so good. Eyes so swollen he couldn't open them. A puffy face covered in blood.

Chin resting on chest. Arms taped to the chair. Unconscious.

Probably just as well until they got this sorted.

"Can you see what I see?" he whispered.

"Yes."

"It looks like Mike will be out of the line of fire once we get positioned. Remember what I told you."

Sasha repeated. "Keep to the stern. Stay in the shadows. Keep you both out of the line of fire. Breathe."

She sounded detached. Like a robot. Good. She was concentrating on what had to be done. That would keep her from thinking about what could go wrong. "One more thing."

"What?" she asked, annoyed. "What now?"

"Safety off," he reminded her.

"Already done. I don't want to spend any more time than I have to playing second fiddle by backing you up."

"Kind of a selfish bitch, aren't you?" His attempt at humor fell flat.

Her response came cold and hard. "You know it."

He halted to listen. Water slapped against the yacht. It would provide minimal cover if they bumped into something. The creaking and groaning against moorings would help. The nattering crew intent on the card game would provide a smaller measure of cover. So far, they remained clueless about their new passengers.

He moved forward.

Sasha followed.

He motioned for her to stop. "Stay."

He could almost hear Sasha's silent Screw you I'm not your lapdog. The safety on the AK clicked. Shit. Why was she putting the safety on? This might not go as smooth as he hoped. If the woman was going to puke, he wanted her to do it silently.

He eased forward and moved into the narrow doorway. It gave him a bead on Mike. He was starting to come around. He shook his head and grimaced. His eyes focused for an instant and he got a bloody, crooked grin past his swollen face.

Easy for Mike.

He wasn't so confident in the outcome as Mike appeared to be.

He did a quick check on Sasha. She was right where she was supposed to be, barely visible on the stern. He couldn't tell if she knew Mike was conscious or not. He pulled out the .45. Eased open the door. Stepped down into the cabin. He raised it and aimed for the kidnappers as he pulled back the hammer.

Dos cabrones recognized the sound. The one sitting across the table jumped up, dumped it, and dropped to the deck.

He cold-cocked the man in front of him and he slid off the chair. He dropped like a side of beef in a cooler.

He fired a round through the table. It shattered and split, revealing the man crouched on the floor.

"Get up. Put your hands on your head. Turn around and get down on your knees."

He made for Mike. Pulled out his knife and slit the tape securing Mike's arms. He helped him up and moved in front. On the way by, he smacked the only cabrón left standing on the head with the butt of the .45. He joined his compadre resting on the deck.

He hoped the two sides of beef wouldn't spoil in the heat.

Mike's face was a mess of dried blood. Swollen almost beyond recognition. His breathing labored. Good for nothing. He'd have to carry him.

"Only two?" I asked.

Mike managed a nod and grunted as he helped him up the steps.

In the darkness, Sasha gasped.

Mike heard her and perked up, but only a little. He wheezed her name. "Sasha."

"Yes."

He nodded again. Whether his wounds came from the plane nosing over when it smacked the beach or from beatings, he couldn't tell. It didn't matter. Mike was free. He put an arm around to help him onto the deck. He groaned louder than he wanted to hear. Broken ribs, probably.

"Can you walk?"

Mike nodded assent, but he wasn't so confident. Mike would never make it down the dock under his own power. He couldn't talk, but then he wasn't about to waste time asking questions. He did the best he could to get the man on deck and onto the dock without shaking him up too much.

The whole exercise was still too easy.

Sasha remained on board long enough to cover the card sharks napping below deck. He got Mike settled on the dock and she caught up. She kept behind us. On guard duty. Just like we talked it out.

It was all good.

Harry tucked the .45 into his belt and hoisted Mike onto his shoulder.

Ten feet.

It was a long, slow go with the injured Mike.

Fifteen.

Mike's constant groaning prevented him from sprinting the length of the dock with the prize on his shoulder. He was concerned he was in worse shape than he could see.

Twenty-five feet and still going good.

Way too easy. There wasn't a sound. He must have really put those boys on the boat to sleep.

The overhead lights switched on, flooding the dock. It was almost brighter than daylight. It would reveal their position to anyone looking.

"Shit. A timer. I knew it. We're sitting ducks and we're not even in a swamp."

Another hundred to get to the van Barbara had waiting at the head of the wharf. How the hell did she get it past the semi blocking the road?

In another minute, they'd be home free.

Sasha screamed.

His hands were full with getting Mike down the dock to the van.

She was on her own and by the sound of it, hell-bent on revenge.

"Come out and dance, you bastards," she screamed. "It's time to rock-and-roll!" The AK barked in Sasha's capable hands.

He couldn't resist. He slowed and turned to look. She was down and aiming at the yacht, peppering the cabin cruiser. Lead flew. Brass skipped off the dock and splashed into the water. She had to have set the AK to full auto, by accident or on purpose.

Barbara worked the van and backed it onto the wharf. She met us halfway. She got out and came around, intending to help. She called out. "Mike—"

"No. He's fine," he insisted. "Open the door and get back in the van. We need you to drive."

The firing halted. He looked back and caught Sasha still kneeling. In that instant, he witnessed her fumbling with the magazine in her attempt to flip it.

He managed to let fly with the .45, laying down cover, and then she was with them. She halted and got down on one knee. The AK barked in her hands. Lead flew. The AK spit brass. It clinked and skipped across the wharf.

She regained control of the AK and continued spraying the cruiser from bow to stern with a steady stream of lead.

Then nothing. Silence. Time for the last mag.

Harry looked back.

Sasha was kneeling. This time there was no fumbling, no hesitating. She had it down. There was no need for covering fire. There was nothing he could do but look and admire, if only for a split second.

He couldn't believe Barbara had the van waiting. In another thirty seconds, he'd have Mike loaded. They'd be on the road.

The AK continued spitting lead and coughing brass in Sasha's capable hands. With that as a backdrop, he loaded Mike into the van and carefully settled him against the opposite wall.

Harry straightened and turned to look back on the wharf. Saw Sasha flinging the empty AK into the water.

He checked on Mike and turned a second time. He drew the .45 from the small of his back, intending to lay down covering fire to allow Sasha to get to the van.

She wasn't there.

19

Give credit where credit is due

"The money is gone. The drugs are gone. We're left with nothing but those two losers. I'm glad I threw them off the bus."

"Do I have to remind you what those two losers ended up doing for us?"

"No, but you're going to anyway, aren't you?"

"You're damned right I am. You're still breathing. So am I. And who exactly kept it that way? I think that deserves some credit. Stop trying to be so tough. Is that too much to ask?"

"You always were the soft-hearted one, weren't you?"

"Yes, but if you don't do the right thing, I'll definitely be showing you all about being a hard-hearted bitch, girl."

20

Mission accomplished.

A bruised and battered Mike was safe in the back of the van. Barbara tended to him as best she could. Mostly, it took the form of holding him in her arms and looking up at me with a questioning look.

Like he knew what the hell was going on.

"You realize your friend has disappeared, right?" he asked, not expecting a response.

Barbara nodded and went back to looking at Mike.

"Did you happen to notice where she went?" It seemed a simple question.

She shook her head.

"How about a direction? Did she leave with anyone? Was she alone?"

"I don't know. I don't know," she insisted. "All right?"

The woman had been so intent on Mike she had lost track of Sasha.

He wasn't innocent, either. "I'm guilty, too," he admitted. "I lost sight of her when I was loading Mike into the van. It's as much my fault."

Sasha was long gone, headed for parts unknown, whether of her own volition or someone else's. He went with the someone else, considering what they had accomplished. "Where the hell did that woman get to? We're not leaving this screw-up without her. Get your act together. It's going to take two to figure this out."

Barbara flew into panic mode, distraught and shrieking, as if Mike's injuries weren't enough when she realized her friend was the one gone AWOL. "She was on the dock. How far could she go? I'll kill that bitch myself if she doesn't show up."

Those were pretty much his feelings, too. "I turned to get Mike into the van, thinking she was right behind us. I saw her toss the AK. When I looked again, she was gone." He still couldn't believe it. "Do you think the cabrones on the boat got to her?"

"I don't think so. The way she was gunning for that boat, there's no way they would have stuck their heads up for anything."

He left Barbara in the back of the van to minister to Mike and took over the driving. He backed up and turned them south, past the big-rig, back the way we came.

Barbara yelled out the window at the driver. "Don't block the road until we come back."

In the rearview I saw the trucker lean out his window. He gave her a huge, shit-eating grin followed by a tug on the air horn. The sound followed them down the empty street.

"That guy is happy to hear from you."

"I'll tell you about it when we have more time," she offered.

"Where the hell could that woman get to? I looked away for a split second. Goddammit, this is no time for her to go shopping." My attempt at humor fell flat.

"She didn't go past the van. I would have seen her. She has to be somewhere close."

"Then someone grabbed her and took her." It had to be.

"I didn't hear any cars or trucks. Could they be on foot?" she asked.

He circled each block that came up, scanning for anything. He came up with nothing and then two men appeared. They were forcing someone into an alley. He took a chance and tramped on the gas before stopping at the alley entrance for a better look.

Doors opened on a white half-ton. Two men forced a familiar-looking woman with long dark hair into the truck. They climbed in on either side and slammed the doors, boxing her in.

The truck raced out of the alley, weaving from one side to the other on the narrow road. It turned and disappeared down a side street.

Our top-heavy van rocked and rolled from side-to-side as the engine strained to keep up in the corners.

In the back, Mike groaned.

"Sorry buddy. Sasha seems to have disappeared on us." Harry wanted to reassure him.

"I knew that woman was going to be trouble, Delaney." Mike's faint words slurred past swollen lips. He turned his head to check as he made a good try at a shit-eater. The effort turned into a grimace and then a groan.

"She's in that truck we're chasing. We'll have her in another minute." He was lying, but Mike wouldn't know. Neither would Barbara, still tending to him.

He caught up to the truck. The men had Sasha in the front, between them. From what he could see, they had to be regretting it. The truck swayed from side to side on the narrow street. It bounced off a wood pole before climbing a curb and crossing a sidewalk. It flew up a short flight of stairs and slammed hard into a church's wooden door.

Mike could add one more to his count.

Harry stood on the van's tired brakes. It screeched and groaned to a halt at the base of the steps behind the smoking wreck. Sasha scrambled to climb over the unconscious driver. She was halfway out the door as the truck reversed down the stairs. Trapped, she hopped down the steps on one foot, keeping up as the truck banged into the side of the van.

The impact threw her clear. She slammed onto the street flat on her back. She didn't move.

Barbara screamed.

He didn't know if it was because of what happened to Sasha, or whether the van's vaunted resale value had just taken a massive dive.

The driver came to as Sasha got up. Wobbling on her feet, she reached for the truck to steady her. The man made a grab, connected, and began pulling a furiously kicking woman back into the wreck. A roundhouse punch to her face brought the scratching and gouging to an abrupt end.

He turned to Barbara. "Where's the shotgun?"

"I threw it in the back. It's there somewhere."

"I'll need the shells if we're going to get Sasha out of that truck."

"There's two. I think they're still in it. I never fired a shot. I got scared when I heard the gunfire on the dock."

"Me too. Funny about that, isn't it?

He dropped the magazine on his .45. It came up empty. He slipped the action. One left. He figured on two in the shotty, and grabbed it. There was no time to check. He yanked open the truck's door. The two in the truck were the same two they had dropped on the back side of the hill.

He wasn't feeling generous with mercy.

The shotgun exploded twice in the confines of the truck's cab as I handed one to the driver. Another for the passenger. He didn't need to count.

Sasha was out cold from the fist that decorated her swollen, bleeding face. He dragged her past the driver and out the door. He picked her up. She was dead weight in his arms.

"Thanks, partner."

Not quite dead. Her words slurred.

"Are you pretending or lazy?"

"A little of both. I wanted to find out if you still cared, Delaney."

"Damn you, woman. The next time you want to go shopping you'd better take me with you. Or else."

"Or else what? You only want to see me naked one last time before you kick me to the curb."

"You're pretty talkative for a woman who just had the shit kicked out of her. And yes, that would be nice. I'll need a paper bag to cover up that mess attached to your shoulders."

She gasped and giggled and protested in a little girl voice. "Don't make me laugh. My ribs can't take it."

"So then, you're happy to see me after all," Harry insisted. He loaded Sasha into the waiting van beside Mike. Barbara was already behind the wheel.

"We're two for two. It's time to go while the getting is good.

We need to get north right now."

Barbara U-turned and took us to the main road. The van arrived at the semi. Headlights illuminated it.

"What the hell is this? You said he'd wait for us." Someone had moved the semi. It blocked the road in front of us. "That's not right. So much for the plan."

The van's headlights played over a body face-down in the ditch. "There's our answer," Barbara said.

Two men guarded the front and rear of the semi. They sported AKs, and they didn't look happy. In fact, they looked downright mean.

"Shit. Stop. Do those two look familiar?"

"I know them," Barbara said. "We're in more trouble than we ever bargained for," she insisted. "We'll have to give it up. If we're lucky, they'll let us get out with our lives."

He couldn't disagree. He had emptied the shotty rescuing Sasha. "We're out-gunned. There's nowhere to go. We can't turn back. It'll take some cojones to talk us out of this one and get our asses past that truck in one piece."

"Let me handle it, Harry. One wrong word and they'll blow us away."

Barbara eased the van up to the semi and called out. "Hola."

He poked the shotgun out the side window, but the empty barrels were all show and no go. It wouldn't do any good to pull the trigger on an empty chamber. He eased the .45 from behind his back and placed it on the console. "We have to bluff our way out of this. Right now," he insisted.

The fat one waddled up to the van and Barbara on the driver's side. "Gringa, we need the drugs."

"They're in the back of the van," she told him. "I'll get them."

Barbara got out and walked behind the van. She raised the gate. "It's all in there." The two men emptied the compartment. She began arguing with the gunman in loud and fluent Spanish. We were all in deep shit. Then it hit me. She could be negotiating a deal for two of us.

He figured he already knew which two it would be.

He followed a smiling Barbara in the mirror as she walked

around the van and opened the door. Was she about to hand him over as the price to pay for getting away free and clear?

"Well, cowgirl, what now?"

"They have our drugs. They promised me they'll let us live," she said.

Yeah, and I'll be getting a yacht for Christmas just like the one we shot up. "I don't know about you, but that's not enough for me. I have a plan."

"Too bad Sasha isn't awake to hear that."

"You can tell her all about it when she comes to. I have one left in the .45. It's time to get down to business."

"That solves half the problem. What about the other half?" she insisted on knowing. She tipped her head toward the two men positioning themselves on either side of the van. In back, Sasha and Mike groaned in stereo.

"I think she's coming around again."

"Good. I'll be able to spank that damned woman as soon as we got our asses out of the mess we're in." The joke fell flat. "On your way past those two, see if you can steer this crate into the one on your side. That'll get me a clear shot at his partner on the right. What do you say?"

"You insist on wrecking my pride and joy, don't you?"

Barbara must have slept through the huge dent in the side of her van thanks to the half-ton.

"It's that or we're done. I don't know what kind of deal you worked out, but I don't trust them."

"I'm a California driver. I can put him up against that trailer so hard he won't make it to tomorrow."

"In that case, I have a simple plan," he said. "Do what you said and duck. Whatever you do, don't stop. Keep your foot flat on the gas. I'll steer when the time comes."

She did and he pulled the trigger on the .45. It barked once. They were home free. He tossed the useless weapon out the window.

Next stop, Ensenada.

21

Barbara wouldn't allow Harry to take over driving duties for her once-prized van. He talked fast, but it didn't do any good. She insisted on navigating north through the treacherous, winding uphill road paved with Mexican good intentions and filled with hairpin turns that threatened the underpowered van.

Undeterred, she leaned over the wheel and peered past the windshield into the black abyss. The single remaining headlight was barely capable of illuminating the faded gray asphalt. The road sucked up the light like a sponge. On the crest of a hill north of Santa Agueda she pulled to the side of the road. Behind us in the distance, lights illuminated the wharf.

The door flew open and Barbara rushed to exit the van like we were doing a Chinese fire drill.

He hurried to take over the seat behind the wheel. He had no idea what they had left in their wake. He was happy to have Santa Agenda's lights in what remained of the mirrors. No one chased after them. They couldn't know what might be farther up the road.

Barbara gasped for air and threw up.

He offered up a bottle of water.

She took it and swallowed greedy mouthfuls.

"You think we're free and clear, Harry? There aren't any lights behind us." She didn't leave him time to respond. "I don't think anyone would be stupid enough to try those turns in the dark with no headlights."

Maybe she never heard of Mexican drivers. He thought it strange, given the time she and Sasha spent driving the Baja.

For the moment, they were home free. In hours they'd be partying it up in Ensenada, getting a well-deserved rest before crossing the border. Mike and Sasha needed time to mend. Provided they could find a place that didn't ask questions, that is. They could hole up for a couple of days.

Reminded of what he didn't want to think about, he turned to Barbara in the back and asked about their passengers.

"Sasha is okay. Her face is beat up, but she'll be as good as new in a week. I'm not so sure about Mike."

Harry wasn't either. "Mike didn't sound so good when I helped him off the boat. He's got a broken rib or two. Maybe bones broken in his face. I need to get him looked at once we cross the line."

Or maybe even before we left Ensenada, to be on the safe side.

"How long do you think we need to stay in Ensenada?" Barbara asked.

"Maybe a couple of days." What the hell did he know? Maybe a week. "I'll try to get Mike to a doctor while we're holed up. I don't want him dying on us now."

The woman looked panic-stricken at the mention of Mike dying. "I don't want him to die either. Do you think we could get him to an emergency room?"

"Works for me. What about Sasha? How is she doing?" he asked again.

"She's moving around on her own. Her face is swollen and bruised and she might have a few loose teeth, but she'll be all right after some rest. Her pride is probably hurt more than anything else."

"You should get back to taking care of Mike." He could tell she was itching to do that by the way she kept looking at him. Trouble was, she didn't have anything she could use to take care of him, outside of some mothering.

The events of the past couple of days were eating at him. Ever since they hooked up with these women, everything had gone steadily south. They were on the down-hill, and it was no toboggan ride.

Could their luck be even worse than theirs? And if it was, why did it have to be passed on to them like a disease? Nothing added up since the two of them pulled into the campsite. And that was only days ago, even if it seemed like a week.

He was in the dark in more ways than one.

It was Barbara's turn in the hot seat, and she wouldn't be happy about it. After what went down in Santa Agueda, everything that led up to it was squarely on their shoulders.

No matter how fast and loose Barbara tried to sweet-talk him, she couldn't deny it by any stretch. Bullshit baffles brains. Well, not this time. He wanted an explanation, and he wasn't about to wait for one. He pulled the van off the road and climbed in the back to check on Mike and Sasha.

At least, that was his excuse.

Barbara cradled Mike's head in her lap. He was sleeping or passed out again.

If ever he knew anything about women, it told him she cared. He'd use it to learn what he could. "We have to wake Mike up regularly. If he has a concussion—"

"I know. I just did that. He hasn't made any noise yet."

"What about Sasha?" he asked.

"She's okay. Don't worry about her," Barbara reassured him.

With these two, he was more concerned about Mike and himself and the chances of getting their asses out of Mexico. They were so happy to find themselves here after departing East Africa in a hurry. It was no longer a footloose and fancy-free R&R.

"Are you going to tell me what the hell that was back there? It's been a hundred miles, and I deserve more than what I've been getting." He hadn't been getting anything. Barbara had to believe that loose lips sink ships. Or, in their case, yachts.

"Sasha can tell it better than I can," she had the nerve to say.

So that was how she was going to handle it.

"Yeah, and she's not talking, as you can plainly see." He suspected Sasha might be playing possum for her own benefit. "Sasha might be mute. Or maybe she's pretending. Otherwise, this rig would be parked on the side of the road a lot sooner. She'd be the one getting the third degree."

Barbara sighed, as though resigned to being forced to come up with some measure of truth.

"You won't like what you hear. That's why I want you to hear it from Sasha."

No way was he about to let Barbara off that easily. The woman owed him, big time. "After what we've been through to collect Mike and your friend, I think I can take it. Talk." He wanted to add Or walk, but he was pretty sure she wouldn't believe him.

Barbara mumbled something and smiled a crooked, insincere smile.

He wanted to hit her for putting them into whatever it was they found themselves in. He couldn't do that. He held back and waited instead.

It took her a while. Eventually, Barbara climbed in the front and loosened up. What she told him finally started making sense.

"We've been running drugs up the Baja for almost two years. We've done about a dozen trips. It's getting to where we're running out of places to cross without raising suspicion."

Sasha had told him something similar. Barbara confirmed it. "The meet-up on the beach. When you pulled into my campsite. Was that chance?"

"Yes. It was."

It was the same story he got from Sasha. He already figured it couldn't have been any other way. No one knew he and Mike would meet there. "Who were the men chasing you on the beach? Mike and I thought they were after us."

"Our plan was to meet our supplier there. It's where we pick up our loads. They must have thought you were in on it with us," she said.

"In on it? In on what? What do you mean?" He had to know.

"This was supposed to be our last trip," Barbara revealed. "We loaded up with everything we could get our hands on and headed north. We thought the pickup on the beach would be a bonus when you were already there. Unfortunately, someone was paying attention and caught on to us. You and Mike were collateral damage. At Coronado we tried to drag you into it. We thought it would help us get away."

"How did that work out for you?"

"It worked out until we started having feelings for both of you. Until that happened, we didn't care one bit."

"Where did you learn your Spanish?" he asked.

"My mother is Hispanic."

It was his turn to sigh. "I know Mike well enough. He won't like finding out he's been played for a sucker. Especially given his present condition. When he learns why he's in the shape he's in, I'd want to be somewhere else if I were you."

"What more can I say? We know we were wrong," Barbara admitted.

But did they? He had his doubts. He let it go anyway. At least he had a glimmer of what the hell had been going on. They had played them for patsies. Given that Mike's present condition resulted from all the bullshit, he'd like it even less than me.

"Get in and drive, woman. Plan on stopping in Ensenada. Those two need time to heal. And I need to get Mike to a doctor."

Dead quiet reigned in the van for a lot of miles.

Harry rode in silence in the back, waking Mike from time to time. He checked on Sasha, too.

"Before we get to Ensenada, we need to dump the firearms we have left. You know the road. Pick a spot to pull off when you feel like it."

Eventually, Barbara turned off Mexico 1 onto a rough trail. The tired van bumped and swayed following the uneven ground. The single weak headlight squinted into the gray dirt, illuminating almost nothing. They bounced and kicked up dust on the way to a clearing surrounded by low brush. Barbara flipped off the headlights. It was pitch-black.

"Do we need to remember this place?" she asked.

"Not unless you plan on the four of us having a reunion any time soon. Do you?"

He got down on his hands and knees in the back of the van. Using the dim interior light he got busy searching for spent cartridges. He found the .45's shell casing and tossed it. He tossed the leftover empty AK magazine as well.

"I guess not. Do you think Mike will be angry with me?" she asked.

So she had been thinking about consequences. Better late than never.

"I don't know. You and Mike are going to have to work it out on your own. I don't need to be dragged into it. Right now, I don't think he's too concerned. He needs to heal. You'll have to wait until he knows what happened."

He sure as hell wouldn't be holding back on that.

They limped into Ensenada in late afternoon. Harry checked them into a seedy hotel where no one asked questions. Barbara helped him carry Mike upstairs. She went back to the van to help Sasha limp up the steps. At least they had actual beds to sleep in.

They took turns running food, bandages and splints for the injured. He let Barbara tend to the cuts, scrapes, and bruises left over. While our patients slept, they wandered down the block for beer and margaritas.

"You're not going to volunteer any more than you already have, are you?" Why wasn't he surprised?

"I already told you." she insisted. "I'm going to leave that up to Sasha. If she wants to tell you, she will."

If he wanted to hear more about their escapades on the Baja, he wouldn't be getting it from this one. They were too loyal to each other. No way would Barbara talk past what she already revealed. He had to admire her for that, even if Mike's condition had been the result.

Getting across the border would be their next problem. The bonus was it wouldn't have the same urgency. The coca and bales of dope were long gone. Even so, he had to ask. "We shouldn't have any problem with the border at Tj. Even if the dog jumps on us, we've got nothing, right?"

"I didn't stash anything for a rainy day. I don't know if Sasha did or not. We better remember to ask her before we head out."

Sasha chose that moment to show us she was paying attention. "What are you two worrying about now?"

Finally. She was awake.

"We'll be crossing at Tj. Barbara says she didn't stash anything in the van. We need to know if you did."

"Not an ounce. I'm busted flat."

"Maybe not so much."

Barbara rolled her eyes. Sasha stifled a giggle. "Christ, don't make me laugh. You're still trying to kill me even now, aren't you?"

"If Barbara hadn't filled me in on your escapades, I'd definitely want to kill you. That's done with. I think we all paid our dues. I might put you over my knee, though."

She ignored me. "I can smell the border in Tj. How's Mike doing?"

"He's in and out since we got out of Santa Agueda. His lucid periods are getting longer. I'd say another day and we can go for it."

"That should be easy enough. What have we got to our advantage?" Sasha asked.

"Nothing. Who wants out?"

Mike groaned through his cracked ribs. His groan overtook the laughter.

There was one last question he had for Barbara. "How did you get that trucker to block the highway for us? Did you use the shotty?"

"Hell no. The driver was from L.A. I climbed in and told him I'd show him my tits if he'd pull across the road. Then I figured I'd park the van off the end of the dock to make it easier for the three of you. I climbed back in and asked him if he wanted a second look. When he turned on the light, I knew I had him."

Mike was awake and paying attention. "They are nice."

"I'll have to agree with you on that," Harry assured him.

Barbara smacked him on the back of the head That was all right.

Even Mike got into it. "You never could resist a look, could you?"

"Nope. And neither could you."

"You're right," he went on. "Sasha has a nice rack too, but somehow I don't think she's going to be showing me the goods."

He already knew Sasha wouldn't let that slide even if she was beat up and hurting.

"Will you guys cool it with the comments about my breasts? Our breasts? It's enough to give us a complex. If you want to keep on getting an occasional look, you both better start showing some respect. And no, that doesn't mean you'll be getting a look, Mike. It's only an expression."

He couldn't argue with that. "Better you're here listening to us fantasize than for us to have left you giving a lap dance to your newfound amigos in the half-ton."

He had one more thing to add. "You do sound kind of cute when you lisp."

22

Three days in Ensenada and plenty of beer flushed the last of the adrenalin that constantly pumped through all of them since the adventure began in Coronado. Harry spent the time getting to know Barbara, and then Sasha when she felt up to coming with us.

Hussong's became a favorite with one or the other after each tossed the coin to determine who remained behind with Mike. More often than not, Barbara volunteered. That left him with Sasha to tour the bars. They ended up doing a lot of drinking.

They were all eager to return to the boring sanity they had attempted to escape when they departed on their separate adventures. After what happened, none of them would be signing up for more fun in the sun any time soon. They were looking forward to the border and refuge.

Only days before, they feared it. Empty-handed, they hadn't the slightest care. They looked forward to crossing the line and getting on with their lives.

Five days later, they piled into the graffiti-covered van stashed behind the hotel. It started without a hitch and Sasha steered them into the street, headed north.

"Last chance to change our minds coming up. Who wants to back out?" He couldn't remember who asked. Nervous laughter followed by silence wasn't what he expected.

Barbara and Mike huddled together in the back, whispering he didn't know what to each other. Maybe they were making a pact to reunite at some future date. If it involved Mexico, he hoped the man wouldn't try to talk him into it.

Ten miles short of the line, Sasha called to Barbara to come up front. Just like that, he was relegated to the back of the bus. He sat down beside Mike and we gave each another a look that said trouble.

After more than a few miles, they decided the trouble lay behind, not in front.

They were hyped when they hit the border. The long line in front of them was disappointing, but they were talked out. Even the vendors walking past ignored them. They must have known they didn't have money to spend.

Cursory questioning by border guards and what must have been satisfactory answers resulted in a friendly wave with hardly a glance inside. Crazy Town's *Butterfly* boomed through the speakers, serenading us as they drove past the barrier.

"How easy was that?" he asked.

No answer. The women were talked out. The deal was done.

Mike and Harry were just happy to be there. He didn't know about the two up front, but he figured they should be pretty happy, too. The van slowed and stopped by an exit ramp a couple of miles north of the border.

"Why are you pulling over in the middle of the 5?" Harry asked.

Cars and trucks whooshed past, rocking the boxy van on the side of the freeway. Sasha's eyes reflected in the mirror, cold and unforgiving.

"It's time for you and Mike to take a walk."

"What? In the middle of an off-ramp on the 5? In San Diego?" Where the hell did this come from? They wouldn't even be able to hitch a ride. "We kept you two alive and brought you this far for this? That's just harsh."

"That's the way it is, cowboys. Get out. It's time to find your way."

Damned if he was going to beg. He helped Mike limp out of the van. Barbara got out, but all she could do was hold up her hands in frustration. She looked embarrassed. Like she wanted to die.

Sasha scrambled into the back. She tossed our bags out the door and slammed it shut with happy energy. "Get in, Barbara. It's time."

Barbara got in. Sasha crawled back into the driver's seat and accelerated away, fleeing down the exit lane from the indignity she'd committed.

He helped Mike pick up his bag, and we began pounding the pavement on the side of the expressway.

"This isn't the first time someone has kicked us to the curb. All we need is a ride in exchange for a sad story and we'll be back on top of the world," he reassured him.

"Yeah, and I've heard that sorry tale before, Harry. I think another tour of East Africa is in order. I heard there are rubies and emeralds to be had for the asking. Let's find a phone booth somewhere and I'll make the call."

"I wonder when the two of them came up with the plan to abandon us on the side of the road like a couple of dogs?"

Mike looked at me and shook his head. "I don't think two people worked it out, Harry. I think it was only one. What did you do to piss off Sasha?"

"Screw it. We're wasting time out here in the boonies. Let's find that phone. If we're lucky, whoever we can bullshit on the other end will wire us cash for plane tickets. We'll be crying in beer paid for by someone else before we know it."

Far ahead on the freeway, a flurry of brake lights flashed and a van cut over onto the shoulder. It began slowly backing up.

"Come on, Mike. Let's get it together. Someone has had a change of heart."

He picked up the pace and quick-stepped down the freeway as fast as he could. Mike had trouble keeping up with his tired limp. "You're slowing me down, buddy. I don't want to miss the explanation for this fiasco because you can't run."

"Don't bullshit me, Delaney. You're hoping to see Sasha naked one last time before she kicks you to the curb in person."

"Not this time. Get a move on, or we'll both be late to the dance."

PART 2

Then and now

23

PILOT WANTED

For Pilatus Porter PT-6 STOL. 1,000 hours turbine time on type required. Mountain, jungle, desert experience definite asset. Rotation three weeks on/one off. Paid in/out. Cable ZANZIBAR.

Mike Williams flipped the newspaper across the table. "Did you see this, Harry? It looks like it could be somewhere in Africa."

Harry Delaney picked up the paper. He studied the ad for too long before tossing it back to his friend. Mike took a second look, folded it, and passed it back.

"Someone must have pull. An ad for a pilot in the *International Times* isn't something you see very often."

The Times rarely carried specialized job ads. It was a three-times-a-week paper for expats wanting to get caught up on the news from around the world.

"And a cable address. It has to be out in the boonies—or off the edge of the map."

Mike regarded Harry and nodded. "Just what you're looking for, Delaney."

It was true. Harry was bored with his present job. It was getting to be too tame for his liking. The difficult flying was done. What remained on the contract was fast becoming routine.

"If it hasn't been filled, consider the cable sent." Harry tore the ad out and pocketed it.

"Don't forget your old friend," Mike said.

Harry knew Mike shared his feelings for the job they were doing. It was time for change. The problem would be to find replacements, but it wouldn't be their problem. It would be someone else's.

"I'll let you know when I get there."

24

Harry Delaney's reputation preceded him. The job flying the Porter fell into place. After a time, he was doing so much flying he became almost too busy to do the aircraft engineer's job. Misery loved company, and Harry felt a need to share some of it with his friend Mike Williams. After repeated attempts at overseas calls from the rat-hole where he was forced to spend his time off, he finally connected with Mike.

"Your presence is requested." Harry grinned into the phone. Mike wouldn't be any the wiser, at least until he arrived.

"What have you got for me?" Mike wanted to know.

"One beat-up, timed-out, tired pile of aluminum. But you know what? It's still flying and so am I."

"Well then, I won't need to be around much to work on it, will I?"

"I wouldn't say that. But don't take my word for it. You'll find out everything you need to know when you get here." Harry reassured his friend. And that was more than the truth.

"I can't wait," Mike told him.

"In that case, cable me when you're arriving and I'll meet you."

Mike Williams wasn't able to secure a room in the small, single-story hotel. He tried, even offering baksheesh. The bribe was turned down, its refusal unusual in this part of the world. Come closing time, another offer of cash up-front guaranteed him a reserved spot. He spent a restless night atop the sketchy hotel's cheap wooden bar-top with his duffel for a pillow. When morning arrived it brought a queasy stomach. Thinking he might throw up, he rushed outside to gulp fresh air.

The high-pitched whine of a PT-6 engine in full reverse and the cloud of red dust it produced announced Harry Delaney's arrival at the airstrip, sitting as it was right next to the hotel bar. The plane slowed and stopped.

Mike choked back the sensation of wanting to puke. If Harry saw him, he'd never hear the end of it, even if the bar where he spent the night was an adventure. He picked up his duffel and tool kit and walked over to the Pilatus and its idling engine parked beside the small bar's outbuilding. Fading paint from too much time spent in the hot, dry climate greeted him. He swung open the pilot-side door.

Harry yelled over the turbine's ground-idle whine. "Throw your tools in the back and hang on."

Mike cracked the cargo door and inspected the compartment. It was empty but for a stainless-steel floorboard. There were no seats or belts. "That's an understatement. Where's my seat belt?"

"I'm the only one that gets the luxury of a belt unless you want up front."

"Thanks for the offer." He gestured to the barren cargo compartment. "I always wondered what it was like to fly cabin class."

Mike walked around the back of the idling PT-6 and climbed up to join Harry on the flight deck. He took the right seat in the Pilatus before strapping in. He looked over at Harry and grinned. "If you thought I was going to get into the back of this tin can, you're sadly misinformed."

Harry grinned across at his good friend. "Don't worry. It was only a test."

The duo low-fived before Mike turned to look past the jury-rigged canvas divider into the sparse cargo deck a second time. He confirmed what he saw at first glance. "Christ, Harry, it was no lie when you said she was a beat-up, ugly pile of flying junk."

The Pilatus Porter was a purpose-built aircraft, manufactured in Switzerland for high-altitude mountain work. It was in high demand for its load-carrying ability at lower altitudes and hot temperatures, too. With an experienced pilot at the helm, it could get into and out of landing areas where a helicopter was too expensive.

"Just think of the experience you'll be able to put on your work history," Harry said.

The Porter Harry piloted was outfitted for cargo-only. Seats and belts were missing. The deck was stripped of every piece of useless weight. The floor was protected by a thin layer of aluminum cut to size and bolted down. Even that modification wouldn't be there if it wasn't needed.

"Yeah, that'll go a long way in this business, all right."

Harry looked at his friend. "I can tell you're impressed with the utility configuration. You should have seen her before I showed up." He dialed in eight turns of flap, stood on the brakes, and pulled the column full aft. An immense cloud of dust and dirt collected behind the plane and drifted toward the hotel and its bar thanks to the noisy propeller's huge bite.

He advanced the throttle on the single-engine plane. At the same time he eased in right rudder to counter the massive amount of torque the PT-6 produced at full power. He looked left.

"Clear right," Mike called.

Harry released the brakes. The plane jumped forward. With the column full-aft, the Porter rotated onto its tail-wheel and became airborne in 200 feet. He set the climb rate and the old friends settled into an easy banter that had developed along with their friendship over the years.

"What took you so long to get off the ground? Have you been slacking?" Mike wanted to know over the turbine engine's whine at climb power.

"The fuel control needs some tweaking. I tried, but that's

the best I could do. Besides, that's why you're here. I didn't want to do you out of a job."

"How long to camp?"

"About an hour."

"Plenty of time." Mike pulled out his notebook and a pen.

Harry leveled the plane and set up for cruise while bringing Mike up to speed on the operation. "I fly out ivory and tanzanite and the occasional ruby in exchange for arms or whatever else will fit into this crate on the back-haul. Money fits, too. Lots of it."

"Tanzanite? What's that?" Mike wanted to know.

"It's a gem-quality mineral, blue in color," Harry explained. "The world's best-known deposit is where we're headed in northern Tanzania, in an eight square mile area."

"And that's all there is to this gig?"

"Well, not exactly," Harry said. "I pack this thing with six or ten people every now and again. It's my job to make sure they get to where they need to be. It's what keeps my people-handling skills from deteriorating."

"That'll be the day. Where's the base?"

"Everywhere and nowhere. We work out of uncharted landing strips, so to speak."

"A true bush operation." Mike put down his notebook. While Harry talked he was listening to the idiosyncrasies of the PT-6, examining gauges.

"If you only knew," Harry said.

"I suspect I'm about to find out." Mike settled back in the seat and closed his eyes. Hungover as he was, there was no sense wasting good sleep time. He suspected he wouldn't get much rest once he arrived at the bush camp.

Mike felt the elbow in his left side. He woke up and blinked before examining the gauges. Satisfied everything was in the green, he turned his gaze out the window.

"Is that it?"

"We're here. Strap in and hang on, my friend."

Harry reached to check flaps zero in preparation for the

short-field landing. The strip disappeared beneath the nose. He throttled back, put the prop into Beta and stuffed the nose into a 45-degree dive. Pitch warning and reverse/Beta range warning lamps came alive on the panel. He ignored the lights.

As the Porter was about to touch down, he pulled back and flared for a three-point landing. With wheels on the ground and the prop in reverse pitch, the turbine-engine Porter stopped in 200 feet.

"It feels like the brakes are shot, too." Mike pulled out his book and made a note.

"You could probably look at them when you get a chance," Harry said. "You'll find plenty of spares available. Whoever heads up this disaster doesn't scrimp on aircraft parts."

Harry held the column full aft and taxied the Porter to its resting spot on the side of the strip. He used the engine and the variable-pitch propeller to torque-turn the aircraft. He backed it beneath the tree canopy before shutting down.

Mike used the time waiting for the prop to halt to rest his head against the seat-back.

"Rough night?" Harry asked.

Mike sighed. "Only if you consider the room and the bed I paid for on the hotel bar."

Harry laughed. He was accustomed to Mike's antics. "Give me some help to manhandle this thing."

The pair exited the Pilatus onto solid ground.

"You never told me the job required actual physical labor," Mike said.

They arranged the Pilatus under the bush cover. Mike helped string the camo netting to ensure invisibility. When they finished, he looked around at the campsite. The dark-colored tents sat off to the side of the strip beneath the canopy. More camo nets covered them. There were no vehicles.

There were no people, either.

"What are the living arrangements, Harry?"

"We'll be sharing quarters. Laundry is done every day. Just leave your clothes on the foot of the bed. At the end of the day, you'll get them back, cleaned and pressed. Clean sheets, bed made, floor swept. Your job is to keep that thing in the air for me. Once in a while you'll get to eat and sleep, too."

"How much time do I have?"

"I told them you'd have the plane tied up until tomorrow morning. They weren't happy about it, but I'm the only one here who can fly it. You make two, but I didn't tell them that."

"In that case, take my bag to the tent for me", Mike told him. "I'm going to be busy until dark. When's your next flight?"

"Tomorrow in the a.m." Harry didn't specify a time.

"Do we have lighting?"

"There's a small generator and a couple of trouble lights if you get desperate. I'd advise against using any light after dark. It's liable to bring down rain from hell."

That didn't bother Mike in the slightest. "In that case, give me a hand getting set up and then you can disappear."

"One more thing, before I forget."

Mike glanced Harry's way. "What's that?"

"You mentioned disappearing. Don't walk past the perimeter after dark. Ever."

Mike got busy going to work on the Porter. He pulled the cowlings to open the Pilatus PT-6's engine compartment. It was clean. No oil leaks evident. No fuel weeping, either. It appeared as though Harry had been working on it to keep it that way. He'd ask later to be sure. The prop seals were good. Fuel and filters were clean—no fungus, at least.

He wiped at the accumulated dust and grime and cleaned up as best he could. He lubed the brake controls twice. The Porter would stop on a dime now. He chocked the wheels before pulling back the camouflage netting. He went through the start sequence, pushed the igniter, and the engine obeyed its start limits. He set it to ground idle, allowing it to warm to operating temperatures. When he was satisfied, he stood on the brakes and advanced the throttle.

A quick check of the gauges showed a limit that didn't look good. Not wanting to chance it with the normally reliable PT-6, he shut down right away. He searched through boxes stacked under the wings and came up with a set of cargo-compartment seat belts and a fuel control unit. By the time he finished, it was dark.

Without light, he couldn't do more. The run-up and test flights would have to wait.

He checked his watch. It was time to eat. Mike ambled over to what he figured was the cook tent and pushed through the flap. Two huge camo-wearing men glared at him with surly looks. Beside them, automatic weapons leaned against the table.

"Greetings, gentlemen."

The answer-back was accented—the first sounded South African; the second, Belgian. Mercs. Mercenaries. Dogs of war.

"How's the grub?"

"It's okay, but we can't talk the pilot into back-hauling enough to make us happy."

He'd be able to solve that problem easily enough. His solution would give him a leg up once the eats arrived. He figured keeping these guys happy would be the least of his worries. He sat down across from the mercs.

"Have I got a deal for you." Mike took out his notebook and began writing.

25

Mike rolled out of bed. His feet landed on the tent's canvas floor. He shook his cargo shorts and pulled them on. He reached for his boots, turned them upside-down, and tapped the sole's edges together before sliding his feet into them. He halted outside the tent to splash the wash-basin's cold water on his face. He shivered and dried off.

It wasn't yet sunrise, but he was in a hurry to take another look at Harry's snag list in the light of a new day. He fired up the small generator and chanced a trouble light. He pulled back the camo netting covering the Porter and went to work on several of the minor items on his list. They wouldn't make a big difference, but the overall improvements would.

Happy with his work, he put his tools away and closed the toolbox. Satisfied everything in his notebook was in the green, as he called it, he turned his attention to the bush landing strip. He walked it from one end to the other, paying attention to the growth of shrubs and trees at both ends. When he finished his walk, he fueled the Porter with minimums, removed the rest of the netting, and stowed it before patting the wad of cash stuffed in his shirt pocket.

He had everything he needed.

He climbed into the cockpit to do his engine run-up and complete his test flight. He looked over his shoulder for stowaways and came up empty. It was an old habit developed out of necessity on some of these isolated bush jobs.

Last night during his confab with the mercs, he got them to agree not to shoot him out of the sky on the test flight. At least, that was his story, and so far, everyone looked to be sticking to it.

He taxied the Pilatus out of the bush shelter in the growing twilight. By the time he positioned on the end of the strip, the PT-6 was warmed and ready to go. He brake-turned into the brisk wind blowing straight down the makeshift rough and rocky bush strip. He cranked in eight turns of take-off flap and pulled the stick full aft.

The way forward was clear. He looked right and then left to the tents. A few of the mercs lined up, perhaps not expecting to see the plane on the runway with Harry still drinking coffee in the mess tent.

He firewalled the throttle and pushed right rudder at the same time to overcome the huge input of torque generated by the 550-horsepower PT-6 turbine engine. The nose pointed straight down the runway. Minus his rudder input, the Porter would be headed toward the tents on the left.

The Porter shimmied and shook, resembling a powerful racehorse ready to bolt. He released the brakes, and thanks to the wind straight down the runway, the plane jumped into the sky. Super-light, the main gear came off the ground. He rotated on the tail wheel. The Porter became airborne in fifteen feet.

If that didn't leave them clapping, nothing would.

At 500 feet, he dialed in a thousand-feet-per-minute climb and had the Pilatus at altitude in jig time. He backtracked on yesterday's route into camp by setting the DG—the Directional Gyro—to the compass. He tuned the ADF—the Automatic Direction Finder—to the town's local radio station.

He was on his way to delivering the riches he promised the mercs.

Harry didn't need to check his pocket watch when Mike and the Porter didn't show up following what was supposed to be a routine test flight. When plane and Mike returned, he was pretty sure the Porter would be loaded to the gills with fresh grub.

No matter where he found himself in the world, food and having enough of it was a constant complaint in every bush camp he had ever been in. Even on the off chance the cook might be a former five-star chef on the outs, everything revolved around food and whether they were getting the best they could.

With nothing to do while he waited out Mike, he eavesdropped on the grumbling around the breakfast table. His friend was taking a verbal beating for keeping the mercs from making their rounds. They had grown accustomed to completing their aerial recons first thing in the morning while campfire smoke still floated over the bush.

The mining consortium depended on the mercs to keep anyone and everyone from interrupting or halting the profit of the mining operations. It was a full-time job. The dozen mercs were broken up into two squads of five each. The sixth was a spare for illness, R&R losses, or casualties. Each team had a responsibility to perform clean-up ops in the region.

The bitch session came to an abrupt end when the Pilatus arrived on its noisy final. It dropped below the horizon. The mercs stood up, not sure what to expect next. They shouldered their equipment and headed single-file to the strip.

Mike danced the Porter onto the strip and plowed his way to the cook-tent on the Porter's spread gear before shutting down.

Harry stayed put to watch the antics as the mercs opened the cargo door to climb aboard. They soon dropped their weapons to unload boxes, bags, containers, fresh fruit and vegetables. All of it ended up at the kitchen, carried there by the sweating mercs.

"You did good, Mike," one grizzled veteran told him. "We will doubt your word no more."

Two AKs complete with packs stuffed with ammunition and magazines, delivered in person by Mike, was the last of it. He dropped the goods on the table in the cook tent.

"What are you planning on doing with those?" Harry asked.

"I made a bargain with the devil last night. All I had to do was come up with the equipment. Fresh food and plenty of it in exchange for small-arms training. In this job, I figure one day we might need it."

"Good. I kept putting it off. You're right. It's overdue. We could both use the training."

"There's no reason to put it off now," Mike insisted. "You can thank me later when you get stranded out there some day." He waved an arm. "The mercs will throw in an RPG lesson for free."

"Here?"

"Hell no," Mike insisted. "When we get back to civilization on an R&R."

Harry shook his head. "So then, you're telling me my next R&R will be spent doing weapons training."

"You betcha, buddy. Like I said, thank me later."

"Just so you know, I'm not doing laps," Harry told him.

Mike grinned across the table. "Yeah. Until you find a woman to chase. Then you'll be doing the laps."

"Is that what they call it back in civilization now?" Harry wanted to know.

Following Mike's arrival, the flying became routine and relaxed. Mike took over the chore of maintaining the Pilatus. Working steadily, he cleared the entire snag list in a couple of days. To ease the boredom, we took turns flying the recon missions. With the Porter in good condition and the engine operating at its peak, positioning the mercs at the bush strips proved to be a lot less nerve-wracking.

Every ten days, a flight into town saw that the kitchen was outfitted with fresh grub and beer. The mercs were grateful, and when six of them flew out for an R&R, they convinced us to start our weapons training regimen. Before long, our own bitch sessions began.

"Damn, Mike, these guys are treating us more like a legionnaire brigade than a couple of guys wanting to learn how to shoot an AK-47."

We huffed and puffed to keep up with the mercs on every run.

"Maybe, but just think of the many ways you'll be able to talk yourself out of being kidnapped with an RPG backed up with an AK and grenades."

"It won't hurt to have the know-how. I'm pretty sure the single merc they leave with us when we're parked out on those isolated strips will be grateful for the extra firepower."

"Especially if we know how to load and fire. That plane is their lifeblood. It's ours, too. Destroy it, and we'll all be royally screwed."

"You're right. We definitely don't have any friends out there."

"Let's get a shave, shower and shoe-shine. I have it on good authority that the bar in this rathole is a real treat."

"Really? Whose authority?" Harry asked.

Mike grinned a shit-eater. "Mine."

26

Harry Delaney looked around at the three corporate jets dwarfing him in Mike Williams' enormous hangar. They were gleaming white spectacles indicative of the stature his old friend gained as he climbed toward the top of corporate aviation's ladder. It was plainly obvious that Mike's business was no fly-by-night operation.

"Well, what do you think?" Mike asked.

He glanced at Mike and smiled. "I think you're into it up to your neck."

"I have to admit it's unusual to have them here all at once. It's a rare occurrence."

"Those 300s are nice. How many aircraft are you operating for the oil patch?"

"All of them," Mike told him. "The Twin Otters are up at our northern base."

"How do you fill vacancies for the jets?" Harry wanted to know.

"We don't very often. Once a pilot gets into one of those beauties, they pretty much stick it out."

"What about the Twin Otter drivers?"

"They're all experienced old-timers. If we get a new hire, he or she will get into the right seat with an experienced captain for a long-term evaluation before we put one of them in a pilot-in-command role."

"That's the way to do it," Harry agreed.

Mike nodded. Harry was just as knowledgeable as he was. "By the time I get my hands on them they're fed up with living in the bush or the desert or the arctic. By then, they've got a ton of flight time in a variety of operations and aircraft. Most of them are IFR-rated."

"The oil business can be chancy. By the look of it, you're doing all right."

"We're making good money. We don't have to go begging to get paid. The blue-eyed Arabs pay their bills on time. It's not like the old days any more."

"Yes, I know those old days well. I'm still living in them."

"You also know you've got a job here if you want it," Mike assured him. He had been trying forever to talk Harry into coming to work for him.

"I'm not ready yet, Mike. One day."

"Then if you're done with your base inspection, it's time we headed to the house." The men grinned at each other, both knowing the other was just as stubborn.

"Are you still living in the same place?"

"Damn, Harry, you should get home more often. No, we moved two years ago."

"Right, I knew that. I just forgot, is all." He didn't remember, but he didn't let on.

"Just so you know, Barbara invited Sasha and Christa." Mike wanted to prepare Harry before he saw his ex-wife and daughter at his home. He knew they got along, but even so, he knew not to blind-side his old friend. "They know you'll be there. That's why they're coming."

"Is Sasha still with that oil guy?"

"Gene? Yeah. He's with CAN-AL Oil, one of our biggest customers. They're all over the world. He might be at the house, too. It's time you met him. He's playing dad to your daughter."

"What's he like?" Harry wanted to know.

"He treats Sasha and Christa pretty good, but he can be a

pain in the ass. He hasn't been out in the world much. He's from one of those oil tycoon families, born into the business."

"No seat-of-the-pants flying, in other words." Both men know what that meant.

"Definitely not. He seems to be a by-the-book guy. That's okay with me. He's trying to make a name for himself. You know the type. Daddy's boy makes good in the business started by his father."

Harry knew the type, all right. "If the bills get paid on time, it's all good."

M ike pulled into the driveway of his new house as Harry marveled at the expanse. "You've done all right, old friend," he told him.

"Life is pretty good," Mike replied. "I'm enjoying the fruits of my labors while I can. I'm going to let you go first. I have it on good authority that there's a little person behind that door that won't be held back."

Harry opened the door. Christa, his daughter, squealed with delight at the sight of her father through the open door. All of the little girl's patience flew out the door as she ran into her father's open arms.

"Harry! I missed you, daddy."

"Hi honey. How's my little girl?" Harry scooped Christa up, hugged her, and twirled her around. She laughed and giggled until Harry set her down.

"I really miss you," she insisted.

"I miss you just as much, sweetheart. I always miss you."

Sasha, Harry's wife, smiled watching the two of them chase after each other as they got re-acquainted. Christa never left his side, and Harry, patient man that he was, gave her all the time she wanted. If only he wasn't so far away most of the time, then just maybe—

She ended the reminiscing and concentrated on Harry and their daughter.

"I've missed you too, Sasha, just so you know," Harry told her.

"It's always good to see you, Harry. It doesn't happen often enough any more. There's something I need to talk to you about. Can we do it after dinner?"

"Of course we can."

"In that case, come with me," Sasha insisted. "I want to introduce you to Gene."

One look at Gene told Harry all he needed to know. Tall and slim going to skinny. Clean cut. Plenty of hair to keep neat and tidy and trimmed just right. Clean manicured hands. Fresh-pressed shirt and pants.

He shut out his thoughts, happy that his ex had found someone. His eyes wandered to Sasha. She was still beautiful. Sill kept her black hair long. There was no gray, but she probably took care of that—not that it mattered. All he had to do now was find someone for himself. He grimaced at the thought.

"So this is the guy who's been stealing my daughter's affections. I finally get to meet you."

"I've heard a lot about you," Gene said.

Harry snapped back to the immediate reality at the sound of Gene's high-pitched voice. "Not all of it bad, I hope."

"No. None of it bad, actually."

The two stood apart, each sizing up the other. Satisfied, Harry backed off and made an excuse to go looking for Barbara. "Where's the real owner of this dump?"

Barbara, overhearing him, called out. "She's trapped in the kitchen. Where the hell do you think? Get your ass in here."

"Yes ma'am."

Barbara looked up from the cookies she was making. "Where's my hug?"

"Right here, gorgeous, where it always is. It's great to see you. What's for dinner?"

"Always getting right to the point, aren't you? I'm not going to ruin it by telling you."

"Your home-cooked meals keep me coming back," he grinned.

"If that was the truth, you'd be back more often," Barbara said. "Did I hear your daughter call you Harry out there?"

"Yes, well, I'm not proud of it. I was hoping no one would notice."

'I'm sorry. I always thought you three should be together, just like old times."

Harry didn't mind Barbara's acknowledgment that she wanted them back together. Sometimes, he wondered why he had pulled up stakes, too. "People change. When Sasha told me she wanted out, I let her know I'd keep paying the bills until someone came along for her and Christa. I'm just glad they stayed close to you and Mike."

"We are too, but we miss you, Harry."

"We've all been through a lot together. It's tough to let go sometimes, but it was the thing to do. I wasn't going to fight her," he said.

"Just between the two of us, I get the feeling Gene is going to ask her to marry him."

That was news to Harry. He figured Mike didn't know, or he would have told him. "Isn't it about time? He's been seeing her for a year, hasn't he?"

"Like I said, you should come by more often. They've been seeing each other for almost two years."

"If that's true, it took the man enough time to make up his mind."

"Well, it looks like he finally has," Barbara insisted.

Harry poked around the enormous kitchen.

"Are you looking for anything in particular?"

He looked up at the shotgun peeking out from the top of the cupboard. "Is that Mike's old shotty stashed up there?"

"It is. I thought I'd keep it around, just in case."

"Just in case of what, Barbara? Better times and happier memories?" he asked.

Exasperated, she planted her hands on her hips and looked at Harry before replying. "Something like that."

Harry stacked the last of the dishes before wiping the counter. Barbara stood back and marveled before teasing him. "You'd have made someone a good house-husband. It's too bad you're so old and set in your ways."

"Don't bury me yet, girl," he reassured her. "I've only got one of my feet in the graveyard."

"Yes, and sometimes you have the other planted firmly up your rear end. You need to do right by that woman, Harry. You're going to let her get away again, aren't you? And what about your daughter? What's going on there?"

Harry sighed. "I think Sasha has pretty much made up her mind about what she's going to do—and I support her in it."

"You're going to lose her."

"You're probably right—and there's nothing I can do about it. Now I have to go and find her. He cast a sheepish glance at Barbara before explaining. "She said she wanted to talk."

Barbara shook her head. "Don't tell me I've got you on the run already. You just got here."

Sasha paced back and forth, anxiously waiting for Harry. It had been two years since they last saw each other, but she knew they'd get along. She still liked him. Maybe she still loved him just a little, too. She smiled anxiously when he arrived.

As always, Harry dove right in. "What's happening with you two—or you three now, I guess," he wanted to know.

She made sure to get right to the point, too. "I get the feeling that Gene is going to ask me to marry him."

"Will he want to adopt Christa?" he asked.

"We haven't talked about that yet, but he'd better if he wants a family with me."

"Whatever you want to do is okay by me." There was no point in objecting. He wouldn't anyway. "I'm her father. That won't change. I trust your judgment. You already know that."

"Yes, but it's nice to hear you say it," Sasha reassured him.

"I hear Gene is going to be taking you overseas on one of his trips."

"Barbara told you, didn't she? Damn that woman," she bristled. "I wanted to be the one to tell you."

"Of course she told me. You know she talks to me about you and Christa—and you'd better not mind, either. Do you know when you're going?" he wanted to know.

"He wants to take Christa, too. I need time with him to help make up my mind. I don't plan on saying yes until after the trip."

"You have my blessing no matter what you decide. Christa needs the stability. I think you do, too." Harry pulled a box out of his backpack.

"What's that?" Sasha wanted to know.

"A little something for my two favorite girls. Thanks to Barbara's advance warning, when I learned where you were going, I picked up a GPS transmitter. It's the latest tech. I know someone and got a pre-release version. You turn it on and press a button and it will transmit your location to a satellite and send out a pre-programmed message."

"Do you think we'll need all that, Harry? We're going for a week at most. Neither Christa nor I will be out in the middle of nowhere. We'll be seeing the sights and doing some shopping in civilization while Gene does some business."

"Of course you won't need it," he reassured her. "Do you know where you're going to be?"

"Gene hasn't told us yet, but I'm pretty sure he will soon."

As Harry suspected, Gene wasn't as forthcoming with his family as he'd like him to be. "I set it up with Mike and Barbara's email address, and their corporate one as well. They know all about it."

"Are you going to put yours in? That's the one I want if I ever have to use it."

"You know I'm all over the place. If you have to press the button, you're going to want to have someone who can take the call."

"Will you show me how to use it?"

"Of course. I'll show you both before I leave."

Sasha already knew Harry would ship out in a few days. Barbara kept her informed, and she was glad of it. "You're still hitting the high spots, aren't you? Where are you off to this time?" She never knew where he worked any more.

"NBO."

Spending time with Harry, once she learned the airport designators, she never forgot them. "Nairobi."

"Yes."

"Please be careful."

Christa pulled the GPS Tracker out of the box in front of Gene. She was proud her father had taken the time to explain how it worked. She wanted to show it off to her mother's boyfriend. "Gene. Look what Harry gave us." She held it out, wanting him to take it.

"Yes, that's nice, sweetheart."

"Harry showed me how to turn it on. He says it will help to find us if we get in trouble."

"It's plastic. It doesn't look very well built. Put it away before you break it," he told her.

She put the Tracker in her backpack and zipped it shut.

Gene turned to Harry. "They won't be needing that thing. They'll be with me the entire time."

"Well, they have it if they want it. It's for them to decide."

"We'll be three or four days at most, then back home in no time," he reassured Harry. "The batteries will probably go dead by then."

"The batteries are fresh. I made sure myself." Exasperated, Harry had nothing more to say to the man. He returned his hands to his pockets and looked across the room at Barbara.

She returned the look, but what she was thinking, he couldn't tell.

"Whatever you say, Gene. If it's needed, they have it."

27

Gene wasn't happy when Harry stuck his nose into his relationship with Sasha and her daughter. He saw the useless GPS junk Harry had presented as an assault on his ability to look after them. When he saw Christa had brought it with her on their trip overseas, he went into full-on denial. "Christa, I thought I told you to leave that thing at home. We don't need it."

"But Harry gave it to me," she explained. "He said I could bring it on our trip for good luck."

"It's a cheap toy. It's not going to bring anyone any luck. The thing probably doesn't even work."

Distracted by the arrival of their car, Gene tossed the tracking device on the chair in the hotel lobby. Christa retrieved it and stashed it in the bottom of her backpack, out of sight.

"Our driver is here," Gene announced. "Let's get going. We have an airplane to catch."

Sasha tried one last time to convince Gene she and her daughter needed to go exploring on their own. She didn't think either of them should be out in the desert. "Is it really necessary to take us out into the middle of nowhere? Christa and I planned on spending the day looking around. We wanted to do some shopping. We'll never have another opportunity like this."

"I want to show you how important this project is for CAN-AL. You can look around town next time."

Christa looked at her mother and rolled her eyes. Sasha waggled a finger at her daughter, but she smiled, too. It was beginning to appear as though Gene was more concerned with himself and his self-important image than anyone or anything else.

"Now come on, we have to get to the airport." Gene hurried Sasha and her daughter out of the lobby and into the beat-up old deux chevaux. In twenty minutes, they were aboard the Beech-18 charter. Wheels-up followed, and they were on their way to the desert strip located a few miles from the oil company camp and well-site.

Sasha wasn't impressed by the plane. The livery—she chuckled to herself as she remembered the term—was faded and peeling in places. She'd been around Harry and Mike long enough to know the Beech was an ancient piece of tin. Even Mike wouldn't be caught dead owning one. The seat cushions were on their last legs and the windows were so scratched she could barely see out. The operator was probably a local, hungry for oil money and running a scam of some sort to get CAN-AL to agree to hire it.

She looked across the aisle at her daughter and smiled. Christa had her head buried in the picture instructions for the GPS transmitter Harry had given her. She turned away from her daughter and inspected the plane's interior with a critical eye. She settled on the beat-up interior and dusty, shabby seats. Considering the advanced age of what they were riding in, she hoped they wouldn't have to put the tracking device to use any time soon.

S asha recognized the familiar sound of power coming back on the Beechcraft's twin engines as the pilot set up for his approach. Sasha cast her gaze outside the plane through the scratched window. A stark desert landscape presented itself. They passed over limitless sand and hills and boulders and rocky outcrops before the wheels touched down. The plane bumped its way across the uneven sand strip. Sasha wondered if Harry at some point might have been here before her.

Across the aisle, Gene surveyed the vehicles outside his window. The plane halted and the engines went quiet. Trucks stirred up dust as they positioned to block it in.

"Those aren't our trucks. They aren't our people, either," he announced.

Sasha's head snapped to look at Gene. "Then who are they?" She looked out the window to observe the weapons mounted on the back of the trucks. Technicals. She recalled seeing them on television and then reading about them at some point.

"I don't know. Stay here."

She wasn't going to disobey, until she spotted the rifles. "Gene, wait. Those look like AKs."

"What's an AK?" he asked.

Of course. If the man only knew. She hoped they were an advance guard. If they were, why were they needed? What might she and her daughter be stepping into if they got out of the plane? "Trust me, you don't want to find out if one gets aimed in your direction. Christa, come here with me. We're getting off now. You too, Gene."

"Let me handle this," Gene insisted.

Sasha took Christa's hand and stepped in front of Gene. She dropped her daughter's hand and held up her own. "Dear. Hold up your hands like mommy is doing and follow me." She stepped in front of her daughter and jumped down onto the sand. Christa followed, keeping her hands in the air. Gene reluctantly followed behind and the three of them moved away from the Beechcraft.

"Gene, half of those people look barely older than Christa."

In that instant, the technicals opened up on the twin Beech, raking it from nose to tail with automatic fire. Christa covered her ears and turned to her mother. Sasha's arms instinctively went around her daughter, but she knew her body would be incapable of protecting her from the ferocity of the weapons raining lead into the airplane's carcass.

By some miracle, the pilot appeared in the doorway,

unscathed by the intense display of firepower. Before he could step down, a second hail of bullets cut him to pieces.

Tracer rounds passed through the wings. Fuel in the tanks ignited, intensifying the fire already burning. Minutes later, the Beech-18 turned into a smoking pile of melted aluminum as the draining fuel did its job. The heat forced everyone to step back.

A tall man approached them. "You will come with us."

Obeying without question, Sasha and Christa started toward the trucks.

Gene hesitated. "I'm with CAN-AL Oil. We're doing the drilling north of here. My people are supposed to be meeting me. Do you know anything about it?"

"Get in the truck," the man insisted.

Gene went on. "But I'm with CAN-AL Oil. I have to get to our camp. I have meetings scheduled."

Exasperated with Gene and worried for her daughter's safety, Sasha was in no mood to put up with the man's whining. He was putting them in danger. "Gene, do what they tell you. Do they look like they're not serious after what they did to the plane?"

"But I have meetings. They can't do this. We're supposed to fly back tonight."

Sasha turned to look back at their plane. "Take another look, Gene. We won't be flying anywhere tonight. Keep it together and let's go. They've got the guns. That makes them the boss."

Sasha finally understood. Gene was incapable of comprehending the desperate situation the three of them were in. He couldn't fathom the danger they were in. The man's mindless ranting was annoying everyone—especially their kidnappers.

Unwilling to give up, Gene kept ranting about getting to the camp for his meetings. An impatient kidnapper jabbed Gene in the gut with the butt of his AK. Left gasping for breath, he was forced to shut up. Sasha helped him climb into a Jeep.

"Christa."

"Yes, mommy?"

"Do you still have that thing Harry gave you?"

"Yes. It's in my backpack," she told her mother.

"Do you remember how to work it?"

"I think so. I looked at the pictures on the plane."

"I know. I saw you." Sasha smiled down at her daughter. "I think now would be a good time to turn it on. Can you do that? Pretend it's a toy if anyone asks."

"All right, mommy."

"It is a toy," Gene said, as if to add insult to injury. "It'll never work. Damn it. I don't have time for this. Don't these people know who I am?"

At a signal from a man in the back of the lead vehicle, the convoy got underway. The procession of vehicles moved slowly eastward, in the direction of the Indian Ocean. She knew because she had seen it from the plane before they began their descent to the desert floor.

Sasha continued to ignore Gene in the heat and the dust trailing from the lead vehicles stretching out in front of them. "Did you get Harry's tracker turned on, honey?"

"Yes."

That was good. At least something was going right. "Did you press the red button and hold it down the way Harry showed you?"

"Yes."

"Good girl. Give mommy a hug."

Gene went on with his ranting through the convoy's thick dust. "Admit it, Harry's junk is useless and you know it. Your ex is still the loser he always was."

Christa rolled her eyes at her mother as she sheltered her daughter in her arms. How was it her daughter knew Gene better than she did?

28

A fed-up Mike finally got hold of Barbara when she picked up. "Where have you been? I've been calling and calling for the last hour."

"I was across the street at the neighbor's drinking wine and telling lies. What's up that's so important?"

"Sasha's Tracker has been sending out emails."

Barbara gasped. "Oh shit. Where are they?"

"According to the position map, East Africa. On the Horn. Hits have been showing every fifteen minutes. I've got the guys installing the utility interior in the jet now."

"I'll try to track down Harry," she told him. "Damn. What time is it in NBO?"

"That's your part of the job," he told her.

She knew that already. It wasn't the first time. "Once I track him down, I'll get our bags to the hangar as soon as I can."

Barbara knew Mike would want her to stay home and safe. He also had to know it would be impossible to keep her away. She and Sasha had become even closer following their shared adventure on the Baja.

"This won't be a picnic, Barbara. It will be dangerous. It won't be an easy extraction. Are you sure you want—" Mike didn't get time to finish.

"You couldn't keep me away with your old shotty," she insisted.

"What we had on the Baja will seem like a picnic compared to this exercise, believe me. There's nothing out there—and I mean nothing. No roads. No towns. Nada. You can't depend on anyone. Life is cheap. People you trust can turn on you in an instant. Sometimes, people you can trust are non-existent." Mike halted.

"We're doing this together," Barbara informed him. "In fact, you and I and Harry need to do this. I'll be with the people I need to trust. I wouldn't have it any other way. I don't think you would, either. I know everything has evened out between you and Harry since the Baja, but between Sasha and me, it will never be even. It will always be equal." If that didn't convince Mike, nothing would.

"All right. You win. I'm getting the guys together. It'll be another couple of hours by the time we're loaded and ready."

"There's no way I'm telling Harry we had a hit from the Tracker," Barbara added. "He'd be crazy by the time we got there. I'll let him know we have a charter into NBO. That should hold him."

"You're right. I'm concerned about him going off on his own. He's got plenty of contacts over there, but he's going to need a lot more than that."

The flight into Nairobi was going to be a long haul for the jet. Barbara knew Mike wouldn't stop for anything until he got to Harry. She opened the door to the fridge and began putting together a cooler of food for the flight. While she waited for a return phone call on Harry's whereabouts, it would keep her busy doing something besides worrying.

Mike wasn't looking forward to addressing his employees. Meetings weren't his style, and he called few of them. He enjoyed dealing one-on-one. It was more personal that way. There were no stragglers when he made his way into the lunchroom. Conversation halted immediately.

"Guys, I've just received bad news. A family friend has gone missing on the Horn of Africa. I'm going to need help. If any of you want to volunteer, I'd be more than happy to have you on board."

There was a murmur among the assembled group before a single employee spoke his mind from the back of the room.

"You want volunteers? What's the pay?"

The question took Mike aback, angry that money came up when he had asked for volunteers. "Pay? Pack up your tools and get out. That's the pay. Don't bother coming back."

Sammy Pollard, one of the old timers with the outfit and overworked by the request to ready the jet for the long haul ocean crossing, overheard the verbal confrontation from inside the jet. An old Africa hand himself, he knew Mike all too well. He approached Mike at the front of the room. He made sure he wasn't overheard. "Take it easy, man. What the hell is going on?" He'd never seen Mike in such a state.

"I just told everyone what was going on, Sammy."

"I'm on board, no matter what," he assured him, "but the young guys need more information than that. They don't work like we used to."

Mike valued Sammy as one of his more experienced aircraft engineers. Instantly, he changed his demeanor to one more easygoing before speaking up. He made sure everyone heard. "I'm going to need at least two. A welder. A mechanic. Someone who knows how to handle firearms. If you can figure out who to bring, do it, Sammy."

Sammy didn't waste any time thinking about it. He knew his people. "Bill was a Huey door-gunner in Nam."

"Then do what you have to but get him on board. Unless someone else shows up, you can plan on being my First Officer. Pack your tools. Treat it like we're going on an extended field operation back in the old days. Load the welding equipment— tanks, hoses, sheet metal, whatever you think you might need. A generator and lights. Throw in our satellite phones. We'll charge them on the way."

"How much time?"

"When Barbara gets here, we're gone, ready or not."

"How many passengers should I plan for on the return?"

"Seats for our own crew plus three."

Without being asked, helpers began assisting Sammy. They stripped the jet's interior. It needed to be light as possible to convert it into a utility configuration. Equipment availability was the least of his worries. He had to get the jet ready for as much gear on board as he could stow.

Even after Harry finally convinced Sasha to marry him, he was forced to spend long periods of time away from home to pay the bills. He was doing the flying jobs he loved. Neither of them was happy with it, but his work provided a level of support for the three that was beyond reproach.

Eventually, Sasha had enough of the never-ending lonely days and nights. She put her foot down. By then, it was too late. The free-wheeling Harry took an extended overseas jaunt and Sasha filed for divorce. He didn't contest it. He allowed her to have full custody of their daughter, Christa. He knew he couldn't offer them a home, given his penchant for around-the-world adventures.

Christa was three when they separated. They stayed on good terms. Harry continued to pay the bills while Sasha raised Christa. He didn't begrudge his ex-wife a thing. He knew she was doing one heck of a job with their daughter.

It was a job he knew he wouldn't be capable of doing on his own.

Sasha remained close with Barbara and Mike. She was always welcome in their home. She knew Barbara told Harry about her comings and goings, but she didn't object. In the back of her mind, she knew Harry still loved her—and in some ways, she still loved him. If the man would come home and stay home, she'd go back to him in a heartbeat.

She didn't dare tell Barbara, though. She kept that part of it to herself. She knew her friend secretly wanted them to get back together and would end up telling Harry.

Barbara arrived at the hangar as the jet was being fueled. She unloaded coolers of food and beer and their backpacks. She recognized Sammy and sighed with relief. He was one of Mike's most reliable hands. She approached him to ask if he needed to get anything from home.

"No, I should be good," he assured her. "I keep a ready bag in my locker. Old habits die hard, you know? I called the wife. She knows I'm going to be away for a bit. I didn't mention where we here headed. Best not to worry the woman."

Barbara was secretly pleased at the man's willingness to devote himself to a cause he knew little about. "Thanks for coming, Sammy. Mike needs more people like you."

He nodded and went back to work readying the jet.

Certain her husband would soon reveal all, she headed for the office. Mike greeted her with a flurry of questions.

"Did you pick up the cash?" he asked.

"Yes. U.S. dollars."

"You packed the shotty, didn't you? Did you bring shells?"

"Yes, and yes."

"Did you locate Harry?" His eyes bored into hers.

"He's in NBO. Holed up at the Flying Club."

"Sammy and Bill volunteered to come along for the ride. See if they need any help."

Barbara hesitated before walking onto the hangar floor. "Will we have access to Sasha's Tracker page?"

"We'll have en route access," Mike assured her. "I told Sammy to put our satellite phones on board. Check that he does. We'll fuel in Gander and Naples. If everything comes together, we should be 25 hours elapsed into Nairobi."

"What about a co-jo?" To be legal the jet required one.

"I ran out of volunteers for this job. It will be Sammy. When he gets tired, it'll be you."

"That's not legal."

"Maybe not, but ten years ago, nothing we did was legal. We've been sitting pretty getting fat, dumb and happy. It's time for a little adventure in our lives again, wouldn't you say?"

Barbara wasn't so certain. "It may not be time, but it sure looks like it found us again. Let's hope this time is the last time."

29

Alerted by Barbara's phone call and never one to doubt the capabilities—or the ETA—of his friend and former bush pilot Mike Williams, Harry Delaney waited anxiously for Mike's 300 to arrive at NBO. He checked incoming flight plans, and he caught sight of the gleaming white jet on final and on time. He was proud as hell as he observed the jet taxiing onto the fixed-base operator's tarmac before shutting down.

He waited for the airstair to deploy before he approached. It was even more obvious Mike was doing well in the cutthroat aviation business. He had no doubt the man had been doing more than a little throat-cutting of his own.

The door opened and Mike waved at Harry to approach. The look on the man's face was too serious. He put it to the long flight. Hell, he'd probably be even more exhausted.

"Come aboard, Harry. I've got some people I want you to meet."

He climbed the stairs into the cabin. "Hi, guys." Seeing Barbara took him by surprise. "Holy shit. Barbara. Playing tourist, are you?"

"No, Harry, I'm not."

He ignored the gruff response, immediately passing it off as fatigue and maybe a touch of air-sickness. He should have known better. "This is a pretty quick trip. What's going on?" Harry's gaze settled on the gear and boxes secured in the back of the jet. Mike didn't give him time to ask before introducing his chief engineer.

"You remember Sammy. He's an old Africa hand from before our time. He's also the best engineer I've got. That's Bill sleeping in the seat. He's a little younger. He gets tired easier."

"Whoever the hell it was that called me in the bar at the Flying Club cost me a round of drinks. You owe me."

"It was Barbara," Mike informed him. "And you're about to get repaid real fast."

It dawned on Harry that something wasn't right. The interior of Mike's jet was stripped bare. All kinds of equipment was lashed to the airframe. His eyes wandered to the seats. There were three for the crew, and three more. "What the hell is going on? You didn't bring your wife and a team all the way over here to brag about it."

"I got an email from Sasha and Christa." Barbara was trying to smile, but he recognized she wasn't quite pulling it off.

"Of course. They must be here by now. Where are they?" Harry wanted to know.

"It was a GPS hit, Harry." Finally she was able to get the words out. "Several of them, as a matter of fact."

Harry's jaw dropped. His look of surprise immediately turned to one of concern. He knew his ex was going to be in this part of the world. She told him. Now Mike was telling him he was right to outfit them with the tracking device after all.

"Damn. Now I know why Barbara wouldn't tell anyone at the Flying Club why she was looking for me."

Mike opened the laptop and loaded the mapping page. He tapped the screen. "That's where she pulled the pin the first time. Since we departed, they've been on the move toward the coast. The signal is intermittent. She's probably turning it off to conserve batteries."

"She shouldn't have to do that, but no matter." Harry said. "Those hits look like they're near one of our old operations. Can you zoom in more?"

"You're right," Mike informed him. "I noticed that, too. At least we've got something going for us."

"They're not moving very fast."

"No, but they're definitely on the move east toward the coast and Eyl. They're staying off the trail, though. Probably—"

Harry interrupted. "The pirate den on the Indian Ocean."

"Yes."

"The easy targets floating on the Gulf of Aden and the Indian Ocean have proved lucrative up to now. Do you think they're branching out into fresh territory?" Harry asked. "Maybe oil company territory on dry land?"

"This is all news to me," Mike said. "As far as I know, the pirates were strictly sea-going. They keep to the waters off the coast. It seems out of character, but I guess they could have moved on to targets on dry land."

"If they have, that means unlimited ransom demands," Harry said.

"There's been some renewed oil interest in that area, most recently by CAN-AL. Don't take this the wrong way, but I'd be wondering if CAN-AL will pay out a ransom."

Already Harry was committed to a rescue operation. "I'm not going to stand around with my hands in my pockets scratching at my balls waiting to find out. That's my ex and my daughter out there. I'm thinking you didn't come all the way over here to talk me out of doing something."

"Of course not, Harry. We're all here to help."

Harry was eager to get started. Standing around talking about it wasn't in his genes. "What have you got up your sleeve, Mike?"

"Here's what I think," he replied. "They're headed overland. Helicopter access will be impossible. It won't have the fuel range. There's no way we could come up with one on such short notice anyway, even if we steal it."

"I agree. We've got work to do and not enough time to do it before they reach the coast. Just off the top of my head, we'll need a DC-3. At least two technicals and people to man them. Maybe a translator."

"And weapons," Mike insisted. "Don't forget weapons, Harry."

Harry ignored Mike for the moment. "Why are my girls out in the open desert? What did that dumb son of a bitch do?"

Harry would crawl through hell to get to his wife and daughter. There'd be no letting up until he had her. "We'll get her," Barbara said. "We always do." She pitied the kidnappers when he found them. "We got her on the Baja, Harry. We'll get the two of them in the desert."

"Don't you mean the three of them? She's with that dimwit that got her into this mess to begin with."

"All of them, Harry. We'll get all of them," Barbara tried to reassure him.

Outwardly, Harry appeared satisfied with that, but Barbara knew the wheels were still turning. She wasn't wrong.

"Sammy, before I forget, there's a few more things we're going to need."

"You bet, Harry. Just let me know." Sammy didn't want to be the one to disappoint Harry. Still, he would have a hard time keeping up with his demands. He didn't want to say no, either. From what he'd seen so far, Harry didn't like to hear the word. "Whatever it is, you've got it."

"You might end up being sorry you said that. We're going to need two .50-calibers."

The look on Sammy's face said it all.

"And five thousand rounds to go with them."

Sammy shook his head again and grinned like a dog trying to screw a football. "I've got some old legion contacts in Djibouti. I'll make some calls."

Barbara handed him a phone. "Get to it. I'm off to find us a hangar."

Sammy moved off to make his calls. Harry wasn't finished with him.

"Before you get busy, Sammy. We're going to need AKs. Extra magazines. A thousand rounds. See if you can dig up RPGs too."

He regarded Harry with a look of wonderment. "Anything else?"

"Yes. See if you can get a line on an old DC-3 to hold it all. We'll need it in Djibouti to launch."

"I'll see what I can do about the Dakota, but I can't make any promises."

Harry's eyes bored into Sammy's. "If you run into any problems, mention my name. Both Mike and I have been around these parts before. We're just not current at it, is all."

"When Mike said you'd been around, I didn't take it to mean you were once on the black market with arms," Sammy said. Harry didn't answer and Sammy disappeared to make his phone calls.

Harry called to Bill. The man scrambled to his side. "Yes, sir."

"Sammy told me in passing you were a Huey door gunner. Is that right, or is it bullshit?"

"No bullshit, sir."

"Don't call me sir. You're almost as old as Sammy. By any chance, could you rig up a dual mount for a pair of .50 calibers? We'd need a floor mount to hang them out of a DC-3. I'll want them pointed out the cargo door. On a swivel would be nice," he added, before thinking he was taking a huge chance with an unknown.

"I could do it better if we had the pair of .50s sitting on the ground beside the airplane. I'd get it done a lot faster, too."

It was music to Harry's ears. "I'll let you know."

Barbara returned from her search. "I found a hangar. There's a tow coming up. We'll be behind closed doors shortly. Fuel is on the way."

Mike was eager to get airborne. "We won't need the hangar." On overhearing Sammy, he knew where they had to be to meet up with the dealers providing the hardware they were buying. "We'll be heading for JIB as soon as we take on fuel."

That was an airport code Barbara wasn't familiar with. "JIB?"

"Djibouti," Mike replied.

Nothing would delay Mike now. If something came up, Harry and Barbara would see there'd be no interference. Hell, even Sammy was proving to be an enormous help.

The fuel bowser approached the jet and halted at the end of the wing. Barbara hurried toward it carrying the briefcase. An agitated Mike searched for his friend. "Where the hell did Harry get to?"

"I'm right here. I don't have a line on a DC-3 yet, but it looks like everything else is coming together." In fact, Harry had a line, but he knew he couldn't tell Mike and Barbara about it. It would be too upsetting. In fact, he hoped Sammy would make good and come up with a plane on his own.

"That was quick."

"All I can say," he told Mike, "is that Sammy better not fail with the hardware acquisition."

Mike ignored Harry's worry. He knew the capabilities of his chief engineer and he trusted him. "How many favors did you have to call in?"

"More than a few, but one in particular is sure to come through for us."

"So you do have a line on a Dakota."

"Not yet. But I managed to get a call through to our old friend in Galkayo."

"Ali? You mean that old bugger isn't dead yet?"

"Not yet. He's got half a dozen technicals sitting around in parts."

"Parts won't do us any good, Harry."

"That's what I told him. Ali says not to worry. By the time we get there, he'll have two put together from what's left of the scrap."

"Then he'll come through," Mike reassured his friend. "He's never failed us yet."

"The man gave his word he'd keep the strip open for us as soon as he could get to it. I told him we'd be another day."

"That's pretty optimistic, considering what we have to get done. In case you haven't noticed, we don't have an airplane."

Harry ignored Mike's comment about the plane. He didn't want to show his hand. "Ali has a condition, though."

"We're bringing that old bugger guns and he has a condition?"

"He sure does. He said he wants to meet the woman that got us both over here at the same time after so many years have passed."

Barbara wasn't about missing a chance to get in a dig. "I'm thinking he must have said something else, too."

"He did. He said she must be quite the woman."

Barbara wasn't about to let Harry off the hook that easily. In fact, she was surprised he was even talking about it. Something must have changed. "Why is it Ali knows that, even though he's never met Sasha? Yet you, who knows her better than anyone, hasn't figured it out yet?"

Harry held up his hands, but both of his friends were on a rant. Holding up his hands in surrender wouldn't do a thing to halt their good-natured ribbing. He also knew it was mostly true, but he'd be damned if he'd admit it. "You just have to start in on me, don't you?"

Mike couldn't resist piling on. "She's right, and you know it. Now what did you have to promise Ali?"

"I told him we could probably come up with some munitions for him if he absolutely needed them."

"At least that part of it is settled. Having Ali's support is one less worry. If someone shows up to shut down the strip before we get there, Ali is capable of keeping it open."

"Bill tells me he'll be able to fabricate the dual mount for the .50s. He wants to have the guns sitting on the tarmac outside of the cargo door. He can eyeball it better that way.

The fuel truck disconnected. Barbara opened the briefcase and paid with cash. She climbed aboard the jet to make the announcement. "We're good to go."

"Great. Now all we need is a couple of .50s and an airplane to put them in."

Mike lit up the on-board APU. The high-pitched whine of the auxiliary power unit alerted Sammy. Huffing and puffing, he rushed up the stairwell looking far too happy. He tapped Mike on the shoulder. "Let's power up this tin can and get to Djibouti. Thanks to some old legionnaire buddies, I've got a line on twin .50s and five thousand rounds. And all for the bargain price of seventy-five hundred."

"That's great. Now tell Harry. He'll be happy to hear it."

"Funny thing about that. When I mentioned his name, they dropped the price. Who the hell are you guys?"

"I'll explain it when we're all sitting in a bar so I only have to tell the story once. In the meantime, Barbara is going to be our new First Officer. While we're en route to Djibouti, you're going to help Bill sketch up a gun mount for the cargo door on a DC-3. That's where the twin .50s will be going. Oh, and maybe you could talk to your suppliers again and find us some RPGs to go along with the .50s.

"Harry already asked me to do that. I'm waiting for a call-back."

Bill slipped aboard at the last minute. He ended up at the back of the jet on top of the cargo. His eyes were closed, and he was breathing easily, already fast asleep.

"Is he always that way? He'd better be one well-rested son of a gun by the time we arrive. Do you think he's going to have any objection to being promoted to door-gunner again?"

"You never told me you wanted a helicopter, too, Harry. Where are we going?" Sammy asked.

"We're on our way to hell and back."

30

Mike **prepped the** jet for takeoff, going through the computerized pre-flight checklist. He paged Harry in the back of the jet. "I need an actual pilot up here, Harry."

Barbara took the bait. "I'm out, husband." She pulled up the armrest and exited the cockpit. She passed a grinning Harry on his way to the front. Mike waited for his friend to settle in before addressing him.

"The right seat is yours, First Officer Delaney," Mike told him. If there was ever an opportunity to encourage the man to consider trading in the foot-loose lifestyle of a lifelong bush pilot for a more stable corporate environment, this was it. "Do you think you could get to like this, Harry?"

Mike continued running through the computerized 300's checklist until he was ready to advance the throttles for taxi.

"Well, it has benefits for sure. Large airports over bush and desert strips. Hotel rooms over tents. Modern maintenance. How's the pay?"

"Are you thinking of applying?" Mike wanted to know.

"I might be," Harry replied.

Mike grinned. "In that case, I'll need you to fill out an application." He moved to reach into his briefcase.

"Not so fast, friend. I'll need time to think about it."

Mike received his clearance and turned onto the runway. "In that case, pay attention, First Officer. We're about to become airborne."

Mike advanced the throttles. Harry covered Mike's hand with his own to back him up. Mike eased the column back and the jet became airborne.

"Why don't you get a feel for it? You have control."

The grin on Harry's face spoke more than words. "I have control," he repeated.

Mike sat back and regarded his old friend as he adjusted the seat and the column to his liking. He followed him on the controls until he settled.

"I'll talk you through the settings you'll need for the approach into JIB when we get closer. For now, just enjoy."

"Roger that."

Mike coordinated his efforts in the cockpit with Harry's abilities at the flight controls. Harry was no amateur. He had plenty of flight time and experience in all kinds of aircraft types. None of them were jet-powered, however.

Even so, Harry's handling was smooth, and his efforts were even and coordinated. It came naturally to some people, and Harry was one of them. It wouldn't be long before he could be jet-qualified if he wanted it.

"All of this is nice, Mike, but it's not taking my mind off of what's coming up. We're out of time. We have to stop the kidnappers in their tracks, fast. If they get to Eyl, they'll be unassailable in that pirate den. We'll never get my girls back."

"You're not alone in this. Sammy is one of the most qualified people on board. Bill, sleepy as he is, is no slouch in the art of metal-working."

"I didn't think you'd bring any slackers on this run. You're not going to like what I have to tell you next."

"Don't stop now. I can take it," Mike replied.

"I was pushed to the edge. I had to sell my soul to get a DC-3 delivered to Djibouti."

"Don't worry about it. We'll cover it off together."

"Not this time, I'm afraid. I gave a personal guarantee so you couldn't be tied to this. There's a lot more to it than I'm willing to tell you." Harry did a quick check of the DME—the Distance Measuring Equipment—before pointing the reading out to Mike. "We're almost there. It's time you started talking me down."

He was thankful to change the subject back to flying.

When Somalia's national airline went bankrupt, several of their DC-3s were acquired by interested parties. Those that weren't ended up mothballed. Thanks to Harry's globe-trotting habits and the contacts he made over the years, he was able to acquire one of the planes. He directed Mike to taxi the jet in front of a deserted hangar. The waiting DC-3 was parked beside it. It still wore the blue and white livery. The airline's name was in faded paint on the side, too.

"Damn, Harry, who did you call to get that thing to meet us here? More important, what's our payback going to be?"

"I can't say. He had to fly it here, so at least we know it's airworthy. That should shorten our down time."

"You're ignoring the payback."

"Don't worry about it," he told Mike. "It's all on me. When it comes, I'll be taking the call on this one."

The mood inside the jet changed for the better as soon as the engines died. Everyone knew the old plane they could see out the window was the missing key to the rescue.

It was Barbara who stated the obvious. "Come on, you guys. We've got work to do. We have twelve hours to turn this Dakota tin can around."

Mike wasn't jumping for joy at getting into the left seat of the familiar airplane, given the reason for it. It would make the task easier. "I don't know how you did it, but this old bucket of bolts is just the ticket we need." He hadn't captained one for so many years he couldn't remember. Still, he was glad the DC-3 was something he was once very familiar with. "Do you have any idea how long it's been since I sat in one?"

The look on Mike's face told Harry he was happy. Nothing would drag him away now.

"Just so you'd know, I'd like to help, but I'll leave rigging the Dakota up to you and Bill. I need to get Sammy over to his legionnaire comrades to collect the goods. Where's the cash?" Harry asked.

"Barbara always handles that. It's her job." Mike called to the woman.

"Christ, stop yelling, you two. You'll end up getting us shipped off to a refugee camp."

"Harry needs cash," Mike told her.

"I know. I heard. Relax. I'm going with him."

Mike's old shotty hung off of the woman's shoulder, concealed by her jacket. It was the way Mike used to wear it back in the old days. She and Mike were twins when it came to some things. At least she was ready. There was nothing but hand tools for anyone else.

Harry couldn't help grinning at the sight. "That's my girl. Always taking care of me. Come on, Sammy. We have places to go and people to see."

Sammy let it be known he wasn't happy at the prospect of a woman coming along to witness his arms dealings, even if she was Mike's wife. He'd seen her around the hangar from time to time, but she never stuck her nose into the operations side of the business. That was a good thing, as far as he was concerned.

He was sure the reason Barbara was a part of this operation was because she was Mike's wife. The ex-legionnaires would not be impressed when he showed up with a woman in tow. It might even scuttle the deal. Needing to talk about it, he approached Harry. "Can I have a word?"

"We don't have time, Sammy," Harry told him.

Sammy pulled Harry away from the group. "What are we doing with that woman here? We don't need her. All we need is the cash. I wouldn't trust her with the men I have to deal with. What if she panics?"

"Sammy, you better tell her yourself." Harry called to Barbara. He knew by the stubborn look on her face she didn't want to be bothered. "Sammy has something he wants to tell you."

Harry worked his way behind Sammy to join Mike. They

were all eyes and ears, certain they knew what would be coming. Mike nodded acknowledgment to Harry. The pair pasted huge grins on their faces while they waited. That alone told Barbara something was up.

Sammy turned to Barbara and went for it. "I don't want to be a spoil-sport, but do you really need to be tagging along with us? We're capable of handling it."

The friendly smile on Barbara's face froze. She blessed Sammy with an unforced, steely eyed gaze. Under more normal circumstances, the look would have melted iron. She had it toned down for Sammy. "Tagging along? It's our money, not yours. If you have complaints, we'll settle our differences later. No one has time for this. We need to get the job done."

She flashed the twin barrels under her jacket. Sammy's eyes turned into saucers. He went silent. At that moment, Harry was glad to have her along. He knew her abilities, and he was damned glad of them.

"She's with me, Sammy, and we're a better group for it. That's all you need to know."

"Then I guess that's the way it's going to be," Sammy said, resigned.

"Yes, it is. What about the AKs and mags to go with them? Plus the thousand rounds. Will your friends be able to hook us up?"

"From the way they were talking, yes. They want to meet you."

Barbara led the way to the truck. "Come on, you two. Enough talk. Let's see some action."

31

Ten years ago
Tanzania

Harry was first to spot them in the dark, dingy bar. Even in the dim light, they stood out like a lighthouse in a desert. One was blond, the other brunette. By the look of it they were too pretty to tango, but the lights were low and so were expectations. A belly-full of beer didn't hurt either.

"Wazungu. What the hell are camo-wearing white women doing here?" Harry asked.

"I noticed that," Mike confirmed. "We have to check this out."

"You're right. Camos can hide a lot. You're closer," Harry insisted. "They are women, right?"

The women weren't shy. One kicked two chairs in the right direction and Harry and Mike became instant prisoners. Irit was the brunette. The blond, Eloria, said, "We heard you're doing bush flying in the area."

Harry gave Mike the look. You could never tell what was going on, and these were two he'd never seen before. There was no sense igniting controversy when none was warranted. "We're doing exploration work for a mining company in the region. By any chance are you new transfers with the company?"

The women finished their beer, slammed the bottles down

on the table, and laughed. "You might say so," said Irit.

Harry's ears perked up. "Your accent. I've heard it before. Israeli?" he asked.

"Good guess, but no. Not even close," Irit volunteered. "We're Canadian."

Harry rolled his eyes. "Don't bullshit us. We've both worked with Israelis. You have the same accent when you speak English. Aleichem Shalom."

Mike disappeared in search of more beer. Harry glued himself to the brunette. "What are two nice girls like you doing in a shithole like this?"

Irit and Eloria answered with more laughter and reached behind their chairs to pull out Galils leaning against the wall behind them. Mike returned with a tray of beer and Harry gave him an in-like-Flynn look.

"If I get in a bar fight, I want you two backing me," he told them.

Mike couldn't argue with that. "And I'm guessing you work for the mining company, too."

There was more laughter while the women stashed the Galils out of sight. "You could be right. Now you know about us, but we know nothing of you. Are you American?"

"Hell no. We're two lost Canadians looking for a place to live and women to love," Harry said.

Irit was definitely interested. Harry wasn't so sure about Eloria, but what the hell, that was Mike's job.

"Canadian? That's okay with us, right Eloria? Come on, you two. Curfew is coming. We have somewhere we need to be."

Harry pulled the covers back. He was hoping for one last morning look at the blond Irit sprawled across the bed on her stomach, arms and legs akimbo. He was trying to figure out how he could turn her over for a better look without waking her up.

It wasn't to be this time. Last night his hand had been forcibly removed from under her pillow when his fingers brushed against cold steel. Whether a gun or a knife, he couldn't tell. She was too quick for him.

Footsteps sounded as Mike stumbled into the bedroom. "It's time to get the hell out," he insisted. "We need to get far away from this trouble until we figure out what's going on."

"I'm with you on that. Mine sleeps with steel beneath her pillow," he said, still unsure if it was a gun or a knife.

"You're lucky. Eloria has a loaded sawed-off under hers," Mike countered. "There's no way I'll be pissing those two off. I'll be counting on you to remind me if I forget."

"In that case, the getting is good right about now," Harry said. "They're both snoring."

The five-minute walk to the plane gave them time to chase away the previous night's cobwebs. Harry began the daily inspection on the Pilatus to ready it for the return flight to base camp. He was half-way finished when two Jeeps screeched to a halt. Dry-heaving, still drunk and hung-over mercs stumbled out.

Mike elbowed Harry. "Check out the drivers."

"Christ. What the hell are they doing here?" Harry wanted to know.

"Well, you did tell them you were looking for a place to live and someone to love."

"I might have made a mistake. It wouldn't be my first," Harry insisted.

He started in on the two women. They were just as hung over as the rest of them and in no mood for an argument. Eloria gestured toward the mercs with her Galil. "Back off. They're with us."

He knew better than to question a women holding a firearm in this part of the world. "You should have mentioned something last night."

"Last night we didn't know who you were," she told him.

Harry knew enough that in these parts it wouldn't have been smart to announce it last night, either. "Get those drunken excuses for mercs on board. You and your friend can wait here with Mike until I get back."

Reverse pitch halted the Pilatus in a thick, swirling cloud of red dust. Harry didn't shut down, but instead set the throttle to ground idle. He opened the door and waved to Mike and his two-woman crew to get on board.

Mike escorted them to the cargo door and opened it. Irit and Eloria took in the ratty condition of the plane's interior. It appeared as though they might change their minds. Mike tossed in their gear. They climbed aboard and planted themselves on the floor. Mike closed the cargo door and went around to the front of the Porter.

The women conversed over the whine of the idling turbine engine. "Doesn't this look cozy. No seat. No seat belts. No intercom. No one told us this would be an accident looking for a place to happen."

Eyes roamed front and back. "Check out the AKs strapped to the bulkhead," Irit said. "Do you think they're for show or go?"

A hung-over Harry was in no mood for backtalk. He turned in the left seat and leaned into the back. "Stop whining, ladies. You're in the army now."

"No, we were in the army back home", Irit said. "To get where we are, we sold ourselves to the highest bidder."

Mike climbed past the canvas separating the cockpit from the cargo deck. He gestured for Irit to move up front with Harry. "There's your seat and harness. Lock in. We're going on a ride." He pointed at Eloria. "Unless you know how to fly, you'll be staying back here with me.

Up front, Harry oversaw Irit as she buckled in. He reached for her lap belt and tugged it tight. "Lean forward and use your thumbs to grab the inertia straps to lock them."

Irit did as she was told. The inertia shoulder straps did their job and kept her upper body from connecting with the dash. She gave harry a thumbs-up to confirm.

Satisfied, Harry advanced the throttle and taxied the PT-6 to the end of the strip. He set flaps, locked the brakes, pulled the column full aft and checked his flight controls. Mike used the opportunity to brace himself in the cargo complement. Eloria took the hint and followed suit.

Harry kicked in right rudder to counter engine torque as he firewalled the throttle. The lightly loaded plane accelerated quickly. He rotated on the tail-wheel, brought the nose up high, and dialed in the Porter for a steep climb-out. He banked and headed in the direction of the bush camp.

"You did that pretty good. How are you at landing?" Irit wanted to know.

Harry grinned across at her. "You'll find out in just a bit."

The camp came into sight and Harry descended the Porter to circuit height. He waited for the strip to disappear under the nose of the Pilatus. He pulled the prop into Beta. At the same time, he dropped the nose to 45 degrees. The Porter descended like a summer fair carnival ride. At the bottom of the dive he flared to get the Pilatus into a three-wheel attitude for touchdown.

The high-pitched screaming wasn't coming from the engine. It didn't stop until the Pilatus gently bumped the runway. Harry couldn't shut down fast enough. Both passengers jumped out, ran to the tail and threw up.

"How was my landing?" he wanted to know.

The response came in stereo. "Screw you!"

"Grab your gear and find a tent. The rest of us have work to do."

Six fully armed men climbed aboard. One handed Harry a map and pointed at several spots marked on it. "When we land, we'll leave one man with you and the plane like we always do. His orders are to let no one touch it or you on pain of death. Understood?"

Eloria and Irit collected their firearms and their gear and humped their way to the tents scattered beneath the canopy on the far side of the airstrip. They pulled back tent flys as they went to check out sleeping arrangements. They weren't happy with the side-by-side racks they'd be sharing with the rest of the mercs. When they reached the end, they turned and retraced their steps. They only halted when they caught up to Mike.

"What is it?" he wanted to know.

"We're moving our gear into your tent," Irit said.

"What's the problem?"

"We're not sharing bunks with those animals. We'll end up mincemeat the minute we fall asleep," Eloria insisted.

"You might have a point. Our tent is off to the side. Look for the one that has the shower," Mike told them.

"All the comforts, or what?"

Mike's grin was bigger than he wanted. "Well, it sure looks like it now."

32

Present Day
Djibouti

Harry had the distinct feeling he was being sized up for something following Sammy's introduction to the ex-legionnaires. Unsure of what it could be, his mind wandered back to the woman who had helped Mike get across the border into Kenya years ago. Thanks to Eloria, he and Mike were both alive.

He took Mike at face value when he told him Eloria had been killed in the attack. He didn't blame Mike for not going back to look for her in the heat of the pursuit with lead flying. Now, he wasn't so sure.

Yes, Mike had convinced him beyond a doubt that Eloria had been killed during the chase north to the Kenyan border. Because of that, he hadn't given a thought to going back. Now, he wasn't sure that had been the right thing to do. Perhaps he should have done just that after getting out of the hospital.

Instead, he ended up taking Eloria's and Irit's Canadian passports to a foreign embassy rather than his own. When he presented them, they disappeared behind a door. It was a long wait until someone came out. That was when he knew his hunch had been right. He ended up being asked to show identification and then he was unceremoniously ejected from the embassy. The women's passports remained behind.

He never told Mike.

Neither he nor Mike told their wives about that rescue exercise, either. How Mike ended up with Eloria's shotgun, now tucked under Barbara's jacket, was never discussed. They both thought it was a story better left untold.

Until now.

When this was over, he wanted to have a conversation with Mike about all of it. He thought it was time to tell their wives.

Money changed hands. A phone call was placed by one of the ex-legionnaires. Following a brief wait, brakes squealed on an overloaded two-ton. It groaned to a slow stop in the dark. The truck repositioned to back against the derelict DC-3's open cargo door. Barbara stood by. The shotgun remained concealed beneath her jacket.

It was all hands on deck to help unload the goods that included the twin .50s and their ammunition belts. The scrap metal and acetylene waited on the ground. The truck pulled away.

Bill fired up the generator and the lights. He arranged the steel and lit the cutter. The gun mount wouldn't be pretty, but once in action, it would be a killer.

"Sammy, do you see any problems with the .50s once we get them mounted?" Harry asked.

"There'll be a couple. In the heat of the moment, we don't want the muzzles arcing into the wing. Two, we want to keep them away from the elevator. Other than that, no," Sammy assured him.

"Is that a big deal? Locking them out, I mean. I know it's a big deal to be shooting up our own airplane." He laughed nervously.

"Not as long as we tie them off with rope or bungee cords. That'll keep things under control when the going gets tough."

Harry still wasn't convinced Bill was capable of doing the job. "We're sitting in the middle of night with nowhere to go for help. Does your guy know what he's doing?"

"Oh, he knows all right," Sammy reassured him.

The words were small comfort for Harry. "In that case, let's start the engines and see what we've got with our airplane."

With Harry's capable hands nursing the throttles while Mike observed, one engine followed by the other turned over and started without a hitch. A couple of run-ups later, Harry was satisfied.

"All the gauges look normal. Agreed?" he asked Mike. Mike was the DC-3 pilot expert.

"I agree. I'll fly her," he told Harry.

Harry went in search of Barbara. He didn't have far to go. She was beyond the fringe of the lights, keeping a watchful eye on their surroundings from the dark. "How about taking the two-ton over to the FBO. See if he can track down some empty fuel drums and an electric pump. We'll need tie-downs, too."

She nodded and hesitated before heading for the old truck.

"Don't lead anyone back here until we're done with the outfitting and ready to launch. I don't want this firepower witnessed by anyone. The Yanks are liable to shoot us down on sight. The French might give us enough time to get away when they wonder what the hell is going on and decide they don't want to be involved."

"What about the pirates?"

"If the pirates have Sasha and Christa, they won't be long for this world."

The gas welder hissed and sparks flew in time with loud and frequent cursing. With Sammy's help, the gun design the two engineers worked out on the flight into Djibouti began to take shape.

Harry pried open boxes like it was Christmas. The AKs looked to be almost brand new. The magazines would need loading and taping. The RPGs and their rounds were there. His old friend Ali would be one happy customer when he got his hands on this load of freight.

"Come on Barbara, give me a hand. We have a lot of work to do. I'll show you how to load the magazines. When we're done,

I'll do the taping. I don't have time to show you."

"How about if I watch you do a couple and then I'll copy you."

"No, I don't think so," he told her. "I'll be on the ground, down and dirty. I need to know the mags will work the way they should. Don't take it personal. Next time, okay?" He knew right away he shouldn't have said it.

"Next time? Next time? If that woman of yours tries this shit again, I'll take the butt-end of an AK to her myself."

"Look. You're supposed to remember how it works. Sasha gets herself in trouble, and we come along to rescue her."

Barbara wasn't about to let Harry off so easy. "Yes, well, this time there's two of them."

"I don't need to be reminded. Thanks to that fool Gene, my ex and our daughter are wandering around the desert at the whim of a bunch of land-based pirates."

"I can't help it, Harry. I'll tar and feather that woman myself."

Harry changed the subject to something more pressing. "Did you get another look at the GPS locator when you ordered the fuel drums?"

"They're still moving overland. It looks like they're headed to the coast, like you thought. It seems to be slow going for sure. They haven't covered a lot of ground since the last time I checked."

"They're probably pirates out of Eyl fed up with their chances on the ocean. They're looking for land-locked ransom targets. I hope Gene is smart enough to keep his mouth shut about what a bigwig he is."

"I wouldn't think that's going to happen, but you didn't hear it from me. Gene likes to run off at the mouth about how important he thinks he is. Mike won't say anything, but he knows the guy can be a jerk."

"We have to get to them before they get to the coast. If they get to Eyl, they'll disappear and we'll never see them again. I'm going to give Ali a call. Keep stuffing those magazines."

"You're going to give me a lesson on how to handle an RPG. When the time comes, I want to know how to light something up, big time."

"No problem, girl. I'll hook you up."

Mike appeared beside his wife. "Hook her up with what? What kind of deal are you two cooking up?"

"Your wife wants to learn how to fire an RPG," Harry informed him.

Mike didn't hesitate. "I'm good with that. Just make sure she doesn't bring one home."

Harry was getting more anxious by the hour. He paced. He wandered back and forth. There was nothing he could do to speed things up. The gun mount was critical to the operation. Without it, they'd be limited to an overland counterattack.

All this time spent on the ground in the dark at a strange airport wasn't good. That it was the middle of the night and they were lit up like a shopping mall parking lot only made it worse. It made what they were doing more suspicious and more likely to draw prying eyes.

His wife and daughter were wandering around in the desert with pirates bent on ransoming her boyfriend to the highest bidder. Dammit, but what the hell was she doing out there? Gene turned out to be a dumbass. He'd have to have a talk with her about that man the next chance he got.

"How's that mount coming along, Sammy?" He asked for the tenth time.

"It's done. We're ready to install, Harry."

"All right. We need to get the drums loaded first."

He called to Barbara. "What time did you arrange for fuel?"

"0400 local," she told him.

Harry checked his watch. "How did you make out with the magazines?"

"They're ready to go. You'll have plenty of time to tape them on the flight."

One thing bothered Harry about the .50s. It was Sammy's description of how they could swing into the wing and the tail. If Bill became distracted or got carried away with the action on the ground, lead flying in the wrong directions would end up being disastrous.

"What did you come up with to protect our wings?" he asked Sammy.

"Once we get straight and level, I'll check the sight lines and cut some rope to tie them off on both sides. It's primitive, but it won't be a problem," Sammy reassured him.

"Sounds good. Now, who's missing? Where's Mike?"

"Right here," he announced. "I just got off the phone with Ali. He'll meet us at the strip with the technicals. If he has to, he'll take it and hold it for us until we get there. He said he'll bring fuel for us, too."

The one thing Harry and Mike had going for them was the location in the desert where Sasha and Christa had disappeared. Years earlier, he and Mike both worked in the area. It was then they met Ali and developed an instant rapport with the clan headman. "In that case, forget about loading the fuel drums. We won't need them."

Headlights blazed a path toward the jet and the DC-3 parked beside the hangar. A black BMW eased to a stop overlooking the tarmac. The headlights remained on, aimed at the DC-3.

"What the hell is this? Guys, we've got company coming up. Douse the lights. We don't need anyone seeing what we're doing."

The generator died and the ramp lights dimmed and went out. Two doors slammed. Two men walked to the front of the car. The headlights served to backlight them, making perfect targets for anyone so inclined. The men lit cigarettes, and the double flash of orange flame illuminated two pairs of gleaming white teeth smiling in the dark.

"I can't get to an AK."

Beneath her jacket, Barbara adjusted the strap on the double-barreled shotty. She pulled back the hammers on both barrels. "Don't worry. I've got you covered."

"You would, wouldn't you?"

"You're damned right, mister. Who the hell is going to look after you two if I don't?"

"I heard that before," Harry admitted.

"You know it. Now get rid of those bastards or I will."

Harry called to the two men. "Salaam. What can we do for

you this early in the day?"

"Salaam alaikum," one responded. "Someone has requested that we collect payment for taking up parking space on this end of the airport."

"Who would that be?" Harry asked. "We don't pay baksheesh unless we know where it's going."

"The people who are accompanying your friends in the desert sent us."

The jungle telegraph. Of course. Harry shook his head.

Barbara heard enough. They were talking about her friend Sasha and her daughter. She raised the shotty hanging off her shoulder. Both barrels cleared her jacket. In that instant the men knew they made a huge mistake.

"In that case, here's your baksheesh," Barbara told them.

The men reached for holstered weapons too late.

"Drop it off on your way to hell." Barbara's finger closed on the twin triggers. She pulled them both. Two shotgun barrels exploded. Buckshot carried past the intruders, dousing the car's headlights. The recoil forced her into a quarter-turn. She recovered instantly, breached, and reloaded.

"Anyone else?" she asked. "No? All right, guys. It's past time to get your pale white asses in gear and get airborne before les flics arrive."

"The men milled around, not quite sure what they just witnessed. Sammy's eyes were as huge as saucers in the darkness. Barbara shouldered past all of them and climbed aboard the DC-3. She turned at the cargo door. "Are you all going to stand around looking guilty? Someone clean up the tarmac and load those two in the trunk."

"Come on, boys. Let's do what the woman says," somebody said.

Barbara turned to address Sammy. "Collect my brass."

Sammy's retort came instantly. "Yes, ma'am."

33

Out of the past
Tanzania

Pilots and operators prized the low-and-slow short-field capabilities of the Pilatus Porter. The plane was designed to give access to locations that would otherwise be inaccessible. Areas with rough ground and extremely short landing runs surrounded by steep approach and departure paths could all be accessed in the Porter outfitted with its powerful PT-6 engine.

But while those characteristics inherent in the design were a positive for the pilots flying the aircraft, there were some flaws in the equation. The low-speed, low-altitude characteristics were a definite liability when it came to hot-zone landings.

Harry was familiar with the bush strip, having used it at least half-a-dozen times. He expected to use it for at least another five or six landings and extractions. He lined up and set up for his steep, high-angle approach.

The Porter disappeared beneath the canopy surrounding the strip and touched down. He stood on the brakes, pulled the control column full aft, and reverse-pitched to halt the landing run. The Pilatus stopped in a thick cloud of dust and sand kicked up by the powerful engine and its massive propeller. Harry stood on a brake pedal and turned the aircraft to prepare for takeoff after the mission was completed.

He was ahead of himself.

Hell broke loose mere seconds after completing the turn. Gunfire exploded and raked the fuselage. The dust cloud the engine strained to produce offered no protection as it drifted off with the wind. Again and again lead poured into the flimsy aluminum fuselage. Harry's crew was in the middle of a hot zone.

The mercs deplaned to confront the gunfire. Flying lead chased them around the aircraft. They returned fire and retreated until they found themselves surrounded by bush. A slight ridge offered some protection. Ensconced behind it, they regrouped and returned a steady stream of fire.

The mercs were out-gunned. The squad leader spotted the idling aircraft exactly where they left it. They beat a hasty retreat into the open, returned more fire, and climbed aboard. Harry firewalled the throttle and fast-taxied the Porter to the far end of the short strip.

He ran out of room and stood on the brakes, forced to prepare for a turn that would line him up with the runway and his exit path. It was the opportunity the shooters were waiting for. They found their mark in the slow-turning plane. A shower of lead erupted inside the cockpit. Harry's last act was to pull back the power and shut off the fuel. He deserted the plane and collapsed on the ground.

The mercs exited behind him. First out set up a perimeter while they retrieved the wounded Harry. Outgunned, the survivors retreated into the bush a second time under a hail of gunfire. They were forced to take cover in low ground covered by shrubs.

The second thick cloud of dust dissipated. As the mercs regained situational awareness, they realized they were trapped. Wounded Harry ended up trapped with them.

I rit and Eloria were in the radio room when the call came in. Eloria ran to Mike's tent. She stormed in and bent to rouse him. "Wake up. Come on. Get up." She poked and slapped at the sleeping man.

"What the hell are you doing?" a sleepy Mike asked. "What time is it?"

Already Eloria was making for the door. "It's late afternoon. Harry isn't back. We heard a radio call. They're under attack."

Still groggy, Mike turned his boots upside down and bumped them together before slipping them on and lacing up. He barely had time to splash water on his face before Eloria grabbed an arm and hauled him toward the ops tent.

The sound of gunfire echoed in the background of the panicked voice behind the radio transmissions. As information trickled in, the gravity of the situation became clear. The Pilatus, their lifeline to the outside world, had been shot up. It was likely beyond repair. There was no mention of Harry.

"See what else you can find out," Mike told the women. "I'm going to suit up."

Mike loaded his backpack with full magazines for the AK and some water and ration bars. He returned to find Irit and Eloria outfitted and waiting. Muted, sporadic gunfire could be heard overland in the distance.

"Judging by the sound it's not far," Mike said. "Are you coming with me?"

"We checked the map. The bush strip is only a couple of kilometers away."

"So then, are you volunteering?" he asked again.

"We're ready to go. What's in your pack?"

"Mags and food. What else do I need?"

"Pick up some grenades. And smoke markers in case we need to pop one. Did you get a radio?" Eloria wanted to know.

"No. I didn't think of it," Mike replied.

"We have grenades," Eloria said.

"Are you sure you want to come with me?" Mike asked again.

"Why wouldn't we? You and Harry treated us all right. Why wouldn't we want to get Harry back? Besides, we're getting paid for this. And we like the way you outfitted your tent with a shower." She didn't mention that they likely wouldn't be seeing the inside of the flight crew's tent again.

Before slipping the map and topographic sheets into his

pack, Mike took a compass bearing. "In that case, I feel a lot safer with you two. The rest of these so-called war dogs sitting on their happy asses in camp can kiss mine."

Mike had already made the rounds of the mercs remaining behind. Not a one volunteered to rescue their comrades. He hadn't bothered to waste time explaining why they might want to help. He knew by their diverted eyes and mumbling voices.

"Let's go. Harry's waiting."

Mike headed off on his compass bearing to the strip. The women followed. No one talked. Progress wasn't difficult. The light ground cover and low scrub provided few obstacles to hinder their advance. As they closed the distance, the gunfire became louder and more sporadic. The women passed Mike. He moved to keep up.

Eloria motioned and called out in a low voice. "Mike."

He recognized he was new at this. He halted in his tracks.

"Wait here. Stay down. Do not move until we return," Eloria told him.

He nodded without comment. The women advanced to flank two thickets fifty meters apart. Both of them disappeared into the brush. A flash of sunlight on steel gave up Eloria's position. Then nothing.

Minutes later, he heard a chirp and Eloria showed herself. She motioned to him to move toward her. He made for the thicket, where two bodies lay sprawled on the ground, one on top of the other.

Irit exited the thicket. "Do not look. You are not accustomed."

The woman's instruction came too late. The capabilities of these women became crystal clear to Mike. In the bar, wearing their camos, he thought they were a couple of camp-followers mugging the part. Even when they pulled the Galils out, they still hadn't been completely convincing. That they had showed up in camp wasn't unusual, either. They could have been a couple of stragglers hired for mess duty.

He was convinced now. They were the real thing. Stone cold killers when they needed to be. He was glad they volunteered to help him get to Harry.

He felt Eloria's hand on his shoulder. It interrupted his thoughts. She looked him in the eye. "Follow me. Stop and drop when I say."

There was no doubt whatsoever. He would do whatever she told him to do.

To the left, Irit crouched and leveled her Galil. Eloria did the same and motioned for him to drop beside her. "Do you see that huge tree and the thicket under it?"

Sweat streamed down Mike's face. He swiped at it and nodded.

"We think the rest of them are there," Eloria said. "Can you put a grenade into it?"

He had no doubt. "Yes." He pulled a grenade from his pack.

"When I give the signal, pull the pin and throw. Don't hesitate."

"I can do that," he insisted.

"The sound of it dropping in the dirt should chase them out if they're paying attention. When they run, start picking them off. Irit and I will finish up what you and the grenade miss."

He knew these two were more than capable of finishing up what he'd miss. Given that he never intentionally killed anyone, it was bound to be—

"Throw it."

Shit. She didn't give a warning. He pulled the pin. Tossed the grenade. Pitched too short and watched it arc and land before it bounced into the thicket. Men cursed and scrambled out into the clearing.

The grenade exploded. The women picked them off. Five men fell in rapid succession. He never had time to fire a round.

Again, Eloria motioned for him to follow. She finished off her targets with the double-barreled shotgun and paused to reload. Irit's pistol echoed the shotgun's boom. These two were something else. This was going to be a hard act to follow.

"Come. Walk with me," Eloria instructed. She whistled into the canopy. Someone whistled back. "Over this way. Come."

He followed the woman. They walked the ridge surrounding the depression. The danger appeared to be over.

With Eloria on point and Irit bringing up the rear, it was minutes until they crossed paths with the crew of mercs.

Mike's eyes roamed the group until he found Harry. "How is he doing?" he asked the men. Harry didn't look so good. His back was against a tree. He was pale and appeared weak. He wasn't talking.

"He's okay. He has a head wound. He took a bullet to his shoulder. It missed all the best parts. He'll be all right. We've all survived worse," a merc replied.

"How are we going to get out of this mess? The plane is a write-off. We're going to have to walk to camp."

"There's no way to get out of camp, even if we wanted to go back to it," Mike said. "The men we left behind will be useless in any event. I expect the infighting to have started already." Mike pulled out the map sheet. "Will this help? How about the rest of you? Any ideas?"

The mercs moved away and began whispering among themselves. In minutes the discussion turned heated and loud. One left the group and approached Mike.

"We're going back to camp. You can stay here with the pilot and the women. We want nothing to do with you."

Mike cast a withering gaze at the man. "Would that be because you were just pulled out of danger by two women?"

The scornful look had no effect on the hardened mercs. They were intent on getting back to camp.

"Those women did more to save your incompetent asses than all of you put together. The rest of your esteemed crew is still sitting on their asses in camp. They couldn't even be bothered to go to the radio room."

There was no response. He didn't expect one. "Leave me with some spare mags and grenades. The women have everything they need. We won't be needing you. Go back to camp and get fat and lazy on the grub I flew in for you. So long."

The sullen mercs headed off toward camp. Mike splashed the still unconscious Harry with water. He groaned and opened his eyes. Mike was in front of him, holding up a hand.

"How many fingers, pardner?" Mike wanted to know.

Harry strained to answer. He looked up, grinned at Mike, and tried to focus. "Do you want the truth, or would you like me to sugar-coat it?"

"Give it to me straight, partner. I can take it," Mike told him.

Harry stared hard at Mike's hand. "By the look of it, I'd say not enough to get us out of this mess. I see you brought the women to cook and clean. Good deal."

The effort was too much. Harry slumped and passed out before Irit and Eloria could get a word out.

"He'll pay for that when he's better," Irit said.

"Somehow, I think he knows that. He's dreaming about it right now," Mike insisted.

34

Mike **Williams ran** through the weight and balance numbers one more time. He checked again with a finger running down the page. A little over 2,400 pounds of fuel on board the DC-3. Half tanks. Satisfied, he considered the estimated 372 nautical miles out of Djibouti direct to the desert landing strip at two hours plus thirty minutes en route. He marked an X on the Michelin road map. It was more like a trail map.

Ali promised to make fuel available at the strip. That meant he wouldn't be hauling dead weight in fuel. He'd be able to take on fuel at the strip for the return to Djibouti.

Once over the target, there would be plenty of fuel remaining. He'd be able to get in a couple of strafing runs before he'd need more fuel. He didn't want it to go that way, of course. He needed to get his passengers deplaned, as well as the arms offloaded. It would make the DC-3 a lot lighter and more maneuverable on those strafing runs.

He looked over the twin .50 caliber machine guns and their jury-rigged swivel mount. He checked the arc. He needed to be sure his wing and tail were good. He tested the straps that would secure the guns as the twin muzzles tracked. Satisfied, he looked over the cargo. It too was tied down and secure.

"I'm sorry there are no seatbelts for anyone on this fly-by-night charter."

Wide grins and nervous laughter came back to him.

"We're good, Mike. No worse than sitting on top of the cargo on a single-engine Otter back in the old days."

Everyone laughed again, but he knew it to be true. The old days weren't all that far away in this part of the world.

"Try to do what Bill is doing and get some sleep," he told everyone.

Mike walked forward and climbed into the left seat. Harry was already waiting in the right. It was time to fire up number one. He tapped the gauges and dialed in the altimeter. Set the mixture. Hit the starter. Number one fired up in blue cloud.

"Old habits die hard. Do you still do that tapping thing on those fancy jets?" Harry wanted to know.

Outside, Sammy circled the flashlight. Number two coughed and came to life.

Both Harry and Mike had learned to fly in the bush pilot environment of single-engine piston aircraft and unreliable indicators. "Yeah. You're right. The guys give me a hard time, but I do it anyway. They keep telling me I'm going to break a glass one day in one of those expensive cockpits."

He began a slow taxi to the end of the paved strip before lining up the nose of the DC-3. He checked the engine temps, released the brakes and advanced the throttles. Harry's hand covered his on the throttles. After a short takeoff run on the smooth paved strip, the tail came off the ground. The DC-3 lifted off the runway with plenty to spare.

Mike called out "Gear up." Harry responded with "Two white".

He followed the shore, keeping the ancient aircraft low over the water until he was far from the city. More comfortable away from the lights behind, he turned southeast and dialed in the twin-engine power settings that would give the old plane a climb of a thousand feet per minute.

He knew he was a little rusty with his seat-of-the pants flying ability in the left seat of the old Dakota. He hadn't done it in years. That was all right, though. He had Harry for backup.

The plane reached cruising altitude. Mike reduced throttles to set cruise power and relaxed only a bit.

Across the flight deck, Harry sensed his concern. "How does it feel to sit in one of these again? You've been getting fat and lazy in your fancy jets back on the oil patch."

"I'd feel a lot better if I had a horizon. This bucket of bolts has no instrument panel."

"What are you complaining about? We've got a turn and bank. I see an artificial horizon. There's an NDB. You monitor the engine instruments. I'll do the flying and look at the panel once in a while." He grinned at Mike in the dim cockpit lighting.

Harry knew he could do it all, but he felt a sense of adventure building in Mike and he wanted to keep it going.

"You're right," Mike said. "Dial in the reverse NDB for the strip we're headed toward. It's been too long since I did any seat-of-the-pants flying."

"In that case, I have control."

Mike released his grip on the column and repeated, "You have control," the phrase to recognize that Harry indeed had control.

"We'll get a daylight horizon soon. You can take her when the sun begins to rise."

"I'm glad you're my co-jo on this fly-by-night charter, Harry."

"I wouldn't have it any other way, old friend," Harry reassured him. "But don't be too hasty. We haven't discussed salary and benefits yet."

In the back, Bill was stretched out flat on top of the wooden RPG boxes. He did what he did best, sleep and snore. The sound of the man's supercharged snoring got the better of Barbara. She relocated to the ammo cases, only to find herself trapped beside Sammy.

He kept looking out the window, and she was glad of it. It meant he wouldn't be pestering her with questions she didn't want to answer any time soon.

Sammy looked at Barbara and went back to staring out the window. It was starting to catch up to him, and he began to wonder exactly what he had gotten himself into with these people. He had more than a few questions. He walked forward and nudged Mike. He pretended to be casual, but the expression on his face was serious.

"Holy shit, you guys, where did you find these women?"

Harry grinned across at Mike. "Is there something wrong with our women, Sammy?" he wanted to know.

"No, no. I'm just sayin'. There's one hanging a sawed-off from her shoulder who isn't afraid to use it. She's married to the guy who pays my salary."

"You're right. That's my wife, and you know it. She's never minded getting her hands dirty. Don't forget it. And if you don't believe it, ask Harry."

Sammy didn't ask Harry. He knew better by now.

"There's another one wandering around out in the desert like she's related to Moses."

It was Harry's turn. "Right again. And that's my ex-wife."

Sammy went on. "When the people who ponied up the arms asked who the buyers were going to be, I was more than a little reluctant to tell them. Then I thought about it and figured that since you're new to these parts, I'd give your names up."

"What did you learn, Sammy?" Harry wanted to know.

"When I told them who you were, they knocked thousands off the price."

"In that case, think of the money you saved us. Barbara will be happy to hear it. Maybe there'll be a little something extra in next week's pay envelope when we get home," Mike said. He wouldn't use the words *if we get home*. He never considered it.

"I get the feeling there's something you're not telling me, but I'm afraid to ask. Who are you, and why haven't I ever heard of you before? I worked all over this continent for years." Sammy held out the shotty's shell casings for Mike. Instead, Harry took them and handed them back.

"We like to keep a low profile, Sammy. Maybe Mike will fill you in when he has time. In the meantime, be sure to give these back to Barbara."

Mike joined in. "Exactly. We're kind of busy using the seat of our pants to keep this bucket of bolts on the straight and level. I wouldn't want to say for sure, but right now might not be a good time to be asking us questions. Go on back and talk to Barbara. She'll tell you all about it."

Sammy left the cockpit. Mike turned and saw him disappear behind the crates. "He bought it. Damn, but he's a brave man. It's going to get interesting back there."

"Barbara will set him straight," Harry said. "Did you see the look on her face when he told her he didn't want her coming along with the cash on the buy?"

"I did, and I was ready to grab the shotgun because it looked like she was going to use it. I didn't want her shooting him right then. He was still useful."

"When she flashed that shotty to show him who was boss that shut him up in a hurry."

Harry looked back to witness Sammy taking up his seat beside Barbara. "There he goes. Any bets on how long it will take Barbara to get to the cockpit?"

Sammy began peppering Barbara with questions. She kept her answers short and to the point. Finally, she had enough. She politely excused herself and headed for the cockpit.

"Which one of you shoved him in my direction?"

Harry and Mike pointed at each other.

"I figured. But don't worry. He's one of us now. He asked if he could see the shotgun but first he wanted to know if it was loaded."

"Did you give it to him?"

"No way," Barbara said. "After I opened it to show him it really was loaded, I closed it up. I'm no virgin, remember?"

"We remember. The Baja wasn't that long ago." The pair high-fived and grinned.

"No woman could stay one for long hanging out with the two of you. Now what are you going to do about your ex-wife, Harry?"

Christ. The woman hadn't changed in all these years. She

was still the same old Barbara, asking questions he didn't want to answer. His ex was the same way.

"First on the list is sweeping her sweet ass up off the desert together with my daughter."

"That's not what I meant, and you know it."

"I know—and I don't know. She seems to be pretty stuck on Gene. Christa seems to like him, too. Besides, Sasha picked him, so he must be quite the guy."

"Well, you're in the hot seat now," Barbara insisted. "That must say something about your feelings."

"Christa is always going to be my daughter. Sasha and I get along well enough that we can share her with no problems. If one of them is in trouble, they're both in trouble."

"You need to do more than pay the bills, Harry. I'm telling you," Barbara said.

"Is there something I need to know?" Harry asked.

"You need to know that you're back in the middle of a desert on the Horn of Africa. You're chasing after your ex-wife and daughter, who are following another man around the continent. That same dumbass with half a brain is leading all of us on a magic carpet ride across sand dunes. If the son of a bitch that put those two into this mess had any cojones, he'd be—"

Harry scanned the instrument panel. His eyes halted at the hydraulic oil pressure indicators. He held up a hand. Barbara knew to stop talking and pay attention.

"Tell Sammy to come up front, please. Right away. I have a question."

Sammy hurried to the cockpit and scanned the hydraulic control panel on the bulkhead. The system pressure had dropped, but so far seemed to be holding steady.

Harry tapped the hydraulic pressure gauge. "If we lose pressure, we lose the landing gear."

"Has the needle moved since you first noticed it?" Sammy wanted to know.

"No," Harry told him. "Are we going to be able to keep this thing in the air for another half hour until sunrise? We'll need until then to look for a track to put her down on."

"How has the landing gear pressure been?"

"Steady."

Sammy ran through a mental checklist for the old DC-3, picturing the diagrams as he went. It had been ages since he last worked on one, but he remembered the manuals well. "The hydraulic pumps are driven off of an accessory gearbox on each engine. Use the selector to switch between them."

"I've been doing that. It looks like number one."

"It should hold until we get to the strip. When you weren't looking, I put on a drum each of hydraulic fluid and oil. We'll be good once you get her on the ground. If it's a leak I can't fix, I'll rig a setup with the drum and a hand pump to keep the tank filled while we're in the air."

"Thanks, Sammy. You're a good man."

"Not as good as Mike's wife. I can't wait to meet the other one roaming the desert."

"Two, Sammy. There's two good women roaming the desert."

Sammy raised an eyebrow before remembering that Harry's ex-wife together with his daughter were roaming the desert thanks to pirates. He retreated aft to sit with the ever-sleeping Bill. He knew by now he wasn't exactly Barbara's cup of tea.

"That's got him. Go easy, Harry. He's not made like the rest of us," Mike said.

"Maybe not, but he deserves a bonus after what he and his buddies did for us by getting all that hardware."

"Don't worry. When we get everyone's asses out of this mess, I'll take care of both of them. I just hope Bill's mount doesn't come apart from the pounding it's going to take from those twin .50 machine guns. If it doesn't hold together long enough to see this through—"

"You don't have a Plan B, do you?" Mike asked.

"No."

Mike turned away from Harry and to stare out the forward windscreen. "Neither do I."

35

Relentless noonday sun beat down on the pirate convoy from an endless blue sky. Waves of heat reflected off the light-colored sand. Sasha reached for the vehicle's metal, testing it. She quickly pulled her hand away from the hot burning steel heated to boiling in the unrelenting sun, shaking her fingers as she did so. The action provided minimal relief.

She rearranged her large scarf, seeking to adjust it in order to provide more shade for Christa. The scarf provided little to no relief from the clouds of sand and dust kicked up by the convoy's leading vehicles. The sand penetrated every fold of clothing and the dust covered every pore of exposed skin.

In the inhospitable environment, the group was sunburned, thirsty, and extremely uncomfortable. Sasha called to anyone who might listen. "My daughter is thirsty again. She's hungry, too."

A passenger in the technical beside her responded. "It is almost noon. We will stop soon to put up shade for you and your daughter."

"Thank you. She needs more water," she insisted.

Water didn't appear to be a problem for Gene. Even Christa noticed the man taking more than his fair share. He had to be bribing the men—at least until the cash in his pocket disappeared. How far would he get when the money ran out?

"You will eat when we get to camp," the same man told her.

"Where is camp? How long will it be?" she asked.

Number two in charge of the convoy answered her. "You will find out soon enough."

Gene, still on his self-important rant, proved harder to satisfy. It seemed as though the extra water they allowed him permitted the man to think he had some influence with the kidnappers. "Will there be a phone there?" he asked. "I need to call my company. They'll be concerned that they haven't heard from me."

Sasha cast a nervous glance at Gene. So far, he hadn't uttered a word of concern for Christa or for her. Just who was this man she had tied her wagon to? Even Christa noticed that Gene didn't care about either of them.

She admitted to herself she should have kept Harry when she had the chance. There were none like him, anyway. Any doubt she had was long gone, chased away by Gene's self-importance and constant whining. She turned to her daughter. "Honey, did you press the button again like I asked you to?"

Unlike Gene, Christa turned out to be a real trouper. Harry would be so proud to know how dependable his daughter was when it came to deploying the beacon.

"Yes," she told her mother. "The little light didn't come on."

Sasha's heart sank. Batteries. Why hadn't she replaced them with brand-new batteries when she had the chance? Surely Harry would have done so. In fact, he probably did. The equipment was new. Knowing Harry, he might even have acquired a test model just for them. If that was the case—

It must be the light. Was the signal even working? Was anyone getting their SOS? Who could possibly be on the receiving end if the equipment was still being tested? Who would be watching?

It had to be the light.

She was worrying, and that wasn't good. If Christa found out she was scared for might what become of them—

She had to be strong for her daughter. Gene wasn't the man

to be strong for them. It was obvious they had been tossed aside for access to water and a phone.

Either the signal had been enough, or they were doomed to be imprisoned in some dustbin on the Horn of Africa until someone sent a ransom demand. How long would that take? There would be endless negotiations. She began to think the mess Gene put them in would never end.

Sasha was forced to accept a measure of blame, too. She was the one to go off with Gene thinking this trip would cement her relationship. It was supposed to be an opportunity to get to know him better. Well, she was certainly getting to know him, but it wasn't for the better. She didn't like what she saw. She liked even less what she was learning about the man.

She doubted it would get any better.

Sasha went back to worrying about whether the distress messages were getting through. She worried even more about her daughter. The situation she found them in was hopeless. It was too much for even a glimmer of hope that Harry would show up to save the day. She hoped anyway. She gained some small measure of joy imagining what would happen when he found them.

If he found them.

"Why are you smiling, mommy?"

"I was just thinking about your father, dear."

Christa smiled up at her mother. "I was thinking about daddy too."

She hugged her daughter even tighter and convinced herself it was all about hope.

Harry Delaney had a difficult time wrapping his head around the fact that Sasha, his ex-wife, had accompanied Gene on his trip. Not only that, but she took their daughter with her. Surely, if she thought about where they were going, she might have re-considered taking Christa.

It wasn't Sasha's first rodeo, either, considering what transpired years ago on the Baja. She must have thought she would spend a couple of nights in a foreign city somewhere and see the sights with Christa. She and Christa would then meet Gene when he returned from the oil company field office.

That was more than reasonable. He would have been happy to go along with that. No doubt Gene didn't tell her he was planning on taking the two of them out to the well-site in the middle of a desert. That it was four hundred miles from any semblance of civilization should have been a concern.

Hell, if she asked, he might have given her a better picture of the problems. He also knew it wouldn't have stopped the woman. That's one of many things he loved about Sasha. She did things her way and on her terms.

My way or the highway, he liked to tease her.

Well, now she was in the middle of a desert on a highway to hell.

Dammit, he should have tried to stop her. At the least, he should have tried to talk her out of taking Christa. Sasha would have gone anyway, with or without his okay. She could have left Christa with Barbara.

It occurred to him she should have been able to leave their daughter with him, but he was in town for only a few days. Now his daughter was a part of Gene's folly. He was trying to show off for them. Cripes, but do men never grow up as far as a woman is concerned?

Harry already knew the answer to that. He was guilty as hell.

Sasha saw that the kidnappers had abandoned the main trail on their way to the ocean. At least, to her it appeared as though they did. The going had turned very slow. It looked like they were on an ancient, dry riverbed, built by many tributaries flowing down from low hills in the distance. It resulted in the flat, sand-covered plain they were on. At least, that's what her high school geography told her. Sand dunes, rock outcrops, ridges, dry wadi, all needed to be traversed to make their goal. It was slowing the kidnappers down considerably.

Why did the kidnappers leave the main trail, she wondered?

The group slowed and stopped yet again. After a heated discussion and plenty of arguing from what she could tell, the convoy got underway. Left even farther behind was any sign of road or trail. The slower pace meant less dust. That alone was a welcome relief in the relentless heat. Sasha hoped for cooler temperatures once they ran up against the ocean.

If they were headed to the ocean. She didn't know for sure. It seemed like days since the plane landed and they were forced into captivity.

A vast expanse of unbroken sand and distance lay ahead. The Jeeps and half-tons were incapable of making time in the loose, deep sand. It turned into wind-formed dunes. Trucks sunk up to their axles in the sand, halting the convoy's progress in its tracks.

She thought it strange that these desert kidnappers would have such a hard time traversing territory they supposedly knew so well. It occurred to her the kidnappers were in too much of a hurry to get to wherever it was they were being taken.

Sasha started out worrying about the kidnappers and what they wanted with them. As the ordeal went on, it became obvious they were after Gene. She relaxed only a little and began to treat it as an adventure for both her and her daughter. What else could she do? They were trapped. There would be no getting out until Harry showed up. At least, that's what she told herself. Were the Tracker signals getting through? She didn't want to think about it.

The convoy halted. "Get out," one of the men addressed her. "There will be no more travel today."

On hearing the announcement, Gene couldn't keep his mouth shut. "Stuck? Do you dumb bastards know how to drive?"

Sasha looked at the man with alarm. Didn't he know he was putting them all in jeopardy with comments like that? "Gene, if I were you, I'd shut up and do what they say," she told him.

Gene barely suppressed the anger in his voice. "What makes you such an expert with these idiots? They live in these conditions and they don't know how to drive a truck across a desert, for crying out loud."

"You must listen to what your woman says," a pirate told him.

"She's not my woman," Gene insisted. "She has to marry me

before I'll ever listen to the likes of her."

It was slow to dawn on her, but Sasha finally realized Gene would be better off without her—and without Christa. Getting stranded in the middle of an East African desert finally illuminated Gene's shortcomings.

Where were all the good men in the world that she had saddled herself with the likes of Gene? She should have listened to Barbara when she chastised her for not getting back with Harry. She made up her mind to tell her that the next time she saw the woman. From where she sat, it wouldn't be soon.

She turned to ask Gene a question and instead witnessed a kidnapper knock him on the side of the head with the butt of a rifle she recognized as an AK-47. Gene collapsed face-down in the sand, finally silent.

She made no move to help the man. Rather, she used the opportunity to get a better look at the weapons the kidnappers were carrying. She had seen them before. They were definitely AKs. Would she be able to get her hands on one?

She flashed back to her time on the Baja when Harry took her under his wing. He trained her how to fire the AK-47. They crossed paths with the weapons when sicarios, killers, bent on finding them, were outsmarted in a parking lot.

She definitely had some thinking to do. She would bide her time and try to come up with a plan. She thought back to Harry and the Baja again. She recalled how he explained to her that the AK-47 was the most reliable weapon in the world.

If it fell in a river, he told her, you fished it out and put it to work. If you slipped and fell into a mud hole, you straightened up and began firing. If you were forced to fish one out of a sand dune, you dragged it out, gave it a shake, and put it to use.

Sasha looked around the Jeep, remembering. That was when she saw them, and she smiled.

Perhaps things weren't so bad after all.

36

**Out of the past
Tanzania**

Mike Williams halted on the edge of a small clearing. He was a mere three hundred feet from the wrecked Pilatus. He took off his hat and wiped the sweat from his face as he regarded his three companions. The women weren't the problem. It was Harry that concerned him.

The man didn't look so good. Sweat poured down Harry's face and saturated his shirt, front and back. He struggled to walk, limping along, sometimes beside, sometimes behind. With every step, he could hear Harry's labored breathing, even with the women supporting him. They would have to stop more often. "Gather round, boys and girls," Mike announced. "You too, Harry, if you can stay with us."

Mike opened the map case he brought from the ops tent. Half-a-dozen aerial photos slipped out and fell to the ground. He smoothed the dirt before unfolding the paper map. He placed it on the ground beside the photos. Lined up his compass on the map. Arranged and rearranged the photos until they matched.

"Well now. This is too good to be true. We're in business." He checked the compass and studied the black and white terrain in the photos. "Does anyone have any input?"

"You two are the pilots. What do you see?" Eloria asked.

"I'm not so sure. Harry, look here." Mike pointed to a spot on a photo.

Harry groaned, reluctant to open his eyes. He swiped at the perspiration running down his face. Blinked. Squinted past stinging salt before leaning back against a shrub. It gave way, and he groaned. Irit bent and helped to straighten him. She remained beside him, helping to keep him upright.

The spot Mike pointed at was open and brighter than the others. "It looks like a mine. What do you think?"

Harry inhaled and groaned. "It's a mine, all right. Tanzanite if I recall." He inhaled again. "If we can get there, we can steal a truck and get out of this mess. What do you say, Eloria? Irit?" He groaned, finished and needing the break from the effort of speaking.

"We're game. We won't be going back to the base camp. Now that we know how those little boys with their tiny penises feel about being rescued by women, we'd be dead meat in no time."

"That's the spirit," Harry insisted. "Does that mean you'll be making it a foursome?" He tried not to laugh. It was a lost cause when his smile turned into a painful grimace. He coughed and wheezed.

"We were looking forward to showers in your tent. It would have been, how do you say, a bonus if you were with us. Now it is out of the question. We will first need a conference." Their grins matched before Irit and Eloria could contain their laughter. "Yes, we're coming with you."

Irit took a bandage roll out of her bag. She allowed Harry to remain with his back against the bush while she completed the first aid job the mercs had started. When she finished, his arm ended up cradled in a rough imitation of a sling. "Harry." She snapped her fingers and shook him. "Harry. Are you able to walk on your own?"

Harry groaned and wheezed, still out of it. Still willing to try. "I think so," he replied. "If not, you'll have to carry me, partner." Harry looked up at Mike and grinned another crooked grin in time to see Mike shake his head.

"Yeah. No. Fat chance of that, stranger," Mike told him. "In no time we'd be fresh meat to whatever caught up to us. You're going to have to suck it up."

The women gathered their gear. "Come on, you two. We can't stay here. In case you forgot, there is fresh feed for the hyenas." Irit gestured toward the downed plane and the bodies.

"You're right," Mike agreed. "I have to get back to the plane to pick up my pack and the AK. Who's coming?"

"We'll all go," Irit assured him. "I saw a survival kit on board. We can check our course to the mine one more time. Judging by the distance, it's going to be a long trek through the bush. At least two days."

Mike didn't want Harry walking any more than necessary. Since he was paying attention to Harry's wounds, it would be a test of the strength the man had left.

Harry groaned again, but this time it wasn't from the pain. "Two days? I'll never make it."

Eloria and Irit exchanged glances. The look didn't go unnoticed. "Yes, you will. You wouldn't want the hyenas tearing you apart while you are alive. Give up and we will have to shoot you."

"The women are right, Harry."

It was Harry's turn to slowly shake his head. "You two aren't going to be any help, are you? I can't get any sympathy."

Mike gathered Harry's backpack, and the group made their way to the plane. He collected the AK from the cabin. "I don't know if you'll be able to carry this. Try it. If you can't, we'll dump it."

Harry was as ready as he could be with a mild concussion and a shoulder wound. "Did you figure out a bearing?"

"We're good. We won't move without you, friend."

"That's comforting. Do I have to stay awake the whole time?" he asked. "Can I trust you to be with me the next time I wake up?"

"Unless the women talk me out of it," a grinning Mike reassured him.

"In that case, I'm glad I didn't piss them off with that landing I put them through."

"I wouldn't be so sure about that, partner."

They made good time, even with the wounded Harry slowing them down. The ground cover was light and mostly knee-high. The underbrush was uneven, yet easy enough to step through. By evening, they found themselves at a narrow stream trickling into a waist-deep pool.

"It's late enough. We will hold up behind that stream until it is daylight," Irit said.

"What's for supper, ladies?" Mike asked with a silly grin.

"We don't cook. We fight," Eloria was quick to inform him.

"That's the truth, and that's all right—this time. Come on, Eloria. We're going for a swim. I need to clean up," Mike said. Eager as he was, Mike wasn't considering the possibilities for fresh game making its way to the waterhole.

"You can't swim in that," Eloria said. "Something will eat you. If there's nothing to eat you in the water, wait until something comes for a drink that will eat you for dessert."

"Don't be a spoilsport. One will stand guard for the other. I'll keep watch first," Mike insisted. "You clean up."

"No, you will go first," Eloria told him. "If there's nothing in the water that wants you, then we will change."

"That's good enough for me," Mike announced. "The rest of you, don't wait up for us if you hear growls and screams."

Harry grinned. "I know. I heard the two of you back in town, remember?"

Mike and Eloria laughed and headed for the pool. Mike halted and looked back. "Harry, if you're feeling up to it, throw some wine and cheese together while we're getting cleaned up."

Already Irit had Harry on the ground and was attempting to make him comfortable. When she was satisfied, she left to gather wood for a fire.

"Would you like a formal white tablecloth, or would checkered be more to your liking?" Harry's eyes closed, and he fell into a restless sleep.

The women were first to wake. Irit and Eloria used the time to go through their gear. They sorted ammunition and grenades and smoke and shared what remained. Irit examined

Harry's AK. She pulled back the slide. Checked the receiver. Extracted the magazine. Satisfied, she replaced it and safetied.

Mike walked into the clearing and called out. "There you are. I was wondering if you hiked back to camp."

"How soon you forget. It was my turn to stand watch while you got your beauty sleep," Harry told him.

Mike was exhausted. Still, he was glad Harry had made it through the night. He didn't look too bad but for bruises and cuts and scrapes. "Is he going to make it?" Mike hated asking the question.

"He will make it with your help," Irit said. "We will help you. We need to go."

They broke camp slowly, all of them fatigued by standing watch for curious animals on their way to the watering hole. Packs were closed. Weapons were slung. They were mobile, but it remained a struggle to keep Harry moving forward. His shoulder wound slowed progress. So did the developing limp caused by his concussion.

Noon of day two saw them come out on a low hill overlooking the mining operation pictured in the aerial photo. Eloria searched in her bag and came up with a small scope. She trained it on the open-pit tanzanite mine. She searched, scanning back and forth. "There's a blockhouse with two guards. The gravel road has a swing gate. No fence. No perimeter road or trail."

"Is it patrolled? What about vehicles?" Irit asked.

"One-tons. A Rover. A small half-ton of some kind. It looks like they're all junk, Eloria replied.

"What about that Rover? Does it look like it might be good? Every car lot has them. Once we hit civilization, we'd be able to make a trade for traveling money," Mike insisted.

"Traveling money? That's a tanzanite mine. All the money we could want is sitting there for the taking," Irit said.

"Maybe so, but we still have to get our hands on it," Mike said.

Eloria continued her search with the scope. "The only guards are sitting by the blockhouse. That has to be where they keep the goods until they're shipped. Why don't we take possession and make the next delivery?"

Harry sighed, disappointed that he'd be unable to take part in the action. "Don't count on me. I'm out of it."

"No problem," Irit told him. "I will move close to the blockhouse to provide cover if it is necessary. Mike will take the Land Rover. Eloria will cover for him if he takes fire."

"There shouldn't be resistance until we get close to the blockhouse. Even then, they won't know who's coming up on them. We'll have the element of surprise," Irit said.

"While we're there, how about if we look for something to eat?" Mike asked.

"On top of everything else, now you're hungry? You Canadians. Enough daydreaming. Let us go."

Mike and Eloria strolled nonchalantly down the hill, making straight for the coveted Land Rover. Mike yanked the wires from beneath the steering column. Cursed and flashed pairs until he found the correct sequence. Sparks flew and the Rover fired up like a dream come true.

They stopped to load Harry waiting by the side of the road and then continued down the rough trail toward the guardhouse. They arrived to find Irit had the blockhouse under control. She was inside, already setting a charge to blow the safe.

They cleared out, and Irit ignited the charge. The strongbox exploded with a bang loud enough to wake the dead. The cloud of dust and debris and smoke cleared. For all the trouble, the inside of the strongbox contained nothing of value.

"Shit. We have to get out of here," Irit said. "Now."

The Rover bounced wildly down the dirt road as fast as Mike dared go. Keeping up speed wasn't easy with the tired suspension on the ancient truck. It jerked and rocked back and forth, threatening to run off the road or toss them out. Mike crested a slight rise. The end of the road came up fast. He stabbed at the brake pedal. Tired brakes squealed and slowed the Rover. Mike yanked the wheel left and the Rover careened onto the paved highway.

Up front, Eloria rode shotgun. She cradled the cut-off

across her lap. She kept the muzzles aimed out the passenger door. She liked to use it only for close-in work. On the run, she found it best to be prepared for any eventuality.

"Harry has stopped groaning," Irit said from the back, where she shared the bench with him as they traveled on the smoother pavement. She spoke too soon when Mike couldn't avoid a huge pothole.

Harry groaned through the rough patch. "It won't be like the road from the mine," Irit tried reassuring him. She pushed and steadied herself against Mike's seat-back. Dutifully, she looked back to scan the road just traveled for anyone who would prevent them from making the border with Kenya. She ministered to Harry the only way she could—by telling him they were almost at the border.

Mike studied the passing surroundings and then the odometer. "We're almost home-free. Only a few kilometers to go."

Irit yelled from the back. "Jeep! Coming up fast."

Mike jammed the pedal to the floor. The Rover rocked and rolled even more violently. A badly aimed RPG round whooshed past and struck a tree. It exploded in the canopy. Tree branches followed by broken glass landed. He called back to Irit. "Where the hell did that come from?"

He heard nothing. He stomped even harder on the gas in a vain attempt to keep them as far ahead of their pursuers as he could. The old Rover was almost done for. There was nothing left for it to give. At top speed, it bounced over the road with a fury.

"Can someone look at a map and see how far we are from the border?" Mike said to no one in particular.

On the floor in the back, Irit lay sprawled across the seat with Harry only inches away. A tree-branch protruded from her chest. Eloria leaned over the front seat to tend to her friend. She tried frantically to resuscitate her. Cursing, she gave up and dropped the seat-back. Both Galils lay across her lap. Grenades bounced on the floor.

"Those bastards won't keep living for long."

Mike called out into the back. "Pop some smoke. That

might keep them off us for a bit. The border can't be much farther."

On a straight stretch, in the open and exposed, Mike caught sight of white buildings surrounded by a grassy plain. It had to be the border with Kenya. What else could it be?

"Mike, take this. It's loaded." Eloria handed off her shotgun.

"This won't be good. Pop more smoke for us," Mike yelled at her. There was nothing. He turned to look in the back. Harry lay slumped in his seat. Irit's body lay where Eloria left it.

Eloria tossed a smoke grenade. The Rover left it in the dust. The distinctive sound of her Galil penetrated the cloud as she tried her best to hold off the overtaking attackers.

"Mike. Slow down. Slow down," Eloria called to him.

Against his better judgment, Mike did as he was told. He knew better than to question this woman while she was engaged in fierce, deadly combat.

Eloria fired and reloaded and fired until her Galil was empty. She grabbed Irit's weapon and emptied it in measured response at the Jeep. It continued to gain.

The gunfire halted. Mike checked his mirror. Eloria was on the ground, rolling. She came up standing and popped smoke to cover her position. A second Jeep was speeding through the smoke. It was gaining. He couldn't make out Eloria in the broken mirror.

The heavy gate at the Namanga border post came up fast. Mike refused to slow. He ducked and plowed through. Guards yelled and waved and scrambled out of the way. The Land Rover careened past.

Kenya was hanging out the welcome sign. A determined Mike was hell-bound for Nairobi and a hospital.

A half-hour past the gate, Mike braked to a sliding stop in the high grass. He pulled Irit's lifeless body from the back of the Jeep and left her on the side of the road with the empty weapons. He kept Eloria's shotgun. He felt for Harry's pulse and decided it was just as well he wasn't conscious.

Mike climbed onto the Rover's hood and looked around.

He was unsure what to expect. Vehicles from the border station should be on the way to apprehend them. There was no one. Nothing but a smoke cloud. He jumped down from the hood and held his hands out in front of him. He wasn't able to still the trembling until he got back in the Rover and gripped the steering wheel.

He eased the Rover onto the paved highway and fled for Nairobi as though in a dream.

37

Present Day
Horn of Africa

It **didn't appear** as though the grin on Mike's face in the left seat of the DC-3 was going away any time soon. Harry wasn't able to ignore it any longer. "I can tell you're getting the hang of it again. I told you it wouldn't take long."

Mike gave him his *What the hell are we doing here?* look, even though he well knew. "You know, I have to admit to a certain amount of luck and good fortune with my business to get it profitable. Would you mind explaining why I gave all that up to be here today?"

"Because we're two of the dumbest sons-of-bitches in aviation," Harry stated.

"Possibly," Mike agreed. "But besides that."

"Your shit-eating grin pretty much says it all, Mike."

"Now you're stating the obvious," partner.

Harry went on. "Look at it this way. You ended up taking Barbara on the vacation of a lifetime. When this is all over, there's no way she'll be nagging you to take her somewhere for a long time."

Two arms came up for the celebratory high-five slap. The high-five came to an abrupt halt when a third hand inserted itself between theirs.

"Will you two stop trying to cheap me out of a vaycay? I deserve better than this," Barbara insisted. "And Sasha certainly deserves more than what she's getting from that loser she's traipsing around with in the desert."

Harry and Mike were unwilling to admit defeat, even though caught red-handed. "Oh miss, you'll have to return to your seat. Fraternizing with the flight crew is not permitted and against regulations. It could distract them from their duties and endanger the well-being of the rest of the passengers and crew."

Barbara put her hands on her hips and looked at Harry, sitting smug in the right seat. He found himself suddenly busy tapping gauges and checking numbers.

"You owe me, buster," she told him, in no uncertain terms. She was about to abandon the cockpit and return to her seat in the back. She abruptly changed her mind. "Furthermore, distract this." She raised her shirt and bared her breasts just as Harry and Mike turned toward her.

"Gosh, Mike. You are one lucky man. She looks exactly the same as she did on the Baja."

The two men high-fived once more. A red-faced Harry couldn't halt the nervous grin. Before anyone could say anything, he went back to checking the gauges.

"You both owe me big time, and I don't mean for the look I just gave you, Harry." Barbara grinned at the two men. "I'm going back to sit with Sammy. You both owe me for that, too."

The temporary distraction took them over familiar territory beneath the DC-3. They looked out windows at the dry wadi that had once been in the far distant past a proud river that scoured the valley between distant cliff faces. It ran roughly from the northwest to the southeast. The now feeble underground stream surfaced at Eyl, on the shores of the Indian Ocean.

Mike checked his watch and added power to climb to 10,000 feet. Dead reckoning had once again taken him to their destination. "We're here," he announced. "Let's see if we can find our girls." On reaching altitude, he put the once-proud DC-3 workhorse in a shallow bank. It allowed him to renew his acquaintance with their old stomping ground.

Mike began scouring the ground out the cockpit's port window. Harry leaned over him. Two pairs of eyes searched the desert as their old service landing strip disappeared beneath the wing. What they were looking at hadn't changed in a hundred years, and it wouldn't change over the next hundred.

"Overland travel in that sand won't be easy," Mike remarked.

"They couldn't be far from their last position," Harry said. "A sighting would make the ground chase a lot easier."

"Here comes the strip again," Mike told him, as the old landing strip appeared a second time.

"Look." Harry pointed. "There they are. Nine o'clock low. Our strip is west of them."

"I'd say they made three or four miles past at most," Mike said.

"They went off the trail. That's what's slowing them down."

"There's no sense broadcasting our arrival" Harry said. "Throttle back and set up for a landing on the other side of the strip."

Mike did as instructed. Harry was the experienced desert aviator. Doing the landing would give Harry the chance to renew his abilities in the DC-3.

"You'll need to come in low and slow from a distance so as not to alert them," Harry said. "Drop the gear when you get as low as you can to that sand."

Harry's words told Mike he would be doing the approach and landing. He couldn't deny he was a long way from home and his office desk. There would be no turning back for any of them.

Harry shared cockpit duties as he talked Mike through the approach and landing checklist for the ancient plane. Mike performed flawlessly, although a little slowly. He was re-familiarizing himself as he went along.

"You're not as rusty as you think," Harry told him.

"Maybe not, Harry, but just the same I'm glad you're sitting as my number one."

Harry continued calling the numbers as Mike lowered and set the flaps.

"Gear," Mike called.

Harry selected gear down. The landing gear groaned and locked into place. The indicator lights illuminated.

"Two green," Harry called.

Mike continued to keep the DC-3 low and slow on final across the wind-swept dunes. Harry's hands backed up his own as he pulled back the throttles and mushed onto the sandy, uneven strip.

"Smooth as silk, Captain," Harry announced. "You're hired. When can you start?"

"I'll let you know when we touch down at JIB on the return."

"I've got her, Mike," Harry announced.

"You have control." Mike was fine with Harry taking over ground taxiing the heavy plane loaded with arms in the mushy sand.

"Sammy did a job reducing pressure in those tires. This thing just about floats over all that sand."

Should the plane bog down in the sand, they'd be trucking it to Djibouti, well over 500 miles overland by road to the northwest. It would force the planned airborne assault to distract the kidnappers into a full-blown ground operation.

It was something they already discussed, and didn't want to do. It would put the women in too much danger.

"I'm going to position for a quick departure, just in case." Harry advanced the throttles to maneuver the DC-3 into position with the nose pointing down the strip. Satisfied, he shut down in a cloud of dust and sand.

A nervous Sammy waited between the seats. "There's a crowd outside waiting for us. Did you see them?"

"They're okay, Sammy. If they weren't, the plane and everyone in it would be shot up by now," Harry assured him.

Sammy visibly relaxed. "How did she taxi?" he wanted to know.

"Like a dream, Sammy. Good job on the tires. I was just telling Mike that he's hired. So are you," Harry grinned. The air in the plane was growing warmer. "You'll have to figure out what's going on with the hydraulics in a hurry. The rest of us will offload the arms we won't be needing."

Young Bill opened the cargo door and an even hotter blast of dry desert air flooded the cabin.

"Ali is going to be happy with his delivery. He's nervous for his clan with all the crazy fundamentalists running around this part of the country. We're giving him enough armament for a small army. I'm glad he's on our side."

Sammy got busy troubleshooting the hydraulic lines from memory. "What do you make of the pressure loss?" he asked Harry.

"I'm worried," he told him. "If this airplane claps out, we're in trouble. Ali might have dug up fuel and two technicals for us, but there's no way he'll be able to deliver a DC-3."

Sammy headed for the back of the plane and jumped onto the ground. He gestured at a technical and motioned for the driver to pull up beneath the number one engine.

The driver hesitated. He turned to look at an old man standing by the edge of the strip. His robes fluttered in the wind. He nodded assent, and the technical moved beneath the engine.

Sammy waved his thanks before climbing onto the back of the truck. He moved past the .50-caliber mounted on the bed and climbed onto the roof with a handful of tools. He began loosening the cowlings and eventually the bottom half of number one engine came into view.

In the back of the plane, Bill fussed over the heavy mount for the twin .50s. Satisfied, he called for Mike and Harry to help him remove the door and secure it. The three of them wrestled the gun mount into the doorway.

Bill bolted it to the airframe. "It's not as strong as I'd like it, but Sammy and I did the best we could on such short notice. She'll hold for what needs to be done. No guarantees after that."

Harry nodded. "If you and Sammy say so. I trust your work. We're not planning on starting a war. All we need is a few thousand rounds and we'll be good to go."

"As long as Mike knows I'll need to test fire the rig in-flight to sight her in," Bill said. He continued with his fussing, greasing the friction points on the jury-rigged gun mount. He swiveled the dual guns in all directions to check the firing arc. On the ground, nervous gunmen racked their weapons and aimed them at the DC-3. A word and an arm signal from the old man caused them to stand down.

Satisfied with the way things were proceeding with the gun mount, Harry jumped to the ground. The man he and Mike had gotten to know so well in the past began striding toward the DC-3.

"Jambo, Ali" Harry called to the man. He returned Ali's grin and stuck out his hand. The old man took it and held on.

"Jambo, bwana Harry," Ali returned the greeting. "Hibari? How are you?"

"Mazuri. Fine, fine. And you?"

"I too am well, old friend."

"You have aged well," Harry told Ali. "It must be your young wives."

"It costs much to have those young wives. I must have old wives to keep them in order."

Harry grinned at Ali. "Mike will be here in a minute. He brought his wife to meet you."

"So I have heard. She did well by both of you in Djibouti." Already the old man had heard of the shooting. It was always thus in this part of the world.

"News travels fast." The desert telegraph, Harry knew. It was never to be underestimated.

"If I did not have many informers," Ali admitted, "I would not still be here in your time of need."

"We are very grateful, Ali. Now come and have a look at what we brought for you." Harry helped the old man into the plane.

"If this were anyone but you, I would be wary of people bearing such gifts." Ali looked over the wooden boxes and the machine guns hanging out of the DC-3 cargo door. "Enough of business for now. You must tell me about the woman that has brought you this great distance one last time."

38

Mike joined **Sammy** on the back of the technical. He already knew the fastidious Sammy would be concerned about getting everyone safely back to Djibouti aboard the plane. He also knew his chief engineer was a can-do guy who had learned from the best how to do his job. He could improvise with the best of them. He had witnessed it repeatedly, most recently with the design of the mount for the twin .50s that would hang out of the DC-3 cargo door.

He waited patiently for a chance to get a word in with the talkative engineer.

"This antique is holding together better than I expected, but for that pressure leak." Sammy went on with his task, talking as though Mike weren't there. "If we can't get it repaired, it will limit our options."

"That's not good news," Mike informed him. "It will mean a running gun-battle on flat terrain with unobstructed visibility for miles. That won't be good for the hostages. Or any of us."

Mike looked off to the east, in the direction of the pirate convoy carrying Harry's wife and daughter to the coast. He couldn't see them, but he knew they were there. He saw them from the air. "Have you figured out what we need?"

"I'll replace number one hydraulic pump. The seals are gone. I don't suppose this crate came with any spares. Get me a hydraulic pump and we can fly this tin can to hell."

Mike grinned at his long-time engineer. "Hell is good. It's where we're going. One problem, though. We'll need to get back, too."

"This plane will get us to hell. I'm not so sure about the getting back part without a pump."

"Harry's the one made the promises for this little gem of an airplane," Mike admitted. "I think he got all nostalgic for the airline he used to ride on for his R&Rs into Mog. I don't know if he bothered to pick up any spares for our brand-new charter business or not."

That wasn't the answer Sammy wanted to hear. He looked nervously in Harry's direction.

"Yes, I lined up a few spares," Harry said, taking the cue. "I told the seller I needed to keep expenses down on my new startup. I asked specifically for a hydraulic pump, and they threw one in gratis."

"You don't know it yet, Sammy, but you're hanging with two of the best can-do guys in this desert. You make number three," Mike told him.

Sammy didn't take time to look for the part. He trusted Harry's word he had a spare available that he could bolt in. He went back to work disconnecting lines and removing the damaged pump.

Mike climbed down from the technical and met with Harry. "Sammy will figure it out, eventually. I think he's still stuck on Barbara and the shotty. Wait until he sees her with an RPG."

"Damn, Harry, I wish you wouldn't. Ever since she missed out on the AK action down on the Baja, she's been after me to take her to a gun range."

"How long has it been since you took the woman to one?" Harry wanted to know.

"Never," Mike admitted. "And I don't want you encouraging her, either."

"Si, mon Capitán." Harry turned to call out to Sammy. "Did you check out that box in the cabin labeled spares?"

"No. I figured that hand-written sign was a joke you two were playing on me."

"No joke, Sammy. I'm sure the pump you need is in there somewhere," Harry said.

It was dark when Sammy finished changing out the hydraulic pump. He gave Mike the okay to start the engine. Harry monitored the hydraulic pressure gauges behind the seat. Under the open engine, Sammy used a flashlight to keep an eye on his work, checking for leaks.

Satisfied, Sammy signaled Mike to shut down. Cursing the entire time, he fumbled in the dark to get the engine cowlings mounted and buttoned up. The technical's weak headlights were little help.

Barbara overheard his cursing and offered to hold a flashlight. Sammy waved the woman away, but she persisted by climbing up on the roof of the technical. Before long, they were working together. Sammy grudgingly thanked the women for her help when the job was completed and the cowlings were buttoned up.

Sammy still wasn't sure what to think of the adventurous band of misfits he had tied his wagon to. Mike was a good man to work for back home. Payday came regularly and there were no problems with airworthiness on his airplanes. Every bulletin was done, mandatory or not. These days there was something to be said for that.

When he agreed to get on board with this operation, he found himself drawn into something completely different. The eagerness with which they had all adapted to the new circumstances in the middle of the Horn of Africa surprised him. Mike's wife had been even more of a shocker.

When she flashed the shotgun in Djibouti, he had cause for concern for his own safety. That concern was eased when he saw how she handled herself at the end of the strip, in the dark of night. Pulling the trigger on the bandits looking for money convinced him he was in with the right crowd.

These people weren't behaving like fresh recruits who didn't know how to handle themselves. The kidnappers had no idea what was about to be unleashed.

Hell, he was going to have stories to tell in the bar when this was over. They'd surpass those of his own of time spent in West Africa when he was a young man doing his own questionable things to make a living.

It was close to midnight before it quieted enough for the crew of misfits to get some shuteye. The DC-3 became the hotel of choice. With nowhere else to go, the plane was crowded with anxious adventurers desperate for sleep. Harry and Mike bunked in the cockpit. Haphazard arrangements allowed Sammy and Bill to hunker down on air mattresses provided by Barbara, who slept on her own.

With Ali and his well-equipped crew providing protection by surrounding the landing strip, no watch system was set up. It wasn't even discussed, given Harry and Mike's trust in Ali's abilities. No one bothered to slip a single magazine into an AK.

There was no need.

Harry slid the cockpit window open, hoping to allow some of the warm air that infiltrated the cabin to escape. That was when he heard the sounds. Ignitions caught and groaned to life on tired batteries. He counted at least three, maybe more. He climbed out of his seat and shook Mike awake. "We're getting fat and dumb and lazy. We should have posted our own guard."

He rushed to the back of the plane, only to be tripped up by sleeping bodies and wooden boxes still scattered across the floor. Mike bumped against him and he almost fell. Lead pinged through the cargo hold of the DC-3 and both men found themselves on the floor out of necessity. They crawled in the dark, searching for the cache of AK-47s they knew were somewhere in the back.

Two loud whumps announced the attack was over almost before it began.

"Those are RPG rounds," Harry announced. "What the hell—"

Ali called out past the open cargo door. "Do not be alarmed, old friends. We discovered enemies within our camp."

Harry and Mike jumped down to confront Ali, who was surrounded by the remains of his men, armed to the teeth with rocket launchers and AKs.

"We have taken care of them," the old man said. "They will be missed by their families but they will not come back to bother us on this or any night."

The three still fast asleep in the back of the plane were none the wiser. No one had so much as blinked an eye at the sounds of the commotion.

"In that case, Ali, let's go to your campfire. We can drink chai and talk about old times," Harry said. It was a good excuse to keep alert and on the watch for further trouble.

"As you wish."

The pair settled on the blankets beside the old man. Ali poured the hot, dark chai into glasses containing rock sugar, cloves, and cinnamon sticks. He raised his glass to Harry and Mike. "To your continued good health, and to that of your wives and families."

The men drank the hot, sweet tea and sighed with enjoyment. "We had some trouble in Djibouti while we were readying the plane for this trip," Harry informed Ali. "We had to take care of two men begging alms. Unfortunately, we had nothing to offer beyond substituting lead for gold."

"So I was informed, as I told you. Your wife is quite the woman, Mike. I would like to have one so dependable in my house."

Mike slapped Ali on the back. "She's not for sale, no matter how many sheep and goats you offer.

The sly old man grinned. "I have many camels, too."

39

Out of the Past
Tanzania

Mike Williams locked his eyes on the old Land Rover's remaining mirror. Dirty, cracked glass reflected an empty road. He was free and clear, thanks in no small measure to Irit's sacrifice. It was Eloria who had volunteered without question to make certain he made the border with his wounded comrade.

He knew his debt to be enormous, but he could give it only fleeting thought. Free of Tanzania and the pursuing mine guards, his major worry was Harry. He was still out cold and motionless in the back seat. His friend was in and out of consciousness. The out was coming increasingly more often and for longer periods.

Harry's concussion had to be worse than he initially thought. Harry needed a hospital. That meant a city. If he could depend on memory, Nairobi was at least two hours distant.

Money was a more immediate problem. The mine's blockhouse yielded nothing of value. They were broke, except for a few local shillings. He might as well have a sack filled with Greek drachmas for all that was worth on the continent.

Mike fished under the seat for the shotgun Eloria passed to him before she jumped from of the Rover. He and Harry owed her everything. She wasn't able to hold off their attackers, but she put up one hell of a fight. How they shut her down so fast remained a mystery.

His hand closed on thick paper taped to the short butt of the sawed-off. He slowed to a stop before carefully slicing through the tape. Two passports revealed themselves. Canadian passports. He checked his surroundings before getting out of the Rover to tend to Harry. He slapped him and Harry mumbled something incomprehensible before he passed out again. Mike climbed into the Rover and steered for Nairobi.

There was no way of knowing if the passports were forged. They could be. The accents of the two women were unrecognizable as Canadian—at least to his ears. They said they were sisters. He would add a stop at a certain embassy in Nairobi to his list once he got Harry to a hospital.

It wasn't only Harry's wounds that concerned him. He wanted to know more about the two women that had plucked them both out of the frying pan and dropped them into the relative safety of another country. He and Harry owed Eloria and Irit everything.

With both women disappeared, payback would be a long time coming.

Mike had few options. He needed dollars, and he needed them fast. Selling the Rover would bring some immediate cash, but not nearly enough. The plan, when he got Harry to a Nairobi hospital, was to hole up at the Flying Club. Perhaps someone there could point him toward an outfit with a need for pilots or maintenance people.

It was slow going into Nairobi with the wounded Harry. He had to stop and minister to Harry too often for his liking. Finally, he reached the outskirts of the huge, sprawling city. He flagged a taxi and convinced the driver to lead him to a hospital. On arrival, he stashed Harry with two concerned nurses. He promised to return before making for the Flying Club.

Mike parked the stolen, bullet-riddled Land Rover in a distant corner of the lot. He would be good until someone walked by and noticed its condition. He made his way inside, where a regular at the bar recognized him.

"I heard you and Harry were working for a tanzanite outfit

south of the border. What brings you up this way?"

Mike usually enjoyed listening to the rumors and gossip, but he didn't much care for it when it was about him. "Harry's plane got shot up at a strip we were servicing. I got him out."

"He's not with you?" the man wanted to know. "What happened to him?"

"He didn't make it out with much more than the clothes on his back," Mike reassured the man. "I dropped him off so he could pick up some gear."

Mike hoped that would put an end to speculation and pointed questions, but he'd have to get out of here fast. No way did he want to explain why Harry wouldn't be showing up any time soon.

"I'm looking for some work to the north, maybe Libya. Have you heard of any leads? Helicopter or fixed-wing, it doesn't matter."

The man thought for a minute. "I heard about some oil work up that way. The outfit is always looking for pilots. I don't know why. Maybe the camps aren't so good."

That could prove to be the ticket. When Harry got out of the hospital, they could head north for a fresh start. "In that case, give me a name and a number and I'll make some calls."

40

Following the failed attack by traitors within Ali's trusted crew, the band of misfits thanked the old man for his help. Without him, their mission would have failed spectacularly. Had the plane's engines been shot up, the rescue plan wouldn't have a chance of working. They found themselves one step closer to success.

They made their excuses and climbed into the DC-3 to huddle in the cramped confines of the ancient plane. The attempt to shut the rescue operation down kept everyone wide awake and on guard. AK-47s were checked and checked again. Harry and Mike made sure magazines were loaded and taped for maximum efficiency.

Nervous chatter kept them all from thinking about what would come later in the day.

Harry and Mike knew if Ali unknowingly brought enemies to the strip, there could be more. No one wanted to be responsible for shutting down the rescue. Come hell or high water—and there would be no chance of high water any time soon—it would be today.

"Rise and shine, you lazy, hopeless bastards," Mike called out. Much grumbling and not a lot of sympathy echoed down the cabin at the sound of the eager call to action.

"If the owners of this airline thought they knew anything about providing passenger comfort, they were sadly misinformed," Barbara insisted.

Harry's grin joined Mike's. "What do you expect from the fly-by-night outfit you're all accustomed to working for?"

"You didn't think we were so hopeless that you remained in comfort back home," Harry told them. "Personally, there's nothing I'd like more than to be sitting in the Flying Club with a hand wrapped around a damp Tusker."

"You're right, Harry. I apologize for hurting your feelings," Barbara said.

"Look. We have a functioning DC-3. We have fuel, oil and hydraulic fluid. We have the old girl outfitted with twin .50-caliber machine guns. We have AKs. We have RPGs. If all that fails, we have a double-barreled sawed-off shotgun. We're ready as we'll ever be and raring to go. Barbara, it's time to do your womanly duty and cook breakfast for the crew." Harry quickly stepped aside as he cast a huge grin in Mike's direction.

"Breakfast? Cook? Screw you. We didn't even bring MREs. We'll toast this adventure when we're back in Djibouti—if the jet hasn't been impounded by the time we get there," Barbara told him.

Sammy took his chances and joined in the merriment. "Don't listen to them, Barbara. They spent the night sleeping in comfortable seats up front in first class. You can cook for all of us when we have the next company barbecue back home."

"Don't push it, Sammy," Barbara told him with a quick grin. "I have a loaded shotgun tucked under my arm."

"That's the spirit, Sammy. We're ready to rock and roll. But first, it's time for a meeting. Does anyone have a plan?" Harry asked.

That was the last straw for Barbara. She threw her hands in the air and raised her voice. She'd be heard or else. "For crying out loud, you two. Are we back on the Baja all over again?"

"Relax, girl. By the sound of it, we won't be getting breakfast any time soon," Harry was forced to admit. "We'll move on to other matters. I actually have a plan."

"Well suck me blue and call me ice woman. Harry has a plan. I can't wait to tell Sasha about this." Barbara looked around the inside of the plane. She saw faces marked with worry, mirroring her own.

Harry spelled out the details as best he knew them. "The kidnappers can't be far past where we saw them yesterday. Barbara and I will be heading out in the technicals with Ali and his crew. By the time the rest of you get this bucket of bolts airborne, we should be within cheering range of the parade."

Mike interjected. "You've got the easy part. I have to figure out how to fly a pattern that will give Bill a good elevation on the target. I don't want him hitting the good guys and girls."

Bill saw the need to put Mike at ease about the operation of the twin .50s. "In Nam we had DC-3s outfitted with mini-guns. We called them Spooky. We nick-named them Puff the Magic Dragon. Orbiting at 3,000 feet and 120 knots in a Spooky, those mini-guns could depopulate an area the size of a football field."

"What rate-of-fire will you get with the .50s?" Mike wanted to know.

"I don't want to burn out the barrels if I can help it," Bill stated. "I'm set up for 300 a side. That should keep them cool enough to do the job."

"Mike, you should be able to fly that pylon all day in the Dakota—or at least until you've put five thousand rounds through the guns.

"No problem," Mike confirmed. "I can hold it to that, but I'd like to do a test run first." Mike had to be sure Bill wouldn't screw up with Sasha and Christa on the ground. If he or Bill made a mistake, he'd never be able to face Harry again.

"After we take off, give me a practice pylon at a three thousand feet above ground. I'll need that to get the .50s sighted in.

"As good as done," Mike assured Bill. Still, he would be doing something he had never done in the DC-3, and that was a pylon turn. Such a turn would keep the guns positioned at a very small target on the ground. The only variable in that case would be the muzzles of the machine guns as Bill sought targets from the stable gun platform provided by the DC-3.

Harry looked over the rag-tag volunteers his friend Mike had put together on such short notice. His eyes moved from the clapped-out DC-3 with the jury-rigged gun mount hanging off the side to Ali and his well-armed crew milling about the remains of their campfire. Mike's crew, nervous, exhausted and aware of everything that could go wrong with their rescue attempt, were quiet and reserved.

Harry, more than the others, knew the airborne rescue attempt could turn to shit in a hurry. If that happened, Sasha and his daughter could end up being on the receiving end of what Harry hoped he'd be able to dish out from the ground.

If he got his way, those kidnapping bastards would suffer through hell from both high and low.

In her past, Barbara was a reluctant witness to Sasha's AK training routine on the Baja. Regretful that she didn't take part, she understood this would be her last chance. The RPGs were calling her name, but she wasn't sure how to convince Harry to allow her to fire one.

"So that's it, Delaney? The briefing is over?" she asked.

"You know it. Just like old times—but wait, there's more. If you want to learn to fire the Rocket Propelled Grenade launcher, it's time."

Harry grinned across at Barbara. He knew, and a huge grin lit up her face. "Now you're talking my language, cowboy. This is a briefing. Let's do it."

Harry picked one from the stockpile. "It comes with three parts. The rocket head or warhead. The booster. The launcher." He held each section up as he named them. He handed the empty tube across and watched as she familiarized herself with it. "Step into my office, woman."

Harry worked his way past the door guns and jumped down. Barbara slung the empty RPG tube across her back and followed him out of the plane. On the ground, Harry continued. "You screw the booster onto the warhead, like this."

Transfixed, Barbara watched as Harry demonstrated. She

would get to fire one of those suckers or else. Nothing would hold her back.

Harry went on with his instructions. "Once the two parts join, the warhead gets inserted into the front end of the launch tube. How do we know it's the front end?"

Barbara didn't hesitate. "The pistol grip. It's like a handgun."

"Exactly. You might get to fire it twice. You won't have time to learn all the ins and outs. Just remember. Twist it on. Stuff it down the front. Shoulder. Line up the sight. Pull the trigger. Bonus points if you remember not to have your rear end pointed at anyone you love. He looked at her and raised an eyebrow before going on. "Why might that be?"

Barbara didn't hesitate. She held the RPG end-to-end and looked through the empty tube. "Exploding gas."

"Exactly." Harry moved off to the side. He didn't aim. Instead, he angled the loaded RPG skyward to the east and pulled the trigger. The round went high and exploded, leaving behind a huge black cloud. "If they're still close by, that ought to put the fear of Harry into them."

Barbara applauded and Harry re-armed the launcher and handed it to Barbara. She got down on one knee, as Harry had done. Instead of shooting for the sky, she aimed at a rock-pile situated off the end of the strip. She pulled the trigger. The impact and explosion showered everyone with dirt. She yelled over her ringing ears. "Holy shit, Harry. This could be fun."

"We'll take half a dozen rounds with us. I want you to pre-arm them, just like I showed you. If I need them, you won't have time to be screwing around. It'll be load, point, and fire," he explained.

"That's good enough for me," Barbara assured him.

"And don't forget where your ass is pointing."

She gave Harry a hug and squeezed his rear. "That's double duty from me and Sasha."

"Good grief, don't let Mike see you doing that. I have enough trouble with Sasha as it is."

"I saw that, you two," Mike interjected. "It's a good thing none of us have had breakfast or I'd be suspicious of your motives."

Barbara rolled her eyes. "If you're not careful, I might bring this not-cooking thing home with me. That would be trouble you don't want."

Mike didn't get a chance to reply. Sammy had finished his pre-flight on the DC-3. "She's fueled and ready, guys. Last night's encounter with flying lead hit nothing of consequence. Once you get airborne, don't forget Bill will want to test-fire the .50s and sight in."

Harry wanted Barbara to be ready for whatever would come next. "Chica, get your soccer-mom ass onto that truck. I need a pep-talk with that man you married." "It's been a long time since anyone called me chica. And you'd better not be saying my ass is fat if you know what's good for you."

A grinning Harry boarded the DC-3 for a last word with Bill. "My ex is in that convoy with our daughter. I don't want to put any pressure on you, but if you mess up, Barbara will turn you into one sorry-assed son-of-a-bitch the next time she sees you."

"Go easy, man," Bill insisted. "I know what I'm doing. I'll get the job done. I've never done it from a Spooky is all. I never got to crew on one. And I already talked to Barbara. She's good."

"I know you can do it. In case you didn't notice, we're all a little jumpy this morning. We haven't had our coffee fix. That's the story I'm going with," Harry said.

Harry walked up to join Mike, already in the cockpit. He was methodically going through the checklist. "You'll be without a co-pilot on this run. Can you handle her?"

"Piece of cake. I kept fuel down to half tanks. We're light and maneuverable. That should make it bearable for the old girl to fly those pylon turns I had nightmares about last night."

"I'll be taking Barbara with me," Harry told him. "Is that okay?"

Mike cast an unbelieving look in Harry's direction. "Seriously? You're asking my permission? I couldn't hold that woman back if I wanted to. She has it set in her mind that she's going to kick Sasha's ass all the way back to home. I expect you'll be there for that. When we're done with all of this, I want to be first to hear your version."

Harry grinned and shook his head. "One more word of warning before you go. Don't get in front of her if she has that shotgun out to cover the bad guys."

"I hear that," Mike said. "Thanks for the warning."

"Don't thank me yet," he warned Mike. "We're not going to be out of this sand-trap for a while. I'll see you back at the strip."

The two men high-fived.

"You know it, partner."

41

Bill **fastened the** strap on his old door-gunner helmet. He had rescued it from his locker back at the hangar, thinking it would be the last time he would get to wear it. He lit a cigarette, exhaled a cloud of smoke, and coughed as he made his way to the cockpit.

"I didn't know you smoked," Mike said

"Not for thirty years," Bill insisted.

"Do you need a minute to tuck the lung back in?" The two men grinned back and forth. Nervous grins. They knew everything depended on them. Knew Harry was counting on them to do the dirty work. The idling DC-3 engines seemed to confirm it.

"No, I'm good."

Mike began his briefing. "After wheels-up I'll move off to the west. When I get us to three thousand above ground, I'll look for a pile of rocks. Shouldn't be too hard to find in this terrain. Overtop I'll go into a pylon turn. You do your sighting in. Let me know when you're finished."

"Roger that."

"From there, we'll make for the convoy. Once I have the target I'll be descending as low as I can to do a single pass at full throttle. That will let Sasha know we're here and on the job. It should also give us good eyes on the convoy." Mike hesitated. He wanted to be certain Bill heard the next. "You'll get your look-see out the cargo door. Be aware that as I go by, I'll be waggling the wings. That's going to tell her who's doing the driving. Don't fall out and don't ask how she'll know."

"Roger that," Bill told him. "When we're done with this operation, I'd like to know more about you guys. Do you think you can manage that?"

"One thing at a time." Mike went on. "When we're doing that low pass, look for a woman with a little girl. Harry's ex has worked with us before. She'll know enough to get the two of them away from the action before we circle back to do the dirty work."

"I'll be on the lookout for them real hard," Bill assured him.

'You can plug into the intercom back at the door."

"I know," Bill said. "I tested it back in JIB. How's our fuel?"

"A little less than half," Mike said.

"Good. We're light."

"I don't want you taking any chances with that .50, Bill. If you hit them, they're mincemeat."

"I know that. The flyby will give me eyes. I need the flyby to sort things out on the ground. Once you get us into orbit, I'll be good to go. With twenty-five hundred rounds a side, I won't leave anything behind if you can keep me overhead."

"Then let's get it done." Mike's tone was final.

They shook hands. Bill headed back to his position at the door and inspected the setup he and Sammy had come up with and rigged. The bungees would help steady the twin .50 muzzles in the DC-3's slipstream.

He swung the guns forward to the wing and pulled hard. He arced them up and then down. Rope kept the twin muzzles away from the wing. He swung aft and checked for the tail. The rope did its job again. Unless something unexpected came up, there was no way he'd end up shooting down the gun platform and any hope of rescuing the women.

Up front, Mike fired up number one engine. It coughed and caught in a cloud of blue smoke. He did the same for number two. Sammy signaled all clear for both engines, and Mike advanced throttles at the end of the strip.

Bill tossed the unfinished cigarette out the door. It would be the last one he'd taste. The only reason he lit it was to commemorate his days as a long-ago Huey door gunner. He plugged into the intercom and called Mike. "Gunner to cockpit. Final check is complete. Guns will remain clear of the wing and tail. Ammo loaded and guns are hot. All I have to do is rack and we're ready to rock and roll."

"Roger that, Bill." Mike put in enough throttle to jockey the DC-3 into position for takeoff. He stood on the brakes and firewalled the throttles. A cloud of sand and dust blasted the empty ground behind the plane and drifted past the open cargo door. He one-handed the column and reached to tap the gauges. Satisfied, he released the brakes.

The lightly loaded DC-3 almost jumped into the air. He reached for the gear lever and listened to the whine as the gear retracted and he got two white. Mike set the throttles and began his climb to a thousand feet. He made sure he banked low to the west in order not to announce the team's arrival.

A babble of nervous voices swept through the stalled pirate convoy at the sound of an approaching plane. The voices grew in intensity as the engine sound grew louder. Anxious eyes scanned the horizon, trying to locate the plane by sound as it bore down on the ragtag collection of trucks stalled in the sand.

It was getting close. Fast. It would be on them soon. Sasha didn't have time to figure out what she would do. She didn't need to. She knew. She had worked it out when the vehicles became bogged down in the sand. The overhead distraction sealed the deal. She addressed her daughter. "Do you see those black things in the back of our truck? The ones with the shiny metal at one end? Do you think you could put as many as you can in your backpack?"

Sitting beside them, Gene overheard her. "You're crazy, woman. You'll get us all killed."

Sasha wasn't having it. She'd had her fill of Gene and his endless whining. "Shut up, you fool." She turned back to her daughter and caught her sticking out her tongue at Gene. "Me too, sweetheart," she told her.

Christa smiled, and her tongue disappeared into her mouth. "Try not to let the bad men see you, dear."

The increasing rumble of the approaching engines at full throttle put the kidnappers in a panic. The exploding airborne round that appeared to the west of their position put them on edge. Sounds of the plane only served to heighten their apprehension.

They scrambled to locate the plane. All eyes moved to the sky, searching high and low. The moment gave Christa the perfect cover to collect the magazines.

Sasha witnessed the plane topping a sand ridge at treetop level as it came into view. Except there were no trees. She thought she saw a puff of dust raised by the low-flying plane's slipstream. Whoever was doing the flying knew what he was doing.

Engines continued their roar as it bore down on the convoy. She observed the wings waggling in continuous slow motion as it flew toward the convoy and passed overtop. It disappeared over a ridge. The sudden silence was ominous.

It had to be Mike at the controls, announcing his arrival. She'd seen a plane he was flying do that before. They were here. She jumped out of the truck and almost danced a jig.

An RPG, or what she thought was one, appeared. A kidnapper climbed on the back of a truck and began searching the sky for the plane. He was too late. It had flown off, hugging the ground before disappearing past the ridge and over the horizon.

Sasha knew no matter what happened, the man with the RPG would have to be her first. But how would she get away? Her question was answered by the kidnappers as they struggled to make sense of what had just happened with the plane.

"My daughter has to go to the bathroom. Is it all right if we go behind those rocks?"

"Yes. Go. Go. Hurry."

"Come on, Christa. Come with mommy and bring your bag. Your father and Uncle Mike are here to take us home." Tears streamed down Sasha's face.

Christa looked up at her mother. "Daddy's here? And Uncle Mike? Why are you crying, mommy?"

Sasha swiped at the tears. "Yes, dear. Harry and Mike are here. I think Uncle Mike's airplane will come back. I think he has a job to do and we need to get out of Uncle Mike's way so he can do it."

She had to get Christa up the hill. If they could get behind it to safety before the plane returned, Mike could do whatever he needed to do.

"Gene," she called. "Are you coming with us? You don't want to be caught out in the open in the middle of whatever is going to happen."

In the distance, the sudden appearance of the climbing DC-3 held the kidnappers' attention. They ignored Sasha and her daughter.

"Did you get the things I showed you, Christa?"

"Yes, mommy. They're in my backpack. They're heavy."

"Good girl. Now let's go." Sasha made a grab for Christa's hand and pulled her around the back of the truck. On the way, she picked up an AK and slung it in front of her.

Gene witnessed her efforts with the rifle and grew more agitated. "What the hell are you going to do with that? You don't have any bullets. You'll get all of us killed, you stupid bitch."

Sasha barely acknowledged him. "Yes, Gene, I'm going to be doing some killing."

Gene wouldn't be placated. "You think that's Harry come to rescue you on his white horse?"

She tried one last time. "You could make yourself useful and grab some of those mags. I think I can hold the kidnappers off from behind that pile of rocks."

"Nice. And what's your little airplane boy going to be doing from up there while you're singing your swan song, hiding behind a ridge like a coward?"

"Harry and Mike will be expecting me to help them any way I can. That's how we work," she said.

"Screw you and that loser. He can have you."

Sasha finally knew what the man was made of. He left her

with no doubt. Her eyes bored into Gene with a cold, distant look. "It's time you picked a side and stuck with it before that plane gets back, Gene. I don't want you to be on the receiving end of whatever hell Harry and Mike are about to unleash on all of you."

She moved to follow her daughter. She halted mid-stride and turned to look back at Gene a final time. Christa kept walking toward the ridge. She stumbled but determined as she was to help her father, she kept going.

"Don't you dare lift a finger to help those people. I'll shoot you dead where you stand," Sasha called to Gene.

Mike wasn't so busy in the cockpit that he was unconcerned about an errant RPG round aimed at the lumbering DC-3. The weapon had a range of about a thousand meters. The shrapnel from the exploding warhead would do a lot of damage once it caught up. He didn't like the thought of ending up as part of a pile of aluminum before his job was done.

He throttled back and took up an orbiting position at 3,000 feet above ground. The altitude would give him only a small edge over the RPG's range. It wasn't much, but it might be enough.

"How we doing, Bill?"

Wind noise and static echoed over the ancient intercom as Bill pressed the transmit button. "Bad news. I didn't get eyes on the women. I need a pass to get a look from the other side of the ridge."

"Dammit. If they get an RPG round off we'll be in trouble."

"I'm sorry, boss. We have to do it. I couldn't see them."

That wasn't good. Mike counted on the first pass to do the job. Now the kidnappers would be on full alert. He wanted to be overhead and in position for Bill to walk the guns through the crowd. The DC-3 lumbering along at low-level would be no match for a well-placed RPG round if it found its mark.

Mike eased the nose down while lining up for his second pass. He flew parallel to the ridge. He wanted the cover of the low hill if someone tried to stuff an RPG up his ass. Bill interrupted his worry with the transmit button. Wind whistled in the headphones.

"There they are. I have them in sight. The woman and the little girl are moving toward the rise. They'll be clear of the action in a couple. Well I'll be damned."

"I'm single-pilot up here and kind of busy right now. What is it?"

"I don't want to jump to conclusions, but it looks like that woman has an AK. Maybe even two."

"You're permitted to make the jump, Bill. That woman would be Harry's ex, Sasha. The little girl is Harry's daughter."

"All right. Got it," Bill reassured Mike.

"You better believe me when I tell you she knows how to use that AK. Don't ever piss that woman off when she's got her hands on one of those things. If you land any rounds close to her, she's just liable to return fire to show you who the real boss is around these parts."

42

**Present Day
Horn of Africa**

Harry taught Sasha well all those years ago, when they were forced to make a desperate, last-ditch effort to rescue Mike from his kidnappers. She remembered how he kept by her side, giving her confidence, as they retreated down the dock with the badly wounded Mike. Then she made the mistake of staying behind to empty her last magazine into the cabin cruiser. That was the move that almost got her killed.

Sasha climbed behind her daughter, allowing the little girl to set the pace. Waited when she stumbled. Encouraged her to keep going. When Christa stopped to look back, she smiled at her. "You're doing good. You're beating me to the top. Your dad would be so proud. We're almost there. Uncle Mike will be back any minute. Keep going."

Christa struggled and stopped to rest and struggled over more rough ground before reaching the ridge-top. When Sasha caught up to her daughter, she too was winded.

"Crouch down, honey. You don't want to let anyone see you."

"I'm sorry, mommy." Christa looked like she was about to cry.

"It's all right, dear. It's all right," her mom reassured her. She hugged Christa and smiled down at her. "You did a good job. I'm proud of you. Now let's see if we can go just a bit farther."

She led Christa past the ridge top and then together they sat. She gripped the familiar AK, needing to renew her acquaintance. It was as heavy as she remembered, maybe even heavier. She remembered Harry's instructions in the gravel pit, and she ran through them as best she could. She began with the safety, sliding it full up to lock the action. She released the lock on the magazine and swung it forward and then back. It clicked into place.

"Can I help, mommy?" Christa wanted to know.

Sasha reached to stroke her daughter's face and smiled. "You can help by keeping down. In a minute we'll look for a place for you to hide."

"All right. I'll be careful."

Sasha recalled Harry's description of the AK-47. It's reliable, he had told her. Drop it in water. Drop it in mud. Drop it in sand. Drop it in dirt. Pick it up. Fire. It'll work every time until the magazine is empty.

She rotated the safety full-down to semi-automatic and racked. A round ejected onto the rocks. It clinked with a solid sound. She was good to go. Comfortable as she could be with the weapon, she safetied.

Do or die, she said to herself. It will be the last time the weapon is safetied.

She would use the ridge for cover. She stumbled over the rock-strewn ground making her way across the back side. She had to stay out of sight. She stopped to wait for Christa, never hurrying the girl. Allowing her to make her own way. Satisfied, she directed Christa into a hollow depression behind her position.

"No matter what happens, you have to stay right there. Do you still have the transmitter?"

Christa nodded.

"Good. Don't turn it off. Every once in a while you can press the button." She wanted to give her something to do. Wanted to make it feel like she was taking part.

"All right, Mommy. Is Harry still coming to get us?"

"Yes he is, dear," she reassured her daughter." Uncle Mike is coming, too. It's time to stay down. Wait for me to call you, all right? It won't be safe until I call for you."

"All right, mommy. I'll be right here."

She remained with her daughter, explaining for a second time that she would have to remain where she was until she called her name. Christa nodded solemnly and settled in the depression. Sasha began placing small rocks all around the edge, hoping they would keep her daughter out of sight and safe from whatever was about to be unleashed.

"I have to go now, honey. I won't be far away. There'll be lots of loud noise. Try not to worry. It's mommy taking care of you, okay?" She hugged and kissed her little girl. It would have to do. If things went bad, she knew neither of them would make it out.

Satisfied her daughter was as safe as she could make her, Sasha moved to stretch out prone on the ridge-top's uneven ground. She wanted the lower profile. It would keep her location concealed for as long as was practical.

It wasn't to be. She stretched prone and discovered the jungle magazine hanging off the bottom of the AK forced her into an uncomfortable position. It kept her profile too high, and would reveal her position to the pirates. She cursed her stupidity and shook her head and suddenly realized she wouldn't have known if she hadn't tried. She was no soldier of fortune, unlike her Harry and Mike.

Sasha eased back from the top of the ridge. She put her right knee down. She decided her old crouch position perfected on the dock in Santa Agueda would serve her well here, too. She recalled how Harry had shown her how to support the weight of the AK by placing her left elbow on her knee. It would allow her to concentrate on accuracy with the iron sights.

She called out to her daughter. "Are you all right, dear? I'm right here with you."

"I'm okay, Mommy. I pressed the button again just like you said."

"Good girl. Now it's time for you to be quiet. It's going to get really noisy and I'm going to be very busy. Remember what I told you about coming out from hiding."

"I remember. I have to wait for you to call me."

She took time for one last look in Christa's direction. The girl was safely out of sight. She nodded and turned her attention to the situation in the valley beneath her. Tears streamed down her face. She swiped them away and began concentrating on what she would have to do.

She placed Christa's stolen magazines on the ground and arranged them by her right knee. She knew she'd fumble the first magazine when it came time to change out. There'd be no flinging the empty AK into any water this time. She'd hang on to this one for dear life—and the life of her Christa. Harry's Christa.

She peeked over the ridge, searching for Gene. He chose not to climb with them. It was just as well. He would have ended up a hindrance. She hoped he had been smart enough to get out of her line of fire. It wouldn't go well for him if he stayed with the kidnappers. She didn't know what the airplane had in store. If Mike was doing the flying and if Harry was on the ground, anything was possible.

If, if.

It was strange how the memories of that day on the dock so many years ago returned, flooding her mind. She silently thanked Harry one last time for getting her ass out of Mexico. She was truly sorry she had forced him to come for her again. It was looking like it was turning out to be his permanent job.

She put it out of her mind. There were things more pressing that needed doing.

Harry shook Ali's hand before leaving Barbara with instructions to stay with the technical and the old man, no matter what. He kissed her on the cheek. "That's for old times. At least you're not naked."

Barbara grabbed him and wrapped her arms around his neck for a last, desperate hug. "If you don't bring them back, I'll kill you myself."

"Thanks for that vote of confidence, woman."

Barbara's face froze in a half-hearted grin, and Harry knew

then how concerned she really was. "You know what I mean, and we both know it."

"Yeah yeah. Next thing I know you'll be grabbing my ass again."

Harry shouldered the AK and a bag of magazines. Without looking back, he began working his way toward the back side of a ridge. The elevation would allow him a clear view of the hollow and the stranded vehicles trapped in it.

In the heat of the moment, he hoped Mike and Bill would remember that part of the briefing. If they forgot and began tearing up the ground around him, it would be lights out.

His plan was to draw Sasha and Christa away from the action. If he couldn't do that, he would have to get down and dirty over flat, open ground. He would need to be within range of the Land Rover and the technicals.

Damn, but Sasha would end up being the death of him yet.

It took longer than he wanted to make his way across the rough, rocky, boulder-strewn ground. Mike and Bill had already made their low pass to get the lay of the land. He hoped they hadn't missed him on their recon. It would be bad news if they mistook him for one of the pirates. The twin .50 machine guns would make mincemeat out of anyone and anything that got in the way once they found their mark. He didn't want to be anywhere close to the receiving end.

He continued the slow trek. He zig-zagged his way around boulders on the way to the back side of the ridge. He walked another 500 yards and angled toward the top. It was slow going uphill over the rocky ground, especially on the up-slope. It forced him to tread carefully. The one thing he didn't want to do was give away his position. Rocks crashing down a hill would do that.

If any of the kidnappers panicked and made their way to the high ground, it would give them a height advantage. They would be able to see the DC-3 approaching over the horizon from any direction. An RPG set loose would make Mike in the lumbering DC-3 very unhappy.

Mike wrestled the DC-3 into a pylon orbit and held the ancient gun platform, port wing low, steady over the stalled vehicles. Sweat poured down his face. His right hand kept busy on the twin throttles, working them to keep the engines in sync. His left worked the yoke, and after a couple of circuits, he had the rhythm. A disembodied voice called out over intercom static and wind noise.

"I've got eyes on the woman and the girl," Bill reassured him.

"Roger that." He looked out the port windscreen to the stalled trucks. They would make the perfect stationary target for Bill and the twin .50s. Suddenly the DC-3's airframe shuddered and began vibrating all the way to the cockpit. Wide-eyed, he shifted his gaze to the gauges. Everything was in the green, and then he realized what it was. Bill was busy in the back as he was in the front.

Two more shudders shook the plane. Bill had to be setting up to get the range one more time. He waited for a lull in the fire before contacting his gunner on the intercom. "I have eyes on a man working the back side of the ridge the women are on. It looks like it could be Harry."

"You sure?"

Mike wasn't one hundred percent certain. He worked the DC-3 out of the tight oval and away from the trucks. He advised Bill to keep an eye out. He dropped flaps and gear to force the DC-3 into a low and slow flyby.

"I'll go past on your side. That will give you a good look. It's on you, Bill. I'll be busy flying this old girl low and slow."

The plan they had worked out was simple. They would disable the vehicles first. That would tie up the pirates and keep them from separating. Once the trucks were done, they could go to work on the men. Now, with the lone man, he had to shut down the aerial operation and chase him down, all while hoping Bill would be able to recognize Harry. If it was Harry.

The intercom crackled and interrupted his train of thought. "The man's waving. Holding a rifle over his head. He's waving some kind of circle."

"Affirmative. It's Harry. We're returning to the valley to get the job done."

Mike raised the gear and flaps and waggled the 3's wings before wrangling the plane back to the valley. He settled the plane in over the target one more time and felt the DC-3 shudder. He took his eyes off the horizon to observe out the window as a technical disintegrated beneath him. Destroying the trucks would give both Harry and Ali's men the edge they needed to reach the kidnappers in the event the DC-3 clapped out or the twin .50s jammed.

The plane shuddered three more times in quick succession. With the pass completed, there was nothing recognizable but for piles of smoking vehicle scrap in the wake of the deadly machine guns.

Mike maintained a steady orbit over the smoking destruction. He came within range a second time. Death from above followed by shiny brass rained down on the kidnappers as Bill's pass with the guns found their mark again and again. Men scrambled, struggling to get out of the way of the advancing .50-caliber guns. It was impossible. Puffs of sand traced their footsteps as lead chased them down.

Bill rained concentrated fire down on the remaining kidnappers. Shelter from the lead pouring down was impossible to find in the open valley. Bill walked the .50s in a relentless march toward each man, as one after the other, they collapsed. The puffs of sand and dirt made it almost too easy as he tracked them with the twin barrels, dispatching them straight to hell.

Mike brought the shuddering DC-3 in closer. The concentration required for the low-altitude flying didn't allow him to remain aware of the situation on the ground. He was more concerned about the ideal range it would put him in for an errant RPG.

Sasha witnessed the air attack in slow motion from behind the safety of the ridge. The huge airplane lumbered onto the scene and began flying what looked like a circle. A man in the doorway was aiming something out. The plane was too far and too high to know if it was Mike.

By the time she figured it out, the first target had been wiped out before her eyes. Puffs of sand were on their way to the second. Her eyes widened. Her heart thumped. Her breathing halted. A kidnapper climbed onto a truck. An RPG hung from his hand. On the truck bed, he began raising it to shoulder height.

She had to stop him. Mike and the plane would be destroyed if he got a round off. She rotated the AK's safety full down to its semi-automatic position and took careful aim from behind the rock pile. She lined up the iron sights on the RPG's owner and slowly squeezed off a single round.

Nothing. She missed. She silently let off a string of curses and took fresh aim. She held her breath and began squeezing the trigger. The man dropped the RPG. It landed at his feet.

What the hell? Had she missed by that much?

Unsure, she looked over the AK's sights. What should she do? The man was falling. He curled up in the back of the truck, clutching his stomach. His body twitched.

It took her a minute to realize there was something else going on from her ridge position. Or somewhere. She looked around. There was no one. She returned her attention to the men scattering on the ground.

She looked up and witnessed Mike's plane break off from its attack. It got lower. She thought she saw the gear come down before it flew parallel to her ridge. The wings waggled as they flew over her.

Why were they doing that? Why weren't they concentrating on the vehicles in the valley? She cursed the plane and whoever was doing the flying for halting the attack before turning her attention back to the ground.

She picked out another man crouched behind the twisted metal of what was left of a truck. She rotated the safety up one notch. She'd give her kidnappers spray and pray for her grand finale.

And then, just before she pulled the trigger a second time, the man dropped onto the sand. He twitched and another puff of smoke forced him to lie still.

This time, she heard the gunshots before the rat-tat-tat assault from the DC-3 reached her ears. Whoever it was, he had to be somewhere on the ridge she was on. There wasn't another one. She checked again, but still there was no one. The shooter was well concealed. Better than she was, for sure.

Sand and rocks kicked up in front of her. She was in someone's sights. Startled, she screamed and pulled back her position. She unleashed the AK in full automatic and unloaded her magazine before withdrawing farther. Her location had been discovered. She'd have to change her position. But where? Where would she go?

She looked around. The ridge ran away from her in both directions. There was no height advantage in one direction or the other. The line was exactly the same.

Confused. Scared. Worried. She hesitated. Immediately, she knew she would not desert Christa. She would never desert her daughter. Harry's daughter. She would stand her ground. She flipped the mag flawlessly and ran for Christa's shelter.

It would be all or nothing.

43

Overhead, **Bill struggled** and fought against the DC-3's slipstream. It caught at the muzzles and attempted to wrest the twin .50s from his grip. The barrels shook and shimmied in the powerful wind whipping past the open door. Experimenting with short bursts, he discovered the best firing position. He would aim down and to the rear of the plane.

The bungee cords and the ropes Sammy rigged did their job and kept the twin muzzles away from the tailplane assembly. He found he could lean back against the cargo door's frame. It provided support and accuracy as he became more familiar with the jury-rigged gun mount hanging out the door.

He had eyes on Sasha on their second flyby. Knowing her position, he could fire at will into the valley. He pounded away with the .50s, concentrating his fire at the static targets on the ground. He proved relentless in his pursuit with the twin muzzles. There was no shortage of targets. Survivors didn't last long as Mike kept the makeshift gunship circling overhead.

Mike glanced out the cockpit's port window. The plane was in an ideal position. He spotted what had to be Sasha on the ridge. She was crouched and had a rifle shouldered. He'd only heard about her abilities from Harry when the duo came to his rescue on the Baja. As far as he knew, she had never mentioned it to anyone.

It was looking good, but now he had to concentrate on flying the plane full time. Bill had rendered the trucks inoperable. There'd be no escape. He had plenty of help from Sasha. From what he could tell, every time one of the kidnappers stood up in an attempt to escape from the lead pouring out the cargo door, she kept the man pinned.

Bill exhausted the ammunition in the .50s and got busy reloading fresh belts. He flipped the intercom button from monitor to transmit and hailed Mike. "It looks like that woman put down at least three. I don't know how many I took out. There might be a couple left. There's a crazy white guy standing out in the middle of it all. He's running around in circles and waving his arms at us."

"Any sign of our technicals?" Mike asked. "They can't be far away."

"There was a dust cloud when we did our recon, but I don't see it now."

"Can you see Harry making his way from the technicals onto any of the elevations?" Mike asked.

"I've been too busy to notice."

"I'm going to descend for another run," Mike informed him. "Send the rest of them to hell."

Bill managed a couple of dozen rounds before his frantic voice sounded over the intercom, interrupting Mike's concentration. "The guns are jammed. Move off. The guns are jammed."

Mike knew not to argue. With no hot lead pouring out of the DC-3 to occupy the pirates, it was a perfect opportunity for an errant RPG to find its mark. He asked anyway. "Both of them?" Mike didn't wait for Bill's answer. He pushed the nose down and made for the cover of a hill to provide an element of protection. Bill screamed into the intercom.

"There's another technical on the back side of the hill. It's making its way toward the women."

"Let me know when you get the guns working."

"Roger that."

Helpless in the front seat of the DC-3, Mike was left to pilot the useless plane until Bill could get the jammed machine guns operational.

Sasha adjusted her position on the ridge and moved back. She needed to stay invisible. She thought her position unassailable as long as she had ammunition for the AK. She had a clear view of the sloping ground in front. She would concentrate on not letting her kidnappers escape.

She set the AK in single fire mode. It allowed her to put round after round in the direction of the men. More often than not, she missed. Ricochets off the damaged vehicles kept the men guessing.

The circling DC-3 moved off into the distance. The hell raining down from above halted. Rocks rolled down the hill behind her. It had to be Gene, coming to his senses and realizing he had to get out of the way.

Whatever or whoever it was, the lower ridge behind kept them out of sight. She put the sound into the back of her mind and concentrated on what was happening in front of her.

She heard the sound again. More rocks. She looked behind. A head wrapped in an Arab burnoose topped the crest of the hill. She wheeled around, leading with the AK. The man was on top of the low rise behind her. He was almost on the hollow where Christa lay concealed. He was steps away. Two more and he'd be on her. She was certain Christa would scream if he surprised her.

"Stop. Simama! I'll kill you where you stand."

The man halted in his tracks. He released his weapon. It clattered to the ground. He surrendered with arms out to show empty hands. "Damn you, woman. You have a one-track mind once you set yourself to doing something."

"Harry!" she screamed.

"Your one and only," he reassured her.

"Pick up that damned thing and give me a hand," she told him. "I'm almost out."

"Here, try one of mine." He handed her a fresh magazine.

"Dammit, who taped this thing?" she wanted to know.

"That would be me, my darling wife."

Sasha grinned and released her magazine before slamming home the fresh mag. "In that case, it'll do just fine."

The look on Harry's face shifted to one of concern. "Where's Christa?"

"She dug a little foxhole behind me. You almost tripped over her."

He crouched beside his ex-wife and shouldered his AK. "Come on, woman. We're not done yet. We need to send what's left of them to hell and then—"

A little girl's voice interrupted Harry. "Do you need more mags, mommy? I have more."

Sasha looked at Harry and smiled. "Not now, honey. I have everything I need. You stay there until I call you, okay?"

Harry shook his head. "I swear. If one wasn't enough, now there's two of you."

"If I tell her you're here she might break cover."

Ali's crew arrived in a flurry of dust and sand to discover they were late to the party. There was nothing for them to do. According to plan, the airborne assault had eliminated the kidnappers' means of transport. Once that was accomplished, Bill went to work on the survivors. Mike made sure he didn't leave until the job was done.

Between the fire from hell and Harry and Sasha's efforts from behind the ridge, there was nothing for Ali's crew to do but collect the armament.

Sasha called to her daughter. "Christa, honey. Stay here, okay? Daddy and I are going to go down. We want to be sure it's safe for you. I'll be right back."

Harry regarded his wife through eyes that knew she seldom obeyed him. If ever there was a time, this was it. "Stay with our daughter. I'll send for you when it's time. You are not to come down until I do. Understood?"

"Yes, dear."

"Never mind the *yes, dear*. This time, do as you're told," he insisted.

The look on Harry's face told her not to argue. She didn't.

"Do you have ammo?" he asked.

"Yes I do," she said. "Christa has more magazines."

"Good girl, that daughter of ours. You raised her well."

Before Sasha could respond, Harry moved off to descend the ridge toward the smoking piles of scrap courtesy of Mike and the DC-3. Gunshots rang out. Ali and his crew were busy finishing off the survivors. He arrived at the bottom to meet up with Barbara. "Are there any left?"

She turned to him. "None to worry about, Harry. Ali is finishing off the wounded." Barbara cast a glance in Gene's direction. He was crouched behind a pile of rocks. "That one wet his pants but he'll be okay once he gets back to his penthouse. The sooner the better, as far as I'm concerned."

"Would you go and collect Sasha and our daughter? I left them up on the hill with instructions not to move until I sent for them."

"And she listened? I can't believe it."

"For once in her life she realized I know what I'm doing."

Barbara shouldered a loaded RPG and cast an evil grin at Harry. "Just in case."

"You go, girl."

Barbara began her climb to the top of the rise carrying the RPG and its solitary round. She allowed herself to get closer before announcing her arrival. "Sasha? Where's Christa?"

Sasha stuck her head over the edge of the rise. "Barbara. You're here too."

"You're damned right I'm here. Where's your daughter?"

"Don't worry," she reassured Barbara. "Christa is where you like to be, eating dirt and dodging ricochets. She's behind me. I helped her dig a little foxhole and told her to stay in it until I called for her. Sasha checked her AK, dropped the empty mag and inserted her last magazine. "I'm good to go. Let's get her."

Barbara adjusted the weight of the loaded RPG over her shoulder. Sasha regarded her friend with fresh interest. "Did

Harry arm you?"

Barbara grinned. "You're damned right he did. I even made him show me how to use it."

"I didn't think you were carrying it for effect."

"Yeah. No. I blew up a rock pile, but I was happy doing it." She grinned back at Sasha.

"We all have to start somewhere. Christa is going to be so excited to see you. Even I didn't think you'd be showing up."

"What are friends for, girl?"

They laughed and in the brief moment of levity did a pinkie shake before proceeding to Christa's hiding spot. As they neared the crest, Sasha held up a hand to halt their climb. "Do you hear it? It sounds like a truck. What's it doing back here?"

The duo advanced the rest of the way along the ridge top in a crouch. Sasha pointed. "Christa is there. Can you see the little rock garden she made?"

"I see it. What about that truck?"

A technical whined in low gear. It was making its way slowly up the back side of the hill toward the women. It halted, and the driver got out, as though listening. Satisfied, he got back in and the truck carried on.

"Do you think he's one of ours?"

Barbara considered before answering. "No. All the vehicles in our convoy are in the valley."

"Then it has to belong to the pirates. Perhaps his plan was to meet up and help them get to the coast."

Barbara set the RPG on the ground. She flipped her serape aside and checked the shotty's action. It was loaded. She closed it and replaced it beneath the serape.

"Is that the one from Mexico? You never wear it back home."

"Yes it is." Barbara retrieved the RPG and finished arming it. "Don't stand behind me. This will give you a sunburn, believe me."

Sasha stepped to the side. Barbara moved away, making certain that Christa's hiding spot wasn't near the path the rocket would take on its journey.

"You're good, girl. Christa is right in front of me."

Sasha went down on a knee and whispered to her daughter. "Barbara is here with us. We're both going to take care of you, okay? There's going to be a loud noise. Stay where you are until we come for you."

"All right, mommy. Is daddy here?"

"Yes he is, darling. That was his voice you heard earlier."

"I thought so. I wanted to come out but you told me not to. Did Uncle Mike come with him?"

"Yes, sweetheart. Uncle Mike is here. They're all here to make us safe and take us home."

In that instant, Barbara shouldered the rocket launcher. She aimed, as Harry showed her. The truck halted and the man got out again. The situation was perfect. She pulled the trigger. In a split second the rocket found its target. The man ducked and covered as the truck disintegrated beside him.

He stood up beside the smoking ruins and looked toward the hilltop. The last thing he saw were the two women. Sasha unloaded the AK on his position. Puffs of sand and rock danced toward him as she found the range. He collapsed and lay still.

Barbara regarded her friend. "I suppose we'd better go down there and check to see if he's done for dinner. We wouldn't want him playing possum on us, would we?"

"There's no possum in this sand trap. And you're right. Let's go."

She called to Christa.

"Stay here, darling. Mommy and Barbara have to check on something."

Sasha racked. She forgot the magazine was empty. She went to Christa in her little foxhole and retrieved a magazine. She handed off the AK to Barbara. "Trade you for Mike's shotgun, girl."

"I'll going to stay with Christa for you, mommy dearest. You go do your thing," Barbara told her.

Sasha made haste on her way down the hill toward the burning technical.

Harry topped the ridge as the shotgun's boom echoed up the side of the hill. "I heard the explosion. You got to fire the RPG. Are you happy now?"

"Yeah. No. I got to fire it. I think I killed another one. Sasha went down to check and finish the job."

Harry called to his daughter. "Christa, you can come out now."

"Daddy!" Small rocks scattered as the little girl climbed out from her hiding place and ran to her father. He took her in his arms and twirled her around. "We'll wait here for mommy, okay? She won't be long."

"I made a foxhole for a hidey place. Mommy helped me. Come and see." She took Harry's hand and led him to her hidey place surrounded by the rocks she had gathered.

"You sure did, sweetheart. You did a very good job."

Harry and Barbara and Christa squatted on the rocks by Christa's foxhole on the crest of the hill. They waited for Sasha to make the climb up the hill. Huffing and puffing, she finally arrived. "Are you two working hard or hardly working?"

Sasha bent to pick up the discarded AK. "Do you have a spare mag?" she asked Harry. "I only have the one."

Harry handed over a magazine. She tucked it into her shoulder bag and slung the rifle over her shoulder. She bent to pick up her daughter. Christa's arms surrounded her. "Let's go, honey. I've done enough for one day."

"I have more mags if you need them, daddy," Christa insisted on telling her father.

"Of course you do, sweetheart. You hang on to them for now, okay?"

The DC-3 roared overhead. Bill flung lead into the corpse of the smoking technical the women had knocked out. Satisfied, Mike did another flyby.

"Bill's guns must have jammed," Harry said. "That has to be why he missed out on the truck. You about shot up everything in sight."

"I had a good teacher," she said. "I'm just a little rusty after all these years." Sasha slung the AK in front of her. It was the same way she carried it on the Baja.

"Woman, there you go again with another AK across your chest."

"It's not the same chest I had on the Baja. And we don't have a Jeep to celebrate."

"It might not be the same, but it's still the best," Harry insisted.

Sasha knew now it was Harry who did the bulk of the cleaning up. She was only the window dressing for his full-on assault from the hilltop. He never said a word to Barbara about his efforts from behind the ridge.

"Thank you for saving my ass one more time, Harry. Why didn't you tell Barbara?" she wanted to know.

"You're welcome. And that's your story to tell. I just happened to be here."

Overhead, Mike did a gear-down low-and-slow, off to the side to allow Bill to cover them with the .50s. The DC-3's wings waggled for the last time. Mike threw it into a bank and headed west to the landing strip.

"We'll meet up with Mike and the crew later. Right now, Ali wants to meet you," he told his wife.

"Who's Ali again?" In the heat of battle, she forgot about Harry's friend from the time he had spent in this part of the Horn.

"He's an old friend. He says he wants to meet the woman that can drag both Mike and me back into action. If I know him, he's going to want to make you his fourth wife."

They made their way down into the valley and halted by the old man's technical. Ali, gray-haired and still handsome in the fashion of a desert dweller, slowly made his way toward Sasha.

"So this is the woman. I am honored. And this is your daughter? This is your Christa?" The old man pronounced the girl's name in the local fashion as one not familiar with it. "This woman gave you this gift? For shame, Harry. Why is she here in my part of the desert and not back in your house taking care of you?"

Sasha smiled at Ali. He had won her over. Even Christa took the old man's hand. She glanced briefly in Harry's direction. His face was beet-red.

"I'm wondering about that myself."

"Perhaps Sasha would rather have a Somali headman to take care of instead," Ali insisted.

Sasha smiled at the old man. "How many?"

"You will be number five, but you will be my favorite."

Harry moved to break up the love affair before Sasha might consider taking the old man up on his offer. "All right, you two. You don't have enough camels to trade, Ali. Even if she wanted to go with you."

Ali laughed. "You are right, my friend. Then let us get back to the landing strip. Come, Christa. You will ride with me."

"Come on, dear," Sasha said. "We're going to go with this nice man who helped rescue us."

"Mommy, he said my name different."

"That's all right, dear. That's how they say your name in this part of the world."

Gene chose that moment to come out from behind a pile of rocks. A huge and growing wet spot anointed his legs. He recognized Harry immediately.

"I knew it. You stupid bastard. You could have gotten us all killed. How am I going to get out of here now? My company will be wondering where I am. I need to get to a phone."

Sasha stared coldly at the man. "These are the only people looking out for anyone, you dumb son of a bitch. Harry, look after Christa for a minute. There's something I need to do."

She unslung the AK and raised the butt. She put her weight behind it a smashed it into her former suitor's face. There was no time for him to be surprised. Cold-cocked, he dropped to the sand like a stone and stayed there, unmoving. "Consider us broken up."

She turned to Harry and Ali. Both men regarded her in a new light. "That ought to hold him for a while. Dammit but that man is annoying. Why did I have to come halfway around the world to find that out?"

Sasha checked the AK's action. She took another magazine from Harry before climbing into the Jeep with Ali, Christa and Barbara. She kept the AK across her lap, making sure to aim the muzzle out the door.

44

Out of the past
Kenya

Mike Williams hung up the Flying Club's phone. A wide grin on his face told the story. He arranged for a wire transfer and two one-way tickets to ride on a Hawker flying to Benghazi. Next stop, the hospital and Harry. Harry would be thrilled when he heard the news.

Mike confronted the door to Harry's room. He put his ear against the closed door and gave a quick listen. The muffled voices made little sense. He walked in without knocking and cleared his throat. It took three tries until the occupants barely noticed.

A raven-haired woman in a white uniform fussed over Harry. She was no slouch in the looks department. His throat-clearing earned him a cross look from Harry and a quick once-over and a frown from the nurse. "Yes? Who are you looking for? Can I help you, sir?"

He ignored them both and refused to take the hint. The nurse smiled down at Harry in his sick-bed. "I'll be back later to check on you, Harry."

She turned away in a huff and did a quick-step march out of the room.

"What's the diagnosis?" Mike wanted to know.

Harry grinned like a baboon discovering a fresh pile of rocks. "Until you showed up, I'd say it was pretty good. After your interruption, I'm not so certain."

"No, you jackass. What's the medical diagnosis?"

"Oh, that," Harry said. "The doc says I can leave in a day. When I checked with my personal nurse for a second opinion, she said I could stay at her place until I get my sea legs."

"That's nice, but neither of us is in the navy. I'll be in Benghazi, waiting for you to tire of your personal nurse." Mike reached into a pocket and withdrew the tickets and the cash. He waved them in front of Harry.

"Benghazi? When do we leave?" Harry wanted to know.

"I'm almost there as we speak. As for you, when you're ready. I figure it'll take you a week, maybe less, to make good your escape."

"Nurse won't be bringing back my clean clothes until her shift starts tomorrow."

Mike emptied his rucksack on the bed.

"No worries. I have everything you need right here." Mike raised a bag and pulled out a shirt and a pair of pants.

Harry eyed the pile of wrinkled clothes. "Who does your ironing?"

"Well, obviously not your nurse, that's for sure."

Mike waited in the hall for Harry to dress. He contemplated how he would tell the man what went down during the pursuit from the mine to the Kenya border crossing. Harry's understanding of what happened was sure to be clouded by his concussion.

"What's the last thing you remember, Harry?" Mike called thorough the door.

"I was watching Eloria revive Irit. I draw a blank on anything after that."

"It's not even that good."

Harry joined him in the hall. "I figured as much when they didn't show up with you."

"Eloria wasn't able to revive her. Irit died in the Land Rover.

I'm sorry, Harry."

It took Harry a moment before he could reply. "And Eloria? Where is she? What happened to her?"

The pained expression on Mike's face told the story all by itself.

"If you're not up to telling me about it—"

Mike hesitated before continuing, unsure of where to begin. Finally, he relented. "Eloria is the reason we're sitting here talking about it. We owe her everything. When she couldn't revive Irit, she collected both Galils. She put her back against the seat and started firing with a vengeance."

Mike paused, remembering. "During a break to reload, she handed me her shotgun and told me to keep it until she got back. *Back from where*, I asked. By the time I got the words out, she was already out of the Land Rover and on the ground."

"Damn," was all Harry could say.

"Yeah. I checked the mirror in time to see her roll and then stand in the middle of the road. She popped a couple smokes and that was the end of it. My only course was straight ahead. Next thing I know, a single Jeep is plowing through the smoke. By then, I was crashing through the border."

"So she got one of the Jeeps. How the hell did they get her so quick?" Harry wanted to know.

"If she was alive, neither of those Jeeps would have come through that smoke," Mike said.

"You're right," Harry said. "Damn. Those two were something else, weren't they?"

"When they learned you were missing at that strip, they didn't hesitate. Between the two of them, they had more uhodori—and bigger balls, too—than all the mercs sitting on their asses in camp. Without them, you'd still be sitting on that strip. Your bones would be stripped clean," Mike assured him.

"Thanks to those two, we're alive and safe in Nairobi. We definitely owe them everything," Harry said.

"There's something else, Harry."

"There always is."

"There were two passports taped to the shotgun. Canadian passports."

"Don't tell me—"

"That's right. Forged or not, I don't know. It turns out they were sisters."

"Sisters? Well, I can believe that. But Canadian? With those thick accents? I don't think so. What did you do with the passports?" Harry asked.

"I still have them. I was going to go to the Canadian embassy tomorrow."

"I don't think so. Give them to me. We'll stop at the other embassy first and drop them off," Harry told him.

"Then let's get it done," Mike said.

"You're right. We've got people to pay back for the advance and the Benghazi tickets. Damn, Mike. Libya?" Harry wanted to know.

"I got us two one-way tickets. You can stay here, broke and listening to the stories in the Flying Club bar that you've heard a hundred times. Plus you have your personal nurse to do your laundry and cook your meals." Mike could almost see Harry's wheels turning. "Your personal nurse would be happy to have you. Does she live alone?"

It was true. "Come to think of it, I never asked her if she lived alone."

"Or you could hole up in a dusty, wind-swept, isolated tent camp in the middle of a desert and get sand-blasted by a ghibli while you earn your pay."

"I've been thinking about that. Can I bring my personal nurse?" he asked.

"Not unless I get one, too. Look, we owe people for the tickets and the advance. Do you want time to say goodbye to the woman?"

"No. You got us a pretty good offer," Harry told him. "But we could turn it into something else."

"What do you have in mind?" Mike wanted to know.

"We could cash in those tickets and make a stop in Spain while we're on our way to Mexico," Harry said. "Have you ever been to Mexico?"

"Well, now that you ask—"

45

Under Mike's capable hands, the DC-3 began its low and slow approach to a landing at the desert strip. It would be the last time. Mike taxied and turned the plane as Harry had done. If need be, it could be started and begin its takeoff run from the same spot.

He hurried to climb on a wing, searching for the convoy making its way to the strip. The dust cloud appeared to be about a mile away. He jumped down and Sammy greeted him. The man was disappointed he hadn't been able to take part in the air show, but he knew if anything went mechanical with the plane, he'd be needed at the strip.

Sammy and Bill began the tedious work of pulling the .50s and the mount. When Harry and the convoy arrived, chased by a cloud of dust, they were still not finished. Mike waited, impatient in the wing's shade.

"It's about time you're back. I was worrying when the gunfire halted. I figured either Sasha was out of ammo or everyone was dead."

"It was a little of both," Harry admitted. "We're all fine. Ali offered to make Sasha wife number five. She might still be thinking about accepting."

"The guys are almost done pulling the .50s. When they're finished, we're good to go," Mike said.

"Yeah. About that." Harry regarded Sammy.

"Now what?" Mike appeared wary of what might be coming.

"I had to give my word to get my hands on that DC-3. Part of it was leaving the .50s in it when we finished."

"Ali won't be happy he's not getting his hands on those guns," Mike said.

"Ali will have to do without. I don't know what the plan is for the 3. I didn't ask. All I know is, they wanted it left as is when I finished with it."

"Then that's what we'll do. You're going to have to be the one to tell Ali, Harry."

"It's as good as done. I told him about it after our camp got shot up. He's good with it," he told Mike.

"In that case, let's get this flying circus airborne."

A troubled Gene remained incapable of comprehending what had happened. That, and the rifle butt to the head convinced Sasha that she'd never set him straight. She was finished with the man.

"How soon are we getting out of here?" Gene asked. Sasha frowned. Gene ignored her, to his peril.

"I already told you, Gene. If you don't stop your bitching, I'm going to open up on you with this AK. Are you deaf, dumb, blind, and stupid, too?"

Sammy looked at Gene and shook his head at the man's stupidity. "If I were you, boyo, I'd listen to what that woman says. She means business."

Sammy and Bill reversed their work on the .50s and completed the reinstall. They busied themselves with rearranging the cabin to make room for the new passengers. The atmosphere on board the plane was charged with the excitement of the day's action. Getting out was high on everyone's agenda.

Mike and Barbara approached Ali one last time. "Ali, my wife has something for you."

"Yes? What is it?"

Barbara pulled the shotgun off her shoulder and presented

it. "I have no more need for this."

"Thank you. I am honored by your thoughtfulness. And thank you, my old friends, for your other gifts. If the need should arise in these difficult times, I will put them to good use defending my village."

"You're welcome, Ali. Harry and I are grateful for your help. We couldn't have done this without you. We will always remember you."

Harry called from the cockpit. "All aboard. It feels like the wind is changing direction. It's time to launch before we get shut down by a sandstorm. So long, Ali. May you live long and have many wives."

Harry allowed Mike to taxi the DC-3 to the front of the deserted hangar in JIB. The modern jet he parked beside presented quite a contrast. It had remained untouched in their absence. Harry hadn't bothered to tell Mike he had arranged for a crew to guard it until their return. "There should be a flight crew waiting to fly this thing away. Leave it running and let them take it while we load the jet," he told him.

"Are you ever going to tell me about it?" Mike wanted to know.

"Some day, maybe."

"It's going to come back to bite us both in the ass, isn't it?" Mike asked.

"It's not for you to worry about. I signed up all by my lonesome," Harry insisted.

"You say that now, but we both know you don't mean it."

"Don't forget to unload Gene and point him toward the terminal building," Harry reminded Mike.

"Yeah. No. About that. He's a good customer. They pay their bills on time. I think we'll be taking him as far as Naples, at least."

Harry looked at his friend. "Are you certain the company wants him back?"

"Well, his father might. I'm not sure about anyone else. In any case, he's coming with us."

Mike received clearance to position the jet for takeoff. In back, all on board were eager to begin the long flight home.

"Christa, Barbara and Harry want to talk to you." The little girl looked up at her mother.

"Am I in trouble?" she wanted to know.

"I don't think so. Let's find out." Sasha took her daughter's hand and walked with her to where Barbara was sitting.

"Christa, honey, you did a good job when you turned on the locator. High five."

Christa beamed, happy to learn that she wasn't in trouble, and doubly happy that she had helped to get everyone out of trouble. She high-fived Barbara. "Mommy helped me with it."

"Yes, sweetheart, but you were the one in charge," Harry said.

"Thank you, Daddy. Thank you, Barbara. I don't think Mommy likes Gene any more. I don't like him either."

"It's okay not to like someone. You just don't say mean things about him to other people," Sasha told her daughter.

Barbara rolled her eyes. "Woman, there's no way I'll be trying that on for size. I've been speaking my mind for too long. Which reminds me—if you ever try something like that again, you're going to have to deal with me. Is that understood?"

Sasha considered crossing her fingers behind her back and then thought better of it. At the last minute, she changed her mind. "Yes, Barbara. Something like this won't happen again. I can promise you that."

Sasha uncrossed her fingers and smiled sweetly at Harry and Barbara. She knew she wasn't fooling anyone.

It was lecture time. Harry already knew Sasha would win at it. She'd been winning with him for too many years. Even so, he had to try. "Do I have to remind you what happened the last time you went on some half-baked shopping trip without me?"

"Is this going to be a test?" she asked. "Yes, I remember. You rescued me."

"You and your daughter could have stayed in Djibouti and

spent the day wandering around the shops and soaking up the atmosphere. It's not such a bad place," Harry said.

"We could have, but then we wouldn't have you here with us now, would we?" She smiled, knowing she had the man.

Harry looked at his ex. All he could do was shake his head. There was no winning with this woman—but that was what drew him to her in the first place. "Do either of you have your players with you?"

"We both do. Why?"

"Dial it up," he told her.

"Dial what up?"

"You know what." Sasha handed Harry her music player. He plugged it into the sound system on board the jet. An old Crazy Town tune, *Butterfly*, started the serenade. "I know you better than you think."

Sasha blushed, but she refused to surrender. "Maybe you do, and maybe you don't."

"Mike says he has a job for me. I'm going to take it. It would mean you'd be seeing me more often," he told her.

"Why don't you ask our daughter what she thinks about that? After everything that happened, you already know how I feel."

An exhausted Christa was fast asleep beside her mother. She had spent most of the day explaining to anyone who would listen that she had been captured by pirates in the desert and rescued by her daddy's team of men.

Barbara reminded her that she, too, had been part of the team. Christa updated her story. It became Barbara's team of men that rescued her and her mother from the pirates.

Which was all right with her father.

It was all right with her mother, too.

M ike checked the autopilot. Satisfied, he moved to the First Officer position, leaving the left seat empty. He paged Harry to join him in the cockpit. Harry didn't blink an eye when he entered. He pulled up the armrest like the captain's seat was meant for him and settled into it. He strapped in and out of habit scanned the gauges.

Mike regarded his old friend. "How does it feel?"

"You're trying to bribe me." Harry pulled the magnetic compass down from the window divider.

"Yes."

"Is that offer of a job still good?" he wanted to know.

"You know it, man."

"Good, because I've got some ideas," Harry began. He turned to look out the window so Mike couldn't see him smiling.

"Hang on. You'll be starting with a co-pilot position on a Twin Otter. If you don't get bumped, you'll make Captain in six months or so."

"You're getting even for San Diego, aren't you? Does that mean you'll be throwing the women to the curb, too?"

"I was thinking a layover on the French Riviera would do those three women a world of good."

Harry changed the subject. "You owe Barbara an explanation."

"I know. I'll tell her the story behind the shotgun before we head home."

"If you don't—"

It was Mike's turn to change the subject. "Would you go back and check to see if those two women brought any weapons on board? French customs will take a dim view and I can't afford to forfeit this airplane."

46

Out of the Past
Eloria

Eloria grew up in the northern seaport of Haifa. She was separated from her sister, Irit, at an early age when she was shipped off to live with her grandmother. It was a move forced by family finances. By the time high school came around, they began hanging out together and become fast friends.

They would walk to school together, meeting in the middle of the street in their working-class neighborhood, forcing what traffic there was to slow down and honk horns to get past them. Later, during school breaks, they'd bus to the beach and hang out. Annoying the boys proved to be a big pastime.

When they turned eighteen, they joined the army and gravitated to the MP Corps, where they went through training together. They ended up getting posted to the Golan. The fights they got in taught them how to back each other up and take care of each other.

When their tour was up, return to civilian life was characterized by boredom. One day Irit noticed an ad for security personnel with an overseas posting. She jumped at the chance. It took little talking to get Eloria to do the same, thus they took a short bus-ride for the interview.

It was a simple process, and given their former experience,

they were offered the jobs. To celebrate, they went to the nearest bar and drank themselves silly in between fights with the other patrons. Eventually, they got thrown out and ended up puking in the alley behind the bar.

The next morning, they showed up at the recruiting office for their travel documents. Foreign passports and identities were given with a minimum of ceremony. Neither of them batted an eye at the forged papers. The next day, they shipped out.

Their first assignment took them to Dar es Salaam in Tanzania. While it turned out to be a cake-walk, it got them accustomed to the security routine of working in a foreign outpost in a large city. Together, they learned to do all over again what they had been trained to do in the military. Even the weapons were familiar. Their rapport translated into an affinity for the work. The pair earned excellent job reviews.

Eventually, their reputation saw them rewarded with ever more tough assignments. They accepted every one without question or complaint. Their most recent had them on a flight to a northern Tanzania town where they were unceremoniously dumped on an airstrip.

A small single-engine plane with engine screaming braked in a cloud of dust and disgorged its passengers. The passengers climbed into a broken-down truck and disappeared. The plane did the same when it taxied to the strip and became airborne. A man shepherding the passengers remained behind.

"I think we should have jumped on that plane," Irit said to her sister.

Eloria only shrugged and gestured to the solitary man remaining behind. "I wonder who that one is?"

The women collected their duffels and walked down a dusty road toward town. They made their way to the only hotel in the sun-baked village. Khat-chewing locals lounging around the entrance greeted them with white-toothed smiles. Following check-in to claim the last remaining rooms, they met with the company man sent to brief them. They were to be flown out to a location deep in the bush the very next day.

The women collected their weapons and headed down to

the bar to discuss their latest adventure. It was to be their last night out before the isolation of the bush.

The bar ended up being a hole in the wall. A dark dingy affair, it smelled mostly of dust and sweat. There was enough light to make out the white faces within. So far, theirs were the only ones. Eloria nudged Irit and the two women observed two men walking in. "Take a look at that."

"Probably Americans," Irit replied confidently. "You can't get away from them these days."

"I don't care," Eloria said. "Fresh meat for us to annoy. If they're looking for white women, they found us." She kicked at two chairs on the dirt-packed floor and they sat down. It was almost too easy. "I'm Eloria. My partner is Irit."

"Pleased to meet you both. I'm Harry. He's Mike."

"You look familiar." Eloria gestured at Mike. "Are you the one that helped unload the plane?"

The look she got said her question made them uncomfortable. All things considered, that was no surprise out here, given what was going on in the bush.

"Mike and I work for a mining company," Harry responded. "Maybe you're with the same outfit?"

"That depends on the name of the mining company," Irit said.

He avoided the question and instead went where the women weren't comfortable going.

"You're Israeli. I can tell by the accents," Harry added.

"No, we're Canadian," Irit insisted.

Mike chose that moment to go for more beer. Harry was left behind, and he called them on it. "Actually, Mike and I are Canadian. And your accents sound like you might be from Montréal. Am I right?"

Shit. Their cover was blown. By actual Canadians. Now what? To change the subject, Eloria pulled a Galil from behind her chair and leaned it against the table. Irit did the same. Perhaps intimidation would work. It had before. "What are you really doing out here?"

"We're a couple of lost Canadians looking for a place to live and women to love," Harry said.

The one called Harry did have a pleasant smile. "Fellow Canadians for sure? That's good with us, right Eloria? Come on, you two. Curfew is coming up. We have somewhere we need to be."

Eloria woke in the dark in the humid room. An arm moved beneath the damp pillow. She rolled and bumped up against an even warmer man. Her hand joined one disappearing beneath the pillow. She almost missed. She swiped and her grip closed on a hand that was attached itself to the barrel of the sawed-off shotgun tucked away beneath the pillow.

"Let it go," she said.

"What?"

"Let go."

Eloria worked her fingers beneath the man's hand. His grip on the barrel was firm, but not so firm that she couldn't press and twist. She extracted the empty hand from beneath the pillow without hurting it.

"Don't do that again if you know what's good for you."

She moved the man's warm hand to her cool breast beneath the thin sheet. In the dark she shifted against the warm, sweaty body lying beside hers. In minutes, she had him convinced and ready to make love again. She lost count of the number of times. Even so, she kept her mind on the shotgun until she lost herself in eager desire for the sweaty body beneath her.

Eventually, need replaced desire for drunken sleep. In her hung over stupor, Eloria didn't hear the man dress and depart in the twilight before dawn.

Eloria looked around in the small room. She was alone. Dim daylight filtered in through a small window. She decided she was still drunk and not yet sober enough to be hung over. She shrugged, reached beneath the pillow, and pulled out the shotgun. Checked the chamber. Snapped it closed. She placed it in her duffel and staggered her way to her sister's room. "Irit.

Wake up. It's time. Let's go." Her words slurred.

"Shit. What time is it? Where did the guys go?" Irit asked.

"I don't know. They deserted us. Come on. We're late to meet up with our people. We need to go now," Eloria told her.

They stumbled to the Jeep and the crew of hung-over mercs waiting to be transported to the airstrip servicing the bush camp. No one wanted to be first to climb on the Jeep, let alone board an airplane for a flight. The unhappy load pulled up at the strip. Those that could threw up. Some only dry heaved. They discovered through experience that it was about par for the course with these people, and they were a part of it now.

The same plane they had seen yesterday was parked by the side of the sand strip. Irit took in two men looking it over. "Look. It's our boys from last night. What do you suppose they're doing here?"

"It looks like they're doing a pre-flight. They must be the aircrew. Shit. Here they come."

Harry spotted the women first. He nudged Mike. "They must have followed us. How are we going to get rid of them?"

"From what I heard, you're the one looking for a place to live and a woman to love," Mike insisted.

"I thought you were busy at the bar. Are you telling me I actually said that?" Harry asked.

Mike regarded his friend. "Yes."

"In that case, they must be all right," Harry told him. Harry's manner went into gruff mode as he approached the women. "What are you two doing here? Did you follow us?"

Still hung-over Eloria was in no mood to take shit from a one-night stand. She pulled the Galil off her shoulder and waved it in Harry's direction. She kept the muzzle pointed skyward. "We're with the mercs. Do you have a problem with that?"

The look she gave him convinced Harry otherwise. He mellowed, and a half-assed grin crossed his face. "Why didn't you say something last night?"

Eloria returned the smile with a nervous smile of her own. "We didn't know who you were last night."

"Now that you do, board those drunken excuses for men,"

he told her. "Be sure to let them know that if anyone gets sick on my plane, I'll toss them out personally."

Even in her drunken stupor, Eloria recognized Harry wasn't a man to be trifled with when it concerned his airplane.

"You and your partner can wait here with Mike until I get back," Harry instructed. "You better be sure your own guts are empty or I'll toss you both out too. One at a time."

Harry regarded the smiling woman. Eloria was grinning like a puppy with a new friend. Already Eloria had her mind made up. Harry and her sister would be a good match. She continued to grin like a puppy at the man Irit had already welcomed into her bed.

Eloria and Iris observed the Pilatus piloted by Harry on its return flight. The plane taxied to a stop in a cloud of dust kicked up by the reverse pitch propeller setting. The engine continued its high-pitched scream. The pilot didn't shut down. Instead, he got out and motioned for them to climb aboard. Eloria looked into the cargo compartment and didn't like what greeted her. No seat belts. No seats. No intercom. "Holy shit. He wants us to climb on board a piece of junk."

Irit pointed a finger over her shoulder to the inside of the cargo compartment. "At least they've got firepower strapped to the bulkhead. I wonder if they know how to use it."

Mike, annoyed and still hung over, was in no mood to take backtalk. "Let's go, ladies. Stop bitching and climb aboard." He unceremoniously shoved Irit past the canvas divide up front with Harry. He took a seat on the floor beside Eloria in the cargo compartment. He removed two lap belts from a small compartment and fastened the clevis pins to the blocks on the floor. He waited for the woman to buckle in before he gave Harry the high sign.

Harry stood on the brakes and firewalled the throttle. The noise was almost unbearable. Mike returned his attention to the woman strapped in beside him. "What are a couple of nice girls like you doing in a place like this?"

Eloria's response was drowned out by the high-pitched

scream of the PT-6 engine as it continued to wind up for takeoff. Harry released the brakes, allowing the Pilatus to gain flying speed. At the appropriate moment, Harry rotated the control column, and the Porter lifted and rolled onto the tail wheel. Lightly loaded, he initiated a steep climb, allowing the purpose-built aircraft to do one of the things it did best.

Eloria's stomach began to churn. Keeping in mind Harry's admonition about throwing up in his plane, she closed her eyes and covered her ears. She put a talkative Mike, glued to her hip in the tight confines of the cargo compartment, on ignore for the rest of the flight. It was tough to do. At the best of times, all she could do was nod or shake her head at the man's non-stop barrage of questions.

U p front, Irit wasn't weathering the flight much better. She was just as hung over as her sister in the back. Harry looked across at the woman, grinned, and looked down at the familiar bush strip before it passed beneath the nose. He pulled the prop into Beta and pointed the nose down at a steep angle.

The Porter dove for the ground. A roller coaster flare and sudden stop coming so fast after touchdown had the desired effect. Eloria opened her door, made a hasty exit, and headed toward the tail. Irit threw open the cargo door and followed.

Together, they leaned against the fuselage and threw up. Neither stopped dry-heaving until Harry kicked them both in the ass. The dirty looks he got for his trouble couldn't wipe the grin off his face. "What did you think of my landing?"

"Screw you!"

Mike threw the duffels out of the plane. "Grab your gear and find a tent. We've got work to do."

Pale-faced and unsteady on their feet, the women stumbled down the rows of faded canvas, hung over and sweating in the bush humidity. They made their way to the bunkhouse. They weren't impressed by the rows of side-by-side cots.

"We can't bunk in with these guys. They'll have us for breakfast," Irit said.

I noticed that, too," Eloria replied. "I wonder how Meeka

and Harry would feel about sharing a tent? They're kind of cute. It wouldn't hurt to ask."

"Ask? Let's tell," Irit retorted. "If they say no, we'll worry about it after we unpack and get set up. Besides, they seemed all right in the bar last night. If we have problems, we'll handle them like we always do."

"They treated us pretty good, even when they were drunk," Eloria said. "I like them."

"So do I."

PART 3

Ghosts

47

Harry Delaney picked up the ringing phone. He got to it late. There was no one there, so he went downstairs to make coffee. In the upstairs bedroom, a second call woke Sasha out of a deep sleep. Groggy, she reached across the night table to answer the ringing phone. It was no big deal. She was accustomed to the late-night calls scheduling the never-ending positioning flights.

Harry called up to her. "Was it flight ops?"

"Whoever it was didn't say," she replied. "I asked if you had to go in early, but she had such a heavy accent I couldn't understand what she said. When I asked who it was, she hung up."

"Probably someone new in dispatch," Harry said. "Sometimes they get uncomfortable talking to wives."

"Which one of them has the accent?" Sasha wanted to know.

"Accent? What accent? As far as I know, none of them have an accent. I'll check in first thing to confirm the rescheduling," Harry said.

It happened during the East Africa excursion to rescue Sasha, his ex-wife. That was when Harry came to realize he still had feelings for the woman. On his return from saving her rear end, he cashed out everything he had to buy the house. That Sasha and their daughter moved in to share the place confirmed that she, too, wanted to give the relationship another try.

He hoped all of it would put an end to the woman's thirst for adventure. As much as he hated to admit it, Sasha's thirst was resembling his own, more and more.

The past eight months of home life had gone by in a blur. His friend Mike Williams had offered him the promised flying job. He accepted and ended up posted in the north to fly a Twin Otter. True to Mike's word, he started out as a co-pilot, but it was looking like he'd get bumped to Captain sooner than expected. The extra money would come in handy now that he had his family back.

Harry grew accustomed to the rotation schedule. It was three weeks out and one week home. Sasha had some trouble adjusting to having him underfoot for seven days at a time. They laughed when she told him, but she knew he wanted to be around for their daughter now that Christa was growing like a weed. He'd be around a lot more when he transitioned to Captain on one of Mike's jets.

The ease with which he fell into the regimented flying surprised him. He had become accustomed to the adventure and the highly paid flying jobs he took in Africa to pay the bills for his formerly estranged family. He realized he should have taken Mike up on his job offer years ago.

He settled in to enjoy the fruits of his labor after the years spent roaming foot-loose and fancy-free across what used to be called the Dark Continent. Who would have known? Both he and Sasha should have gotten a kick in the ass from someone a lot sooner. That someone was Mike's wife, Barbara, but rather than kick them, she let them be. Somehow, she knew the inevitable would happen.

And it did, no thanks to his wandering ways. Things were going so well in the relationship department with Sasha that they talked about getting pregnant again. It wasn't always so.

The phone rang again. Annoyed by the interruption to his early-morning coffee routine, Harry picked up the phone. His hello was an empty greeting. He never had time to say another word. It was all he could do to understand the thick accent of the woman who wouldn't stop talking. He listened carefully. What he heard was unbelievable. When the woman finished, he put the phone down. He knew immediately that all thoughts of a marriage proposal and plans for a wedding had literally flown out the window.

In his former life, he would never have bothered to tell Sasha a thing. He would have packed and left. Now, with Sasha and their daughter Christa as a part of his renewed life, he committed to telling her everything. He had to. It couldn't be any other way.

Reluctantly, Harry made a trip to the garage. It took a couple of minutes to dig out his old duffel. He recalled how he had almost tossed it, given his new life. Duffel in hand, he made his way to the upstairs bedroom. Every step he took weighed heavily. Already he knew Sasha wasn't going to be happy. He hesitated at the door to the bedroom, trying to collect his thoughts.

"What's going on?" Sasha asked. "Do you have to leave early? Give me a minute to dress and I'll drive you." Sasha swung her feet to the floor.

"Damn it. I don't want to do this. I thought I'd have more time," Harry told her.

Sasha's attention was drawn immediately to what Harry had dropped on the foot of the bed. She recognized the tan-colored and dusty old desert bag Harry hauled across the African continent countless times. The look on his face and his words warned her something was bothering him.

"It's two a.m. It's not time for you to leave. What's going on?" she asked.

"I just had a phone call—"

She didn't allow him to finish. "It wasn't about work, was it? The woman's accent—"

He confronted Sasha straight on. He couldn't lie. Not any more. "I'm going to have to leave for a while."

"Yeah. No. You're not," she insisted. Her resolve was firm, and he knew it. He waited her out. "There's no way you're leaving us behind ever again. I don't care what's going on."

"It's something I have to do. I gave my word," Harry said.

"Then I'm coming with you, Harry Delaney," Sasha insisted.

Harry flashed back to his meeting with Sasha and her friend Barbara on the Mexican Baja. He and Mike took the women out of a dangerous situation on the Baja and brought them across the border to safety. Even so, Sasha wasn't a trusting person. She was dead set against marrying him. In fact, she wanted nothing to do with him. Mike didn't think he'd be able to crack her. Barbara knew differently, but she never said a word about it until after the two married.

That told him how close the women were. At the time, he made a promise to himself to never come between their friendship. So far, so good. Up until now.

He saved Sasha's sorry ass one last time on the Horn of Africa after her kidnapping adventure with Gene, her fiancée and the self-styled oil baron.

It was about time he asked Sasha to marry him again. He thought that ought to keep her out of the hot seat and close to home for the duration. That had flown out the window with this latest revelation. He committed himself to asking her before he left on his next rotation. She would have three weeks without having him underfoot to think about it.

Harry was confident it wouldn't take her even that long to get her to bite the bullet for the second time.

Grim-faced, Harry looked at his partner. Together, they had been through so much. Stubborn as the woman was, he knew there was no way he'd be able to convince her to stay behind. He needed to try anyway. "I can't take you. I refuse to let the mother of our child put herself in harm's way ever again. You'd better know that by now."

That was all he had. He already knew it wasn't enough.

"If you leave, I'm going with you and that's all there is to it. If it's what I think it's about, you're not doing it without me, and damn you to hell if you sneak off in the night," Sasha fumed.

"In that case, Christa will have to stay with Barbara and Mike. I can't tell you a thing until after you drop her off. I won't take a chance on Mike finding out. Or Barbara."

Harry's ashen face said more than he wanted. He busied himself with packing while Sasha hurried out of bed.

"I'll be as fast as I can. Barbara is going to give me the third degree. Judging by her reaction the last time I took off, she's liable to chain me to the balcony," she told him.

"I know. Throw some things on the bed and I'll pack your bag while you're dropping off Christa."

"What am I packing for?" she wanted to know.

"Africa. I already made reservations for us into NBO."

It secretly pleased her that Harry had anticipated her refusal to stay home. But Nairobi? What was going on with that? "Barbara is going to have a fit when I arrive in the middle of the night."

"You can't say a word to her," he cautioned his wife. "Mike will want to know what's going on. It's bad enough that I have to send you to tell him I won't be at work tomorrow."

"Why can't you call him?" she wanted to know.

"He'll have too many questions and I'll feel obligated to answer. It wouldn't be fair to either of them," Harry said.

"It's about the women who got the two of you across the border and out of Tanzania, isn't it? Just how many years ago was that, Harry?"

"Not long enough, apparently," he replied. "I didn't let on, but it's been eating me up for quite a while. I need closure."

"You can tell me all about it on the way to the airport."

48

Present Day
Canada

Barbara opened the door for Sasha and Christa and ushered them into the kitchen. She knew right off by Sasha's ashen face something was up. That, and her friend's arrival with Christa in tow alerted her. They were friends too long and spent too much time together for her not to know something was up. Without a word, she took a groggy Christa from Sasha's arms and took her upstairs to bed before hurrying back down to confront her friend. "It's oh dark-thirty. What the hell is happening, girl? Is it Harry?"

Sasha regarded her friend. In an instant, all the troubles they'd been through and shared over the years flashed through her mind. If she only knew how hard it was for her not to give up Harry's secrets. It was too late now. She had promised Harry.

"I can't tell you on pain of death by nagging," Sasha admitted. "Or worse." Harry would leave her behind, and that wouldn't happen in this lifetime if she had anything to say about it.

"If you're going off on another one of your expeditions, I'll have your hide. Sit and we'll have coffee." Barbara was hoping to pry information out of her friend.

"I can't. I don't have time," she told her.

"You will or I'm waking Mike," Barbara insisted.

"Harry will kill me for this."

"He won't kill you as bad as I will if you don't tell me," Barbara said. Their friendship developed over the years was too strong. She couldn't deny it.

"I'm swearing you to secrecy, girl. Like old times."

Barbara took a deep breath and nodded. "Here's to old times."

Sasha settled back in her chair and regarded her friend. "I don't really know much of anything. He wouldn't tell me. All I know is he's making reservations for Nairobi."

"NBO? Reservations? As in two? What's going on?" Barbara wanted to know.

"Yes. Two. It took some doing, but I convinced him. He's not getting away again, no matter how dangerous he says it is," Sasha said.

"Are you thinking what I'm thinking?" Barbara asked.

"Whatever it is, it's my fault for traipsing off into the desert with that dimwit of an ex-boyfriend. If it wasn't for that—" Sasha hesitated.

"If it wasn't for that, the three of you wouldn't be together," Barbara said.

"True, but even so. He made some deal to free up that airplane you all used. Harry wouldn't tell me what the arrangement was. Now I'm thinking it's time to pay up."

Both women knew their men would move mountains if someone who once helped them ever asked for help themselves.

"We both know Harry is good for his word. Mike, too. Always. If someone called in your man's marker, Harry will move heaven and hell to make it good, Sasha."

"That's what I'm afraid of. There's one more thing. You're going to have to tell Mike that Harry won't be at work for a while," she told her friend. Sasha stood up and made for the door. Barbara followed her. She hoped it was all the information Barbara would demand of her. She opened the door, allowing a blast of cool air into the house

Mike chose that instant to reveal himself. "Not so fast, woman."

Sasha turned, taken by surprise at the sound of Mike's voice. Barbara closed the door behind her, trapping the woman. An anxious look froze on her face.

"You tell that son of a bitch if he needs something, he'd better call. He doesn't have to go begging for anything. And be sure you tell him hard so he understands," Mike insisted.

Sasha looked across at Mike as she hugged her friend again. "Thank you, Mike. I will. But not right off. He made me promise not to mention anything."

Barbara followed Sasha to the car. "I knew it. I gave away that damned shotgun way too soon."

"Oh, I hope not."

Harry felt bad insisting Sasha not divulge anything to Barbara. He knew how close the women were, but still. It had to be that way. Mike would have too many questions. He'd want to know too much. In any event, he didn't have enough concrete information to tell either of them anything.

It was bad enough he'd have to tell Sasha more about the two women that rescued them from the Tanzanian crash site. It was thanks to them they got across the border into Kenya. He'd fill her in, but it would be Mike's recounting of the details that he passed on to her, reluctant as he was to do even that.

He remembered nothing. The head wound suffered from the firefight at the landing strip had completely erased any memories of the drive to the border. He had no recollection of his escape across the border from Tanzania into Kenya.

It was enough that Mike finally showed up at the hospital in Nairobi, minus the women. When Mike told him the firefight killed the women, he almost lost it. He owed those two women everything.

Harry waited for Sasha to return by going online to check flights. They could get into Galkayo from Mogadishu. Mog wouldn't be any fun with the rebels in control. He hoped a layover wouldn't be required, especially now that his wife was coming along.

Dammit, but he didn't want to put her in harm's way again. This would be number three, and this time it would be on him if anything went sideways. With his wife coming along, it was time to call in some of the favors he was owed.

Harry searched through his Africa kit and retrieved an old leather notebook. Many of the pages were dog-eared and wrinkled. He flipped through it and the faded writing. A small bit of desert dust and sand filtered out. That was how long it had been since he needed it. He flipped back and forth, remembering, halting, remembering more, anxious for the number he needed until he found the name. He put through the call. The man on the other end of the line in Frankfurt listened patiently to Harry's instructions. He didn't ask questions.

It wasn't the first time Harry had dealings with Frankfurt. He had trusted the man in the past, and had no reason not to now. He ended the call. The arrangement was for a shipment into Entebbe. It was guaranteed to meet up with his flight into Nairobi.

Harry's phone rang a second time. It was the information he was waiting for. Satisfied, he hung up and made one last call to an old acquaintance. The man ran an airline in Somalia. The former Somali Air had been the source of the DC-3 he and Mike used to rescue Sasha on the Horn of Africa.

The phone rang a third time. This time it was his old friend Ali in Galkayo on the other end of the static-filled connection.

"I need you, my friend," was all the man said.

Harry didn't ask why. "We're already on our way."

It was looking like payback would be a convoluted affair.

Sasha didn't soft-shoe around letting Harry know that both Barbara and Mike knew something was going on. "They put two and two together. Mike as much as said so as I was leaving. He must have been listening when I was talking with Barbara. He wasn't very happy, to say the least."

"Mike is going to have to live with it. I won't involve him." Mike had his own family now. To bring him into what was going on might jeopardize his friend's happy life.

"What's next on the agenda? Did you get my bag packed?" Sasha wanted to know.

"Yes," he told her. "Our tickets are waiting at the airport. The taxi is on its way." He parted the curtain and looked outside. "No. It's here already."

"I'm ready."

As enthusiastic as he knew his wife was, Harry himself wasn't. The atmosphere in the taxi was subdued. He was committed, but having Sasha along was something he hadn't counted on. He should have known he wouldn't be able to stop her. "We'll be in Montreal tonight."

"I know, Harry."

"That will be your last chance to back out." It was fruitless, and he knew it.

"I think you can be certain that isn't going to happen."

"I know, but I have to say it. You know why," he said.

"Yes, and I love you, too. Even when I wouldn't admit it, and booted the two of you to the side of the freeway after you got us out of Mexico."

Sasha finally admitted what he knew to be true after all these years. He turned away and looked out the window, smiling. Perhaps things wouldn't be so bad on this expedition after all.

49

Harry Delaney had little to go on. As best he could, he brought Sasha up to speed on the events of the last few hours. He re-hashed what he remembered of Mike's conversation in the hospital in Nairobi. "I can remember pretty clearly when we hit the blockhouse at the tanzanite mine. The intent was to put some cash or gems in our pockets for traveling money, since we didn't have any money. We came up empty-handed."

"Did you hurt anyone?" Sasha wanted to know.

"No. When we found out there was nothing in the blockhouse, we got out as fast as we could."

"Are you sure?"

"I remember that part pretty clearly," he insisted. "We were in and out in minutes after we got our hands on a vehicle. We made straight for the blockhouse. One of the women already cleared it. I think it was Eloria."

"And?" She regarded Harry, wondering if she was getting the full story.

"That's when it gets fuzzy. The last I remember clearly is high-tailing it down the road headed for the border. I can recall bits and pieces after that, but nothing that makes any sense.

Believe me, I've tried."

"That's understandable. You were suffering from the double whammy of a concussion and a shoulder wound," she said.

"Strangely enough, I can remember the landing at the strip and getting shot up. I remember being bandaged up by the mercs. I recall the firefight. Even the almost two-day trek to the mine is pretty clear. But after we hit that blockhouse, that's the end. Everything went downhill from there."

Harry went on to recount Mike's version of events. Eloria rode shotgun. Irit sat in the back, taking care of him. Mike caught sight of a Jeep in hot pursuit. He never slowed. It was full speed ahead.

It all went to hell when the RPG hit the tree just as the Rover passed beneath it. Irit took a branch full on. It went into her chest. Eloria crawled into the back and tried to revive her, but Irit was already gone.

So there was no chance that Irit was still alive by the time Mike got you across the border?" she wanted to know.

"Not according to Mike. He told me he had the pedal to the metal headed for the Kenyan border. Eloria manned up and returned fire. She popped smoke. Handed Mike her shotgun and rolled out of the Rover onto the side of the road." He hesitated, trying to remember.

"Mike said the last thing he saw was the smoke engulfing her. She had her Galil shouldered, and she was giving it a workout. A single Jeep penetrated the smoke, still in pursuit all the way into Kenya."

"And that was the end?" she asked.

"Pretty much. He crashed through the border. A couple of klicks later, he pulled Irit out of the Jeep and stashed the firearms, except for the shotgun." He told her about the passports taped to the sawed-off shotgun's stock. "After I got out of the hospital, before we left, I took them to the embassy. I showed some I.D. and got the third degree for my troubles. The embassy rep wouldn't tell me a thing. I never saw the passports again."

"Could Eloria have been alive after the Jeep came out of the smoke?" she asked.

Harry thought for a moment before responding. "It's a possibility. She was a professional. She might not have wanted to shoot after the Jeep passed her. We would have been in her line of fire."

Harry took his wife's hand. There'd be no talking her out of anything. He settled back in the seat and closed his eyes. Now that he'd told Sasha everything, there would be no turning back.

I t was silent in the passenger airline. The night lights were dimmed. Most of the passengers were sleeping. Sasha mulled over Harry's story. "Do you think Mike ever told Barbara about Eloria and Irit?" If he had, Barbara had never said a work to her about it.

"I have no idea. All I know is it was never a subject of discussion between us once I got out of the hospital."

"What happened with the passports?" Sasha asked.

"Despite the passports, I knew they weren't Canadian. Their accents were too thick. I dropped the documents off at what I thought was the proper embassy and ended up getting the third degree for my troubles. My answers must have satisfied them, because they let me go about my business after a couple of hours."

"That was pretty momentous for both of you. You think Mike would have at least mentioned it to Barbara." And Barbara would for sure have said something to her by now.

"I don't know, Sasha. Like I said—"

"I know. Like you said. So if he told her, why didn't you let Mike know about the phone call?"

"Because lining up the DC-3 that we used to rescue you was entirely my deal," Harry said.

"But you must have known eventually someone would want to get paid back."

"I knew. I didn't think it would be so soon," he said.

"What aren't you telling me, Harry?"

He sighed. Foggy memories flashed through his head. His brow furrowed. Did Sasha need to know? "Eloria might still be alive." Now, for sure, there would be no going back.

Sasha's head whipped around. Long, dark hair drifted across Harry's shoulder. She looked at him with wide eyes. She grabbed Harry's forearm. Her grip tightened. "What? Are you sure? The woman with the accent on the phone?" So that was the reason he hadn't told her anything about the phone call before they left Mike and Barbara behind.

"There's a chance Eloria could still be alive," Harry admitted. At least, that's what it sounded like to him. The female voice on the other end of the line was heavily accented. Not only might Eloria be alive, but she was somehow connected to Ali in Galkayo. How could that even be possible? And where had she been all these years? Why was he getting calls from her only now?

Harry shut his eyes. In another thirty-six hours, he would know, one way or the other.

Harry was having second thoughts. It was unavoidable. The comfortable life he made for his family had just been turned upside-down. Not only that, his once and future wife insisted on coming along. That could turn out to be huge trouble. And if it wasn't, it could at the least be a terrible idea. He took another stab at it.

"It's not too late to turn back. For either of us," he added hastily.

"I've been thinking about that, too. Do I really want to pull up stakes and go on a hunt with you for people who may or may not want us interfering in their lives? Do you even know who it was on the phone? By your description of the voice, it could be anyone."

"I've known Ali a long time. I don't think he'd let himself be used if he didn't think it was the right thing to do. He wouldn't call me over there for something trivial."

"Perhaps you're right," Sasha said.

Harry's phone rang. He answered and his face turned ashen. The phone went dead on the other end. He wrote down the number and turned it off. "If you want to call Barbara and check on Christa, do it now." He already knew what Sasha's response would be.

"There's no need. I trust Barbara. Our daughter will be fine, no matter what."

"We're ditching our phones. We'll be picking up burn phones in NBO. Take out your SIM card and the memory and toss the phone in the trash. I'll flush the rest."

"Are you going to tell me who that was?" she asked.

"Yes."

"Well then, do it, Harry. For crying out loud."

"It was Eloria," he admitted. "At least, it sounded like it could be her." Sounded like? What was he saying? That he'd embarked on this adventure on a whim? That he was putting his wife in danger for a could-have-been?

"She's alive. After all these years. What did she say?" Sasha asked.

"Not much. She didn't have time. She's with Ali in Galkayo."

"With Ali? How did she get there from Tanzania?" she wanted to know.

"I'd say we'll be finding out soon enough."

"Yes, we will," Sasha said. "There's no way you're going to convince me to go home now."

He smiled, thinking Sasha was just as stubborn as he was, if not more so. "There's one more thing. Her last words before she hung up were, Please help us."

Sasha turned to Harry. "Us? Help us? Are you sure?"

Harry couldn't believe it either. He considered the possibilities. Was Irit alive too? Was it Ali? Who could it be?

"But I thought Irit was dead, Harry."

"So did I."

50

Present Day
En route

Harry looked across the aisle at Sasha. He wasn't pleased he was unable to shake her determination to accompany him. He made one more attempt, but already he knew it wouldn't work. "When we land in London, I have a meeting to go to. You're not invited."

Sasha wasn't having it. "In that case, when we land in London, we'll be staying overnight. I'll make a reservation for us in arrivals so you'll know where to go."

"I'd like it better if you flew home from there," he told her.

"Yes. I love you, too."

"Damn you, woman. Do you ever listen?"

"Harry, if you haven't learned one thing about me by now, you never will. When was the last time you were able to talk me out of anything?"

He didn't have to think. He had no answer, either. Instead, he tried humor. "Well, there was that one time on the Baja. In the Jeep. You were—"

"If I remember right, it was me who did all the talking then, too."

There was no getting around it. Sasha had his number. "You're right. I did all the talking when I convinced you to marry me. You ignored me for so long, I thought you were deaf."

"Yes, dear."

He changed the subject by reaching into his carry-on and pulling out some old aerial photos. He described the long trek the four of them made across the bush to the mine site. That he remembered most of it was probably because he had to work so hard to overcome his wound and the concussion. The forced march had given him something to concentrate on.

He left out how he and Mike met the girls the day before and ended up spending the night. If Sasha had questions, she could ask. He tucked the photos away when the seatbelt sign lit up. "I want you to use your American passport to get through customs," he told her.

"Why?"

"If anyone is fishing through the databases, they won't expect it."

"All right, if you insist," she said.

"Once you're admitted you can destroy it. From then on, you'll be a full-blooded Canadian, and attached to me."

"I think they call it married, Harry."

"Some do. Some don't. We're divorced, remember? Where we're going, it could make all the difference when you can drop my name into the conversation." He changed the subject again. "After you find us a room, I'll be heading to a meeting with an old Africa hand. I tried to make arrangements before we left, but with all the electronic snooping going on these days, I wanted to finalize things in person."

"How many markers are you calling in?" Sasha wanted to know.

He ran through the list in his head. He'd need an airplane and munitions to go with it. He already decided on a two-seater. He was familiar with just the one. If only he could get his hands on it. It would be perfect for getting two people out of trouble. Sasha wouldn't know it, but she wouldn't be one of the two. If he had anything to do with it, she'd be sitting poolside at a resort in Nairobi when hell was breaking loose.

"All of them," he finally said.

This time, when he was finished, there'd be no returning to the Dark Continent.

Harry thought back years ago to the job ad Mike had shown him. It didn't take long to decide. He had cabled a response almost immediately. When adventure called, he always answered.

He didn't know at the time where it would take him, but eventually that job ended up earning him and Mike a position in the huge African arms market. It was one that Harry suspected he would have to use to its full advantage now that he had a last mission to accomplish.

He wasn't privy to what transpired back in the camp when Mike was rounding up help to come to his rescue. He was only grateful that someone finally showed up. In fact, after he got himself shot, he thought he wouldn't be getting out alive. Then he heard the explosion of a shotgun blast in the middle of a firefight. He knew right away a sound like that wasn't a part of any rebel arsenal.

Even more surprising was how the rescued mercs wanted nothing to do with the rescuers. He guessed being saved by two women wouldn't be a story they wanted to hear when it got told in a bar. An event like that would follow them for life. He never stopped hoping the chickenshit sons of bitches were left to guard shithouses in a flood plain.

Harry had no recollection of their run to the Kenyan border. Whether both Irit and Eloria were still alive before they crashed through was beyond his conscious memory. It was all he could do to recall being admitted to the hospital in Nairobi.

When Mike told him what happened to the women, he took him at his word, and he took it hard. If it wasn't for the two mercs that took a shine to both of them, he would have been a goner.

Together with Mike, they committed without question to rescuing him at the bush strip. When he heard they were killed trying to get him across the border into Kenya, he crashed for the second time in his hospital bed.

The phone calls in the middle of the night shot all that to hell. He was left to figure out what went wrong and how he could fix it.

If he could fix it.

Harry returned from his London meeting and met a harried-looking Sasha in the lobby. She didn't look happy. "Someone searched our room," she announced.

They rushed up the stairs to the third-floor room. Signs of the search were everywhere. They were traveling light, but the backpacks had been stripped and their contents thrown around the room. Anything with a seam was ripped open and examined.

"I thought you were a better housekeeper. Perhaps I was misinformed," he joked, attempting to make light of the situation they found themselves in.

"I was away for only minutes. I went to the lobby to get something to read."

"It's a good thing. You might have taken a beating, or worse," he said.

Sasha's hands went to her hips and she tapped a toe. "As I recall from our last expedition, Ali in Galkayo had an eye for both me and Barbara. Unless you want to make plans to ship me back to him, you'd better start talking."

Harry sighed. "Allow me to refresh your memory. Our last expedition, as you call it, was put in place to rescue you and our daughter."

Sasha's feet were planted firmly on the floor, and her hands were still on her hips. The look in her eyes wasn't good, either. He was going to have to tell her everything. Well, almost everything. He didn't have it all put together yet. He'd go with what he had. "Where would you like me to start?"

"How about with the phone calls you got at home in the middle of the night?"

"The first was from Ali," he told her. Harry stopped, but he knew he wouldn't get any peace until he came up with a reasonable explanation. This time, he wouldn't have to make anything up.

"Keep going if you know what's good for you. And don't take time to make it up as you go along." Sasha never cut him any slack, but that was a good thing. He didn't want any. Not now.

"Ali called me because he didn't want to involve Mike. He wouldn't tell me everything on the phone because of all those American listening agencies, but I got enough to know he needs some help. He was practically begging me."

"And you can never turn down a friend in need, can you?"

"Well, you were in on the last episode with Ali. After what he did for us, would you be able to say no?"

Sasha didn't need time to think. "Of course not."

"Before this is over, I want you to put that in writing and sign your real name," Harry quickly added with a grin.

"You only wish."

"There's one other thing. That second phone call that came in at the house—" Harry hesitated.

Sasha held a questioning expression on her face long enough to know he would have to come clean.

"It was Eloria on the other end. It's been a long time since I heard her voice, but yes, it sounded like her. She's not dead by a long shot."

"Then what was Mike—" Sasha's voice trailed off.

"I don't know. That's why we're here. And no matter what went on, no matter what we'll be walking into, Mike and Barbara must never know. Is that understood?"

Sasha took a long time contemplating her answer.

Harry knew the two women were closer than sisters. Closer than best friends. Closer than he and Mike had ever been. Their adventures kept them even closer. Neither one of them had ever told anyone about their escapades before the four of them got tangled up. Harry had asked no questions either. He never would. "Well?" he finally asked."

"You bastard. You're forcing me to cross Barbara, aren't you?" She gave him a hard look, and he knew he was into it with her, whether or not he wanted to be.

The look softened. "All right. I promise. And both my hands are in plain sight, so you can see no crossed fingers."

"Good. Now come over here and give me a hug. It might be the last chance we get for a while." Harry swept the clothes off the bed and pulled her onto it. "It's not a Jeep, but we'll just have to make do with what we've got."

She pushed him down and climbed on top. "Yes, we will."

51

Harry slowly eased the covers off of his sleeping wife in the hotel bed. His eyes roamed down and back up on a body that kept him just as interested now as when he first met her. He grinned an evil smile and slapped her naked rear. He didn't give her time to protest. "Hustle it, girl. We've got ninety minutes to make the airport."

Sasha left the covers down and sat up. She quite enjoyed Harry's eyes enjoying her. "You never told me what happened yesterday." She smiled coyly.

"If we're going to make that plane, cover up, woman. You know my weaknesses too well."

Secretly pleased that her body still excited him, she made a show of doing only a part of what he suggested. Her forearm moved to shield her breasts and with a shake of her head, long, dark hair tumbled over her arm while she returned the grin. "Is that better?"

He ignored her. She knew he would. He was all business when he had to be.

"I set us up for two scenarios. I figured I had to. We could end up with four people to get out of there. I'm counting on you to be one of them."

"Four? So? Who are they?" she wanted to know.

"I'll tell you in the cab. Now let's get it in gear."

Sasha held up a small chip. "I just found this." She held it up. "What is it?"

"Don't tell me. That was in your bag." He opened his own and poked and pried. He found nothing.

"Now what, Harry?" Sasha's tone was worried. "Should we attach that thing to the taxi? What do you think?"

"I think we're into it now, whether we want to be or not. Someone is trying to monitor us, that's for sure. I hoped it would take them longer."

They finished packing in a rush, wordless, throwing clothes into bags, concentrating on getting the job done as fast as they could before rushing to the lobby and a waiting taxi. Harry loaded the bags into the car and forced the bug behind a seat. "That'll have to do for now. Did you flush it?"

"My passport? Yes," she assured him. "Good. We're headed to Schipol. After a bit of a layover, we'll hop a milk run into Frankfurt and from there deadhead into Nairobi."

"And once we get there? Then what?" she wanted to know.

"At first I wanted a plane," Harry said. "When that didn't come through, I had to settle for a boat of some sort. I'm out of my element there, but I was promised a knowledgeable crew."

"What if that doesn't work out?"

"I'm depending on you to see that it does, dearest wife of mine."

Sasha looked across at Harry. "Me? What are you talking about?"

"You're the smarty-pants that came up with the plan to board that yacht down in Mexico," he asserted. "With all of your experience, you're promoted to be the admiral of my merchant marine."

"Shit, Harry. I haven't seen hide nor hair of a boat since then. And if I knew how to sail one, I'd have climbed on board before I ever crossed paths with you two Baja bums."

"Look at it this way, my sweet." Harry raised an eyebrow and smiled. "You're just starting out, and already you're an admiral. At least you know enough not to wear spike heels and your bottom should be covered with just enough cloth to give the sailors a reason to sign on and daydream."

She dug an elbow into his ribs. She didn't return the smile. "You won't be so happy when I run us aground on some Indian Ocean shoal."

"See what I mean?" he teased her. "Your knowledge of nautical geography is astounding. Apparently, I chartered an old tub that was salvaged and refurbished. I hope you won't be upset when I tell you there'll be a small crew already on board."

"That's good to hear. I can't wait to have drinks served while I improve my tan."

"I don't want to be the one to splash Indian Ocean seawater on the vacay of your dreams. Not only will you be my admiral, but you're going to be on galley duty."

Sasha recognized the sound of the power being pulled back on the commercial jet's engines. She checked her watch and realized it was early to be landing in Nairobi. "We can't be close, Harry. It's too soon."

The captain's voice came over the PA. "Ladies and gentlemen, there will be a slight delay on our arrival in Nairobi. Presently we're set up for an approach into Entebbe. We estimate twenty minutes on the ground before becoming airborne for our final destination of Nairobi."

Sasha regarded Harry. "You told me this was going to be a direct flight."

"It is."

"But—" Sasha halted. She knew better than to ask.

"Is your seat belt fastened?" he asked her.

The jet banked left to line up on final and Sasha watched the runway lights flicker three times and go out before they disappeared beneath the plane. They must have come back on, because once the jet touched down, the field went dark a second time. "It's pitch-black out there, Harry. Not even the terminal is lit up."

"I told you. We're on a direct flight to Nairobi. Now relax and enjoy the spectacle that's about to unfold."

Lights dropped from the wings and switched on to allow the jet to turn and taxi in the pitch-black night toward the terminal building. The same lights that reflected off the glass of the old terminal illuminated a dark ramshackle building. The jet pulled even with a rough-looking hangar and braked. Lights went dark. The jet's turbine engines hummed through the fuselage.

The front door on the jet opened. A stairway bumped against the plane's fuselage. A man in a long tan overcoat entered the cabin. He walked the length of the passenger deck, dispensing the contents of two spray bombs. He did the same on his return trip down the aisle to the exit. He halted for a second at Harry's seat and dropped a piece of paper in his lap. The man left the plane and an attendant closed and secured the door behind him.

A vehicle's dim lights cut a path through the dark night. It accompanied a forklift. The lights illuminated a large wooden box across the forks. It turned for a 90-degree approach, slowed, and eased up to the side of the idling jet. The plane shuddered as a heavy pallet slammed down into a cargo compartment. The cargo door slammed shut, and the trucks departed. The engines spooled up. Wing lights illuminated the taxiway. The plane made its way to the end of the strip.

The plane turned to line up with the runway. Runway lights turned on. Engines advanced to a loud roar. Brakes strained. On release, the plane accelerated and became airborne. Runway illumination went out the instant the wheels left the ground.

"What the hell was that all about, Harry? Sasha asked. "You just can't be loading cargo on planes in the dark of night. Who were those people?"

"I have no idea. We'll find out in NBO if we have everything we need."

"Christ, Harry, when are you going to tell me what you and Mike did over here?"

Sasha never asked questions about what he and Mike did during their overseas adventures. Harry never once asked her about the time she and Barbara had spent on the Baja. They both sensed there was no use dredging up things that had long been behind them.

"I will when you and Barbara volunteer to tell me what you were doing down on the Baja all those years."

"Touché. You're never going to ask, are you?"

"No. And neither are you."

Sasha sighed. "I have a feeling I won't have to ask. I think I'm about to find out first-hand."

The captain announced their arrival in Nairobi. He taxied the passenger jet to a halt on an empty stretch of tarmac far from the NBO terminal building. The engines remained running. He switched on the PA and made a second unscheduled announcement. "Ladies and gentlemen, we're making a brief stop on the north end of the airport for cargo delivery. The passenger door will open momentarily to deplane two. Please remain in your seats with your seatbelts fastened until we can proceed to the Nairobi terminal building."

Harry stood up to retrieve their bags from the overhead bin. "Come along, Sasha. It's time to deplane." He grinned down at her.

The flight crew cabin door opened in time to greet Harry and Sasha. The gray-haired older man with four bars on his shoulders looked at Harry and then flicked his eyes over Sasha. "This is for you, Harry." He handed over an envelope. "I received it in-flight. Good luck, you two."

"Thanks, Don. We're going to need it."

Sasha smiled warmly at the man before following Harry down the airstair. Warm night air greeted the pair as they left the confines of the plane and stepped onto the tarmac. Harry put his arm around Sasha. He looked up the stairwell in time to see the wave before the passenger door closed.

Harry eased Sasha in the direction of the forklift already hoisting the pallet out of the open cargo bay. "Climb on and we'll ride with the goods."

A hangar door slid open, and the forklift disappeared into the brightly lit, cavernous space. The forklift passed the door and it closed. The box was deposited, and the lift moved away. Harry collected a pry-bar and began lifting tops off crates. He ran through a checklist only he knew.

"RPGs. Good. Shells. Good. Four Kalashnikovs. Magazines. Grenades. Personal packs. Vests. A satellite phone. A GPS each. We're good to go."

Sasha could only look at Harry as he listed the details of his haggling to no one in particular. "I'm afraid, Harry."

He put an arm around Sasha and hugged her. "So am I. It's natural. It's also good to keep busy. Help me get these spares loaded on our truck."

The forklift operator hoisted the crates on the back of a dilapidated two-ton. He had planned for the truck with his Africa connections. The pair climbed aboard and wrestled the boxes into position. When they finished, sweat poured down front and back.

"Merci, Jean. Thanks for all your help."

"Pas de problème. No problem, Harry. The truck doesn't look like much, but I went over it myself. She will be bonne to get you to Mombasa, at least. I have the burner phones, too. They're charged and ready to go. Bonne chance. Good luck."

Harry handed Sasha the envelope the pilot had passed to him earlier. She withdrew a single sheet of paper before telling him, "Phone numbers. Two of them."

He turned on his flip phone and sent a text to the first number. "Ali will get my number from that. You should do the same."

He dialed the second number and handed back her phone and watched her type, Sasha is here too.

"Good. Now he'll have us both." Harry turned on his GPS, scrolled to Mombasa, and marked a dock in the port as their destination. "Do the same for yours."

"So then it's Mombasa to pick up a boat and head north? What about the airplane you wanted?"

"Yeah about that. I was forced to change plans in England. No plane," he told her.

"You're going to be a fish out of water, Harry."

It was true. Harry without a plane would be a fish out of water. It might be a bad pun, but it was true. "Pretty much. Except for the water part and the boat waiting for us in Mombasa."

"Shit, Harry. We don't know anything about boats."

"I don't know anything about boats. You do," he insisted.

"I know just enough not to wear spike heels and when to put on a bikini, remember?" she reminded him.

"That might be just enough. Now come on. You're driving."

He already made that decision. It would allow her to worry about something other than their mission. Whatever the hell it was turning out to be.

"Pick up Mombasa Road. It's also the A109. Stay on it until we hit water 400 kilometers away. And turn off your phone. We don't need to be pinging towers, in case anyone is looking."

Sasha followed Harry's directions and turned left into the black night, driving on the wrong side of the road. It was the right side, as far as she was concerned.

"Eventually this four-lane will go down to two. Don't forget you should drive on the left-hand side."

Late at night as it was, there were no headlights bearing down on them in the heavy truck.

"The left side? That doesn't seem right, somehow."

She wrestled the two-ton's manual steering wheel, swerved into the ditch and onto the opposite side of the roadway. "Are you sure?"

"I'm sure. Carry on." He grinned in the darkness. He considered himself fortunate he had such a plucky woman sitting beside him. Harry caught the side-eye in the reflection from the dash lights. He smiled, knowing how feisty the woman beside him could be. "By the end of the 400 kilometers to Mombasa, you'll be accustomed to driving the wrong side. It'll be second nature."

"If you say so," was all Sasha said.

"Just remember. The 109 dwindles to two lanes. It's a dangerous road. We'll be on it at night all the way to the coast. Don't hesitate to take the ditch and head cross-country if you see the need."

"After all those miles on the Baja road to nowhere I'm not about to end it on some highway to hell in the middle of Africa," she assured him. "You can take that to the bank."

Harry opened Sasha's backpack and rummaged through it. He found her passport and stuffed it down the front of her pants.

"Ouch. That hurts. What the hell are you doing?" She wriggled to adjust her position behind the wheel.

"Don't go anywhere without it, even to the bathroom at the tail-end of this truck. Having my name on you might make all the difference."

"Yes, master. I'll be sure to get your name tattooed on my ass as opportunity presents."

Harry teetered on the edge of threatening to put the woman over his knee. He immediately tossed that thought out the open window. It wouldn't do any good, even as a joke. "You're not on the Baja any more. It's not a day-long drive to get to the safety of home. You're in unknown territory. If anything happens to me, you'll be screwed. Probably in more ways than one. Don't listen to me at your peril. Understand?"

"Yes. I understand." A crestfallen face regarded Harry in the cab's dim lighting.

"Good. Now stop looking so miserable and cheer up, partner. We've got a lot of miles to cover. I don't want my driver thinking about quitting on me before she gets our sorry asses to Mombasa." Harry grinned.

Sasha squirmed as she adjusted the passport stuck in her pants. She grimaced and gave Harry a dirty look. She was on his ground now. Grudgingly, she knew he was right. She would do what was called for to make sure they got home safely with the human cargo they were on the way to retrieving.

52

**Present Day
Mombasa**

Sasha continued to wrestle with the unfamiliar vehicle's enormous steering wheel. Minus the power steering she was accustomed to, she struggled to keep the ancient truck on the strange road in the dark. She couldn't help over-correcting, causing the truck to ease from side to side on the highway. She tested the brakes. They barely worked to slow the heavy, underpowered truck. She bent over the steering wheel and squinted into the darkness barely penetrated by the weak headlights.

Finally, she had enough. She wrestled the truck to the side of the road and coasted to a stop. "Harry, this road is blacker than a Baja night. I can't see a damned thing. I think a headlight is out," she insisted.

Harry sighed, got out, and walked to the front. He assessed the situation before manhandling a fender and kicking it into submission. When he finished, the headlight shone onto the roadway directly in front of the old truck. "That's going to have to do. We're wasting time. We need to make Mombasa by sunrise."

"Is that another one of your deadlines?" she asked.

"No. A lot of the streets are unlit and too narrow for a

vehicle this size. I don't want you wedging this thing between buildings in the middle of a donkey path."

Sasha sighed and remembered to check the mirror before fighting to get the two-ton back on the highway. "There's something following us. Another truck, I think. I don't know if he's been following us for a while."

"Slow down and pull over to let him go past. I'm going to get in the back."

Harry opened the door and vacated the cabin before climbing into the canvas-covered bed. He opened the bag with the AKs and took out two. He checked the actions. In the dark, he felt around for the magazines and picked up two.

The truck bumped and swerved back onto the highway. The canvas flapped. He loaded the magazines and passed an AK through the driver's window. It bumped Sasha's shoulder hard. The truck swerved and straightened. She yelled into the back. "What the hell are you doing? Are you trying to knock me out?" Her voice was lost in the diesel truck's overworked engine.

"No bananas for you, dearie," Harry called to her. He chuckled to himself as he remembered explaining what they were such a long time ago. "You'll have to do with a single. I'll be back here for the duration."

He felt around for more wooden boxes and found a couple of grenades. He stuffed them into his vest pockets. He loaded more magazines and sat them by his foot. Just in case, he told himself. He settled in and fell asleep in the wake of diesel fumes, serenaded by the whining engine on the bumpy road in the swerving truck.

Sasha brought the lurching truck to a sudden halt in the middle of the dark road. She killed the lights. Harry's head bumped against his knees. He rubbed the sleep from his eyes, stuck his head out from beneath the canvas, and leaned into the window. "Why are you stopping?"

"There's a vehicle across the road in front of us." Sasha inserted Harry's magazine into the AK. She adjusted the muzzle across her lap and pointed it toward the door. She made sure to push the safety full down before she racked.

"Go slow. I'll stay out of sight back here."

The headlights barely reached two men crouched by the orange glow of a fire on the side of the road. They stood up and left the fire's warm comfort and cautiously approached the two-ton. AKs hung carelessly off their shoulders. They were evidently unprepared for an argument.

The men addressed her in Swahili. Uncomprehending, Sasha called out. "English. Speak English."

Startled, the men stepped back. A flashlight turned on and swept the cab through the front window. "What are you doing all alone in the dark, white woman?" the man asked in heavily accented English.

Harry poked his head out from behind the boxes. The AK registered immediately with the men. He covered them off with the muzzle of his own aimed directly at them. "Kiasi gani kupita? How much?"

"Nothing for you, bwana. Pass by."

The men stepped aside and waved the truck through. Sasha shifted into first gear and the truck groaned into the ditch past the makeshift checkpoint. Harry followed the two men with his eyes until they were out of sight in the dark. "You handled that like a pro. You're hired, girl."

"Hired or not, you're stuck with me. According to you, the odometer says there's another eighty klicks to Mombasa. Go back to sleep."

"One more thing before I do, sweetie."

Sasha concentrated on keeping the truck on the road in the pitch-black night. Busy and annoyed, she tried to wait him out and failed. "Well, what is it this time?"

"You can turn your lights on."

"Damn you Harry Delaney. I swear—"

Harry returned to his nest in the back of the truck. The sound of gunfire only minutes later brought him standing up again. "What we passed was probably a sentry for the main checkpoint up ahead. Be prepared to motor through whatever is in front of us. I'll do the talking."

Sasha doused the lights. Not wanting to leave anything to chance, she steered the truck off the road into the shallow ditch.

"Whoever you do, don't stop the truck unless you absolutely have to," Harry told her.

Headlights and a fire pit winked in the distance. In the back of the truck, Harry loosened his belt. He tucked two RPG rounds into it. Satisfied, he armed the RPG with a round. "Get back on the road. Leave the lights off. Go slow and keep your head down. I'll be staying back here."

"We need another driver," Sasha insisted.

"You're doing a good job. Don't quit on me now."

"You're only saying that because you don't have anyone else to do the job," Sasha complained.

"No, I'm saying it because you're doing just fine and I love you. And because there's no one else that needs a compliment right now." He chuckled, and he wondered if she overheard.

In the dark, Sasha checked the safety on her AK. It was still off. "I don't like being all alone up front."

"Get used to it. We're almost in Mombasa. There can't be much more of this."

"You forgot to add, *Unless someone is tracking us.*"

"Yes. Well. There's always that.".

Rounds twanged through the rusted cab. Sasha ducked and kept driving toward the fire. Harry stood straight up in the back of the truck. He shouldered the RPG. Launched his first round at the fire pit. He reloaded immediately. The second round banged against the blockade in the road. It disintegrated into scrap metal.

The twin explosions quieted the gunfire. Only the orange glow of the fire remained.

For spite, he released another round. There was nothing left to hit. He tightened his belt and climbed into the cab. "Keep driving. Don't stop for anything until we're in the city."

Sasha walked the truck through the smoke drifting past the road through Harry's RPG carnage. She sniffed the air, and unseen in the darkness, made a face. "What's that sweet smell?"

Harry hesitated before answering. "It's burning flesh." He slipped closer to her in the seat. Sasha shuddered against him.

He left her to process the information

"I don't want to smell that ever again," she insisted.

"Fair warning. You'll never forget it as long as you live."

Sasha shuddered again. This time she stayed silent.

Sasha bumped the truck through a ditch, realized what she had done, and angled along the shallow depression back onto the 109. "I can't see a damned thing with the sun in my eyes."

"Then slow down. Mombasa is right in front of you," Harry said.

The brakes on the rusty two-ton screeched as she brought it to a halt and climbed out. "If you can do it better, have at it."

"Are we only bickering, or are we about to have our first fight on this safari?"

"I'm exhausted," she admitted. "I'm a nervous wreck. You're going to drive this tank to wherever the hell you want to park it," she insisted.

"Well, why didn't you just say so?"

"Don't bug me. I'm going to try to get some sleep. See if you can wrangle this thing through the streets without bumping and grinding, okay?"

It pleased Harry to see Sasha upset with him. She was coming along nicely. In fact, she passed the test. "Si, madame. You did a great job driving through those checkpoints. I didn't expect you'd keep going, but you did. I like knowing I can depend on you."

Harry hugged Sasha and kissed her on the mouth like there was no tomorrow. If they weren't in the middle of a highway— He slapped her rear and stepped back to observe as she climbed into the passenger seat in her tight fatigues. When had she changed into them? Damn, but she was hot.

"Harry."

"Yes dear?"

"Did you forget it's your turn to drive? Stop staring at my ass and get in."

Harry entered the outskirts of Mombasa and eased the truck along a narrow street toward the Indian Ocean and the sun rising over the horizon. He halted about a hundred meters from shore. No dock. He stopped and rummaged through his backpack for a GPS. He came up with a dated paper map. He left Sasha, curled up and sleeping on the seat beside him.

He walked the narrow streets, searching for where he thought the dock should be, trying to find a way through the congestion for the big truck. When he returned, Sasha wasn't curled up on the seat any longer.

Damn it, where did that woman get to this time? He yelled her name. There was no response. He turned toward a whistle and she appeared, bags in hand and sporting a different top.

"This time I wanted to actually go shopping. I was getting smelly in those old clothes and thought I'd try to track down something lighter."

"You know how to worry me half to death, don't you? If anyone had been curious about what's on board the truck, we'd be begging in the street to replace it."

"No, we wouldn't." She pulled up her shirt and the butt of a handgun peeked out of the top of her jeans.

"Besides, the shop is just there." She tilted her head. "I picked up warm fresh bread and cheese and cold water. What more could a woman want going on an Indian Ocean cruise with the man she loves?"

Harry grinned. It was all he could do. Damned if she hadn't gotten the better of him yet again. "In that case, let's eat. The boat can wait. It won't be going anywhere without us."

They wolfed down breakfast, hardly tasting it in their haste to find their way to the wharf. In the mirror, Harry kept his eye on a man leaning against a building. It wasn't unusual. The man shuffled his feet from time-to-time, looked nervous, walked back and forth, but never looked in the truck's direction. That wasn't usual.

"We're being watched," he announced.

"By that man in the blue shirt?" Sasha wanted to know.

"Christ, woman, how long has he been there?"

"I noticed him when I came out of the shop."

"And you didn't tell me because—"

"I didn't tell you because we'd have missed breakfast. And I was right, too. He hasn't done anything except stand around and look innocent."

"Get in." Harry climbed in and started the wheezing diesel. He eased the clutch and steered the noisy two-ton through the narrow street in the direction of the wharf. He checked his mirror. The watcher was talking on a phone.

The explosion rumbled off walls. A cloud of black smoke rose over the harbor and hovered over buildings blocking a clear sight of the harbor.

"Harry?"

"Yeah. That's not good," he told her. He steered the two-ton into a roundabout toward the rising column of smoke. By the time he made it to a clear view of the docks, it became plain where the smoke was coming from.

The boat was attached to the dock by its mooring lines. It wouldn't be going anywhere laying on its side. Smoke poured from whatever openings weren't submerged. There would be no boat in their future. He backed the truck up and turned around.

"Now what, Harry?"

"So much for the crew of mercs I hired. Now it'll be our famous plan B."

"You have another plan?" Sasha wanted to know.

"You betcha, baby. It's plan B, for the *Be adaptable* plan. It's the airport or nothing. We'll pick up a plane," he told her.

"A plane? How do you know there's something there that will do the job? What about security? What about—" She halted.

"I don't know. We'll stake it out until we have a likely prospect."

"In that case, we better lose whoever is following us." Harry backed the two-ton around for the second time and pointed it north along the coast.

"Are you drunk? We passed the airport on the way into

town," she told him.

So she was paying attention after all. "We're not going to the city airport. We're making for Bamburi. It's a no-service strip, exactly what we're looking for. Survey pilots prefer it because it's close to the kind of resorts they like to stay in when they're on someone else's dime."

"So there could be a plane there? How do you know it'll be the right kind?"

"We're looking for a Twin Otter or a Porter," he told her. "If we're lucky, it'll be a Twin with tundra tires. We'll need something like that to haul what we've got in the back of our truck."

Harry knew he'd have to make a move to lose their tail before he took the turn for the road to Bamburi. He halted the truck on a corner and manhandled it into position, blocking the road. The ancient Willys chasing them wasn't able to brake in time. It rammed into the rear of the heavy truck. The driver flew into the street.

Harry picked him up and shoved him into the cab with Sasha. "Wrap some of that tape around his arms and legs. That ought to be the end of whoever is following us for now."

"We can't take him with us. Can we?" she wanted to know.

"We'll dump him in the bush on our way to the airport. In the meantime, if you pass a sign announcing the road to Butterfly Park, you've gone too far."

"While I'm doing the driving, what the hell are you going to be doing?"

Harry climbed into the back of the truck and began loading magazines for the AKs. "You'll get spare mags when I'm done," he called past the canvas. "It'll give you something else to tape if you remember how. Now don't bug me. I'm busy."

53

Sasha eased the ancient two-ton up a slight rise. She pumped the brake pedal. Squealing brakes brought it to a crawl. The end of the landing strip came into view through the front window. Sasha eased the two-ton onto the down-slope and halted. The truck stalled and jerked to a stop. "Harry. We're here," she announced.

"Drive onto the asphalt and follow it until you see a building on the right. That'll be the old hangar."

She did as she was told. She cleared the bushes and recognized the familiar shape of a Twin Otter parked in front of a dilapidated hangar. "Harry."

"Woman, what is it now? I'm busy back here."

The plane was in Williams Aviation's yellow and black livery. "The Twin Otter." The paint scheme was definitely familiar. "It's a Twin Otter. How did you know?" she asked.

Harry put down the AK and stood up. He ducked quickly, barely avoiding the wing as Sasha squealed to a halt beneath it. "It's one of Mike's. We just hit the jackpot."

Harry cast an eye toward the building. He didn't see any cars. "Keep an eye out for the crew. If they show up, we're done. I'll never be able to talk them into giving us the plane."

"We could just take it from them." Sasha racked her AK and returned it to safety.

"We could. But I'd rather not. There's no sense in annoying Mike any more than I have to. Let's get a move on."

They didn't waste time talking. It was go time. If the survey crew showed up, he'd be forced to chase them off. He didn't want to do that. It would make it harder to explain to Mike. If Mike caught wind. But would he? "Back us up to the cargo door and we'll unload. If we can't lift it, it stays behind. minus the weapons. I'm going up front to check fuel."

"Who was your last slave?" Sasha asked.

Harry ignored her. He opened the cargo door and climbed on board the Twin Otter. He made his way past the survey equipment to the cockpit and flipped the battery switch. He was confronted by a familiar glass cockpit. The fuel gauges indicated low fuel. He switched off and went aft to help his wife. He began by disconnecting and unloading the survey hardware in the cargo compartment.

"Come on, woman, lift that barge. Tote that bale. We have to get out of here in case anyone I know shows up. They're liable to talk me out of this exercise. Worse, they'll let Mike know I tried to steal his airplane."

Harry helped Sasha drag the heavier boxes from the truck into the cargo compartment. "You should be able to handle the rest. Get as much as you can on board." He jumped down and ran to the landing strip's electric fuel pump. He switched it on and brought the nozzle to his nose. His sense of smell was assaulted by turbo fuel fumes. He wrestled the hose to the Twin, drained fuel to flush the nozzle, and began fueling. "How's the loading going?" he asked, as he inserted the nozzle into the forward tank. It provided fuel for number two, the starboard engine.

"If you wanted a slave—" Sasha continued dragging the lighter boxes into the Otter's cargo compartment. She opened the heavier boxes remaining and hand-carried the contents on board.

"I love you too, dear. Hop to it or we'll never get back home."

Harry finished fueling the forward tank and switched the nozzle to the aft. He went back to help Sasha finish unloading the truck. He made a trip to the cockpit and flipped the battery switch to check fuel load. He was satisfied.

He switched off and returned to the fuel nozzle. That the tanks weren't full wasn't a concern. He had a backup plan for taking on additional fuel to get them into Galkayo. He closed both front and aft fuel caps and returned the fuel nozzle to the pump and switched it off.

He made his way to the cockpit and settled into the left seat to begin starting number one. Sasha got into the two-ton and moved the truck out of the way. She left it to drift toward the dilapidated terminal building, got out, and pulled the Twin's wheel chocks. She threw them into the back and walked around the end of the wing to give Harry a thumbs up through the cockpit window.

"That's my girl. She's worth every nickel I spend hauling her rear end out of trouble around the world," he muttered to himself.

Number one engine whined to a start. A van appeared on the edge of the strip with horn blaring, unheard by the occupants of the Twin with the turbine engine whining at ground idle. Men jumped out and ran toward the plane. "Incoming!" Sasha screamed. She leaned out the cargo door, grabbed the latch, and moved to pull it closed. She was too late. One man raised a camera.

Harry advanced the throttle for number one and taxied over the rough ground on the single engine. He pointed the nose toward the downwind end of the strip. Sasha closed and secured the cargo door. Harry started number two. When he had the Twin turned into wind, he set throttles for takeoff.

Sasha struggled to climb over the cargo on her way to the cockpit. She settled into the co-pilot's seat and fastened the seatbelt. The Twin Otter accelerated down the bumpy strip. Harry pointed to a lever above the control panel on the Twin's glass cockpit. "See that control? Crank it until the indicator lines up with 30 on this gauge." He pointed to the flap indicator on the panel.

Harry followed her hand with his eyes as Sasha did as she was told. The heavily laden Twin Otter floated gently off the runway and became airborne. "See how easy flying is? You're starting to listen. I'm proud of you."

"Don't let it go to your head," she insisted. "I think someone got a picture of us," she added.

The Twin Otter hugged the shore and disappeared low over the Indian Ocean, headed north up the coast. The men on the ground looked at each other as one of them said, "Did you see what I just saw?"

Mike Williams, their boss, wasn't going to be happy when he heard what they had to say. The captain took out a phone and called to report the theft. At the end of the conversation, he mentioned the woman looked like Harry's wife. Mike, on the other end of the call, was unconvinced.

"We're sure," he insisted. "We both saw her. I'll send you a picture."

"What direction did the plane go?" Mike wanted to know.

"It stayed low enough to wash the wheels, but I watched it until it disappeared. It was headed north, up the coast."

Mike hung up and paced back and forth. Who would want one of his survey planes? He called Barbara. If anyone knew what the hell was going on with Sasha, it would be her best friend. "Has Sasha left Harry?" he wanted to know.

Barbara's nervous laugh carried over the phone. "Not that I know, but I haven't talked to her for a couple of days. Why do you ask?"

"You can do better than that. What the hell is going on with Harry and Sasha? He's been gone for two days. We're babysitting his daughter. I've got a survey plane missing in Kenya. By the sound of it, Sasha is involved."

"That's impossible," Barbara insisted in a nervous tone. The woman's voice became even more high-pitched. "She doesn't know how to fly." She was pretty sure, at least.

"Whoever was doing the flying taxied on one engine and

started number two while lining up for takeoff," Mike told her. "Does that sound like anyone you know?"

Light on fuel, Harry knew the plane would get them into Dhobley. It was a sand strip just inside the Somali border. He used it on occasion when he needed to refuel and not be tracked. He reached into his shirt pocket and pulled out his little black book.

Sasha noticed his action from the right seat. "Are you trying to find a phone number for a date? You realize your wife is sitting beside you."

He handed her the book. "Look for Dhobley and get me the airport code please. I need to dial it in. It's spelled *D-H-O-B* in there somewhere."

"We're not going direct to Galkayo?"

"I didn't get enough fuel on to do that. I need to take on fuel to get us the final 625 statute."

Sasha found the page and give him the airport code.

"Is there a phone number attached?" Harry wanted to know.

"Yes. Do you want that too?"

"Yes please." He handed over his phone. "Dial the number for me."

"It's ringing," she told him as she handed the phone back.

Harry's phone call arranged for four 55-gallon drums of turbo fuel to be delivered to the Dhobley airstrip. His friend, Yuusuf, promised he would deliver it.

"Yuusuf is a contact I made in another life," Harry told Sasha. "He provides fuel off and on. I take care of his family with a contribution, and he goes home happy and satisfied. Even more important, his wife is happy for the husband's contribution to her household."

Sasha continued to flip through Harry's black book. She halted at pages. Skipped through to others. He held out his hand for the book. She handed it back and he returned it to his shirt pocket.

She nervously looked out the windows during their

approach and landing at Dhobley. Unsure of what to expect, she didn't want to be surprised. She took no chances on deplaning until she knew what was waiting. She picked up her AK, slammed a mag home, racked, and checked out the windows on both sides before opening the cargo door. There were no vehicles waiting.

The pair arrived at their fuel stop exhausted, sweaty, hungry and worn out. There was a sense of relief. She felt equipped for any eventuality, and comfortable on the warm, sandy airstrip. She found the breeze refreshing as it blew her long hair. She turned to face the wind and shook her head to shift it away from her face.

Harry observed Sasha from the cargo door. She was nervous on the strange ground. The fuel hadn't arrived yet. He thought about calling Yuusuf again and then decided against it. "We'll wait him out. How much cash do you have left," he wanted to know.

"Just about all of it," she said.

"In that case, hand it over. I have to pay the man," he told her.

"All of it? But—"

Harry interrupted her. "All of it. You don't need it. I do."

A cloud of dust approaching the strip warned them of an approaching vehicle. Sasha's eyes followed it with an easy laziness. It slowed and halted beneath the shade of the Twin Otter's high wing. The AK-47 hung off Sasha's shoulder. If someone planned on anything more than giving up a little fuel, she was prepared for an argument.

A grinning man got out and approached Harry. "Jambo, Harry Delaney. Hibari? How are you?"

"Yuusuf." Harry returned the man's smile. "Mazuri. I am well. I want you to meet my wife, Sasha."

Yuusuf nodded and bent into the truck. "I mentioned to my wife that you had not eaten. She prepared food for you. A little injera. Some meat and sauce to go with it. I hope it is enough."

"It sounds like a feast, Yuusuf," Sasha said. "Be sure to thank your wife for us."

Yuusuf's two companions placed the hand pump into the

barrel of jet fuel and tightened the bung. Harry reached for the nozzle and inserted it into the forward tank. "Let me know when two drums are empty. I need to fuel both sides."

Refueling went quickly after the men figured out who was supervising and who was working.

"I'm going to do my best to secure the cargo," Sasha said. She retreated to the cargo hold and closed the door.

A second vehicle approached the strip. "That will be my cousin, the police chief," Yuusuf told Harry. "He likes to keep an eye on things. I will get rid of him."

Sasha stuck her head out the cargo door. "How's the refuel coming along?"

"We're almost done," Harry said. "We're on Africa time. You'll get accustomed to it once you're over here long enough. Did you get the cargo secured?"

"As best I could," Sasha said. "It shouldn't shift."

"I probably could have taken on less fuel, but it's 625 statute miles to our final destination. I don't know the availability from here on. We're going to be crossing some ground that I'm not familiar with."

"It took all day to get this far," she said.

"That's all right." She looked up at him, and he grinned at her. "Africa time, remember?"

Harry remained crouched in the cargo door, taking in the picture presented by his ex-wife. He was happy to be checking her out after all these years. The wind caught her hair, causing it to shimmer in the late afternoon light. She kept it long and dark, the way she had it when they first crossed paths on Mexico's Baja.

Perhaps there were a few silver strands now, but she was still the same beautiful woman. Even better looking, as far as he was concerned. A little older. So was he. She had learned to be more patient, too. Damn, but he was falling in love all over again. He reached down and offered his hand to help her into the plane.

"What are you grinning at?" she asked. "Suddenly I have the feeling that I'm being checked out by a pervert."

"You might be right, but we don't have time if we want to make Galkayo before dark. We have to get going."

"Four drums empty," Yuusuf called out.

Harry jumped down and removed the nozzle from the aft tank. He closed the cap and handed the hose to Yuusuf. He took out an envelope and handed it over to the man. A little something for your wife to thank her for the excellent food. We weren't expecting that. As usual, I put a little extra in it for you." The men grinned.

"So long, my friend. Until next time." Harry waved and joined Sasha in the cargo hold as Yuusuf drove off with the empty fuel drums.

He ran through the pre-start checklist. Sasha closed the cargo door and settled into the right seat. He started number one and advanced its throttle to begin taxiing while he fired up number two. He carried on to the end of the strip, stepped on a brake, and the Otter shifted and straightened into position to initiate a rolling takeoff.

"Flaps ten," he called out.

Unprepared for the command, Sasha jumped before setting the flap. "Flaps 10," she repeated, as she reached to dial it in. She checked the flap indicator and repeated the call when she had it. Harry followed her movement with his eyes to confirm. The overloaded Twin Otter lurched into the air. Harry kept it as low as he dared until he disappeared over a dune.

They were airborne and bound for their final destination.

It was almost dark when Harry had the Twin lined up off to the side of the Oshaco landing strip. The long shadow of setting sun and approaching dusk chased after them off their starboard side.

"Why are you lined up for the dirt? The strip looks good."

"We're wearing tundra tires. I don't want to risk damaging them on broken rock. The long shadows produced by the low sun makes the rocks stand out."

She saw what he meant when the plane touched down. Rocks were everywhere in the desert sand.

Harry taxied onto the dirt tarmac and shut down in a cloud of dust. A parade of technicals and SUVs surrounded the plane and waited. He didn't recognize Ali in the crowd of men and technicals. He was too exhausted to question the man who met them. Sasha opened the cargo door and Harry preceded her to the ground. She kept the AK at the ready.

"Greetings. You have made it safely. I am Waheed, son of Ali. He sends his greetings to you both."

"Nothing the two of us couldn't handle. Where is Ali?"

"My father is not able to meet with you at this time. He is ill. When he recovers, I will take you to him."

Sasha came up behind Harry and leaned into him. "Do you see her?"

Waheed insisted on unloading the arms. He directed a truck to the cargo door. "I have a place for you to stay in town. You will be safe there. My men will guard you." He made no further mention of his father.

Sasha was unconvinced the offer was genuine. "It sounds more like we're being kept under guard."

Waheed regarded the woman through narrowed eyes. He wasn't accustomed to being questioned, especially by a woman. A white woman, at that. "Perhaps. But you have no alternative. Come. Let us go." Waheed escorted them to a truck.

"I don't like this, Harry."

"Neither do I, but we're here now. And no, I don't see her. I wouldn't expect to until tomorrow, maybe."

He still expected Ali to come and meet with him. After all, the whole reason for this little get-together was because the old man had requested it. It was unlike him to not to greet his familiar visitors.

Waheed's convoy trailed through the city. He stopped at a primitive hotel. The pair were relieved of their weapons, searched and escorted to their room.

"I'm still not liking this. What do you suppose has become of Ali?"

"If what Waheed says is true, he's probably too weak to show up tonight. He's not a young man any more. I hope we'll get to see him tomorrow. By the look of it, Waheed is in charge. I wonder how that's working out."

"We need to get that woman and get the hell out of here as soon as we can."

Harry hesitated before replying. What were the chances that both Eloria and Irit could be alive? He didn't know, but whoever they left behind would be coming out with him.

"There might be two women, remember?" he reminded her.

Large, heavy trucks bouncing and groaning over the dirt road in front of the hotel woke Harry in the primitive room. The dust whipped up drifted in past missing doors and windows, long considered unnecessary in the desert climate. He peered out one of the missing windows at the heavy equipment being ferried to points unknown.

The non-stop action was caused by oil-company big-rigs on the move with trailers loaded with drilling equipment. They would be heading for a place to settle and bore the next dry well.

The locals were still being sold the bill of goods that there was oil underground. From what he gleaned so far, Waheed was convinced. He was able to convince his followers to believe it, too.

It was all pie-in-the sky, but no one could sway the locals. Oil companies threw around plenty of cash. It was almost as though they were seeding with it. Money always bought more arms than happiness. He wondered which of the oil companies were responsible for this latest madness, until he recognized the logo.

CAN-AL.

Of course. CAN-AL was key to the craziness that had taken over. CAN-AL had to be the one that convinced Waheed to buy into the prospects of oil in the region. Lots of cash handed to the right people probably didn't hurt. Payoffs were common in the oil business. In fact, it was standard operating practice. Hell, he'd done his fair share over the years, too.

Harry stopped caring about it when he realized Sasha wasn't in the room. Surely she hadn't wandered off again. He went to the door and checked the hallway. The chair was empty. The guard was gone. He walked to the end of the building and came across another guard.

"Go back to your room," the guard ordered.

Harry did as he was told. He waited a few minutes before climbing out the window to disappear down an alley toward what he hoped would be the local market. It occurred to him Sasha might have gone on another of her shopping expeditions.

The unlit streets proved difficult to navigate

More likely, she a guest of Waheed, taken to his compound. Failing that, perhaps a compound outside of the city. He'd have to find her on his own. Damn but he'd be chasing her shadow again. That woman would be the death of him. The more things changed, the more they stayed the same.

A little girl wearing a garland of bougainvillea around her neck peered past a darkened doorway and motioned. "Mr. Harry. Come. Come."

The girl spoke in heavily accented English, barely understandable. He approached and she retreated into the alley's shadows. "You are Mr. Harry."

"Yes. I am Harry," he replied.

"I am sent to bring you. You must come. There is someone who wants to see you," she told him.

Harry had trouble understanding the girl. She spoke with an accent he never heard. He hoped the girl would lead him to his ex, shopping spree or not. That, or he was being taken to a mugging.

He approached, and the waif grabbed his sleeve. She tugged him on a journey through the narrow streets and back alleys. They blurred into one as though she was leading him in circles. When someone approached the girl was unsure of, she pulled him out of sight into the shadows.

"Are you taking me to Sasha?"

"Sasha? Who is Sasha?" she wanted to know.

"Sasha is my wife," he informed the girl.

"I know nothing of her. I cannot say where is your wife," the girl said. "What has become of her was not our doing. Come. We are almost at the place."

Place? *What place*, he wondered. The girl continued to lead him until she came to a walled compound. She released his sleeve and opened the gate. She pushed him through the opening and followed after him. She slid the bar into place behind them, locking them in. She grabbed his hand once more and led him across a small courtyard into a dark room.

Someone turned up a gas flame. The room's sole occupant stood up in the dim light. A hand pulled at a scarf, revealing a face. Harry's jaw dropped. He couldn't believe his eyes.

54

Out of the Past
Eloria

Eloria made for the comms tent. She raised the flap and rushed into the empty tent. She cursed at the stupidity of the men in camp. During an ongoing operation, the radio was to be manned until the plane returned. A hum accompanied by a steady crackle filled the tent. A voice filtered through the background signal. She found it difficult to make out the transmission. Explosions overpowered the voice. She cranked up the volume and bent an ear to the speaker.

"... under attack ... pinned down ... aircraft destroyed ... pilot—"

The staccato of automatic fire and booming grenades left no doubt about the trouble the team flew into. There was no time for hesitation. She ran out of the tent and slapped Irit on the shoulder. "Come on. We need to get ready."

Eloria ran to Mike's tent and shook him awake. "You have to get up. Now."

Mike groaned and rolled over. His shirt was covered with sweat in the warm tent. "What the hell is going on? Is he back already?" He sat up, groggy with sleep, and looked at the woman.

"A call for support is coming from the airstrip Harry is

working. There is so much gunfire in the background I could barely make out what they were saying."

Mike scrambled out of his cot and pulled his pants on. He flipped his boots upside-down and knocked them together. Eloria allowed him time to splash water on his face before physically dragging him to the comms tent.

The status updates came in spaced five to ten minutes apart. Waiting for the next only increased the unbearable tension. With every transmission, the situation got worse. Gunfire and explosions continued to be broadcast along with the sitreps, or situation reports. The mercs were holding their own, but they were pinned down and taking heavy fire.

Irit and Eloria disappeared and returned with packs and supplies to get them to the site. Eloria called out to the mercs still in camp. No one responded. She aimed her Galil high and fired a burst into the air. It too was ignored. Not one merc volunteered to accompany them on the mission to extract. It would be up to the three of them or no one. She turned back to Mike.

"What's in your pack, Meeka?" Eloria asked.

Mike opened it to show her the rations and AK magazines.

"Throw in some smoke," she told him. "And grenades. Do you have a radio?"

"He shook his head." "No."

"That's all right. We have two," she assured him.

Mike had enough of the broadcasts coming from the endangered men. They were difficult to understand and only kept him on edge with concern for Harry. He turned down the radio until it was a hum in the background. He went through the documents in the tent and found a chart of the area. He used his compass to take a bearing to the strip. Using a pencil, he drew a line and slipped the aerial photos and the chart into his pack. He shouldered it and joined the women in the suddenly silent camp.

The women turned their backs on the camp and followed Mike into the brush as he headed off on the compass bearing. Eloria brought up the rear. Irit was off to the side, a close third. The ground cover was sparse and uneven. It made for easy walking. They made good time.

As they drew closer, the gunfire became more intense. Eventually, it grew sporadic. Eloria was worried about the condition of the team. She halted Mike and ordered him to get behind. "You do not walk past us. Remain between if you must. Do what we tell you to do. Do not ask questions."

Mike gave a silent nod of agreement. This was new ground he was traveling.

Eloria concentrated on the situation at hand. Judging by the sporadic gunfire, both sides had settled in, secure in their positions. It was that, or it was game over and the attackers were mopping up. She didn't let on to Mike, and instead advanced.

Eloria called to him to stop at the edge of a thicket. She made him sit and take cover behind a dead tree trunk. Using hand signals, she motioned for him to stay put. She walked with Irit to flank two thickets separated by forty or fifty feet. They disappeared into the brush. The pair reappeared in minutes brandishing bloody knives.

Eloria regarded a slack-jawed Mike. His demeanor was different, too. He was finally waking up to the fact that the women he and Harry had spent the night with were capable of more than drinking and screwing around. It pleased her to know that he knew it.

"Follow me, Meeka. Remember. Do what I tell you," Eloria insisted.

He nodded curtly and fell in behind the pair once again. Eloria was secretly pleased that he obeyed her orders without question. Maybe he wasn't such a soft man after all. She glimpsed Irit off to her left. The woman crouched low and gestured toward another thicket surrounding a much bigger tree.

"Irit is saying the rest of them are where she is pointing. When I signal, pull the pin and throw one of your grenades."

A sheen of sweat covered Mike's face. He reached into his pack with a sweaty hand. White fingers settled on a grenade and pulled it out. He had no time to think about what he was doing before Eloria called to him.

"Now, Meeka. Throw it now."

Mike hesitated for only an instant before pulling the pin and tossing the grenade. It fell short, thumped the ground, and bounced into the thicket. Five men scrambled out just before the grenade exploded. One by one, the girls picked them off before they could run and disappear.

Eloria headed for the thicket. She gave it a visual and then finished off the men, one at a time, using her shotgun. She paused to reload twice. Irit backed her up with her pistol.

Mike moved to follow the pair into the brush of the thicket.

"Do not go there," Eloria said. "Keep away. You do not want to see it."

Mike did as he was told. Eloria nodded. He would make it.

Irit whistled, and the three joined up. Someone whistled back from where they suspected the downed crew was located. They walked toward the sound. The job was finished.

"It is safe now, Meeka. We are here." Eloria had some difficulty pronouncing Mike's name, even from the very beginning.

I rit fussed over a reluctant Harry, talking to herself the entire time. His feeble attempts to convince her that his shoulder wound was no big deal fell on deaf ears. "Be quiet, Harry," she told him.

She partially unwound the bandage to expose the wound. She poked and prodded and tried not to hurt him too much. She made sure he knew she was in first aid mode, and he was going to take her medicine or else. She finished stripping away the merc's dressings, exposing his wound. "You're going to live," she said. "The bullet went straight through. No bones broken. No major blood vessels damaged." She re-bandaged him and rigged a sling. While she was at it, she cleaned his bloody head wound and bandaged that, too.

"You have a concussion. There's nothing I can do about that." It worried her, but time would take care of it if it wasn't serious.

While Irit busied herself with a wounded Harry, Eloria regarded Mike. It was obvious he would have been helpless in the firefight and subsequent mop-up. That he took the time to express his gratitude to her for coming along to do the dirty work was a plus.

He was humble. Eloria liked that. He was all business, too. He wasn't about wasting time. It was evident when he pulled the map sheet from his pack and began looking for an escape route.

What she wasn't prepared for was the reluctance of the rescued mercs to acknowledge they had been freed by two women. Like she and her sister, the mercs were supposed to be professionals. They refused to contribute anything, and after a brief discussion, one cowed son of a bitch approached and as much as told her so.

Mike wasn't happy with that, either. He called them cowards and demanded they leave some ammo before they departed. The only thing left to do was to laugh at their antics. Although, their routine with the fingers and Harry's response turned out to be pretty accurate, even if no one knew it.

At first, there was some confusion about whether the foursome should return to base camp. Harry was adamant that they make for friendlier ground, even though his condition was worsening. His words slurred and his movements were shaky.

The decision was made for them when Mike pulled out the charts. There would be no retracing their steps. He pointed at a clearing on one of the photos. Harry came around long enough to volunteer that it was a mine. It didn't look to be far away. If it was active, it would provide them with a vehicle to make good on their trek to civilization.

"We're going to need some traveling money," Harry slurred. "Maybe the mine will have a safe."

"Is Harry going to be able to keep up?" Irit asked.

Mike didn't hesitate. "If he can't, I'll be staying with him until he can."

That sealed it for Eloria. She realized Mike would be a keeper—if only they didn't get stuck in this mess.

She joked with Irit, but they let the guys know they would be marching right along with them. Whether Harry could keep up wouldn't be an issue. They would live or die together.

Mike's response came quick. "About that dying part?"

The women looked at him before he went on.

"Damn but I hope not."

Eloria took point after making certain to check on directions with Mike. Irit brought up the rear. Between the two, Mike helped Harry limp along by his side. From time to time, they stopped to allow the wounded man to rest. Mike used the opportunity to check the map and photos and their course. They made good time through the light ground cover, even with the disabled Harry.

Late in the afternoon, they came up on a pool of water. It looked to be deep enough for a swim. Without consulting Harry, the trio quickly agreed to end the trek for the day. To go further would jeopardize their safety, especially if a shortage of water became an issue. Sunset would come soon, too. If they proceeded, it would leave them in the dark in inhospitable ground.

Eloria led them to high ground overlooking the water. She consulted with Irit, and the pair agreed. It afforded them a vantage point over any big animals wanting to drink. "It's an excellent water source. We will stop here. If nothing comes along to eat us, we will be in good shape for tomorrow."

Mike agreed with a silly grin. He made a joke and suggested the women prepare something to eat while he lounged by the pool. Eloria's eyes flashed, and she gave him a dirty look. "I'll be taking a swim. You can join me or you can do what you want."

He wasn't so sure about that, and she sensed his reluctance. "Don't be shy, Meeka. I will stand guard while you undress. If nothing comes along to eat you, then I'll get naked and take my turn in the water."

It worked, and they spent the early darkness making love in the full-moon shadows of the bushes surrounding the shoreline.

No thirsty animals showed up to interrupt the celebration.

The foursome spent the cool night huddled together sharing body heat. Come morning, they struggled to untangle. Eloria suspected Harry would be worse off with his shoulder and arm stiff from no activity. They had neglected to wake him regularly, and she was concerned.

Following a brief wound inspection, Harry appeared ready to march. It would be slow going, but they'd get him to the mine. They started slowly to allow the kinks out of Harry's body. It helped get them warmed up in the early light of dawn. By mid-day, the sun and the heat of the day took over. Wet clothes were stuck to overheated bodies. Perspiration ran down faces. Flies got swatted away, only to return instantly, drawn by the heat and the moisture.

Mid-afternoon saw them on the edge of a low escarpment overlooking their destination. It was bulldozed to protect the mine. Eloria went on ahead to allow Harry to rest. She was concerned about him. He was becoming weaker by the hour. She scouted the way down the hill, marking her trail as best she could. Harry would have a tough time with it, but with effort and their help, he would make it.

At the bottom, she trained her scope on the open pit and its surroundings. She was looking to count people and armed guards involved in the operation. Satisfied, she turned the scope toward the blockhouse guarding the only access road.

She returned the scope to her pack, shouldered it, and made her way up the rough trail, returning to the group the same way she had descended. Irit left Harry and greeted her at the top.

"How many?" Irit asked.

"Two guards at the blockhouse. A swing gate blocks access into the mine. I didn't see any fencing. No perimeter," Eloria told her.

"Any vehicles we can use?"

"Mostly heavy trucks. They look to be junk. There's a Land Rover."

Mike kept quiet until the mention of the Rover. "A Land Rover is good. We can trade it for traveling money when we get to civilization."

The women ignored him. "There could be a safe in the

blockhouse. That would make it easier."

"If they're stupid enough to keep anything there, it would," Eloria said.

"You're right. They would want to get their profits off the property as soon as possible."

Irit regarded Mike. She liked Eloria's lover. Both men had treated them well in the short time they had known them. "We will chance it, in the case there is something of value."

Irit's plan was simple. She would be the one to move toward the blockhouse and secure it. If needed, Eloria would provide covering fire to enable Mike to make his way to the vehicle. He would get it started while the two women kept watch for anyone that might come up on them.

With the plan settled, Irit made her way to the blockhouse, one slow step at a time, cautious that she might be heard. Two guards kept up their card game, oblivious, talking and laughing.

Irit poked her Galil and her head past the door. She knocked the muzzle against the frame, interrupting the card game. She motioned with the muzzle, and the guards exited the blockhouse. She subdued them with tape around hands and ankles.

The safe was old and dust-covered. She taped a grenade to the face, pulled the pin, and ran outside. The dust settled, and she returned. She slipped a finger into the opening left by the missing dial and twisted, working the tumblers. Following a couple of tries, she was able to twist the handle and pull the door open.

Eloria and Mike arrived with the open-top Land Rover. Irit moved Harry from the shade to the side of the road and helped him into the back.

"What news?" Eloria asked.

"There was nothing. A few shillings on the guards." She waved the paper. It was worthless. "They need it more than we do." She tossed it out the window.

"We are wasting time. We must go," Eloria said.

Up front in the Rover, Mike drove. Eloria rode shotgun. Irit sat in the back with the wounded Harry. She ignored the now constant groaning as best she could. Her eyes kept busy roaming the surroundings in their wake for anyone who might chase after them. So far, it looked like they would be home-free.

It was tough going on the rough and tumble access road. The Rover jostled and bounced its way toward the main highway. Harry moaned and groaned with every bump. At the junction, Mike cranked the wheel and steered the Rover north to the border with Kenya.

On the smoother highway, it became easy for Irit to keep Harry settled in the back. Even so, she worried about his condition. He no longer woke up.

The Rover passed beneath a tree. The RPG round whooshed out of nowhere and exploded when it contacted the tree. Branches scattered and crashed into the Rover. Eloria looked into the back to check on Irit and Harry. She screamed. "Irit! Irit!"

There was no answer from her sister. A branch stuck out of Irit's chest. She crawled over the seat into the back. Immediately she tried to resuscitate Irit. It was no use. Her sister had no pulse. The branch had impaled her just beneath her heart.

She stayed in the back of the Rover and took up a position facing backwards. Silently, she hoped, she prayed, that whatever, whoever, was behind them would show themselves. In minutes that seemed like hours, a Jeep rounded a corner. It was gaining.

She pressed her forearms against the Galils in her lap to hold them secure in the bouncing Rover. She wrestled with the pin on a grenade and tossed it. It exploded ahead of the pursuing Jeep. She popped smoke and leaned into the front, where she poked Mike with the butt of her shotgun. She yelled over the screaming engine. "It's loaded. Take it."

She popped a second smoke and jumped out of the moving Rover. She hit the ground and rolled into a kneeling position. She stayed down, shouldered her Galil, and began measured fire in the direction of the pursuing Jeep. It came at her, bearing down fast. At the last second she jumped out of the way and tossed a grenade. It rattled as it landed in the Jeep. Twenty feet later, it exploded.

Eloria had no time to finish off the occupants. Instead, she popped two smokes in succession. Her concern was for another vehicle that might be coming up behind. She was proved right when she was forced to jump out of the way to avoid the second Jeep.

By the time she oriented herself in the cloud of smoke, her only line of sight was toward the disappearing Rover. She chose not to risk hitting Mike and Harry with her fire. Instead, she began jogging along the road toward the border.

She knew she would make it.

It would be that, or she would be the one to die trying.

Eloria heard yet another Jeep speeding toward her through the smoke. She looked over her shoulder. It came straight at her and didn't slow. She was out of ammunition. She had already turned her shotgun over to Mike. All she could do was run. She veered off the road and stumbled across a shallow ditch. She got onto flat, rough ground and headed cross-country.

The Jeep overtook her fast in the open grassland. It circled wide and pulled around in front of her. Exhausted, she doubled over to catch her breath. She struggled against the Jeep's occupants, but there were too many. They knocked her unconscious.

She came to. Hands roamed her body, searching for weapons. Not satisfied with that, the men began beating her. She parried the blows as best she could, but there were too many captors with too many boots kicking at her. Rifle butts landed blow after blow. Defeated, she collapsed, unconscious in the tall grass.

Eloria regained consciousness in the back of the Jeep. Blindfolded and trussed up like an animal about to be hauled to the slaughter, she continued her struggles. She felt every bump the Jeep took as it bounced over what had to be a dirt trail. Beyond knowing they were off the main road she had no idea where she was or where she would end up.

She passed out again.

When she came to, the Jeep was stopped. Still bound and blindfolded, she wiggled toes and fingers and tried moving limbs to assess the state of her injuries. Everything worked. She was incredibly sore. Though blindfolded, she knew she would be bloody from the beating she took. She considered herself lucky to be alive.

With the damage assessment over, it became time to figure out what she could do to escape her captors. Blindfolded and tied up, that would be impossible for the present.

Eloria concentrated on making herself aware of her surroundings. Muffled voices, birds, animal sounds. Shuffling. Snuffling. Roaring.

Hard as it was to believe, she decided she had to be in someone's private game preserve. Possibly the animal compound, judging by the sounds assaulting her from all directions. What was going on? Who wanted her here, and why?

Above all, why hadn't she been killed and left for animal feed?

55

It **took a** minute for Harry's eyes to adjust to the dimly lit room. He reached for the scarf and eased it aside. A face that appeared in many of his nightmares was in front of him. The woman took his hand and cradled it in hers. Warm breath and soft lips brushed his fingers. Her other hand lay protectively on the little girl that brought him here. She peeked out from behind the woman.

"Eloria." He didn't have to ask. "It is you." He removed his hand from the side of her face as a tear streamed down.

"Yes. My daughter has been waiting for you. As have I." The girl moved to stand beside her mother. She looked up at Harry, proud and defiant, as though he might deny her mother's words.

It had been many years since Harry laid eyes on Eloria. In Tanzania. During the trek through the bush to the mining camp. It was a long way from where she stood now. It wasn't only that. He had believed her to be dead. She had to be. Mike had told him it was so.

"What the hell? What are you doing here?" Harry's eyes were accustomed to the darkened room. The little girl moved to stand beside him. A scarf obscured the girl's face. She looked up at her mother. "Mr. Harry asked about his woman."

Eloria removed the scarf covering her daughter's face. She regarded her for a moment with a look of pride before touching the girl's chin and gently turning her face to Harry. "I would like you to meet my daughter. This is Meeka."

She pronounced the girl's name in the same manner Harry recalled her saying Mike's name all those years ago. Meeka smiled up at him.

Eloria turned up another lamp. It was enough to cause Harry to do a double take. How long had it been since their Tanzanian adventure? Nine or ten years? The girl was tall and gangly and had a grin that resembled Mike's more than he wanted to admit. To say she was a spitting image wouldn't cover it. The girl was Mike's younger twin.

Memories of their trek across the Tanzanian bush came flooding back. The downed aircraft. The firefight. His rescue by Mike and the women after they eliminated the attackers. The almost two-day overland trek to the tanzanite mine. Stealing the truck and attacking the blockhouse. The race to the border to escape the gunmen chasing after them.

That chase was the sketchy part. By then his concussion had kicked in for the worse. He had no memory of it.

How would he ever tell Mike about this? Worse, how would Barbara take it when she found out? If she found out. He had completely forgotten that he was now searching for his own wife in all of this.

"Get Mr. Harry a chair, Meeka. He looks like he will fall down soon," Eloria observed.

Harry didn't fall down. He thumped into the chair. His breath escaped with an audible groan. "We have a lot to talk about, Eloria."

"Yes, Mr. Harry. But first you must eat. Meeka, bring Harry chai and roti. Some chicken, too, with a bit of injera."

The girl went to the stove to retrieve a tray of tea and warm bread. She placed it in front of Harry. She pulled a chair close beside him and sat down to watch him devour the food. Eloria rested a hand on her daughter's shoulder. "She likes you already. That is good."

He washed the bread down with a mouthful of hot, spicy chai and nodded his approval before managing to speak. Even then, it was only a question. "Is it good?"

"Yes. It is good," Eloria assured him. "I will explain everything after you finish."

Harry needed time to process what he just learned. He took his time pushing the plate away. He took another drink of the excellent chai to wash down a last mouthful of roti and spicy chicken. Hunger satisfied, he eased back from the table to position his chair to face Eloria.

The little girl did the same. She placed her elbows on the table and rested her chin in the palms of both hands and studied Harry.

"So you know, Eloria. When I found out who was on the other end of the phone, I couldn't let it go. I owe you and Irit everything for getting me out of that mess at the airstrip. That you were alive and asking for help had me cashing in every favor anyone ever owed to get to you."

"Your wife is here, too, I have been told."

"Yes. It's not the first time she has backed me up," he told her. "She is a very strong-willed woman. When she learned it might be you, I couldn't keep her away."

Meeka's eyes shifted back and forth, trying to follow the conversation.

"I know all about you," Eloria said. "Ali has told me many stories about you and your friends. And of Barbara's bravery also."

"I didn't tell Mike I was coming here. Mike's wife, Barbara, and Sasha are best friends. They have been for many years, even before she met me. I forced Sasha to swear she wouldn't tell Barbara or Mike what we would be up to over here—not that we had any idea."

"Why is that?" she asked.

"Because I don't want to threaten their marriage. I have no idea how Barbara would take news of you being alive. Initially, I thought it was you and Irit who wanted our help. Now I find out that it's you and your daughter. Mike's daughter, too, by the look of it. They killed Irit that day, didn't they?"

"Yes. She was killed."

"You weren't, and now I think it's time for you to tell me what's going on."

A truck approached the courtyard. Eloria halted to listen. Meeka cocked an ear. The truck backfired and halted. Instantly, the atmosphere in the house changed. The welcome Harry had received turned to one of caution. Eloria motioned to Meeka, and she scurried into a back room. She called to her daughter. "Meeka. One for Mr. Harry also."

The girl returned, cradling two heavy AK-47s in her arms. A familiar-looking old shotgun hung off of Meeka's shoulder. Harry took the second AK and moved to the shadows in the dimly lit room. He wasn't given time to check the action.

"You must come this way." Meeka took Harry's hand and pulled him into the back.

Sandals slowly slapped their way across the hardened dirt toward the door to the house. Eloria remained in the front room. A man's voice called out. "It is Ali. I am coming in."

Eloria didn't relax until Ali was inside and the door latched.

"I have heard talk that a visitor—an old friend—has come our way," Ali said.

Meeka took Harry's hand and led him back to the front room. Harry slung the AK over his shoulder and greeted the old man with a handshake and a warm hug. "Salaam, old friend. It is good to see you."

Harry stepped back to regard the man who was his friend all these years. The passage of time wasn't kind to Ali. He appeared pale and weak even in the dim light. His hands shook. He slowly made his way to a chair and eased into it.

"And you, Harry. I am glad you could be here on such a short notice," he said.

"As I told Eloria just minutes ago, nothing could keep me away when I learned who it was that needed my help."

Ali didn't waste time. "I have some news of your wife."

"Yes, Harry. Why is your wife not with you?" Eloria asked.

So. Eloria hadn't known his wife was missing. Perhaps that

would bode well when he asked for her help to find Sasha.

"Sasha is very capable of taking care of herself," he told Eloria. "I didn't want to burden you with my problems until I found out what yours might be."

Eloria touched her daughter on the shoulder and smiled down at her. "Meeka, make fresh chai for us, please. I think we will talk for a while."

"Yes, mother. Would you like roti, Ali?" the girl asked, as she moved to the stove and the boiling water.

"No, child. Thank you for the offering."

"Come, Ali," Eloria said. "You must tell Harry what has become of his wife. Surely you will not make him wait any longer."

Immediately Harry suspected Eloria of knowing more about the whereabouts of his wife than she was letting on.

The old man sighed and shifted in his chair.

Harry sensed Ali had bad news about his wife. The man knew he was not someone who sat idly by when threats were made against his family. He learned that when Harry asked for his help to rescue his wife the last time she was missing in this part of the world.

"My son has taken your woman," Ali finally admitted. "He has taken your Sasha."

"Waheed. How do you know?" Harry asked.

"Eloria's child followed him and saw your Sasha being delivered."

It surprised Harry to learn that Eloria's daughter could be so knowledgeable. "It seems you've been teaching Meeka what she needs to know to survive in this place."

"I think you are right, Harry. I hope she will not be here much longer." Eloria retrieved a burnoose for Harry.

"You will need this to blend in," she told him. "Unfortunately, I can do nothing for the color of your skin."

"In that case, I'll have to keep my eyes open and stay lucky," he admitted.

Eloria disappeared into the bedroom and came out with a handgun and ammunition. A k-bar in a sheath and a belt and holster appeared.

"You've been stocking up," he told her.

"It is necessary for a white woman and for her daughter. People know not to mess with me or Meeka. It helps to be aligned with Ali also."

"That might not be such a good thing for long," Harry was forced to admit. He shifted his gaze to a tired-looking Ali.

"You are right, Harry. That is why I called to ask you to come here," Eloria said.

"Ali, why did Waheed kidnap my wife? She has nothing to do with his problems," Harry said.

"I think he wants to put pressure on you to ignore our friendship," Ali said. "He thinks I asked you here to help me convince our people that the oil companies are not good."

"We both know that to be true, don't we, Ali?"

"Waheed has fallen in with a certain oil company and their treachery. He believes their lies about underground oil reserves in our clan territory. He thinks he will become rich beyond his dreams."

"But there's no oil here. Every hole has come up dry since drilling began decades ago."

"You are right. We both know it. Even so, the company is telling him there is oil in the ground. I tried to explain how the companies have been pretending to look for oil for a generation, yet they have found nothing. It is a front for American interference in my country. Now even a company from Canada is in on the treachery."

"Damn, Ali, we were all here when the last round of exploration was going on. There was nothing, not even water. Only sand and dust," Harry said.

"Waheed doesn't believe it. He thinks it is being kept secret. He has taken the side of the oil company and their interfering leaders. He has allowed them to come here and do as they please."

"You will become another arm of American interventionism. Do you want that?"

"No, Harry, I do not. But there is worse to come."

Harry didn't like the sound of that. He pushed back from the table and stood up. "How so?"

Ali went on. "For some time my son has had a liking for Eloria. Unfortunately, he has no use for her child."

Tears welled in Meeka's eyes. She moved to her mother sitting across the table. She stood beside her, looking at the men and finally her mother. "Will you leave me, mother?"

Eloria's arms surrounded Meeka. She hugged her close and tight. "No, my daughter. I will not. Never in my life will you be here without me if I have to die to keep you safe."

"Did Mr. Harry come to help us go away?" Meeka wanted to know.

Harry thought back to the promise he made to himself in the Tanzanian bush at the site of his downed aircraft. The appearance of the women earned his respect and undying gratitude when they came to his rescue. He would do anything for Eloria and the girl.

"When I learned you and Irit had been killed, I was devastated. I've been haunted knowing that I would never get the chance to honor the pledge I made. You are going to get everything I promised I would deliver, and then some," Harry assured Eloria and Meeka.

Heaven and hell would do for now. If there was something else he needed to bring, he would handle it when the need arrived. Harry turned to the little girl, still surrounded by her mother's arms. "Meeka, my promise is to you and to your mother. You will not remain here."

The little girl moved to Harry's side and took his hand. Eloria smiled and nodded. "Thank you, Harry. It means much to me. And to Meeka."

The look she gave Harry convinced him she took him at his word. She knew he meant what he said. "Ali, you are with us, are you not?"

"Yes," the old man admitted.

With that settled, Harry was certain he could put his efforts into locating his wife. "Now then. You must tell me where Waheed has taken Sasha. Before you do, you'd better know I am not happy to learn that he has my wife as a prisoner, for ransom or for any reason. I promise I will dispatch straight to hell anyone who gets in the way or harms her." He looked directly at Ali.

The old man sighed and stood up. "I am afraid of that. So be it. My son is now a grown man. He must be the one to answer for the sins of his actions." Ali steadied himself against the table. He was extremely weak.

The old man's attention shifted to Eloria. "She knows where your woman is. Inshallah, you will have her soon."

That was news. Harry's gaze moved to Eloria. He gave her a hard look. "You didn't tell me."

"Forgive me. I had to know where your loyalty would lie."

"Now you know. It is with my wife and my promise to you and your daughter. You have no reason to doubt any longer."

56

Sasha woke up in a sweat in the hot, stuffy room where she and Harry had been imprisoned since their arrival. Even the missing window and door in the broken-down excuse for a motel didn't allow for a whisper of a breeze. She looked over at Harry on the second bed. How he was able to sleep in the heat and humidity annoyed her. She considered waking him and then thought better. He didn't need to be bombarded with a list of her complaints.

She moved to kick away the sheet on the filthy bed. Her feet swiped empty air, and she remembered the sheets were missing, just like the door. She sat up and reached for her boots. She remembered Harry's instructions and turned them over and knocked them together before putting them on. On her way to the courtyard she passed the guard.

He followed after her in silence, close behind, his footsteps giving him away. She reached the dark, empty courtyard and he was on her. He grabbed her hair and pulled her toward the street in front of the motel. She couldn't keep up. She lost her balance and fell to her knees. He traded hair for arm and yanked her to her feet. She fought. Kicked. Struggled. It was no use. The man's grip was too powerful.

She stumbled and fell again and bumped head-first into a truck. Rendered semi-conscious, she could no longer struggle. Two men easily loaded her into the truck and dropped her in the middle seat.

Sasha came to with a vengeance when she realized they were taking her away. She kicked. Bit. Scratched. The men found out they made a huge mistake in not restraining her. She doubled down on her attempt to escape. She flailed her fists and then her feet at both men. She could only land weak, half-hearted punches. Her efforts were rewarded with a single punch to the head. Quieted at last, she slumped against the seat.

The truck made its way out of town on dark, narrow streets. It wound its way north of the city toward Waheed's isolated compound. Sasha came to and discovered the truck was stopped. The men were busy digging it out of soft sand. She jumped out and ran. She dodged a shovel swung her way and ran into the second man. He swung a fist into her stomach and she collapsed. She ended up with arms and feet tied before they tossed her into the back of the truck.

"If this one was my woman I would leave her in the desert to die of thirst," said the first man.

"I think this one will follow you home and kill you," the second said.

"Perhaps you are right," the first admitted. "Why does Waheed want this woman??

"I do not know. I do only what he tells me."

"Let us go. I want to be rid of her. Sooner is better. She will be Waheed's problem."

Sasha played at being unconscious in the back of the truck. She recognized Waheed's name, but had no idea where she was being taken. If nothing else, she knew who was responsible. When Harry found out, there was going to be hell to pay.

Waheed paced impatiently within the walls of his fortified compound. He was anxiously awaiting the arrival of the Sasha woman. He would use her to distract the man who was to give help to his father. No matter how many times he attempted to convince his father that the oil companies were for the better, the old man wouldn't listen. He didn't see the need for oil-company interference in the affairs of his region.

He, Waheed, son of Ali, would get his hands on as much of that oil company money as was possible. The companies were willing to pay handsomely for help in obtaining their leases. The money would be used for arms and munitions. It would enable him to buy the favor of many in his clan. He grinned and rubbed his hands together, anticipating what would soon be falling into them.

The noisy truck motored up to the entrance of the compound. Brakes squeaked and Waheed knew the Sasha woman was delivered. He smiled and opened the compound's door. The men dropped the dark-haired white woman at his feet. Still reeling, Sasha moaned in pain. Waheed grabbed her hair and dragged her into the compound. "If you promise not to try to escape I will untie your feet."

The man's knife slowly sliced through the thick rope that had replaced the tape wrapped around her ankles. Sasha's eyes darted around this new location.

Waheed helped her to stand. She stumbled and leaned against him for support. Her hand moved to the knife he replaced in his belt. As though reading her mind, he caught it, twisted, and slammed his fist into her stomach. Sasha doubled over. The knife slipped and fell into the sand. She went down with it, unable to breathe.

She stayed down.

There will be a time soon enough.

"You have been brought here alive at my command. Do not try that again. If you behave, you will be treated well. If you do not, I will leave you to starve and die of thirst in the desert. The vultures will pick your bones clean."

Sasha caught enough breath to reply. "Not if I see you first."

The expression was lost on him, as she knew it would be.

"You will be guarded. You must not attempt to leave my compound. If you do, my men will shoot you. If you make it out to the desert, you will be hunted down and killed. Your body will not be found. Do you understand?"

"I understand, all right. You must understand something, too. If harm comes to me, your father's friend, Harry, will hunt you down and kill you. He'll kill your wives. He'll kill your children. He'll kill your camels. He'll kill your sheep and your goats. He'll kill your dogs. He'll salt your land."

Waheed considered the outcome and dismissed it before laughing. "No one will get in here and live. Were I to write this Harry name in the sand, it would blow away in the wind like so much dust before he will take you away from me. He will not rescue you. He will die trying."

"You forgot to add Inshallah," Sasha told him.

"I do not need God's will," he said, before turning away from her.

"Then you are about to learn that God and Harry are two very different things." She flung the words at his back.

Sasha pushed and pulled and fought against the men dragging her toward the building. She flailed. She kicked. The men rewarded her struggle with a punch to the head. It stunned her into complying. She became a more willing subject.

Waheed addressed the men fighting with her. "Prepare this woman for the trip to the brothel. See that she has the clothing."

Someone tossed a robe at her. Defiant, she let it drop at her feet.

"If you do not put it on, we will force it upon you."

Sasha reconsidered. Her struggles had gained her nothing. There was no sense continuing to resist. She swallowed her pride and complied. The men turned to allow her some measure of privacy. She covered her face with the hijab. Someone secured it around her neck, probably because the men thought she would rip it off given the chance.

When her body was covered, a man secured her wrists and shoved her toward the truck. Securely seated between two men, they drove off, headed toward the outskirts of town. In the tight confines of the small truck, there was no room to struggle.

Sasha's mind reeled, confused. Surely she couldn't have heard right. A brothel? What did a whorehouse have to do with anything? She had to have misheard. Wherever she was going, a whorehouse had to be last on the agenda.

She considered making at least one more escape attempt, but the shovel to the head she took on the last truck ride convinced her otherwise. She had no idea where she was. There was nowhere to go. She wasn't about to take any more fists if she had a say in the matter. "Why am I being taken to a whorehouse?"

"A white woman will command huge fees from the oil workers that come to visit." As if she needed further explanation, the second kidnapper chimed in. "Christian men are not permitted in Muslim brothels. All the women in Waheed's brothel are Christian. There are no Muslim women allowed to be there."

So that was why Waheed was so interested in her. He was going to pimp her out for the benefit of his bank account. She wondered how much a white woman went for in an East African whorehouse these days. Just how long would it take Harry to find this whorehouse on the Horn? She wasn't liking her new job description. He needed to rescue her expensive white ass, she muttered to herself.

Son of a bitch, but I'll never hear the end of this.

"What was it you said?"

She didn't have time to answer. The truck halted at the bunkhouse. The men dragged her out of the truck and into a back room. A window on the opposite side was shaded. The room contained a bed and a washstand. There was a frilly pink top and short-shorts on the bed.

"At least you got the props right."

One man forced her into a chair and held her down. A man wielding scissors approached. She thought it best not to object while he cut long hair into something resembling a close-cropped mess.

"How many women are here?" she wanted to know.

"You are four."

"Is it busy?"

"Very."

"How do they pay for the services?"

"They pay with U.S. dollars."

Sasha sighed. *Damn you, Harry Delaney, get your ass over here. The sooner the better, before those oil workers ruin me for life.*

With nothing else going for her, she changed her tack and pretended to play nice. Perhaps she'd be able to figure out where they kept the cash. She didn't get time to do it. The men turned out the lights.

One of the men shoved Sasha. She ended up landing hard in a corner of the darkened room. She hit a wall and slid to the floor. The door closed. The last thing she heard was a bar sliding into place.

57

Present Day
Northern Somalia

A muzzle poked through a window. Harry shouted. Automatic gunfire erupted and ricocheted through the room. He made a grab for Ali and pulled the old man to the floor. Eloria and Meeka dived for the ground beside him. The firing halted as quickly as it started. Feet slapped the ground outside the window as someone took off running.

Ali moaned. Harry moved to help him sit up. The old man's dissipated body provided no help. He carried Ali to the safety of a back bedroom. Ali moaned again and went silent.

"Ali, you must take Eloria and her daughter to safety. They do not deserve any of this."

Harry's plea went unanswered. He checked for a pulse. It was too late. The old man exhaled and his breathing halted. He came all this way to help Ali with his problem and ended up getting him killed in the process. He held back rising panic. Where the hell was his wife?

Harry regarded the old man coldly in the dim light of the room. One problem down, another one to go, but there was no sense in losing sight of the objective. He would track down his wife without Ali's help. But first he would need more obvious help.

One by one, he searched through the rooms looking for a stash of weapons. He found an AK-47 and some ammunition and an old backpack. He filled the pack with magazines and grenades. An RPG came with three rounds. He took those, too.

He checked outside, looking for a truck. Every time he turned around, there was a truck parked in a street. When he needed one, there was nothing. Word must have gotten out to keep away from Ali's compound.

Harry delayed the inevitable by inventorying the weapons. He checked and re-checked the condition and the actions. All were well-used but freshly oiled. Ali knew how to keep things functioning, and for that he was grateful.

Next on his agenda was locating Sasha. A piece of cake but for one small thing. The damned woman had disappeared yet again. He had no idea where to start. For that, he would need Eloria. He turned to her and discovered another woman in his life was missing.

Harry shouldered an AK-47 and proceeded to go from building to building in Ali's compound, searching for Eloria. The entire place was empty of people. Every building he checked was vacated but for the furnishings. His search proved fruitless. The woman and her daughter had slipped away while he was distracted by his search for weapons.

Was her disappearance intentional? If it was, he'd be searching for Sasha on his own. Everything was becoming impossibly difficult.

Ali's death had certainly freed him from one obligation. His second, to Eloria, now seemed to have receded into the background with her disappearance. He was left to wonder if, by her sneaking off, his obligation became one of getting her daughter—who he now knew without a doubt to be Mike's daughter—out of this hell-hole.

That would be kidnapping if the child's mother wasn't in agreement. He had no stomach for that, even though Meeka, based on nothing more than her looks, turned out to be his friend's daughter. He just couldn't put himself or Mike and

Barbara in that position.

A door creaked on its hinges. A high-pitched voice called out. "Mr. Harry."

Meeka. So she hadn't disappeared with her mother after all. With everything else going on, he'd forgotten that the girl might still be in Ali's compound. He had looked everywhere. At least, he thought he had.

Could she help, or would she turn out to be a hindrance? Given how competent he knew her mother to be, perhaps she had passed on some of her abilities to her daughter.

"We need to get out of here, Meeka. Now that Ali is gone, this place will be taken over by Waheed and his followers. Do you know where your mother went?"

Meeka looked up at him with one of those looks Christa, his own daughter, gave him when she thought he had all the answers and could do no wrong. "No. I do not know."

Harry bet that wherever the woman went, a trail of death and destruction would follow in her wake. Avenging Ali's death to her satisfaction would be paramount. "Is it possible that she might have gone looking for Ali's killer?" he asked the girl.

"Yes. It is possible."

Great. He was left to babysit a ten-year-old. How the hell would he ever find his wife if he had to drag a child around? That he was calling Sasha his wife even though they weren't yet married told him what he had to do. "I think we better look for Sasha on our own. Do you think you can help me?"

"Yes, Mr. Harry. I will help you."

At least one of them was confident. "Where do you think we should start?" Shit. Now he was attempting to come up with a plan based on a child's reasoning.

"I think we should go to the girl place," Meeka insisted.

The girl place? What the hell? "Where is that, Meeka?"

"It is on the way to the airport. A building close to a hill," she said.

It was looking more and more as though he would be postponing plans for a wedding until he could come up with the bride. Christa wouldn't be a happy camper if he showed up at home minus her mother. Not to mention what Barbara would do to him. The woman wouldn't wait until he fell asleep.

Damned if he didn't know how he got to where he was. Sasha was missing. Eloria was nowhere to be found. He was stuck with a ten-year-old. Well, perhaps stuck wasn't the word, but that's how it felt. What would he do with a girl while he was trying to track down his wife? He answered his own question when it suddenly occurred to him yet again that Meeka was his best friend Mike's daughter.

"Meeka."

"Yes, Mr. Harry?"

"Would you like to go back to your house to wait, or do you want to come with me?" There was another problem. He had absolutely no idea where he had to go in this hot, dusty hell-hole of a town. He made the decision on the spot. "Instead of that, perhaps you would like to be my guide."

Immediately, he regretted the words.

Harry had a new problem—as if problem one, the missing Sasha, wasn't enough. He couldn't put the daughter of his best friend in more danger than necessary to solve problem number one. Add a missing Eloria into the mix. How would he manage that while searching for two women?

He asked again. "Meeka, I'm going to need a guide. Do you know anyone?" A last-ditch attempt at keeping her safe. If she knew someone—

"I can show you, Mr. Harry. I have learned the streets very good. My mother taught me I should put everything inside my memory."

A ten-year-old for a guide. Perhaps it wasn't so far-fetched after all. "In that case, we need to sit down and have a pow-wow."

She looked up at him quizzically. "What is pow-wow?"

He squatted beside her, and they sat together. The girl smiled at him and his heart melted. "It's kind of like a meeting to figure out what is going on," he explained. "Where we need to go. Who we need to see to get there."

How would he be able to make rescuing his wife a priority

over finding the girl's mother? In his mind, he already knew what he had to do. How would Meeka take the decision? Instead, what came out of his mouth was the complete opposite of what was running through his head. "We're going to find your mother."

Because no little girl should be without her mother. He immediately pictured Christa when he arrived home without Sasha.

He wasn't being entirely honest with himself. He knew adding Eloria to his team of one would be a huge bonus. The trek across Tanzania the four of them made the day his plane was shot up taught him that. Without her and her friend Irit, he and Mike would have been dead meat in short order, food only for the screaming hyenas.

Now he was left to figure out a way to get it in gear for the girl's sake, hit the proverbial road, and locate the women, all while keeping the girl safe. If he could pick up Eloria's trail of death and destruction in her attempt to avenge Ali, they should be good to go.

Another piece of cake. He was getting fat just thinking about it. He would put Sasha over his knee later, after he found her.

"Here's what I think we should do, Meeka."

Harry knew he had to get it together in short order if he was going to find Eloria and his wife. Now he had to worry about Sasha being number two on his honey-do list. If he ever made it out of this alive, he could never admit that to her. She'd remind him until the day he died—which might not be that far off, considering how things were going up to now.

He had no idea where to start. With his old friend Ali dead, there would be no help there. Then there was the mysterious brothel. Why would Sasha be shipped off to a brothel? In this country, men wanted women of their own faith. A man wouldn't be out looking for a Christian woman to screw.

Then it dawned on him. Waheed. Bought by the oil companies. Perhaps he had a side business servicing the roughnecks. Could his wife have been put to work in a whorehouse? It made more sense than anything else he could come up with.

Finally, he had ammunition for when she accused him of putting her in the number two spot on his list of things to do before he died. Speaking of which, that damned woman might still be the death of him. If he wasn't left with a child to take care of, he'd be a lot keener to get started.

If only he could track down Eloria. He was convinced finding her would make things a lot easier. Well, perhaps not a lot easier. A little easier, maybe.

Which wasn't saying much.

58

Out of the past
Eloria

Eloria came to on a metal floor in a tin building. Weak and disoriented, the steady drone of an engine penetrated the fog created by the beatings. Her mouth was dry. She was thirsty. Her clothes were drenched in perspiration. She twisted her head. Flexed her hands. Twisted her ankles. She did it again and again. The bonds loosened only a bit. Slowly, the blood flow increased to her extremities.

She recognized the engine noise. She wasn't in a tin building. She was on an airplane. Groggy and hurting beyond belief, she went back to concentrating on her hands and feet. Everything seemed to work. She wasn't so sure before she passed out after the last beating. It had to be hours ago. When she was still on land.

The plane's stripped interior revealed bare metal. It resembled the inside of the plane Harry flew, although this one was larger and had two engines. No seats. No belts. Heavy-looking wooden crates piled haphazardly on each side of a makeshift center aisle. She recognized them as boxes containing arms. She had to be on a flight to deliver guns. But where?

The engine noise subsided, and it reminded her of Harry doing the same on the plane that took her and her sister to the job in the Tanzanian bush. She was smart enough to know she wouldn't be subjected to the same gut-wrenching landing Harry put her through. Even though she wasn't hung over for this landing, the beatings left her weak and confused even now.

Working her knees, she slid a backpack to within reach of her hands. She worked stiff fingers to open a flap. Rummaged through it with one hand. A weapon. She needed something to put up a fight. There was nothing. She came up with a bottle of water. It was almost as good. She fought to open it and doused herself. It helped to bring her around.

She groaned and pushed with her feet to slide upright against the bare metal. She twisted and stared out a cabin window. There was nothing but dry desert. Before she could position herself for a better look, wheels bumped onto sand.

The opposite window revealed some kind of four-engine plane parked on the side of the sand strip. Her plane taxied past and stopped beside a dilapidated, tin-roofed outbuilding.

Wherever she landed was surrounded by even more desert.

The cargo door opened from the outside. She twisted again to get a good look. As best she could tell, there were many technicals surrounding the plane.

A man unlocked the chain securing her wrist to a box. He dragged her to the open door and pushed her out. She fell on her back on the soft sand. It was no cushion. It knocked the wind out of her. She fought to maintain consciousness as she struggled to catch her breath in the hot desert air.

Where was she? Why was she still alive?

Eloria didn't want to show defiance. She pretended to be weak. She kept herself in check. Considering she hadn't had water or food in what felt like forever, it wasn't difficult. It would do no good to struggle against her restraints in the stifling heat.

She had to find out where she was. Why she was still alive? What was going on? She knew her life lay in the balance. She had to keep alive as long as she could. If she could do that, perhaps there would be a chance to escape. She didn't concern herself with where that would lead.

Men were preparing to shove the crates out the airplane's cargo door. Somehow, she managed to roll away before one of the heavy boxes landed on top of her. The boxes were jimmied open and the contents carried to the trucks surrounding the airplane. AKs, bags of magazines, boxes of ammunition, grenades, mortars, RPGs all disappeared. When the job was done, the trucks moved away in a cloud of blowing sand and dust.

Two men checked her bindings and threw her into the back of the remaining truck. It caught up to the others and followed along a rough trail onto a paved road. She passed a crude, hand-lettered sign, and a village came into view.

The sign was no help. She never heard of the place.

The crowd of men surrounding Eloria parted and a tall, regal man approached. He looked her over, appraising. Others in the crowd deferred to him. No one spoke. She felt the vague beginning of fear.

The man was obviously a leader. What would he do with her? Was she to be his wife? How many did he have already? A mother to his children? Babysitter? She wondered how many babysitters there were in this neighborhood. Probably few—if any at all.

She would wait before showing her hand.

The man removed her bonds and handed over a bag of clothes. He grabbed her, hauled her off the ground, and yanked her toward a tin-roofed building without windows. She would have no chance to escape.

He shoved her into the building. In the dark, she undressed, took the niqab out of the bag, and put it on over her head. The man appeared pleased when she came out wearing the clothes. She took a chance. "Where am I?"

"You are in Somalia," he volunteered. "North."

The voice was guttural, difficult to understand. "Who are you?"

"I am Waheed, son to Ali. Ali is the leader of the clan to

which I belong."

The man's English was heavily accented. "You speak English. Where did you go to school?"

"In Kenya, on the outskirts of Mombasa," Waheed said.

"Your family must be rich if they could afford to send you there."

"Perhaps. But that is not important." He spoke a name, and a woman appeared. "She will take you to get clean."

The woman motioned for Eloria to follow. In another room, she stripped and stepped into a tub and lowered herself. Hot water surrounded her, soothing her injuries. She relaxed and submerged herself in the hot water. She scrubbed at the accumulated dirt and dust and grime accumulated over the last several days. She languished as the hot water soothed her aches and pains. It came as a welcome relief, and she forgot all about her troubles until it was time to get out of the tub and get dressed.

The woman led Eloria to a kitchen. Her attempts to make conversation were rebuffed. Either the woman didn't speak English or she had been told to ignore her. She was offered a plate of bread and a cup of hot, spicy chai. It was exactly what she needed after the bath. It helped to bring her around. Her one worry was how long she would have to stay here by herself.

How long would it be before she found a way to escape?

Waheed turned Eloria over to the women in his camp with instructions to nurse her back to health. For the most part, she was left alone. She was allowed to wander unaccompanied around the town. She used the time to get her bearings. By the time she had committed the town's streets and back alleys to memory, she was moved to Galkayo. That was where she met Waheed's father, Ali.

That was also where she learned she was pregnant. She hid it from everyone until the last months. By then, it became impossible to arrange the flowing robes around her rapidly enlarging belly. The pregnancy gave her a degree of status. Everyone thought the baby would be born into Waheed's clan.

That was fine with her, and she didn't deny it.

Without a doubt, Eloria knew it to be Mike's. When they met that night in the bar, she had trouble pronouncing his name. She took to calling him Meek. He didn't care, and she liked him right away.

It all seemed so long ago.

When the baby girl was born, Eloria had a name ready. Meeka. From that day she was never without a weapon to protect her daughter. If she ever had to fight for her life, the result would not be pretty. By the time she finished with whoever threatened either of them, death would come. Worried as she was, it never happened. She was left free to roam the city, accompanied by her daughter.

As the child grew older, Eloria taught her the skills she would need to become self-sufficient in the event they became separated. Or worse. That's the word she used when she told Meeka about it. What she meant was that she might be killed, or moved, the same way she had arrived here. Still, she lived in constant fear that the two of them would end up separated.

Ali, Waheed's father, kept his eye on Meeka. He liked both mother and daughter. It showed in his manner and his way of talking with them. They became regular visitors to his compound. Eventually, they ended up moving into a place the old man provided in his compound. She felt more secure there than with Waheed.

By then, relations between the old man and his son had become strained. Tensions relating to oil company business in the region were high. Waheed began keeping his distance from his father.

By association, he kept away from both Eloria and her daughter, also.

Over time, Eloria and her daughter gradually became accepted in Ali's camp. Years passed and Meeka grew like a desert flower, always under the watchful eye of her mother. As the girl grew older, she showed her how to disassemble and clean firearms. With Ali's blessing, she took her into the desert to teach her how to hold, load, and fire those same weapons.

In time, the young girl became proficient, an equal to the rebel children photographed with automatic weapons slung over their shoulders. Those same images became popular in the press. There was one difference between the photographs of the rebel children and Meeka, however. When Eloria was finished with her, Meeka could hit her targets. In fact, she rarely missed. That, and she was white.

As the years progressed, changes slowly overtook the region. They were being forced on the people by the oil companies and the clan leaders they bought and paid for. All the companies were trying their best to buy their way into being permitted to drill for the black gold. The companies convinced almost everyone that unlimited riches would be discovered underground if only they were permitted to drill.

So much money was changing hands with the clans that the situation had deteriorated into open warfare. Her mentor Ali was in favor of maintaining distance from the greed and outright lies and trickery of the foreign oil companies. Not his son, though. Waheed was in bed with the companies and was busy selling out to anyone with the cash.

Much strife between father and son ensued. Eloria believed the status quo would not be maintained for much longer. She began searching for a way out of the situation that wouldn't jeopardize her safety or that of her daughter.

She kept her eyes and ears open.

Eloria began taking Meeka to Ali's campfire in the evenings. She would help the old man wrap himself in his blanket against the cool, dark nights. They would keep him company while he poured his sweet, spicy chai for them to enjoy.

He gathered his blanket against the cool air and tell stories of his adventures in northern Somalia. Sometimes he began with tales of enduring massive drought that caused entire villages to relocate into huge relief centers.

He spoke of owning many camels that made him a wealthy man. He told them of leading camel caravans along ancient trade routes that were still being used in these modern days.

It was during one of those story-telling nights that Ali began a story of two men who came back into his life from long ago. The men started their friendship and got to know one another while they were employed by one of the very first oil companies that came into the region.

Long after they left the region to return home, Ali received a phone call asking for help in recovering the wife of one of the men. The man, Harry, had asked Ali if he could provide some assistance in the form of a couple of technicals and some men to operate them on a trek across the desert.

The two men, accompanied by a woman who he later discovered was Mike's wife, arrived by plane at their old landing strip located west of Eyl. He met the plane as requested and discovered it had been modified and outfitted as an airborne technical with twin .50-caliber machine guns mounted in the cargo door.

When the men arrived, they came complete with fresh arms for Ali's men. It impressed him that they came equipped to do some serious damage, consequently he lent his full support to their undertaking.

By the time Ali's story ended several nights later, Eloria was convinced the two men he spoke of were the same two men she had met in Tanzania in the bar. If that was true, Ali knew the father of her daughter.

Ali's story gave her much to think about over the next weeks and months. The identity of the woman that accompanied the men on the rescue mission had to be Mike's wife. That meant that there would be no way she could involve him in getting her daughter away to safety.

On the other hand, with her sister Irit, they came to Harry's rescue in the bush after his plane was damaged. Perhaps that meant he could be convinced to return to help her. After all, he owed her his life.

It was time to collect.

59

**Present Day
Northern Somalia**

Waheed kicked open the door to the brothel and shoved Eloria into the room. She slammed into a wall and collapsed on the floor. The door banged shut and a bar thumped against it on the outside. Someone yelled and another door slammed. A vehicle drove off. The brothel went quiet in a drifting cloud of dust. Eloria understood she was no longer under Ali's protection.

Sasha moved to comfort the woman groaning on the floor beside her. "You're safe for now," she told her. She waited for the woman to quiet before helping her sit upright. She got the woman's back against a wall. In the darkened room, it was difficult to discern anything about the woman. "I don't know what they expect of us."

The woman responded with an accent so strong it was difficult to understand. "English woman. What are you doing here?"

Sasha took an educated guess. "Eloria?"

"Yes. I am Eloria. What are you called?"

"Sasha. I'm Sasha."

"Sasha? You are the wife of Harry, are you not?" Eloria asked.

The woman's response took Sasha by surprise. Her confused brain went into overdrive, trying to come up with why they were both in so much trouble. She put it aside when recognition dawned. Sasha reached for the woman and hugged her. "We've been looking for you. Did Harry find you?" She almost said, *Both of you,* meaning her daughter also, but caught herself.

"Yes."

"What did you do to end up here?" Sasha wanted to know.

"My friend and protector Ali is dead. I wanted to go in search of the enemies who put an end to his life. To do so, I left my daughter with your man. I think he will take good care of her."

"Oh yes. You're right. He'll protect her to the death." With Eloria on the floor beside her, Sasha suspected Waheed would end up searching for her daughter and Harry next. "Welcome to the crowbar hotel, girl. I knew we would meet up eventually."

Eloria wondered at the words. "What do you mean?"

"Crowbar hotel. Jail. Prison."

Eloria nodded in the dim light. "Ever since I learned Waheed has his eyes on Meeka, my daughter, I have been wondering how long it would take him to lock me here. Now I know."

"Do you have any idea where Meeka and Harry have gotten to? Sasha asked.

"The last I saw they were together."

"Harry will take good care of her." Sasha repeated the words, knowing they would be small comfort for the woman.

"Meeka will take care of him also. He needs someone who knows the way. Meeka knows all the streets and alleys of this city. I made her learn. I told her to learn the best vehicles also."

"I don't think a Mercedes Benz is the way to go here."

"You are right. A technical is better. Meeka can drive one," Eloria said.

"She must be a bit short to reach everything," Sasha doubted.

"Not at all," Eloria said. "She does so while she stands up."

"My goodness. You've kept her a busy girl."

A smile crept across Eloria's face. "Yes. I try to keep her out of Waheed's sight the best I can. The way is to send her off to discover things for herself was the best way. It was a good thing to do."

"I hate to change the subject, but how are we going to get out of this aluminum jail?" Sasha was referring to the trailer walls.

Eloria got up on the bed and motioned for Sasha to hand her the chair. Unsteady on top of the soft mattress, she climbed onto the wobbling chair. Unasked, Sasha steadied the chair. Eloria reached for the roof vent and pulled the screen off. She forced it open and stuck her head through. "I do not see any guards. We are the only people here."

She reached for her jilbab and pulled a knife from an opening. "I knew this tent they forced me to wear would become good one day." Eloria worked at the thin aluminum with the blade. She sawed back and forth on the roof. She succeeded in enlarging the opening after only a few minutes. When she had it big enough to climb through, she pulled her head down and motioned to Sasha. "Push," she commanded her.

Sasha released her grip on the unsteady chair and moved to support Eloria as she struggled to climb up through the hole. She shoved with both hands and Eloria's upper body slowly rose above the roof. The jilbab caught on the sharp aluminum, putting a halt to Eloria's progress. From below, Sasha tugged and had enough success to allow Eloria to climb through the hole and get on top of the roof.

Eloria reached down and gripped Sasha's wrists. She grunted and pulled her torso through the opening. She got a knee on the roof and pulled harder until Sasha succeeded in joining her. The women held out their arms to greet the strong breeze fanning their robes. It made them appear to float above the trailer.

"You're right. There is no one around. Now what are we going to do?" Sasha wanted to know. There were a couple of other buildings. They were smaller than the trailer they shared. Sasha doubted there would be weapons in any of them.

"We need to find weapons. Do you understand how to fire a gun?" Eloria asked?

"I am a little familiar with an AK-47 and a rocket launcher," Sasha said.

Eloria smiled again. "Harry married well."

"We're not together any more."

"Yet you both are here. I think you will not be apart for long if he values talents such as those," Eloria told her.

"To tell you the truth, I never thought of it like that."

Eloria regarded the woman standing beside her. "Then perhaps it is time you did."

Harry put his arm around Meeka and hugged her close, as if to say everything would be all right. She smiled up at him, and it became obvious he won her over. His heart melted. He knew he wouldn't be able to disappoint her. If only he felt as confident in the final result of his decision as he appeared to her.

"Are we going to search for your woman now, Mr. Harry?" the girl asked.

"No, Meeka. We will find your mother." The little girl's face beamed with an even wider smile. It was the right thing to do. Sasha would have to wait.

"There is a truck we can borrow," she said.

I was a technical with a machine gun mounted on the bed. It was old. Battered. The front suspension sagged. "That won't be much use. I can't drive and shoot." Even if it was brand-new, it would be useless to him.

"I can drive, Mr. Harry," she told him.

What the hell? He would have to see this. "Then let's get started on our quest."

"What is a quest?"

It was his turn to smile. "It's a search. Together, we will go on a quest for a good truck."

Meeka took Harry's hand and pulled him through the maze of streets, past narrow, shaded alleys fronted by dark doorways. When he stopped for a better look, she went back and dragged him away from whatever caught his attention. "Mr. Harry, we quest for a truck. This alley it is too narrow."

Harry regarded the girl and thought of her mother, Eloria. Once committed, Meeka too wasn't one to stray from the objective.

Meeka led them to a square at the end of a street surrounded by squat rows of shops, all closed. Siesta. Everyone was off chewing khat or sleeping away the oppressive afternoon heat. Two technicals came into view, parked under a shade-tree. He looked around. There was no one.

"Which one do you like, Mr. Harry?" she asked.

In the first beat-up wreck of a technical, he opened a squeaking door, reached in, and retrieved ammo and an RPG. There was no one to object. "We'll take this one. It looks better." It was an obvious lie, given how dilapidated they both looked.

"Come on. You're driving, Meeka."

It was almost like Mike was with him. The girl reached under the dash, felt around, and pulled out some wires. "No one uses a key," she said. She sparked a couple and the four-cylinder engine rattled to life in a cloud of blue smoke.

He fought with the seat on the driver's side until he got it moved full forward and retreated to the passenger side and climbed in. That was her cue to use her long legs to balance against the seat before flooring the clutch pedal.

Meeka white-knuckled the wheel with one hand and worked the shift lever with the other. She let out the clutch and the truck jerked into first gear and began porpoising down the street. She relaxed on the edge of the seat, and by the time she found second gear, she had it down, all while standing and then sitting behind the wheel.

He checked behind. No one seemed to mind the disappearing truck. Her mother would be proud. So would Mike. Hell, he was even prouder. "Where do you think we should start, Meeka?"

"Waheed would like my mother. She did not want to do anything with him. Perhaps he put her in the girl place."

"Girl place? What's that?" Meeka mentioned it earlier, but he was no wiser.

"Yes. Sometimes I follow him there and wait behind a hill. It is where himself likes sometimes to go to."

Harry had no clue what she was talking about. *Girl place?* "Perhaps you should take us in that direction."

Meeka wound the truck through the familiar narrow side streets, jerking through stops and jackrabbit starts. She obviously knew the streets, having walked them for years. Sometimes she would miss a shift, but she recovered and carried on as if it was normal to grind gears.

"Who taught you to drive, Meeka?" He knew it was her mother, but he wanted to put her at ease. Besides, she was doing such a good job with the driving, even with the jack-rabbiting.

"My mother. Sometimes she takes one of these for me to practice. She wants me to learn. She says I must prepare to take care of my own self when she will be sent away."

Well, Eloria had definitely gone away. It was up to the two of them to find her. Finally he felt as though he was doing something, even if it was only being chauffeured around town by a ten-year-old twin to his best friend.

A cloud of dust trailed Meeka and Harry in the technical as she drove, bouncing and bumping, toward the outskirts of town. She took a turn off the main road and ended up on a sand trail. She followed it along the back side of a rocky ridge. In no time they were beyond the town's edge.

"The girl place is past here." Meeka gestured through the hill. "We must go to the top."

Harry needed to get eyes on the place before he moved on it. He worried more about Meeka than what he would have to do once he found the women. Eloria would never forgive him if something happened to her daughter.

"We should check out the high ground first. Try to keep us below the top so we are invisible."

Meeka steered the technical almost like a professional but for the grinding gears. She kept it behind the crest overlooking the trailer. She brought the technical to a gear-grinding halt. Harry took Meeka's hand. He wanted to make sure she didn't rush ahead and become visible against the backdrop of the sky.

They got down and crawled their way up to the crest. Together they peered over the ridge. The trailer's tin walls shimmered in the late afternoon sun. It would be twilight soon. Darkness would provide good cover for what needed to be done. He wondered if it would provide the same cover if the women he was looking for weren't inside.

A cloud of dust drifted behind a van pulling up in front of the trailer. The CAN-AL logo stood out on the door. Half-a-dozen men exited. Laughing and back-slapping, they were eager to get down to business in the trailer. The men ran toward the building. Opened the door. Fought each other to be first in. Slammed the door closed.

The trailer had to be the whorehouse. He would need to move fast if he was going to shut this thing down and retrieve Eloria. If she was even there. He fired a burst in the truck's direction. The rounds ricocheted through the flimsy tin. That wasn't so smart.

He readjusted and directed two single-fire rounds at the swamp cooler on the roof. It amplified the sounds as they reverberated through tin walls. If that didn't get the men moving, nothing would.

The door slammed open and smacked against the side of the trailer. Men stumbled and tripped into the open. Single rounds kicked up sand to keep the men moving in the right direction. Before long the truck disappeared even faster than it arrived. In its wake, only a cloud of dust remained to announce that it had ever been there.

Two armed men exited the trailer. Confused by the gunfire and unsure where it was coming from, they separated. That was Harry's cue to get down to the business at hand. He flicked the firing lever on the AK to single action. He aimed the iron sights and squeezed off a round. A man went down. He aimed at the second and a split second later the man joined his partner in the sand.

Job one completed, Harry's attention switched to the area surrounding the trailer. Nothing moved. Then, from the rear of the building, two more appeared, making their way toward town on foot.

Something twigged, and Harry motioned for Meeka to drive the truck over the hill. He leaned on the horn to draw their attention. They halted and looked toward the crest of the hill. Damn if it wasn't the women he was looking for.

"It's your mother, Meeka. It's Eloria. And Sasha, too." He was pumped at finding both women.

The girl leaned on the horn and jumped up and down, waving her arms and screaming at her mother. The woman waved back and made for the hill.

Puffs of sand walked their way toward the women. The shooter found his mark. One of the women stumbled and fell to the ground. The second bent over her. She looked up and scrambled for cover.

Harry couldn't be sure. He tried to remember what Sasha had on the last time he saw her. A head covering. A robe. What color? Dammit. He was certain that was her laying in the sand.

Harry pulled the pin on a grenade and tossed it in the direction of the gunfire. A satisfying whump followed and a sea of red-tinged sand exploded into the air. A direct hit. It was one down and a lot more to go.

"Come on Meeka, let's do a quick run along the perimeter to check for bad guys and then get our rear ends down the hill." Harry climbed onto the back of the technical and manned the .50 caliber. He scanned ahead as they worked the edge, but there was no one. "All right, let's get down there."

He held on to the .50 for dear life as the girl maneuvered the truck down the hill, bumping and grinding the gears all the way. He was scared to death of what he was certain he would find.

Meeka halted the truck. The woman pulled off her hijab and Harry tossed an AK at her. He jumped out and leaned over the woman on the ground. A thick pool of blood formed in the sand beneath her. Harry bent to listen to the woman's labored breathing.

"Meeka! Come quick."

He pulled Meeka down with him. Eloria's lips moved. The head covering muffled her words. Harry drew his Buck and sliced through it, allowing Eloria's last words to escape. They were barely audible through her shallow breathing.

"Yes, Eloria. Meeka will be safe. I give you my word."

He turned to the girl crouched in the sand beside her mother. "Did you hear your mother?"

"Yes. I listened."

"What do you think?" he asked her.

"We do that, Mr. Harry," Meeka assured him.

Harry reached to close Eloria's eyes. He bent to pick up the woman's lifeless body and carry it to the truck. He checked for a pulse one last time to be certain.

Meeka stood by as he covered her mother's face. The girl seemed unsure of what to do.

"Do you want to say goodbye?"

"I did that, Mr. Harry."

"Then let's go. You're still the driver." She wiped away a tear and smiled.

Harry turned to Sasha. "We'll be off to a rough start, but once Meeka gets going it will be smooth sailing. Get in beside your god-daughter."

Sasha hesitated. "I'm not ready. Give me a minute."

60

Sasha's trembling hands fumbled with Harry's pack. The gravity of the situation she and Harry were in was taking firm hold. She just met Eloria, the woman they both came to save, and now she was dead. Responsible or not, she was less than happy to be hauling Eloria's body around in the truck. "I want to see that picture again."

Harry took the pack and pulled out a picture of Eloria and her daughter. "What's the problem?"

She sighed, out of desperation or fear, or both. "We can't leave Meeka here. Ali is too old to take proper care of her. His son, Waheed, isn't the swiftest camel in the desert. We need to get her off of this continent and take her home with us."

It was a no-brainier for Harry. The decision was already made, Sasha just didn't know. "Ali is dead. Now her mother is, too. We're taking the girl to Mike and Barbara."

"Just like that?" Sasha asked. "What if—"

"Just like that," Harry insisted. "If they won't have her, we will."

"Somehow, I don't think it will be a problem."

"It had better not be." Harry couldn't suppress his grin any longer.

"What are you looking at?" Sasha asked.

"You in that robe. Damn, woman, who outfitted you in that getup? And what's underneath it?"

"If you know what's good for you, you won't say another word."

His eyes took in the ragged, close-cropped haircut. "Nice hair. I'd do you."

"You won't ever again if you're not careful."

"How much were they asking?" he wanted to know.

"In my estimation, not enough. Can we get out of here? We have a job to do, in case you forgot."

"Can you walk on your own, or do I have to carry you?" Sasha kicked sand in Harry's direction and he laughed. "In these parts I don't think that's how the women treat their men. Come on, it's time."

Sasha picked up a discarded AK and a second magazine. She shook the sand out of both before following Harry up the hill to the technical. Meeka started it and took them a hundred meters before Sasha instructed her to stop.

"We cannot, missus Harry," she told her." We have to go from this place."

"What about the others? Are we going to leave them there?" There were others in the trailer's small rooms, she was sure.

Harry nodded to Meeka. She ignored Sasha and kept busy at the wheel, grinding gears and taking them away from the prison brothel.

"Meeka is right. We have to look after ourselves first. Stop for only a minute. There is something I need to do."

Harry exited the cab of the technical and reached into the back. He came up with an RPG, filled the tube, aimed, and fired. In seconds aluminum and sand settled in a huge cloud of dirt and dust. "My responsibility is to you and to Meeka and her mother. Do you want to pile on more? We need to get out of here. There's a truck behind the trailer. It's free for the taking if you want it."

"Since you put it that way—" Sasha hesitated before going on. "I was scared I wouldn't see you ever again. What the hell took you so long?"

"After Ali's death, Eloria disappeared and left Meeka with me. It wouldn't surprise me if she left a trail of bodies on the way to the brothel attempting to avenge Ali's killing. It took us a while to find a truck. When we did, we meandered through the streets to here."

"You got lost?" she asked, incredulously.

"More like momentarily displaced. The faster we get away, the less we have to deal with it and the better off we'll all be."

"What's the plan?" Sasha asked.

"Where have I heard that before?"

Sasha turned to the girl. "Meeka, Harry isn't so good at making a plan. What do you think?

Meeka already knew what she wanted. "I would like to look for my father now."

Harry didn't hesitate. "If that's what Meeka wants, who are we to hold her back?" Harry hummed an old song. Sasha recognized it and hummed along with him.

Sasha rode shotgun beside Meeka in the technical while Harry stood guard in the back with the .50. She kept a studied eye on the girl as she maneuvered the vehicle. How a ten-year-old could do it standing up was foremost on her mind. The girl had trouble keeping the thing moving without jack-rabbiting down the streets.

"Meeka can really handle this thing, Harry. Who do you think showed her how to do it?"

"Why don't you ask her?

Meeka took her eyes off the street and looked across at Sasha. "My own mother showed me to do it." Tears streamed down the little girl's face as she smiled through a look of pride at Sasha's compliment. "We are going to Ali's house on the long way. It will be dark when we arrive."

"How's your AK, Sasha?" Harry asked.

"No doubt full of sand."

"It will be all right, Sasha. The AK-47 is very reliable, my mother says."

"See? They're reliable that way," he reassured her. "Sand.

Dust. Mud. Water. Nothing stops an AK-47. That's why they're the weapon of choice in these parts. That, and they're cheap and widely available.

"Yeah. I remember you telling me about that reliability a long time ago. And the widely available is thanks to you."

Harry ignored Sasha's dig. "You're doing good, Meeka."

Ali's compound came into view. Meeka released the clutch and brought the technical to a shuddering halt in front. No light escaped the windows. Harry got out and looked through a window, but he was unable to see anything of value in the dark. "I didn't think there'd be anyone. What's our situation with munitions?" He contemplated going in to look for ammunition.

"I've got two partial mags." Sasha wasn't satisfied. She wanted more. She grew accustomed to handling the rifle over the years, despite all her objections. After Harry taught her how to use the AK-47 on the Mexican Baja, it proved to be a reliable weapon, even for her. That she was accustomed to it surprised her even more.

"There's one can for the .50 and a single round remaining for the RPG," Harry said.

"I have this." Meeka pulled back her jacket, revealing a shotgun. Sasha gasped, taken aback and unsure how to deal with a ten-year-old carrying a gun.

Harry was quick to interject. "Don't let it worry you. There are children younger than Meeka who routinely walk around with AK-47s over their shoulders."

"Yes. I've seen pictures of those kids," Sasha admitted. Sasha looked closer at the shotgun in the dim moonlight. "I know it's been a while, but doesn't that look like Mike's old sawed-off? Is it my imagination or just the poor light?"

"You're right. It is," Harry told her.

"How did it get here?" she wanted to know.

"Where do you think Mike got it the first time?"

Sasha allowed her thoughts to go back to when she met the two men on the Baja. "All of this is too much for me to take in right now," she admitted. "Let's get out of here. You have a plan, right?"

"Yes I do."

"Are you going to let us in on it, or are we back on the Baja, Harry?"

"Woman, we're divorced, remember? I don't want any back talk from you," he said.

"Mr. Harry, you told to me that you would marry missus Sasha," Meeka said in her matter of fact manner.

The cat was out of the bag, thanks to Meeka. Harry blushed.

"Oh Mr. Harry, you're turning into such a romantic in the dark of night beneath the Southern Cross and an almost full moon." Sasha grinned at him.

"I haven't asked you yet, woman."

"There are no priests in Galkayo or Garowe. They are killed a long time," Meeka told them.

"See? Listen to Meeka. That's why I don't have a ring for you."

Sasha suspected Meeka wasn't the only one who hadn't forgotten about her mother in the back of the truck. She reached for the girl, hugging her close.

"I am good now, missus Harry. We will go." Meeka climbed into the truck and crossed the ignition wires. It coughed to a start in a cloud of exhaust.

Meeka's mother. In the back of the technical. It was more than Harry wanted to deal with. It never once occurred to him it would end this way. He figured on taking Eloria off of the continent with her daughter. Now he was rescuing the girl. He was rescuing Mike's daughter.

One traded for the other.

In a way, he was thankful for that. He wouldn't be presenting a woman Mike thought long dead. With Barbara—

Immediately, he felt guilty and shook off the thought. He wasn't able to save Eloria. He had her daughter. He had his wife. Mission accomplished, as far as it went. The only thing left was to make good an escape as fast as he could. He tossed it out—one idea at a time.

"We're going to the airport. Can you take us there, Meeka?" he asked her.

Her reply was matter of fact. "Yes. I know how to go there."

Meeka turned the technical around and headed toward their new destination. She found her way through the dark, deserted streets and alleys, illuminated only by the technical's misaligned headlights.

"Meeka, can you pull over for a minute? There's something I need to do." Harry went around to the front and smashed the lights. He did the same to the brake lights. When he finished, he climbed up to the .50 mounted in the bed of the technical.

"Your young eyes are good to see in the dark. There's no sense drawing attention to us if we don't have to."

"Yes. The moon is good. No one will see," the girl replied confidently.

Harry's hopes were pinned on Mike's stolen Twin Otter still sitting unmolested and in one piece on the concrete pad where he left it. If they shot it up, there'd be no telling what shape it would be in.

In his mind, he was running through images of leaking fuel tanks, failed electronics and engine damage from gunfire or worse. If the Twin wasn't airworthy, for whatever reason, it would be a long truck ride to Djibouti to collect plane tickets home for three. He tried not to think about the phone call he'd have to make to Mike.

Sasha checked the two mags and racked the AK before putting on the safety. She called to Harry through the technical's missing back window. Nervous, she tipped the magazine's release, again and again. "Do you think we'll have trouble?"

Harry recognized the sound for what it was. "I'm hoping the strip will be unguarded. During daylight someone will punt an artillery shell or a mortar and get lucky when it lands close. Mostly, they're misses. I'm counting on the plane being serviceable—if it hasn't been looted."

"Dammit, Harry, we can't make an overland trip in this thing. Isn't Djibouti five hundred miles north of here? Probably longer by dirt road. And gas. We'll need gas and water and food."

He didn't tell her about the paved road. He didn't want to

give hope when none was available. "I know that. That's why we're headed to the airport. We'll fuel up and be airborne in no time."

If only. His silent two-word prayer. The condition of the plane was a big if, and he'd be taking a chance. They'd have to wrestle with the fuel bowser and get it to the plane. If there were guards asleep in the outbuildings, they couldn't alert them. Gunfire would sound the alarm for more of them to come to the airport to investigate the attackers. Their chances were slim.

Accept it and move on, he told himself.

"You're used to refueling by now, woman. We'll be out of there in no time. What's the problem?"

"We have someone else to think about now, Harry."

He ran through everything. They had Meeka. Unfortunately, misfortune and a well-aimed bullet guaranteed that Meeka's mother wouldn't be making the trip. They had armament left over in case shooting started. With any luck there wouldn't be a prolonged gun battle.

A quick inspection would tell him if the plane was serviceable and capable of becoming airborne to take them to Djibouti. That the plane needed fuel was the problem. If they could get the fuel truck up to it without alerting anyone. Could there be a chance someone would be awake and paying attention?

What could go wrong? What did he have to think about beyond getting them airborne and on the way to Djibouti? The mental checklist was done. It was time to ask.

"What else is there to think about?" he asked no one in particular.

Sasha didn't hesitate when she questioned Harry. She never did. It was one of the things he liked about her in these situations. "I don't like to be the bearer of sad tidings, but we have Eloria's mother. Have you forgotten?"

"Not likely," he said.

"You have a plan, right?"

"You betcha."

"Are you going to tell us, or are you going to put us even deeper in the dark in the middle of the night in this hell-hole?"

"Meeka, pull over for a little bit. I want to spank your missus Sasha."

"That is not good, Mr. Harry," the girl advised him.

Harry's grin was barely visible in the moonlight.

"Don't you worry, Meeka. Your Aunt Sasha has an AK-47 in her lap," she told the girl. "And Mr. Harry, if you please, don't be saying things like that when your god-daughter is within earshot. You could get more than a measly AK up your rear end."

Meeka looked at Sasha. She talked back to Mr. Harry. She ignored it because it seemed to her as though it was expected. "What is god-daughter?"

There was no time to explain. Already Meeka was steering the technical onto the airport road. Harry instructed her to stop. He released his grip on the .50 and jumped from the back of the truck. "Here's the plan. Meeka, you'll drive us to the fuel truck as quickly and quietly as you can. Sasha will get out and start it while I stand guard. If it goes well up to then, we'll convoy to the plane."

The girl looked at him. "Convoy?"

"Yes. Convoy. It means we will drive the trucks together."

Sasha remained unconvinced. "That's too easy."

"Maybe," Harry said. "But it's the best we've got. Meeka, this is important. You don't have any lights, so you must watch out you don't drive your truck into the airplane. If you do, it could break."

"I watch, Mr. Harry."

"Do not stop the technical past the plane or in front of it. We need a clear view of the buildings in case we see people who want to stop us." If they were lucky, no one would have an RPG to launch up their asses while they were held up refueling. Once airborne, it would become a more serious matter. "When I start the gas pump, Sasha will fuel the plane. I'll stand guard with the .50."

"What are you leaving out, Harry?" Sasha wanted to know.

He didn't have a ready answer. He changed the subject. "It's time."

Meeka made sure to circle away from the dilapidated buildings. She kept the engine as quiet as she could in order not to disturb anyone. Standing up to drive the truck didn't make it any easier for her, even with Harry's encouragement.

Sasha made for the fuel bowser and struggled to get the ancient truck started. The engine caught. She did a jack-rabbit start with the clutch, copying Meeka's driving style. The ancient fuel truck bounced and jerked and sloshed its way to the Twin Otter. She hit the brakes. Nothing happened. She twisted the wheel and let out the clutch and the bowser lurched to a stop a few feet from the wing. Fuel continued to slosh. The truck rocked back and forth.

"Good job. You're learning. Another couple of trips over here and we'll get her trained up in no time, right Meeka?"

Meeka knew better than to agree with him. "Mr. Harry, I think Sasha has carried a rifle over her shoulder before right now."

The girls clasped hands and Sasha did a dance around Meeka.

Harry started the gasoline engine on the fuel bowser. "I'll be busy doing the inspection. Keep an eye out in case anyone shows up to cause trouble.

61

Sasha squeezed the nozzle to drain fuel onto the ground. The motion washed out any sand and dust that found its way inside. "Harry, the fuel doesn't smell right for a turbine engine. It's hard to tell in this light, but it doesn't look right either."

He handed her the flashlight. She illuminated a patch of fuel already on the ground.

"It's pink. Isn't that for piston engines?" she asked him.

"Don't worry about it. Pink will do," he reassured her.

Sasha uncapped the front tank and began fueling.

Harry took the light and flashed it quickly over the Twin Otter's exterior. It was the best he could do. He inspected the engine cowlings. The propellers. The tires were undamaged and full of air. He finished and returned to Meeka and held out his hand. The little girl took it in hers.

"I'm going to load Meeka in the right seat. When you're done filling both tanks, climb aboard. Don't forget your AK. Get the shovel from the fuel truck and bring it with you."

He lifted Meeka into the Twin Otter and led her by her hand to the seat in the cockpit. He bent over her and strapped her in. She looked at him the entire time.

"I know. I won't forget your mother, sweetheart. I promise."

Reluctantly, he left the girl to go aft to load her mother's body before returning to join her in the cockpit. The girl's eyes were big as saucers. They grew even bigger when he switched on the cockpit lights, overwhelming the moonlight streaming in through the windows.

"Is Sasha coming with us, Mr. Harry?"

"Yes, Meeka. Your mother is with us, too. We're all together." He put a headset over her ears. She giggled when he spoke into it and heard his voice.

"Do you think you might like to leave out the Mr. and call me Harry?"

She looked at him and nodded. She looked on in wonder as her eyes followed Harry's hands moving over the switches and dials. With no time to pull out the checklist, he worked quickly from memory. When he finished, the start sequence was complete. He fired up number one.

Sasha completed the fueling. She capped the aft tank and checked she did the same for the front. She dropped the nozzle on the ground without shutting it off. Fuel gushed onto the tarmac. She climbed aboard and donned the headset by the cargo door.

"Go! Go! Go now!"

Harry eased in throttle and pushed on the rudder to keep the capable bush plane straight. The Twin Otter shuddered and rolled off the concrete pad, leaving the fuel bowser behind. Sasha stumbled and fell against the door frame, righted herself, and made a grab for her AK. She fired a burst into the fuel pooling on the ground. The bullets ricocheted into the fuel truck's tank. Fuel spilled onto the ground. She fired another burst into the tank for good measure. The fuel ignited.

Engine draft from the powerful PT-6 fanned the exploding orange flames, forcing them toward the tanker truck. While Harry busied himself taxiing toward the end of the strip on one engine, he fired up number two. They were good to go.

He addressed Sasha over the intercom. "You better be strapped in back there."

"The cargo door is closed and locked," she lied. She didn't

want to spend any more time on the ground.

He turned onto the strip and firewalled the throttles while reaching for the flaps. He dialed in and the Twin Otter bumped down the strip, not yet ready to limp into the air.

Sasha didn't dare tell him she was too busy. She struggled against the slipstream, fighting to close and lock the cargo door.

Flaps adjusted, and the Twin leaped into the air. Sasha succeeded with the door and locked it. She dived for a seat and struggled to fasten her seatbelt. In that instant, Harry looked back. She smiled sweetly and gave him a thumbs up.

"You just got strapped in, didn't you?" he called to her.

She shrugged her response and he knew he was right. "You're on board. That's all that matters."

Using moonlight for illumination, he kept the plane low until the orange flames disappeared from sight behind a hill.

Sasha sighed into the headset. *Finally*.

"What was that, dear?"

She leaned back, relaxing from the adrenalin rush that came when she forced the cargo door closed. She pushed up against something soft. *What the hell?* She flipped on the cabin light for a better look and screamed into the intercom. "Harry!"

"Yes, my sweet?"

"Don't give me that my sweet shit. There's a body back here."

"Yes, dear. It's Meeka's mother. How soon you forget. Did you remember the shovel?" he asked.

At once Sasha regretted what she said, knowing Meeka heard, too."

"I'm sorry, Meeka. Yes. We're all here."

Meeka looked across at Harry and nodded. In return, he grabbed the back of her neck and gave her a gentle shake before smiling down at her. For good measure he gave her a thumbs up.

"That's my woman," he told Sasha. "Now relax. Find a seatbelt, strap your butt down and enjoy the ride across the moonlit desert. Meeka, how are you doing?"

Grinning still, she looked back at Harry and nodded.

"I'll be busy here for a bit. It's like when you were driving the technical all by yourself."

The girl nodded and turned away to look out the window at the desert passing beneath.

'How are you doing back there, Sasha?"

"I'm good. Are we headed for Djibouti?"

"We should be." Harry checked his fuel gauges. "If you gave me full tanks, we're on our way to our first stop. We're going to a good place for Meeka's mother to rest."

Meeka turned to Harry. She nodded. "I would like that for my mother."

Harry thought he heard a sniffle over the intercom. It wasn't Meeka.

Harry pulled back the throttles on the Twin Otter. The powerful engine whine decreased as it shuddered and slowed. Sasha listened over the intercom to Harry as he described the flap setting control to Meeka. He explained how to turn it in terms the girl would understand.

He finished and pointed to the numbers, and then called for her to set flaps ten. It sounded as though he'd be walking her through all the settings. Good. It would take the girl's mind off what would happen when they landed.

"Have you got a spot picked out, Harry?" Sasha wanted to know.

"We're headed for the road by the old campsite. Remember that?"

"Oh I remember it all right," Sasha told him. "There should be a burned-out old Beech 18 and a pair of some guy's shit-stained pants there somewhere."

"Well you're just plain harsh, don't you think?" he wanted to know.

"Who is the man with dirty underwear, Harry?" Meeka wanted to know.

Finally. Meeka was over the mister part of his name. "He was an old boyfriend of your Aunt Sasha's. She sort of dumped him there after she shot the hell out of some pirates. The poor guy has probably never been the same since."

"Harry, this isn't about me. It's about Meeka now," Sasha

told him.

"I was only trying to lighten the atmosphere. Speaking of which, Meeka, you can set flaps twenty now." Harry looked up to follow Meeka's handiwork as she stretched in the seat to complete the job.

"That's it, just like that. Easy, isn't it?" He reached for her shoulder and squeezed his encouragement. When the Otter stabilized, he called flaps thirty and Meeka reached up again. "That's great, Meeka. Okay everyone, stay buckled up until I give the word. It will be a bumpy landing in the moonlight."

Sasha waited, knowing Harry would soon be throttling back to allow the Otter to mush onto the sand. Before she knew it, the Otter had kissed the ground with nary a bump, and Harry was busy working the throttles to position the plane in the opposite direction. She knew it would allow him to use the familiar ground over which they had just landed for the take-off.

The engines went quiet and he made them wait until the propellers windmilled to a standstill. "Come, Meeka. It's time." He took her hand and walked with her to the cargo deck where Sasha waited.

"Meeka, I brought you here because it's one of your father's old places. It's an old place for me and for Sasha, too. It's quiet and peaceful and far from the roads." He placed his hand on her shoulder and drew her close before going on.

"There are many old trails. Camel caravans and nomads still pass by. The wind doesn't blow too hard. The sands shift slowly. Sometimes, it will rain a little bit. When it does, beautiful flowers bloom and carpet the sands.

A flood of tears streamed down Meeka's face on hearing Harry describe her mother's resting place. "My mother will like it very much. I do like it also. I am glad you brought us here."

Sasha wiped away her own tears and hugged the girl. "Come, Meeka. Let's gather rocks to prepare your mother's resting place."

Harry retrieved the shovel and began to dig a depression in the rock-strewn sand. When he finished, he carried Eloria, wrapped in the shroud, from the back of the plane. Sasha helped him place her gently in the opening. He collected Eloria's dog tags, but left the second behind. Old habits. Eloria still had them after all these years.

He had a few old habits of his own. "Meeka, your mother would want you to have this." He handed her the metal tag, and together with Sasha, hugged the little girl.

Harry and Sasha helped the girl gather rocks to place on the mound of sand. When they finished, they were exhausted. The rising sun was coming up to the east over the Indian Ocean.

"Take all the time you want, Meeka," Harry said. "When you're ready we'll be at the plane."

He handed her a bottle of water before leaving the girl to reflect.

Harry and Sasha watched over Meeka as she sat by her mother's grave. They waited patiently.

"She's certainly a tough little thing," Sasha said. "I keep trying to picture our daughter in a similar situation, and I can't."

"She had to be tough judging by what her mother was forced to put up with when she was raising her."

"All that's about to come to a crashing halt, Harry. I wonder how she'll handle the change."

"Without too many problems, I hope. I'm getting attached to her just as you are."

Both knew it would be difficult for Meeka once they got her home. She'd be out of the environment she was most familiar with and dropped into one unknown and unfamiliar.

Harry sighed, not wanting to contemplate the job Mike and Barbara would have on their hands. "See if the satellite phone is in the tail compartment. It's past time to check in with Mike," he told her.

Sasha retrieved the phone and dialed voice mail. There were half-a-dozen messages. She put the phone on speaker and played the last one first.

Barbara's voice came over loud and clear. She wasn't happy. By the time Sasha's friend talked herself out and hung up, Barbara ended up sputtering into the phone. The bad satellite link didn't help.

Sasha looked at Harry. "Well, I guess that's that. If we want to get home, we'd better get it in gear or we'll be off to Bamburi with the Twin to finish that job. We only have until noon. Can we make it, Harry?"

"We'll make it. Wait. What day is it? And when did that call come in?" he wanted to know.

"I lost count. I'll call her and find out where they are, just in case."

Harry took the phone from her. "No. I'll do it. You should be with Meeka."

Sasha joined the girl sitting beside her mother's grave. She put her arm around her and pulled the little girl close. She trembled and Sasha hugged her tight, wanting her to know she wasn't alone. She was uncomfortable interrupting the girl's mourning. There wasn't a lot of time left to get airborne and en route to their rendezvous with Mike and Barbara.

Come to think of it, she was with Harry on that. There would be hell to pay with Barbara and Mike. Finally, Sasha couldn't wait any longer. "It's time, Meeka." She helped the girl place a few more rocks over the sand covering her mother. They finished as the sun began rising over the horizon.

"I am ready," Meeka announced. She stood up and took Sasha's hand.

"Would you like to sit with me for a bit, Meeka? When you're ready I'll take you to the front to help Harry."

"Do you think he will be able to fly the plane without me?"

Sasha was touched by the girl's concern. Harry would be tickled pink to know. She smiled at Meeka. "Maybe for a little. Let's see how it goes. You climb into your seat beside mine. I'll be there in a minute."

Sasha steadied the girl as she climbed into the back.

Harry turned off the satellite phone.

"What's the word?" Sasha asked him.

"They're waiting. Same spot we took up the last time we rolled into Djibouti. And Barbara is spitting mad."

"If Barbara is angry at you, just imagine what Mike is feeling when he found out he had to do another trip overseas in the jet to bring us home."

"That's why she didn't pass the phone to him. He'll change his mind when we show up with his daughter. Do you think he told Barbara?"

"That's not my business," Sasha said. "You'd better not make it yours, either. If Barbara wants to tell you anything, she'll do it. Otherwise, my advice would be to stay completely away from that part of the equation."

"You're right. I just hope Mike and Barbara don't have a lot of trouble taming the girl. I think she's going to turn out to be a handful."

"I'm not concerned with that. We'll be paying this cruise off until we're dead," she told Harry.

"You think?" he asked.

"Nah, it's all good. Let's go. I know a little old-time diner that needs a hash slinger last time I checked," Sasha said.

Harry worked his way through the full pre-takeoff checklist. He called to Meeka for flaps, forgetting she was in the back with Sasha. He made his announcement over the plane's PA. "Clear for takeoff, ladies. Hang on. It will get a little bumpy rolling over the sand until we get airborne."

He dialed in JIB on the GPS and leveled out at ten thousand. Four hours later they were on final. Meeka occupied the seat beside Harry. He instructed her to dial in the flap setting one last time. His eyes followed her hand before he looked across at the girl. He patted her shoulder, smiled, and gave her a thumbs up.

"Perhaps one day you'll have the seat on this side of the airplane."

62

Under **Harry Delaney's** capable hands, the Twin Otter's wheels kissed the Djibouti asphalt like it wasn't even there. He contacted ground and requested clearance to taxi to Mike Williams' jet parked in the all too familiar location.

Mike checked his watch. "Not even noon. He made good time. He's ahead of his ETA."

"Mike. There's no one in the co-pilot seat," Barbara's panicky voice announced. Worried about her friend, she grabbed Christa's hand and squeezed. With her other, she gripped Mike's arm and dug in her nails, hard. "Where's Sasha? She's not there."

Harry braked slowly and turned the Otter to line up with the jet. The open cargo door revealed Sasha and her custom hair-do. She grinned and waved to an anxious Barbara. Christa waved and waved and danced up and down. Mike's face was far too serious for her liking.

"I am going to kill that woman," Barbara announced. "She won't be grinning when I'm through with her, either." She finally noticed Sasha's short hair. "What did she do to her hair?" She let go of Mike's arm and rubbed where her nails were busy digging holes an instant ago.

"That's nothing," Mike said. "I told accounting to send out a bill for use of the Twin. Wait until that shows up. They won't be able to deny it, either. I included a photo one of my guys took that shows Sasha hanging out the cargo door in Bamburi."

"Harry will know you aren't serious," Barbara said.

"Yes, he will. But I'll enjoy knowing that for a glorious split second, I had him at my mercy."

Harry cut the throttles to both engines and they whined to a halt. Everyone waited for the propellers to stop windmilling.

Barbara called to Christa. She took the girl's hand and walked down the jet's airstair together. Mike called out a warning. "Mind the propellers."

Sasha waved excitedly before hurrying up front for Meeka. "Everyone is here, dear. It's time for us to go."

Sasha jumped to the ground. She wasn't able to help Meeka deplane. Before she could reach for her, Barbara gripped her and hung on for dear life. With the women occupied, Harry lifted Meeka down and walked with her to Mike. Harry released Meeka's hand and Christa grabbed it and took it in her own.

"Who's this?" she wanted to know.

"That's your new friend. Her name is Meeka," Harry told her.

Christa looked from Harry to Mike and back, and then smiled at Meeka. "Meeka? You look just like Uncle Mike. I'm Christa."

Meeka repeated the girl's name in her thick accent.

Christa turned to her mother. "Dad? She says my name just like Ali says it."

Meeka's ears perked up. "Do you know Ali? The Ali that I know?"

"Maybe," Christa replied. "Our Ali saved us when some bad men took us out in the desert."

"Ali saved me too. He saved Eloria my own mother also."

Satisfied, Christa looked around for her mother. She kept close to Meeka. They had something in common, after all. They held hands, seeking a measure of comfort. This was all new to both of them. "Dad, have you seen mom?"

"I think Barbara is lecturing her out of sight behind the

planes," he said. "That's all right, though. They'll get everything sorted out before long."

Meeka hung onto Christa's hand while she looked up at the tall man standing beside her friend, Harry. The two men were speaking quietly.

"Who is Mr. Harry talking to, Christa?"

"That's Mike, my dad's friend," Christa said.

"Meek?"

Mike's head turned to the girl. He walked up to her, took her in his arms, and lifted her off the ground. "Yes. I'm Meek."

Tears streamed down the girl's face. "Mr. Harry helped me to look for you."

"Yes, I know, Meeka. He told me about finding you and your mother."

"Eloria my mother did not make the trip. He tried. Sasha tried, too" she announced in her thick accent.

"I'm so sorry. I didn't know." Mike swiped at the tears running down his face.

"It is all right. I am here now. You are here, too."

Harry took Christa's hand and led her away. "I think Mike and Meeka need a bit of alone time. Let's go find your mother."

He found the two women standing toe-to-toe at the back of a hangar. Both were locked in a deep and heated discussion. Their hands were locked to their hips and they were busy staring each other down. It was obvious to Harry the stubborn wasn't over yet. It didn't appear either of them was winning. Barbara giggled and he figured he'd better find out what the hell was going on if he knew what was good for him.

"Did I hear you right?" Barbara asked.

"Hear what right?" Sasha countered.

"That you're pregnant. When were you going to tell me?"

"Well—"

"Williams!" Harry yelled at Mike. "Get your ass in gear and get back here." Mike showed up with Meeka and Christa. Harry got down on the tarmac on one knee before pulling the ring out of his pocket. He looked up at Sasha. "Will you marry me? Again?"

Sasha hesitated. "You want me to be Mrs. Delaney number

two?" she asked. "I'm not sure I like the sound of that. Let me think about it."

Barbara elbowed Sasha so hard she knocked her off balance. "Say yes, bitch."

Harry knew better than to let Sasha's comment slide. "You know what they say about number two, don't you?"

"I think I'm about to find out," Sasha told him.

"Number two tries harder."

"Well, I'll try to remember that about you when we have our first disagreement."

"Wait a minute. Is that a yes?" Harry wanted to know. He looked at Mike for support, but there was none coming. "How did I get to be number two?"

"Yes." Sasha left the second question unanswered.

Mike reached to shake his friend's hand. "I'm glad to see you're trapped again, just like the rest of us."

Harry tried, but he couldn't ignore Mike. His friend kept looking back and forth at his two planes, neither of which should be parked side-by-side on the tarmac in Djibouti. Finally, Mike gave in to allay Harry's fear.

"Stop worrying. I brought a pilot over to get the Twin back to Bamburi. Will you all please get out of the way so he can get moving? I need to start making money to pay for this flying circus."

Mike waited for the Twin Otter to depart before closing up the jet. He halted at the cockpit door and turned to address his passengers. "Is there anyone on board who knows how to fly? I'm going to need some help in the left seat up here."

Harry grinned like a banshee and rose in his seat. Christa looked up at her dad and then at her mom. "Is daddy going to go to work?"

"Well, dear, some might call it work, but others—" Sasha halted.

"Now dear," Harry smiled sweetly. "I'm not giving up a chance to fly left seat in one of Mike's jets, and you know it. And Christa, it's very hard work. Just ask Meeka. She helped out on the Twin Otter to get us all here." Harry walked up front to discover Mike already in the right seat.

"Excuse me, Captain, but—"

"Everyone's on board that's getting on board, Harry," Mike interrupted. "Take a seat and let's get going before one of them changes their mind."

Mike walked Harry through the startup procedure and taxied the jet to the button. He called back his clearance to the tower and settled back in the First Officer chair.

"You have control," he told Harry as the man called it back.

Harry advanced the throttles and Mike followed through. He called out V1 and then V2 and they were airborne. As with their old-school training, both tapped the display screens, but it was more for show than anything else on the glass cockpit. Harry reached for the center post and pulled down the magnetic compass. "Old habits die hard," he announced to no one in particular.

In back, a party atmosphere was starting to develop. Sasha was forgiven. Rather than be angry, Barbara was intent on hearing the story of her adventure with Meeka and Harry.

"Even better than that, picture this," she told Barbara. "Harry had Meeka in the right seat on the Twin Otter. I think she'll make a pretty good pilot if it turns out that's what she wants to do."

"Christa, maybe you should take Meeka up to the cockpit and show her what her father and Harry actually do up there." The two women grinned like a couple of cats headed for a pair of canaries.

"I have seen it already, Barbara. Mr. Harry wasn't very busy. He made me do all the work."

The two women regarded the girl in a new light and began laughing. "You are absolutely right, Meeka," Sasha said. "There's always someone up front to do all the work while the other one rests." The women high-fived. "We are so going to be in trouble if they find out we said that."

"What's with the we? You said it all by yourself, Sasha."

Meeka twisted in her seat, and Sasha noticed a bulge beneath the girl's jacket. "Meeka, what's going on, honey?

What are you hiding under your coat? Is it what I think it is?"

"Yes," the girl replied.

"Can I have it?"

"Yes. I have no need now." Meeka took her jacket off. She unslung the shotgun from her shoulder and broke it to eject the shells. Barbara jumped out of her seat and hurried to the cockpit. She wanted to bear the bad tidings in person.

Mike showed remarkable restraint on his walk back to the cabin. He was accustomed to the antics of the women. It wasn't like it hadn't happened before. He sighed and resigned himself to the fact that Meeka would be just like the rest of them. "Take it apart and put it in someone's luggage. Don't stash it anywhere in the plane. I'll forfeit it for that. Shit. Here comes Harry."

"Don't worry about it, ladies," Harry added. "Whose bag are you going to put it in?"

"I'll put it in mine, Harry. It's my fault," Sasha said. "I don't know what I'd do if Mike lost the plane on my account. It never occurred to me to check her for anything like that."

"Well, we can't fault Meeka. She didn't know any better," Harry said.

"But we should have known. Now it's too late."

"It could be too late for Meeka, too. We don't have papers for the girl."

Sasha instructed Christa to take the girl to the cockpit. She didn't want her to overhear their conversation. "She can watch Mike do all the work while Harry twiddles his thumbs."

"The one thing I did before we left was to ransack your house for Christa's old passport," Barbara said. "Fortunately, in the mess I left behind, I found it."

"I wish it had occurred to me back in Djibouti. We could have picked up papers for anywhere in the world," Harry said.

'What are we going to do?" Sasha wanted to know.

"Brazen it out," he insisted. "Now go take off your bras and ice your nipples."

"Shit, Harry, I've been doing that for years and look what I ended up with." Sasha smiled at him.

"The intent isn't to bring the immigration department

home with you, sweetheart. It's to encourage them to take eyes off the documents. And try not to distract your flight crew while you're doing it."

"Harry, if there was any sand on this floor, my foot would be kicking it in your direction," Sasha told him.

"I know, dear. That's why I proposed to you on the tarmac," he smiled just as sweetly at her. "I'm going up front to twiddle my thumbs now. Be good back here."

Harry and Mike piloted the jet toward Naples for the requisite fuel stop needed to begin their trans-Atlantic flight. Mike set up for the approach before relinquishing the aircraft. "You have control."

Mike looked across at his old friend in the jet's Captain seat. Harry's hands went to the throttles and Mike's hands followed as standard practice.

"How does it feel?" Mike suspected he already knew Harry's answer.

"You're trying to bribe me."

"Yes. Yes I am."

"Is that offer of a jet job still good?" Harry wanted to know.

"You know it, man."

"Good, because I've got some ideas," Harry said.

"Hang on," Mike said. "You'll be starting in a co-pilot position. If you don't get bumped, you'll make Captain in six months or so."

"You're getting even for San Diego, aren't you? Does that mean that you'll be throwing the women to the curb like they did to us?"

"I was thinking more along the lines of a layover on the French Riviera would do those three women a world of good."

"You owe Barbara an explanation," Harry reminded him.

"I know. I'll tell her the story behind the shotgun before we head home."

"If you don't—"

The jet was lined up under Harry's control. Conversation halted and the plane touched down. The buckets came out, the jet slowed, and they made for the taxiway and the fixed base operator. The jet halted, the engines spooled down, and the door opened followed by the airstair.

"Would you go back and check to see if those two women hid the weapons? Italian customs will take a dim view and I can't afford to forfeit this airplane."

Sasha called to her daughter. She wanted to stretch her legs in advance of the flight across the Atlantic. "Come on, Christa. We're going for a walk. Meeka has to stay here." She gathered their papers and took her hand as they strolled across the tarmac in the warm sunlight.

They picked up souvenirs from the charter operator's office and walked back into Barbara's crosshairs. The women were friends for too long to hold anything back. "You knew you were pregnant before you left, didn't you?"

She was forced to admit she suspected it. Barbara wasn't about cutting her any slack. "And you went anyway. I always knew you were nuts. You just confirmed it. What the hell is wrong with you, woman?"

"I needed some adventure in my otherwise dull life. Speaking of which, you'll have an adventure of your own with Meeka a part of your family now."

"I know it. It will be a tough few months until things settle down. And with Mike being away a lot, you know where the burden will fall."

"Tell me something I don't know about raising a child when the husband is always missing. I'm there for support if you need me, girl."

"I know you are. Thank you."

Sasha's friend deserved an explanation. "The thing is, I wasn't about to let Harry go alone. Neither of us knew what we'd be getting into. Mike and Harry both believed Eloria to be dead. Harry didn't know if it was her or someone pretending to be her. Ali didn't tell us much on the phone. Then the woman called a second time. That and her accent convinced Harry it was the real deal."

"There's no holding those two back once they make up their minds. Nothing ever goes smooth for the four of us, does it?"

"No, it doesn't. Speaking of which—"

"Oh-oh. Now what?" Barbara asked.

"This is between the two of us," Sasha said.

"You're swearing me to secrecy for a second time after what you just put me through?"

Sasha ignored Barbara's protest. "I thought I saw one of our old Baja friends showing just a little too much interest in the plane and who was on it."

"Meaning us."

"Yes."

Barbara's jaw dropped. "Are you sure? Is that even possible? You'd think they'd have forgotten about us by now. It's been years since we were down there."

"They're everywhere, Barbara. Who knows, someone might still be harboring a grudge. We took off with cash and carry, remember? In the process we broke a few hearts. And don't forget, Harry and Mike weren't innocent in all of it either."

"True. They had their own reasons for running up the Baja. I'm not going to lose any sleep over it. I'm more concerned with Meeka and Mike," Barbara said.

"You're right. It's not the time to be worrying about it." Sasha changed the subject. "Meeka sure looks like Mike, doesn't she?"

"Yes, she does. We always wanted children. I know you and Harry are here for us—when you aren't getting yourself in trouble and dragging his ass all over the world to save yours."

"Well, all right. But this is the last time, I swear," Sasha assured her friend.

Up front, Harry received his clearance. The jet taxied onto the runway.

Unseen by anyone on the plane, a man and a woman followed the departure with binoculars until it lifted off on its long journey home.

"Las drogas," one announced.

"Si. Canadá. El avión es registrado en Canadá."

UNCHARTED

Harry Delaney is back on the Horn of Africa, smuggling guns and falling in love while partying it up on a Nairobi R&R. When Kari, his latest love interest, ends up in his desert camp, she saves a squad of his men during a shootout. The episode only serves to convince Harry she is the one.

A DC-3 flight into Djibouti drops Harry and his crew into the middle of a revolution. Will it be a harbinger of things to come, or will Harry and his ragtag band of brothers conquer all and make good their escape?

Hawaiian shirts, a night of dancing and drinking, and explosions all play a part in putting Harry on the warpath to revenge.

Available now from the usual suspects in print and e-book.

UNCHARTED

Harry Delaney leaned over and kissed his wife on the cheek. Satisfied Sasha was still sleeping, he eased his way out of bed. He opened his closet and dug through it for the faded pair of cargo shorts and the old Hawaiian shirt. He put them on and buttoned the shirt. Considering the number of years that had passed, the fit of both was remarkably good.

He made his way downstairs to the kitchen and turned the counter lights on dim. He usually put the coffee on. Instead, he went straight to the garage and a beat-up, old army-green metal ammo box. He slid it off the back of the shelf and took it to the kitchen table.

He inserted a key and unlocked the box. Instead of opening it, he looked off into the distance, remembering. It was so many years ago. He had been younger, on the run from a couple of back-to-back relationships that had gone south. Africa had seemed like the perfect escape at the time, thus he had answered the job ad with a cable.

It surprised him when a return cable arrived, accepting him for the flying job. It was a hell of a deal. When he eventually got the lay of the land, he sent a wire off to his good friend, Mike Williams, to join the party. Mike didn't say no, either.

He smiled, opened the box, and removed the objects carefully wrapped in blue and yellow silk. It had become faded with age.

When might that have happened?

Again he hesitated, remembering as though it were only yesterday.

Kari Nurmi had called the men to attention in the hotel lobby. She watched as they lined up in their squads, with Iván at the head of one and Jofre at the head of the other. She grinned as she stood in front of each man and held up a shirt she had picked out. Each was special for the man in front of her. To a man they had accepted every shirt without complaint.

And why would they complain? Kari was one of them. They had been proud to accept her. She had earned their respect when she stood by in the comms tent when Mike and his squad were under attack.

Harry carefully unfolded the remainder of the silk to reveal the woman's passport. He opened it to her head shot. She looked so young. He hesitated before flipping through the pages covered with visas. A picture slipped out. It was the photo of the men in the cargo hold of the DC-3.

The battle hardened, tough as nails mercenaries wore the colorful Hawaiian shirts Kari had presented to them. She had told them that if they didn't like what she picked out, they could trade. Not one man had traded. That each shirt had been Kari's choice was enough.

He set aside the passport and removed the handgun, a French MAC50, still in its canvas holster. The web belt remained wound around it, as it had been presented all those years ago by Captain Renard.

He spread the colored cloth on the table, then laid out the rag and the oil and the bore brush. He uncurled the web belt, flipped open the holster, and removed the handgun. He began stripping it down to its seven components. A noise behind him caused him to halt.

"Dad? What are you doing up so early?"

Christa. As usual, she was checking up on things.

"Oh, I couldn't sleep, so I found something to do."

Stripping and cleaning the handgun had become an occasional ritual, although it had been more than a few years since he had taken it out to check it. This was the first time through the decades he had been caught out.

"Let me finish what I'm doing, please."

Christa dragged a chair beside her father and curled up to

observe and learn.

"This once belonged to a very special friend. It was presented—"

He hesitated, unable to go on. His voice caught. He was happy to have something to do. He cleared his throat and finished oiling and wiping and re-assembling the handgun.

"The safety is critical with this particular weapon. If you don't pay attention, in the heat of things—he almost said *heat of battle*—you can flip it on and not realize it."

He demonstrated how it might happen, as he and Kari had been shown by Renard so many years ago.

"Then, in a panic, you'll try to pull the trigger and it won't fire." He put the pistol down on the table beside the box of 9mm cartridges. "In any case, this one has never once been fired."

He replaced the pistol in the holster and fastened the flap. He wound the belt carefully, almost reverently, around the weapon.

"What's that writing on the box, dad?"

"It's French."

He hoped that would satisfy her. Behind him, hands rested on his shoulders.

Sasha. How long has she been standing there?

"What are you two up to down here?"

The sun wasn't yet up. It was only beginning to turn the horizon a dull gray.

"I don't know, Mom. I came downstairs to find Dad sitting at the table."

Sasha took a chair opposite Christa and looked at her husband. "Well? What's up, Harry?" Her eyes moved to take in the steel box and the silk cloth the package rested on. "That's a colorful way to wrap a handgun."

"Yes. It is, isn't it?"

Harry still hadn't looked at his wife.

"Whose passport is that?"

"I think I'll put the coffee on." He moved to stand up.

Sasha, sensing her husband's discomfort, put a hand on his forearm. "I'll do it, dear."

He sighed and settled back in the chair. After all the years, it was time.

"I never told you about the time Mike and I were living in the desert..."

Harry's voice trailed off. The desert had been good to all of them, until it wasn't.

"It was a long time ago. Well before you and I met. We were camped in the sand, with a damn fine crew backing us up..."

About the author

Peter Duke is a Canadian author. He resides and writes in a small college town in Southern Ontario, Canada.

Peter's gypsy spirit has taken him to some strange places in the world, but now he's content to limit his adventures to riding a motorcycle and whatever he might encounter when he's on the road. Consequently, he's worked in bike shops doing odd jobs from planning and putting on rides down Mexico way, taking care of computer networking and security, and to picking up and delivering motorcycles from the L.A. basin to Las Vegas, among other things.

It's pretty boring stuff, isn't it?

He's ridden over a lot of North America at one time or another from Canada to Mexico, and from Atlantic to Pacific. By far his favorite ride is up and down the length of the Baja Peninsula, where the people are friendly, the sun always shines and it's warm in the winter.

Of everything that he has experienced in his all-too-brief life, Africa is perhaps the greatest enigma. It's a beautiful continent, rich in people, nature and resources, yet poor in all of those areas, too.

https://pxduke.com

peterxduke@gmail.com